"Lock the door," she said, heading into the other room.

Kai ignored her and just closed it behind him. Anyone mortal who came through the door unannounced would not survive.

"What did your minion have to say?" he asked, helping himself to a glass of wine. It was a heavy red that was slightly sour and fizzy as if already spoiled. Apparently it had come from a vineyard in the volcanic mountains. It almost tasted like blood, which made him top up his glass. A poor substitute but it would have to do for now.

"That woman, she's still after me," said Akosh, flopping down into a chair like a stroppy child. "This is embarrassing, having to hide in my own city."

"You're right. It is," said Kai. "And to make matters worse, Vargus is on his way here to destroy you."

Praise for Stephen Aryan

"[Stephen Aryan] enlivens his tale with abundant politics, intrigues, double-crossings, and plot twists to keep the pacing brisk and whet readers' appetites for future installments."

—*Publishers Weekly* on *Mageborn*

"A propulsive combination of thrills, mystery, and magic."

—*B&N Sci-Fi & Fantasy Blog* on *Mageborn*

"A vivid and rousing adventure with the kind of magic that punches you right in the face."

—Jen Williams on *Battlemage*

"This is epic fantasy for readers who appreciate extra helpings of carnage with their backstabbing."

—*Publishers Weekly* on *Battlemage*

"Stephen Aryan puts the epic into epic fantasy. This is a ground-shaking debut, full of fiery promise."

—Den Patrick on *Battlemage*

MAGE
BANE

By Stephen Aryan

THE AGE OF DREAD

Mageborn
Magefall
Magebane

THE AGE OF DARKNESS

Battlemage
Bloodmage
Chaosmage

MAGE BANE

The Age of Dread: Book Three

STEPHEN ARYAN

www.orbitbooks.net

Copyright © 2019 by Stephen Aryan
Excerpt from *Cold Iron* copyright © 2018 by Miles Cameron
Excerpt from *The Gutter Prayer* copyright © 2019 by Gareth Ryder-Hanrahan

Author photograph by Hannah Webster
Cover design by Nico Taylor – LBBG
Cover images by Shutterstock
Cover copyright © 2019 by Hachette Book Group, Inc.

Orbit
Hachette Book Group
1290 Avenue of the Americas
New York, NY 10104
orbitbooks.net

Simultaneously published in Great Britain and in the U.S. by Orbit in 2019
First U.S. Edition: August 2019

Orbit is an imprint of Hachette Book Group.
The Orbit name and logo are trademarks of Little, Brown Book Group Limited.

The publisher is not responsible for websites (or their content)
that are not owned by the publisher.

The Hachette Speakers Bureau provides a wide range of authors for speaking events. To find out more, go to www.hachettespeakersbureau.com or call (866) 376-6591.

Library of Congress Control Number: 2019930802

ISBNs: 978-0-316-55485-5 (trade paperback), 978-0-316-55486-2 (ebook)

Printed in the United States of America

LSC-C

10 9 8 7 6 5 4 3 2 1

For JMS, for all of the stories

CHAPTER 1

Kai sneered at the line of beggars that trailed after him as he walked through Herakion, the capital city of Zecorria.

His sneer grew more intense as he passed the front doors of several large churches and temples dedicated to his brethren. Huge stone buildings that spoke of permanence, giving mortals the illusion of comfort in their endless quest to confess their sins. None was eternal, with perhaps the exception of the Maker, but no one had seen him in centuries and yet somehow His faith endured.

Kai knew the others dreamed of having as many followers as the Maker so that they might extend their miserable and empty existence for another century or two. They were sheep. And like all livestock, one day, they would be ripe for slaughter.

Somewhere deep inside himself Kai heard the faint whimpers and pleas of those being consumed and a wolfish smile spread across his face.

The beggars saw only a handsome, richly dressed man striding down the street with purpose. A few cried out, asking for a coin to buy a crust of bread, which he completely ignored. One man, with blue stains at the corners of his mouth and open sores on his arms, made Kai smile. With nothing but the clothes on his back, not even his health, the man chose to spend his money on venthe, numbing himself to the world. The marks on his face were a clear sign of his addiction. Kai flicked the man a small coin, helping him towards his imminent and painful death.

The mortals were even worse than his brethren. Greedy. Desperate to belong. Frantically trying to feel something to give their life meaning. They weren't sheep. They were like ants, swarming around in search of food and shelter.

Kai wasn't paying attention and almost tripped over another beggar sitting on the street. The blind man pulled in his legs while raising a cracked bowl in one grubby hand. Ignoring the wretched creature Kai was about to move on when he felt a familiar but insistent pull.

Part of him wanted to disregard it and keep walking but, as ever, appearances had to be maintained. This wasn't a summons he could ignore without attracting attention. Closing his eyes the world around him faded away. There was a brief moment of disorientation and then he was standing in the familiar banqueting hall.

At the far end of the table the huge chair of the Maker loomed over everyone in the room. Even in such a large space with a high vaulted ceiling, ribbed with beams like the innards of a vast beast, the chair drew everyone's attention. At some point they all glanced at it, half expecting it to be occupied by His indomitable presence. Perhaps, one day, it would be. That was the one thought that scared Kai.

As others began appearing out of thin air, and the room gradually filled up, Kai noticed the pool of empty space around him. He smiled at their fear while carefully studying the faces he hadn't seen before.

Vargus and the others paid little attention to the newcomers, probably didn't even know half of their names. Even among their kind most of the newborn were like moths. Here one day and

gone the next. But some were stronger than others. Some flour-
ished and grew. Some were lame, ready to be culled, and others,
on the cusp of greatness, were ready to be consumed. Licking his
lips at the thought of feasting on the delicious treats that surrounded him, Kai moved towards his chair. The others moved
out of the way without being asked.

Halfway down the table someone blocked his path, refusing to
step aside. Looking up he saw that it was Elwei. Unlike most of
his brethren, the Lord of the First People was inscrutable. Even
now, as Elwei stood in the room with everyone, part of his attention remained elsewhere, focused on distant events. His face was
turned away from Kai and most of his features were in shadow,
partially hidden by a headscarf. The faded tattoos on his black
skin were so ancient that even Kai didn't recognise the symbols.
Powerful and mysterious was never a good combination. He
skirted around the old Pilgrim, nodded politely to Summer and
Winter, and then sat down.

Towards the head of the table the old sailor, Nethun, took his
seat. Everyone else took that as a cue to cut short their conversations and get comfortable. Normally quick to smile, Nethun's
expression was as grim as those around him. The Blessed Mother
seemed troubled and Vargus distracted, suggesting that both of
them were privy to whatever was about to be said. Kai maintained
his air of ignorance, waiting to be told while working hard to keep
the smile off his face.

"As you've noticed, a few of our number are absent," said
Nethun, wasting no time on preamble. "But Akosh has not passed
beyond the Veil. She has ignored several summonses and, as we
agreed, Vargus was tasked with finding out why."

"She has been dabbling in the affairs of mortals," said Vargus,
drawing gasps of surprise from several around the table. Kai shook
his head in disappointment, biting his bottom lip to crush the

mirth rising up inside. "Recently she was seen in Herakion, the capital city of Zecorria. Aren't you in the north at the moment?"

It took Kai a few seconds to realise the question was directed at him. As all eyes at the table turned his way the half-smile slid off his face. Lying and deception were second nature to him, but sometimes the truth, or at least a version of it, was better. It was also easier to remember under scrutiny.

"I am in Herakion at the moment. There was a huge disturbance last night," he offered.

Vargus continued to stare at him with an unreadable expression. Despite the help Vargus had given him in the past, Kai knew better than to trust his dear old friend. Vargus would try to snuff him out if he found out even a little of what he'd been doing over the last few years. Kai had promised to play by the rules, to be a good sheep, but he was fundamentally different from all of those around him. They all knew it on some level. They felt it, deep down. It was why he unsettled them so much. In this place everyone wore a mask of flesh, but few had the bravery to look upon his true visage, stripped of all illusion. He belonged to another era that everyone wanted to forget.

"Akosh was partially responsible for what happened at the Red Tower," Vargus said eventually, breaking the uncomfortable silence. "One of the mages who survived found out that she was to blame. I'm told it was this mage who attacked Akosh last night, seeking vengeance for her murdered family. Their battle collapsed one building and several people died. Akosh fled the area and has not been spotted since. You told me she wasn't in the north."

Another arrow hurtling through the air towards him. Vargus definitely had a boil that needed lancing and it seemed as if Kai was the pus-filled target. One of the reasons Akosh had remained hidden for so long was that he'd misdirected Vargus away from Zecorria and the capital city in particular. Her plans had been developing nicely, which he'd permitted to continue, but now that would have to change.

"She wasn't at the time. Perhaps she recently arrived in Zecorria," he suggested but Vargus didn't seem convinced. Kai couldn't tell if his old friend was angry because he could hear the lies or he just had unfounded suspicions.

"Vargus, where are you now?" asked Nethun.

"Travelling through Shael. It's going to take me a while to reach Herakion."

The old sailor didn't look pleased. Perhaps Nethun was wishing he'd given the task to someone else, but this kind of work was always left to Vargus. Apparently no one else could be trusted, which was probably an accurate assessment. "Get there as fast as you can. Akosh broke the one rule He passed down," said Nethun. All eyes briefly turned to the empty chair at the head of the table. It amazed Kai that a piece of furniture could inspire so much fear and awe. The majority of those sat around the table had never even seen the Maker and yet they were absolutely terrified of him. "The Queen of Yerskania was recently attacked. My sources tell me it was in retaliation for something she did."

For all of his little birds whispering secrets into dark corners, Kai's reach was limited. Nethun had followers in every port and on every ship in the world. They were crawling all over Perizzi, which explained how he knew so much about what went on in the city. It was one of the reasons Kai avoided travelling there. Another was that it stank of fish.

"Why do we care?" asked Kai.

Nethun's frown deepened. "Because Akosh gave the order."

"The humans have attempted to dissolve Akosh's power by rededicating her orphanages," said Vargus, stepping in smoothly. "It's a good start, but it's not enough."

"We will ensure her end is final. We will rip her up, from root to stem," promised Nethun, clenching his ham-sized fists. "All of us will do this."

The Blessed Mother and a few others made noises of agreement, which was a surprise.

They had been planning this. Vargus, Nethun and at least four or five others must have met earlier to discuss a plan of attack. Normally attending these meetings was a waste of time. Just an opportunity for the new faces to bask in the glory of their elders. Asking everyone to get involved was new and unexpected. Moving forward Kai would have to be increasingly careful.

"What do you want us to do?" asked one of the youngest, eager to please.

"Find every orphanage belonging to Akosh, in every country, and make sure it is converted to another faith." Nethun's tone of voice left no room for debate. Without new followers it meant in a hundred years Akosh would cease to exist when all of the current ones had died. But Nethun was intent on utterly destroying her much sooner than that. "She was also responsible for replacing a number of significant people in Perizzi with her own followers. We must ensure she's not done this in other cities. Report any such interference directly to me," said the old sailor.

"What will be done about Akosh in the meantime?" asked the Blessed Mother.

"Kai will have to keep watch on her until I arrive," said Vargus.

"I will be happy to, brother," said Kai, forcing a smile. He knew exactly where she was at the moment, running scared from a mortal. It was so pathetic he almost laughed out loud.

"Is there anyone else in the Zecorran capital?" asked the Blessed Mother, turning towards the Lady of Light. Zecorria was her stronghold, after all, but she shook her head sadly. Everything about her was sad. From her droopy mouth to her sad eyes, always so full of compassion and love. It was sickening.

Kai would have been offended by the Blessed Mother's lack of trust if not for the fact that the old hag was right to be suspicious.

"I am in Shael," said the Lady of Light. "There are many here who are lost and dispossessed." Her benevolence made Kai want to vomit. She'd been scared into her new subservient role by Vargus after he'd destroyed her consort. It had been a mask to begin with, but now she had become that which she'd pretended to be in the past. A pious priestess. She was a prisoner and didn't even realise.

"Anyone else?" asked Nethun.

Remarkably there were few in the country and no others in the capital city, a fact Kai knew very well. Those who had travelled to Herakion mysteriously disappeared and were currently nourishing him.

"Should we travel to Herakion to lend our support?" asked a desperate youngster. He was like a hungry puppy, begging for scraps from his master's table.

Nethun barely considered it. "No. It's not worth the risk."

Kai noticed he didn't specify who or what would put them at risk. Even if they destroyed Akosh's future she still had a large number of followers, particularly in the north, providing her with strength. A youngster bumbling into the city would be easily noticed. Akosh's followers would soon warn her that someone else was on her trail.

"I will do my best to keep you apprised of her whereabouts," said Kai, his smile bordering on a grimace.

Ever a raconteur of witty banter the old sailor merely grunted.

"Is there any other business?" asked Summer.

"No, we're done," said Nethun, talking over one of the youngsters who'd raised his voice With that they were dismissed. The majority of those assembled immediately vanished, returning to the mortal world.

"I'll see you soon," said Vargus, making it sound like both a promise and a threat. With that he too vanished. Kai thought his old friend looked distracted.

A few stayed behind and a group of four were having a frantic whispered conversation. They were too far away for Kai to overhear but their petty concerns were of no interest to him. He'd lingered only to ponder about what to do with Akosh and how to manoeuvre Vargus when he arrived. When the four youngsters concluded their discussion and vanished Kai realised he wasn't alone in the hall.

Sat only a few seats from the head of the table was Elwei. He'd not spoken a word during the meeting and Kai had to admit he'd forgotten he was even there. His head was still turned away, staring at something in the distance, perhaps half a world away. Kai might have thought the old Pilgrim had lingered because of him if not for the distracted stare.

Kai returned to the mortal world, stepped around the blind beggar, and hurried away down the street. It wouldn't take long for Vargus to arrive in the city. A few weeks at most. It might be possible to delay him for a couple of days, but Kai knew he was relentless. It was better to deal with Akosh now, make plans for when Vargus arrived, and hold other schemes in reserve in case those failed. Experience had taught him to prepare for the unexpected where his brethren were involved.

Garvey, the blind beggar, had watched with his mouth agape, as the man-shaped being paused in front of him on the street. It moved like a man but it wasn't human and he doubted it was even mortal. It was more like the chalk outline of a man. Inside it was filled with a vast ocean of swirling energy that was both alien and somehow familiar. Even without the use of his eyes his remaining senses were being flooded by the creature in front of him. Energy radiated from the being in waves, like ripples on a pond, which he translated into distinct impressions and emotions. Darkness, despair and a sea of blood across time were the strongest. The number of deaths connected to it appeared endless. There was so much blood he could taste it in the back of his mouth. Garvey would have screamed if his throat hadn't been constricted with terror.

Everyone else on the street was oblivious to the weight of its presence, but he could feel it pressing against his mind. Its immense power made his teeth ache and his bones hum. Being so close it felt as if his skin were on fire.

It was also what he'd been searching for since escaping from the palace. The first time he'd sensed it had been in his cell. Somehow it had noticed him reaching out across the city. If not for Tianne's distress Garvey would've been discovered and, he suspected, torn to pieces. It was malicious and he knew it could crush him with ease, but like a moth he was drawn towards it. Such a being was beyond anything he'd encountered. Its existence was both terrifying and intoxicating.

He'd expected the being to move away down the street, but something happened. It paused, right in front of him, staring off into the distance. Even masking his own magic, Garvey had sensed a peculiar shift in the air. Energy unlike any he'd felt before saturated the area and a doorway opened. The being of light remained immobile, staring into space, while the larger part of its presence travelled elsewhere. Garvey felt its focus move away from the street and he decided to take a risk.

Reaching out to the Source he drew energy into his body. His fatigue and the pain in his muscles instantly vanished. His hunger became a distant niggle and the strain from being so close to the being also faded.

In the rest of the city time was almost standing still. All sounds became distorted. Voices stretched on and on in an endless shout that never wavered. Overhead a seagull wailed, its mournful cry grating on his ears. Garvey was caught within a bubble as he could still hear his heart beating at a steady rhythm.

Carefully, with delicate strands of power, he explored the surrounding area. Only a few minutes had passed when Garvey's instincts screamed at him to run. He instantly severed his connection to the Source and masked his power. A doorway to the other place reopened. The man-shaped being returned and marched away down the street, muttering under his breath.

Garvey was about to follow when the air in front of him flickered again. Time had resumed its normal pace and yet a schism remained. No one noticed as he moved towards it and reached out with one hand. The moment he made contact the street disappeared and Garvey found himself standing inside a huge building. Even without his eyes he could sense the vast space surrounding him and the high ceiling. His breathing echoed loudly in the empty room, rebounding off bare stone walls.

Something ancient and huge sat in the middle of the room. It held a distant echo of life. As soon as his fingers touched the surface of the table he knew the tree it came from had stood upon the world centuries before he was born. It was impossibly long and yet was made from a single piece of wood.

At first Garvey thought he was alone, but soon he became aware of a tall figure seated at the table. The stranger stood up and approached on sandalled feet that whispered across the tiled floor. His presence was as overwhelming as the other being, but Garvey sensed it was being masked, to make it bearable for him.

"No mortal has set foot in this hall in over one thousand years," said the tall man, his voice deep and sonorous. The other had radiated malice but Garvey didn't feel afraid of the being in front of him. "And now, two Sorcerers have been here in only a handful of years."

"Balfruss?" asked Garvey.

"Yes."

"Who are you?"

"A Pilgrim. More than that is not important."

As silence filled the hall Garvey thought the Pilgrim was waiting for him to speak. "Why am I here?" he asked.

"I sensed you were nearby."

"I was following someone like you," said Garvey. "But he was different."

"How?"

"He's coursing with malicious, dark energy. Blood and violence cling to him like a second skin. I've never felt anything like it."

"Tell me more," said the Pilgrim.

CHAPTER 2

As she was led through the streets of Oshoa, the capital city of Shael, Wren's mouth gaped in wonder at her surroundings. The contingent of Royal Guards marching beside her didn't glance at the buildings, but even after a few days of being in the city she was still astonished.

Rooke, the western district of Shael where she'd established her community of refugees, showed little in the way of local culture or history, but Wren knew it was a country renowned for its art and creativity. The contrast between the abandoned west and the thriving city around her was significant.

Paintings by several famous artists from Shael were so popular they had even found their way into homes in Drassia. In her country a renowned artist meant someone who had been honing their craft for decades. For her people to embrace an outsider's art, regardless of their age, meant their talent was considerable.

Wren had been hoping to see equally remarkable feats of creativity in the architecture and had not been disappointed, despite the anarchic layout of the city. In the hands of someone less capable it would have been a mess, but whoever had planned the streets had an artist's eye. Tall buildings, that reminded her of the Red Tower but without the eerie feeling, stood cheek to cheek with glass-domed structures that sparkled in the sun. Spires and towers stood in rows behind the common two-storey businesses lining the wide streets. Ancient temples, decorated with dozens of stone gargoyles, sat beside blocky schools of learning. It looked random but after a while she discerned a pattern in the chaos. Everyone else in the city was immune to the rare beauty around them but she spent a lot of time craning her neck to look at her surroundings.

In addition to the buildings the people's artistry showed in the fountains and statues found at almost every crossroads in the city. Every square and meeting place was dotted with more statues, mingling with the crowds of people that filled the streets.

There were so many remarkable things to take in it spoke to her of the nation's ingenuity and creative spirit. She delighted in seeing what the country had been before the war, and could become again in the future, if it prospered.

Wren and her three companions were currently guests of her royal majesty, Queen Olivia of Shael. She'd briefly met with the Queen to formally present her with Boros and the other raiders, but since then Wren and her friends had been given free rein to explore the city. Wren had spent most of her time since then in the large park at the centre of the city. Half a dozen pathways had taken her on tours of brightly coloured flowerbeds, orchards laden with fruit, a small pond surrounded by trees and decorative gardens filled with hedges cut into fantastic shapes. It was a remarkable and peaceful oasis at the heart of a busy city.

A short time ago she'd received a summons and was now following the guards through the vibrant streets towards the palace.

Despite being modest in design compared to some buildings in the city, the palace was still a magnificent structure that combined several creative elements of architecture. Built from white marble that sparkled in the sunlight, the pillar-fronted building

had seven crystal-topped spires set around a huge decorative
dome. Every window in the building was lined with coloured
glass depicting historic moments and rulers that were so detailed
the figures seemed alive.

As her escort led her through a set of large double doors Wren
discovered that the interior of the building was no less opulent.
But despite its ornate design she noticed a few absences inside.
At several points along the hallways she spotted empty spaces on
the walls where paintings must once have hung. There were also
a large number of plants sat upon pedestals which she guessed
had been resting places for gifts and artefacts.

A pair of heavily armed guards, each carrying a sword, spear
and crossbow, in leather armour stood on either side of an iron-
banded door. Despite her escort the two guards stared at her with
suspicion. Up to this point Wren's reception to the city and palace
had been friendly. It made her wonder if she had misjudged the
Queen, or if one of her friends had done something stupid in her
absence. One of the new guards, a middle-aged woman with red
hair, searched Wren thoroughly for weapons. She didn't react or
protest despite the intrusiveness and the fact that she had been
searched only a short time earlier.

Eventually the guard was satisfied she wasn't carrying a con-
cealed weapon and stepped back. The heavy door opened on silent
hinges and the guard gestured for her to enter the corridor. Doors
on either side were closed but the one at the end stood open. Wren
expected to find herself in the throne room but instead saw a
private dining room.

Queen Olivia, a tall young woman with golden skin, flowing
brown hair and green eyes, waited for her inside. Standing beside
her chair was Thias, her husband and the King of Shael. Broad
and tall like most men from Seveldrom he made his slender wife
seem even thinner by comparison, despite her swollen stomach.

"Please, come in, sit down." Olivia gestured to one of the seats beside her. "I would stand up but I've been told to rest and stay off my feet." She instinctively cradled her belly and the child within with both arms.

"Thank you, Majesty," said Wren, making sure she bowed to the Queen and her husband before sitting down.

"I apologise if my guards were rough. They're a little over-protective."

"They were very professional."

Olivia smiled. "I can see why you're in charge of your village."

"You'd make a good politician," said Thias, with a rumbling laugh. He bent down, kissed the top of his wife's head and she touched him on the cheek. It was an intimate display of affection that made Wren uncomfortable. Most days it was difficult to believe it had been less than a year since she'd left Drassia. It was little moments like this, highlighting the differences in culture, which still caught her off guard.

Every day she was learning to adjust to other people's customs. Most didn't shock her but some required that she take a breath or bite her lip so as not to cause offence. To hide her embarrassment she looked around the dining room but there was little to see besides a crude painting of four people. The brightly coloured misshapen figures, possibly two adults and two children judging by the sizes, had been framed and proudly hung on the wall.

"My eldest daughter painted that. Perhaps she'll be good at languages," said the Queen with a hopeful smile.

"Perhaps," agreed Wren, not wanting to insult her child's ability.

"Since becoming Queen I've had several meetings with senior figures from Drassia, so I apologise for meeting in such modest surroundings."

"Your Majesty, I'm not here as a representative of my country," said Wren, forcing a smile so the Queen didn't think she was offended. It was something she'd seen other people do and had adopted.

"Nevertheless, we would normally have met in the throne room, but you came to me in very unusual circumstances." The Queen shook her head sadly. "Since the beginning of our records the throne of Shael has maintained strong ties with the Red Tower. I wanted to personally tell you how deeply saddened and shocked I was by what happened."

"Thank you, Majesty," said Wren, not knowing what else to say. Queen Olivia wasn't responsible but a mob of people from Shael had burned down the school. Wren also knew that ultimately even they weren't wholly responsible. It was the people who had manipulated the mob that deserved to be punished.

"Ever since the end of the war the western district has been difficult to protect." Wren knew the population across the country as a whole had been decimated during the war. Many had fled east ahead of the invading army to the capital city or beyond in the hope of protection. The Shael army had been crushed, their Queen murdered, and thousands butchered in torture camps. A rebellion came, throwing off the invaders, but not without further loss of life. This was the country that Olivia had inherited from her late mother. "After the war, we welcomed survivors into the capital city, but it has put a strain on our resources."

Wren wasn't sure why the Queen was explaining this but she waited patiently for the reason. "The city seems to be thriving."

Olivia smiled. "It is, but there's always so much work to be done. I'm sure that's something you're familiar with, which brings me to the reason for our private meeting." The Queen adopted a more formal tone and Wren instinctively straightened in her chair. "The people are still angry and distrustful of magic. I know the Red Tower and Seekers weren't to blame for what happened, but people in pain aren't rational. At the moment they're unwilling to hear the truth and they won't accept it. Therefore I cannot officially praise you or offer you a reward for what you've done in the Rooke district."

"I understand." Wren had been expecting something like this.

"But I want you to understand. Your actions against the raiders saved the lives of hundreds of my people. And for that you have my deepest thanks. After everything that happened to you at the school, I'm humbled by your selfless actions."

"Thank you, Majesty."

"As I said, officially I can't say that. However, there is much I can do, unofficially," said the Queen, quirking her eyebrows.

"I don't understand, Majesty."

"Babies, Wren. I need babies," said Olivia. It was the last thing she had expected the Queen to say. "I need people to resettle in the west and for the population to grow across Shael. The Rooke district has fertile land for farming and plenty of open space for raising cattle and families. It's been fallow for years now and is ready for new crops. I need people to reclaim and rebuild old communities. To set up new villages and start building homes. If the district is safe, then I can gradually persuade people to travel west and resettle."

"The western road, and all travellers coming into Shael, will remain safe," promised Wren. "My people will continue to patrol it and keep an eye on the local settlements."

She had left detailed instructions with her people. Her grandfather had told her many stories where a powerful enemy was killed only for another to fill the void left behind. They had not worked so hard, and lost six people fighting Boros, only for another group of raiders to move in and take over.

"Thank you, Wren."

"It's my pleasure, Majesty."

"You're so young to take on so much."

"I'm not the leader, Majesty. There are others who advise the community, teachers, farmers and those with skill at various crafts. I merely coordinate them." The Queen smiled as if she'd said something amusing which puzzled Wren but she let it pass. She was still getting used to the way people outside of Drassia behaved.

"And do you have many young mages in your community?"

"Almost fifty," said Wren, running through the list of names in her head.

"I must admit I am concerned. Some of my advisers think I'm naïve. They believe you're training an army."

Wren had expected this. "Your Majesty, may I speak plainly?"

"Of course, and please, call me Olivia."

Wren appreciated the offer but she could not. While she was learning to bend in the face of other people's customs, there were some she proudly clung to from home. "Your Majesty, how much do you know about Garvey and those who left with him?"

"I've received a few reports about his rampage."

"He was one of the most trusted mages at the school, and he broke with centuries of tradition, going against everything they were teaching us." Wren didn't realise how angry she was about what he'd done until she noticed her hands were curled up into tight fists. Taking a deep breath she relaxed her hands and stopped clenching her jaw. "When the school was destroyed I refused any of the choices we were offered by the Grey Council. To run, to live in hiding or to fight. For a time, magic may be forced into the shadows, but it cannot be destroyed. More children will be born with the gift and a time will come when skilled mages are needed again." Wren knew this wasn't news to the Queen but she felt that it needed to be said.

"You're creating a new school," said the Queen.

Wren didn't like to publicly criticise her former teachers but she needed to earn the Queen's trust and make her understand. "I believe the Grey Council made a mistake." Queen Olivia raised an eyebrow but gestured for her to continue. Wren had taken her first step down the path of being disrespectful about her elders, so there was no point in stopping now. "I understand the reasons why the Red Tower was so remote, but in keeping so much about the school wrapped in secrecy, I believe it created more problems. People were scared about what happened inside its walls. They did not see how, in many ways, it was mundane and familiar."

Fear of the unknown was often more terrifying than the truth. While magic itself was wonderful and mysterious, daily life at the school was fairly ordinary. Like students in every school across the world, the majority of their time was spent in classrooms. They had spent a portion of each day practising with magic, but if they had been painters or dancers, it would have been the same.

"Then if not a new school, what are you proposing?" asked the Queen.

"The mages in our community are learning how to protect themselves. But first and foremost, they're learning skills that will help others."

"Despite all that you've done, the people in the Rooke district will continue to be afraid of magic for some time."

It was something Wren had spent a great deal of time thinking about. At first, setting up the community had simply been about surviving and finding somewhere to live. Then it had grown into a school of sorts, combining many practical skills and daily tasks with magic in order to sustain themselves. Boros and her raiders had forced Wren to adapt her plans again, changing the community in ways she hadn't considered.

Travellers on the road and young people in the west struggling with their magic were now aware of her community. It had become the only real haven with the fall of the Red Tower. If a school was to be a part of the village then she was determined not to repeat the mistakes of the past. She'd forged her own path once and would do so again.

"I do not expect people to thank us, or welcome us, but eventually I think their attitudes will change. We will let them know where we are and what we can do. We will offer them healing and whatever else we can. My hope is that in time we will not live separately and one or more mages will live in each community."

"Your parents must be so proud of you," said the Queen, running a hand over her stomach again.

"Thank you, Majesty." Wren thought her mother would be ashamed and deny all knowledge of knowing her when asked. But at least her father would smile at her accomplishments in a way that warmed her heart.

"I would like to see that happen. There's even a form of precedence for integration in Shael."

"There is?"

"In a way. In the cities we have apothecarists and doctors. But in Shael it used to be common that every village and small town also had a Wise. A man or woman skilled in herbalism, folklore and, perhaps, a touch of magic. The practice has faded in the last hundred years."

Wren smiled. "Then perhaps, in time, the village Wise will return."

"In time," agreed the Queen. "So, what can I offer you to help with your growing community?"

"Our numbers are slowly increasing, and we have some skilled people, but we lack certain tools. We're also in desperate need of a glassblower." It sounded such an odd thing to request from the Queen, but this was an unusual meeting in a non-formal setting.

"You'll have whatever tools you need. And I'm sure we can find a willing gaffer."

"Thank you, Majesty. You would be welcome to visit our community at any time, or send someone in your stead," said Wren, gesturing at her baby bump. "Our door is always open. We don't want to keep secrets."

"I think that's very wise," said the Queen.

CHAPTER 3

Munroe pushed open the door of yet another tavern in Herakion. This was the sixth place she and Dox had visited tonight in pursuit of Akosh. A few heads turned as she came into the room but quickly went back to their business, which she took as a good sign. A number of rumours had been flying around the city since her fight with Akosh a few nights ago. They mentioned two mages fighting but little else. She suspected any real eyewitnesses had been silenced by the Regent while his Royal Guards pursued their own investigation. Munroe had no idea if they knew what she looked like but she was doing her best to keep a low profile. The Regent's pet mages were also patrolling the city but she wasn't spending much time worrying about them. Her focus remained on finding Akosh.

"I'm tired," complained Dox. "Can I go to bed?"

"Soon," said Munroe, not giving her a definitive answer. It was incredibly annoying to have a conversation with someone who always knew when you were lying. Munroe was getting better at giving vague answers so that Dox couldn't use her Talent. In a typical teenage fashion the girl sighed dramatically and made her way to one of the empty tables at the back of the room. Munroe paid for two mugs of ale at the bar and then joined her.

"Anything?"

Dox shook her head and ran a finger through the foam of her ale before tasting it. She grimaced and pushed her mug away. "It's disgusting."

Munroe sipped hers and smiled. "I've had worse."

For the next hour the two of them watched the room while studying the people and flow of conversation. Channelling a small amount of power enhanced Munroe's senses, allowing her to clearly hear people talking across the room. After four nights in a row she had become adept at focusing on one conversation at a time.

In turn Dox was using her Talent to study the people. After the first night she'd confessed that it had dented her faith in humanity. She was shocked at how often, and with such ease, people lied about both the mundane and the important things in their lives. Gradually Dox was becoming immune and more cynical as she used her Talent to dig through the rumours flying around the city.

Munroe suspected there were dozens of people in Herakion with a direct connection to Akosh. Followers who hid in plain sight until they were called upon by their Mother to commit a horrible or murderous act. Finding the other orphanages dedicated to Akosh had been easy. As had identifying and following all of the members of staff. It was proving more difficult to work out which of them were loyal to Akosh.

Normally Munroe would have adopted her less than subtle technique of scaring a confession out of them with magic, but unfortunately it wasn't an option. If Akosh heard even the faintest whiff that Munroe was still tracking her she could disappear and leave the city. That meant Munroe had to swallow her rage, proceed with caution and focus on that most hated word. Patience.

It was sickeningly slow and tedious work. So far they had whittled down the list of people who worked in the orphanages to a handful. Their latest target was a boisterous man named Edwin. He seemed an unlikely follower of Akosh, but appearances could be deceptive and these days Munroe was taking nothing for granted. Edwin worked as a cooper for half the week and spent the rest of his time teaching children to read at one of Akosh's orphanages. He appeared to be a kind and generous man but that would change the moment his Mother gave him an order. And not once would he think about the victims or what would happen to his life afterwards. The loyalty of her followers was absolute and had been ingrained into them since early childhood. There was no way to reason with that level of zealotry. If Munroe ever needed a reminder she only had to remember Guardian Brook who had killed herself rather than be taken in for questioning.

Edwin was currently chatting to some old friends, reminiscing about the city as they remembered it from their youth. Their conversation sounded innocuous but she noticed Edwin was unusually nervous. The room was busy with people and the windows had been thrown open to let out the heat on such a muggy night. The fireplace was cold and yet he was sweating. Damp patches were spreading under his arms and he kept mopping his forehead with his sleeve.

Four large men came into the room and immediately made a beeline for Edwin's table. He visibly relaxed and chatted briefly to one of the men while the other newcomers scanned the room. Munroe noticed all of them were carrying weapons and had the stiff bearing of soldiers. One briefly stared at Munroe but he looked away with a frown when she winked at him. And just like that the bodyguard thought she was harmless. She hid a smirk behind her mug as she took another gulp of sour beer.

Some money discreetly changed hands and then Edwin went out the door, surrounded by his new bodyguards.

"Let's go," said Munroe.

She kept Edwin and his bodyguards just in sight until they were a few streets away from the tavern. They were using quiet streets, which made the next part easier.

"Go back to our room. I'll see you there soon," said Munroe. When Dox looked as if she was about to protest she added, "It's going to get bloody. Can you help me with that?"

Munroe waited and eventually Dox shook her head in defeat. Sometimes speaking the truth was useful. Leaving the girl to find her own way home she jogged for a little while before settling into a fast walk. She could hear the scuffle of heavy footsteps and was so intent on catching up she raced around a corner and walked into someone's chest. Looking up at his face Munroe recognised the mercenary she'd winked at in the tavern.

"Why are you following us?" he asked, resting a hand on the dagger at his waist.

Munroe was about to feign interest in him when she noticed his eyes. They were flat with no hint of warmth. Either she really wasn't his type or he was the most professional mercenary she'd ever met. Something in her stance proved alarming as the mercenary drew his dagger while trying to push her away. Before he could warn the others she slid a dagger between his ribs and pulled him close. A wheeze escaped his lips and she gently eased him to the ground. He'd probably live but wouldn't be protecting anyone for a while.

Further down the street the three remaining bodyguards were waiting. Edwin was behind them, wedged in the closed doorway of a shop. When they saw Munroe they didn't go for their weapons until they saw the blood on her hands.

One of the men drew his sword and raced towards her, only to get a dagger in the face. She'd mistimed her throw and it went through his cheek into his mouth. He howled in pain and fell back, his face torn open. The second man stayed to protect Edwin while the third came forward more cautiously. Munroe drew a pair of long daggers from her baldric and laid them flat along her forearms. Dancing back she ducked and sidestepped his sword, watching his movements to discern his style.

When he lunged she used her Talent and his front foot slipped on the ground, making him stumble. She sliced him across the back of his hand and buried her other dagger into his thigh. He dropped to the street when she wrenched it free, hissing in pain between his teeth. Almost immediately he pressed a hand to the wound to stem the bleeding. This wasn't the first time he'd been injured, confirming her suspicion they were former soldiers.

The final bodyguard went for his sword but Munroe didn't give him a chance to attack. Mysteriously his sword had become stuck in its scabbard. The moment he looked down to find the problem she raced forward, kneed him in the groin and elbowed him behind his ear on the way down. He collapsed into a crumpled heap on to the street and didn't move.

Munroe put a dagger against Edwin's neck, forcing him on to his toes. "You have one chance. Lie to me and I'll slit your throat," she promised. "Where is Akosh?"

Edwin's eyes darted around the street, looking for anything to save him. He licked his lips and Munroe had the distinct impression he was about to lie. She pressed the blade a little harder, drawing blood. "Choose your words very carefully. They could be your last."

"I don't know where she is. Wait!" he cried, as she tensed her arms. "But I heard a rumour she was hiding somewhere close to the palace."

Munroe shook her head. "That's vague."

"The jewellery district. I heard she was somewhere in there."

"You're lying," said Munroe.

"He's telling the truth," said Dox, coming up behind them.

"I thought I told you to go back to your room."

Dox shrugged, stepping over the bleeding and unconscious men on the street. "It's boring there."

Munroe turned back to Edwin. "Do you know anything else?"

"Only that she's on the run and that she's scared. A crazy mage is after her. I heard she's unbalanced."

"Oh, you have no idea," said Munroe as blue flames blossomed across her shoulders and upper arms, wreathing her in fire. Edwin's eyes widened in terror and he tried to pull away as his clothes smouldered from the heat. The fire continued to creep down Munroe's arms, getting closer and closer to him. "Anything else you want to tell me?"

"No. That's all I know. I swear!" Munroe didn't need to ask Dox.

"Edwin, tomorrow morning you're going to pack a bag and leave the city for ever. If you try to warn someone, if you speak to anyone, I'll know." Munroe let the fire creep even closer until it singed the edges of his hair. "Do you understand?"

"Yes."

"Swear it."

"I swear! I swear!" he pleaded. Munroe glanced at Dox who bit her lip and nodded. She released her grip on the Source and the fire vanished. Stepping back, she waited until Edwin had finished patting down his clothes before sheathing her dagger.

"Run," said Munroe, gesturing at the empty street. Edwin's feet pounded on the road as he sprinted away. Leaving the unconscious men lying in the street, Munroe set off for their room at the Salty Squid.

"Why didn't you kill him?" asked Dox. "Or the bodyguards?"

"Dead bodies would attract a lot of attention. We need to stay hidden so that Akosh doesn't see me coming. I won't let her get away again."

"That wasn't my fault," said Dox with a pout. "You're the one who destroyed the building."

Munroe bit her tongue, swallowing a sarcastic remark. She knew several people had died in the orphanage when the building had collapsed. All of her focus had been on destroying Akosh. She'd barely noticed the damage they'd caused until the end. Her warning to get out of the building had come too late for some.

"Where are you going now?" asked Dox.

"Bed. Tomorrow we're visiting the jewellery district."

Munroe started to walk away when she stopped suddenly. There were a few people on the street but they weren't what had caught her attention. There was something in the air. A faint echo. At first she thought it was Dox and her connection to the Source, but this familiar type of pulse was further away. Yet with each passing second she could feel it getting closer and stronger.

"Move," she said, dragging the girl along by her arm. Dox started to squawk in protest until she saw Munroe's face.

"What is it?"

They jogged down a couple of side streets away from the echo of power when Munroe sensed a second, much stronger pulse coming towards her from in front. The longer she stayed in the city the more inevitable this meeting had become. If she'd learned how to conceal her connection to the Source then she could have avoided it altogether. All she could do now was choose the place.

"Follow me," said Munroe. After a short run she found a deserted space that was suitable.

In the day it was probably a bustling market square but this close to midnight the stalls were empty shells. Wooden frames topped with canvas awnings filled two sides of the square. A fountain with a statue of a fish sat in the middle happily gurgling away to itself. The rest of the square was open space. More importantly it was abandoned and all of the surrounding windows were dark.

Hopefully that meant there would be few witnesses for what was about to happen.

There were four ways in and out of the square and Munroe put her back to one, facing towards the oncoming enemy.

Dox was about to ask who was out there when Munroe saw her expression change. She was still learning about her connection to the Source but every day her senses were becoming more acute to those with magic.

A short time later six young people entered the square. All of them were dressed in black-and-white palace uniforms marked with a blue star. Bizarrely all six had a matching tattoo on one side of their face above and below their right eye. They were all locals with the typical dark eyes and pale skin. Munroe didn't recognise any of them, which would make it a little easier if things went badly. Behind them came a dozen Royal Guards in their famous brightly coloured armour.

Munroe drew heavily from the Source, heightening her senses and filling her body with raw primal energy. One of the young mages stumbled to one knee and the others seemed disorientated as she readied herself for a fight.

"My name is Kalina," said the tall Zecorran girl at the front of the group. "You need to come with us." She was perhaps a couple of years older than Dox, which still made her young to be in charge. The Royal Guards were following her lead but there was some obvious tension. "No mages, except us, are allowed in Zecorria," she insisted.

"So, does that mean I can join your little gang?" asked Munroe, playing for time. The other mages were looking to Kalina for guidance but she kept glancing at one of the guards who seemed on the cusp of violence.

"That would be up to the Regent to decide."

"And what happens if I don't want to come with you?" asked Munroe.

"We have to take you in. Both of you."

"Both?" said Dox. It was the first time anyone, other than Munroe, had realised she had any magic.

"Really? And how would you do that?" asked Munroe.

Kalina hesitated and the Royal Guard, a woman with a scarred face, actually elbowed her in the ribs. "Take her down. She's toying with you."

"Shut up," said Kalina, startling the guard. "You've no idea what it's like. You can't feel how much it hurts."

"What's wrong with them?" asked Dox, gesturing at the young mages. They were all grimacing as Munroe started to bring her will to bear. The echo of her connection to the Source was disorientating them. One of the young mages was so dizzy she stumbled into the person beside her. Dox rubbed the skin on her arms which were suddenly covered in gooseflesh.

"Take her!" shouted the Royal Guard.

"We can't," said Kalina.

"Then we will." The Royal Guard gestured at the others, who all drew their swords.

"I think not," said Munroe. Bringing her Talent to bear she made twisting motions with both of her hands. The steel breastplates on all of the guards tightened against their chests, bending around the contours of their body, squeezing their ribs and chests. At the same time all of their swords shattered into dozens of pieces as if they were made of glass. With cries of pain the guards fell to the ground, struggling to breathe in their constrictive armour. The scarred guard ignored the crushing pressure, drew her dagger, and ran at Munroe. With a flick of a wrist she sent the guard hurtling through the air. She collided with an empty stall which broke into pieces upon impact. The guard fell to the ground and didn't get up.

"We can take her," said one of the mages to Kalina.

"Walk away," said Munroe, focusing on their leader. "You don't know who you're dealing with." She was suddenly aware of Dox staring at her with a renewed sense of fear.

Kalina and the other mages had a brief whispered argument before coming to a decision.

"We have to take you in," said Kalina. It was clear she didn't want to do this but felt she had no choice.

"Run," said Munroe, urging Dox to clear the square. The young mages let her go, focusing on the larger threat. As soon as they'd gathered their will two of the mages attacked, trying to drive her backwards. It felt like a gentle breeze against her skin. A third added their strength to the others but it made little difference.

Munroe shook her head. "Walk away."

"We can't," said Kalina, lashing out. Her raw attack had no effect and Munroe easily turned it aside.

When they didn't try anything else it became clear they'd not received any formal training. The extent of their magic was the most basic and the first thing pupils were taught at the Red Tower. The physical manifestation of their willpower.

"Magic is so much more," said Munroe, pushing back for the first time. Venting some of her anger at Akosh she knocked them all over with ease. Blue flames erupted from the palm of both hands but it quickly spread across her whole body, wreathing her in fire, making her into a living candle. The mages scrambled back and two of them tried to run but she hurled a ball of fire ahead of them, blocking the exit. The flames leapt up and as shadows danced across the walls of the square Munroe raised one hand towards the sky. The air cooled and rain fell on the young mages, soaking them to the skin while the flames hissed but kept burning.

She herded them around the square like sheep, sending them one way and then the other with fire, ice and light. One of them curled up in a ball and refused to move while the others danced to her tune. With a final flick of her wrists Munroe ripped the blue stars from all their uniforms and knocked them to the ground. Exhausted, soaking wet and bruised from being thrown around like ragdolls, the mages had not only been defeated but utterly humiliated.

"Do not come after me again. I will not be so kind next time," said Munroe. She waited until Kalina nodded before cutting her connection to the Source and walking away.

Dox was waiting for her at the edge of the square, her mouth agape.

"You saw everything?" asked Munroe.

"Yes."

"I'm tired. Let's go back to the tavern."

"No."

Munroe raised an eyebrow. "What?"

"I'm not going to help you any more unless you train me," said Dox. "You promised."

"Dox—"

"No!" shouted the girl. "That's the only reason I came north with you. Show me how to do that," she said, gesturing at the square behind them and the scattered bodies. "Otherwise you can find Akosh by yourself."

Munroe took a deep breath and considered her choices. It would be more difficult, but not impossible, to find Akosh without the girl. With Dox's assistance there was no need to coax the truth or try to discern it from someone's words and body language. It was instant. Without Dox it required patience and subtlety, which she was struggling with more and more every day. Sometimes all she could think about was tearing Akosh apart with her bare hands. Hours could pass with Munroe inventing new and increasingly painful ways to make her suffer before she finally let her die.

On the other hand, if she kept Dox around she was a liability and Munroe already felt responsible for her. She was an undisciplined, stroppy teenager who had never been taught anything about her magic or the Source. She would be a distraction and in every fight Munroe would have to think about protecting her.

"You need me," said Dox, sensing the real possibility that Munroe would leave her behind.

"If you slow me down—"

"I won't. I promise," insisted Dox.

"The next time we find Akosh, make sure you run, because I'm going to do whatever is necessary to kill her."

"Deal," said Dox, holding out her hand.

A brief smile played across Munroe's face. "Deal," she said, shaking the girl's hand.

CHAPTER 4

There were no smiles or friendly greetings when Tammy arrived at the outer gates of the palace in Perizzi. Her Guardian uniform, her position as Khevassar and her history with the Royal Guards meant nothing. Everyone was a suspect. No one could be trusted.

The guards at the gate took away her weapons and searched her thoroughly before escorting her to the next gate where she was passed off to another pair of guards. This continued, with two more searches, before she was finally allowed inside the palace. Even then she was shadowed the entire time. Her boots rang out loudly on the stone floor as an unnatural silence gripped the building. Normally it was a hive of activity with an army of servants attending to their duties. Today the whole palace was holding its breath.

When she finally arrived at the doors to the Queen's private chambers she was pleased to see the Old Man waiting beside four Royal Guards. He was dozing in a chair but his eyes snapped open as she approached. It was strange to see him out of uniform but she was gradually getting used to it. All of the guards watched her closely, hands twitching beside their swords, but she did her best to ignore them.

"Sir," said Tammy, shaking his hand. "How is she?"

"Grumpy, but alive, so that's good," said the Old Man, getting to his feet with a grunt. The guards continued to block the door but before she could object the Old Man's patience ran out. "Move your fat, lazy arses!" he yelled. "Perhaps if you'd done your job, we wouldn't be in this fucking mess in the first place!"

Any of the guards could have cut him in two with little effort but all four flinched at the sound of his voice. She understood their overprotectiveness, and their guilt about what had happened with Dorn, but she and the Old Man weren't the enemy. Besides, their bruised feelings would keep them on edge for new threats against the Queen. Despite their skills, in the absence of any real danger, they'd become more than a little complacent. Hopefully they'd learn from this.

"Open the door, please," she said, keeping her voice calm.

A consensus was reached and they were let inside, the Old Man grumbling all the while. They walked to the end of a corridor past several closed doors to the Queen's private bedroom.

It was the first time Tammy had been in this part of the palace and unlike the rest the decorations had been chosen by Queen Morganse. They served no other purpose than to suit her tastes and were more modest than Tammy had expected.

The room was fairly large and at its centre was a wide bed. Everything else she could have found in her sister's house. A side table covered with framed paintings of Morganse's children and grandchildren. A dresser with a hairbrush and a make-up-spattered mirror. An oil painting of a brook tumbling through a rich green forest. A stack of half-finished knitting, several books and a breakfast tray with the remains of her last meal.

Lying in the centre of the bed, propped up on a vast assortment of colourful pillows, was the Queen. Sitting beside her, reading quietly from a report, was a balding scribe Tammy recognised from previous visits. The Queen's face was pale, her torso wrapped in bandages and her normally luscious hair was lank. There were dark smudges under her eyes and for the first time since they'd met Tammy thought she looked frail.

"Ah, thank the Maker," said the Queen, her voice slightly hoarse. "You've saved me from another tedious report about grain." She waved away the scribe, who bowed and shuffled out of the room.

"No sign of your friend Balfruss, I assume?" asked the Queen.

"No, Majesty."

"A shame." They'd both hoped he would soon pay a visit to the city. Then it would've been up to Tammy to try to persuade him to heal the Queen and speed up her recovery. Unfortunately it looked as if she would just have to do it the old-fashioned way.

"How are you feeling?" asked the Old Man. He sat down beside Morganse and took one of her hands in his. The Queen squeezed his hand and smiled.

"Bored, tired and annoyed. But my doctor assures me I'm going to live." The Queen's tone was waspish and Tammy saw her make an effort to relax. She was undoubtedly frustrated at being bed ridden. Morganse was so active it must have come as quite a shock to realise she was as mortal as the rest of them and couldn't keep going indefinitely. "What did you find?" she asked, looking at Tammy.

"We searched Dorn's home. We found an idol and a book devoted to Akosh. I have several people investigating his history."

"He came to me highly recommended. I was told he was the youngest son of a minor house."

"I'm confident that's a lie as all of Akosh's followers are orphans. We're also looking into the people who recommended him," Tammy assured her. It was likely the nobles who had put Dorn's name forward had been tricked or blackmailed, but as ever she wasn't taking anything for granted. Trust was at a premium right now and it would have to be earned again.

"I'll leave you to it," said the Old Man, getting to his feet. "I just came to see how you were doing. I'll visit again soon and we can share a pot of tea."

"That would be nice," said Morganse.

"You can stay, Sir," suggested Tammy. She still valued his opinion and didn't want him to feel that he was being forced out of the room.

The Old Man shook his head. "You're the Khevassar now. You know what you're doing."

They both watched him leave then listened to the sound of his footsteps receding down the hallway. The Queen gestured at the seat beside her bed and Tammy sat.

"He's very fond of you," said the Queen.

"I was about to say the same thing."

"Do you know where Balfruss is?"

The truth was she didn't know but had a few theories. If Balfruss had not left a note in her office then she would have been extremely worried. Even so it had been strange to see the empty octagonal cell beneath Unity Hall. She had no idea how he'd smuggled all of the young mages out of the building without being seen. It served as another reminder that as well as being her friend he was also a renowned Sorcerer and member of the Grey Council.

"He's still in the west, but I don't know exactly where. He left a note saying he'd found somewhere more secure to imprison the rogue mages."

The Queen tried to adjust herself on the pillows and hissed in pain. Tammy went to help but she was waved away. Morganse took a few deep breaths and the lines of pain on her face eased. "That's a matter for another day."

"Yes, your Majesty. Now, more than ever, we need to make sure the palace is secure. It's my first priority."

"As much as I hate all of this coddling, I agree."

"My people are carrying out discreet checks on everyone in the palace, but it is going to take some time," said Tammy.

There were more people than she realised coming in and out of the building every day. As well as the Royal Guards there was an army of servants who worked in the stables, kitchens, household staff and gardens. In addition to them dozens of strangers were allowed inside the palace to make deliveries, petition for appointments, as well as to meet with scribes and money-lenders. Even though most of the visitors never came anywhere near the Queen it was possible one of them might slip away without being noticed. They couldn't put a guard in every corridor but they could double the number of bodies around important areas.

"I have some people who can help with the searches," said the Queen. "But I need you to keep their identities, and what I'm about to tell you, a secret."

Tammy knew the Queen had a network of spies in the country and abroad but had never met with any of them. "I won't reveal their names to anyone," she promised.

"It's more than that," said Morganse, suddenly reluctant. "No one can know. Not a single Guardian or friend. I want your word on it."

"You have it, I swear," promised Tammy.

"You've heard of the Silent Order?" asked Morganse, waiting for Tammy to nod before continuing. "Tell me what you know of them."

"They're a group of assassins. Apparently the organisation is hundreds of years old."

"That's what everyone has been told for decades. The truth is the group was founded a hundred years ago by my grandfather," said Morganse. "They work for me."

Tammy sat back in her chair, taking a moment to mull it over.

She knew that assassination was a tool used by rulers, but she hadn't considered that such a well-known group would be part of Morganse's government. She didn't know if that made her naïve or the Queen more ruthless than she'd realised.

"Your contact will be a man named Ben. He and one of my agents, Faith, have people who can help you with the searches. They're waiting in the next room. Give them a list of names and they'll discreetly find out if they're loyal to Akosh. I've told them to report their findings directly to you."

"Thank you, Majesty." Morganse's eyelids drooped and her head briefly dipped towards her chest. "I'll leave you to rest."

Tammy was almost at the door when the Queen asked a question that had been running through her mind. "Do you think Akosh will send someone else to finish the job?"

They both knew that Dorn's attack had been retribution for killing so many of Akosh's people in the city. Tammy had thought a great deal about what she would've done in Morganse's position if she had been facing the same choice. The truth was after much deliberation she still wasn't sure. To do nothing risked Akosh's network slowly chipping away at the foundation of everything the Queen had built. An open, honest and free city that welcomed people from across the world, regardless of their religious beliefs. Then again, such a bold move was always going to come with a high price.

She considered lying to the Queen about another attempt on her life but Morganse didn't need comforting lies. The truth would serve her better.

"I think it's possible. But we'll do everything we can to keep you safe."

Morganse's expression told Tammy that she understood what was unsaid. It was impossible to guarantee her safety.

Surrounding her with a ring of people they could trust was a good start. But if an individual was absolutely determined, and had no concern for their own life, then it would be possible to find a way. Dorn had proven that.

In the next room Tammy found a lean man with grey hair who moved with the grace of a cat. His ash-coloured beard was neatly trimmed and she noticed Ben's hands were extremely clean and hairless, suggesting he spent a lot of time wearing gloves. With no unusual features and dressed in drab grey and black clothing, he would be easily forgotten, making him an ideal assassin.

The woman beside him could not have been more different. Faith was an attractive, curvy and vivacious brunette dressed in a colourful and fashionable dress. A heavy gold necklace hung around her neck and more gold decorated her fingers and ears. She exuded confidence and when she smiled it reached her eyes, unlike the man beside her whose emotions were tightly locked away. Tammy might have thought Faith was a prostitute, if not for the fact that they were standing in the Queen's private quarters. Her poise and signs of wealth suggested she was someone used to spending a lot of time mingling with high society. Tammy was confident the ruby around her neck was not coloured glass.

"My my, you're a big one," said Faith, craning her neck. "What do the other Guardians call you? The Steel Giant?"

"I've not heard anyone using a nickname," said Tammy, shaking her hand.

"Then it must be bad," said Faith with a wry smile.

"And you must be, Ben," she said to the assassin.

"Khevassar," he said, inclining his head slightly. His grip was firm but not crushing. While Faith was warm and welcoming he was polite but focused purely on the matter at hand.

"To business. I need you to check into the history of every cook, baker, guard, farrier and anyone else who works in the palace. My people have already started checking into the servants, but we don't have enough bodies. Tell me where and I'll send you both a list of names."

"What are we looking for?" asked Faith.

"Orphans. All of Akosh's people were raised in orphanages dedicated to her. Dorn lied about his background, so some digging may be needed. Failing that, look into those who donate a portion of their wages every month to the orphanages. My best guess is a number of people deposit the money with a local bookkeeper. You're also looking for something like this in their homes." Tammy held up one of Akosh's idols they'd previously recovered.

Faith inspected the idol briefly before passing it to Ben who held it up to the light. "Crudely made. Common stone."

"Which makes it difficult to trace where they come from or who makes them. I've looked into it already, but that isn't important at the moment. That's for later, understood?" she said.

"Understood," said Ben, passing back the idol.

"Once we've cleared all those with immediate access to the palace, we'll expand the search to suppliers. People regularly delivering goods, and so on. Our first priority is to create a ring of silence around the palace. If Akosh sends word to one of her people in Perizzi, whatever their purpose, their actions won't directly affect the Queen and put her life at risk."

Ben pursed his lips. "Her network of people could still cause all manner of chaos in the city, even if they don't directly target the Queen."

"I know," said Tammy, thinking of all the people who had been killed in one night on Morganse's order. "These people are zealots. They're not afraid to die and believe their cause is righteous."

"Are you saying it's going to be dangerous?" asked Faith.

"Most likely."

"Wonderful," said Faith with a grin.

CHAPTER 5

Vargus steered his horse to the top of the ridge with his knees and gently brought it to a stop. A little distance behind him Danoph was coming up the trail, staring around at the western district of Rooke with fresh eyes. He'd been like this ever since they'd left his village.

His perception of the world had changed overnight.

Now, when he looked at the rolling hills and patches of forest, Vargus knew he wasn't looking at grass and trees. His eyes saw the distant past of Shael and what had been there centuries ago. He would also be able to see the thousands of people that had passed through the area. The cities of yesteryear long fallen to ruin, then dust, and eventually forgotten by every living soul and even the history books. A closer look, turning back only a few years, would show rich farmland with dozens of sleepy communities thriving with herds of cattle. Vargus thought that if he focused he could almost hear the whistle of a shepherd and the cackle of two mothers talking across a washing line. But it was only his imagination. He wasn't the Weaver any more and all that he'd seen and experienced lived only in his memory. Now the mantle belonged to Danoph.

"Come on, Danoph. We need to make better time."

"Sorry, I was distracted," said the boy, glancing to the west. Vargus couldn't see anything but Danoph kept lifting his right arm slightly and there was a distinctive glow in the palm of his hand.

This was one of the reasons Vargus had not taken him to the last meeting with his brethren. For the first two days after telling him the truth Danoph had drifted along in a fugue state. Every day he did just enough to feed and bathe himself then climbed into the saddle. The rest of the time he was in what seemed like a drug-addled stupor, staring at the world through a lens only he could see.

To expose him to the others at such an early stage would have been overwhelming and potentially dangerous. Some of his brethren would seek to use Danoph's naïveté, and his power, for their own gain. To a mortal's eye his unusual family might appear divine, but few were benevolent and like any cornered animal, they would fight hard to survive when facing death. There was also the possibility that if Danoph dug too deeply he might uncover secrets they wanted to stay buried, putting him at further risk.

"We're not too far away from Wren," said Vargus. Mentioning her name brought Danoph out of his daze. "We could pay her a visit."

"I'm not sure that would be a good idea," said Danoph.

"Why not?"

"I can't help her. You said that was the one rule we couldn't break. To interfere with the natural course of mortal events."

"You could just go and talk to her," suggested Vargus.

"I'm not sure what I'd say."

"She's still your friend, Danoph. What you are doesn't change that."

"Do you have friends?"

Vargus chuckled. "Of course. And most of those aren't members of our peculiar family. We may be connected, but I don't see eye to eye with many of our brethren."

"But isn't it hard?" asked Danoph, steering his horse closer. "Seeing your friends grow old and die."

They rode in silence for a while as Vargus tried to think how best to answer. It was something he'd spent a lot of time thinking about over the years.

All of his brethren had chosen to look human. Most of them, at some point in their long existence, had spent one or more lifetimes as normal men and women. They'd move to a town or village then live and work alongside their neighbours as if they were ordinary people. They'd build friendships over decades, sometimes get married, grow old and eventually die, or so it would seem to everyone in their community. Sometimes the only way to understand mortals and their daily struggles was to become one of them for a lifetime or two.

But with such lives came the death of friends and loved ones. After each painful loss Vargus would ask himself if it was worth it and he always came to the same conclusion.

"I won't lie, it's hard to have mortal friends, but it's worth it. The alternative is isolation from everyone. In which case you might as well seek oblivion in the Void where you'll feel nothing." Unable to cope with the pain a few of his kind had done just that.

"We're not mortal, but we have so much in common with them, and we live in their world. Many of my friends have died, but in some ways that's no different for mortals. Children watch their parents and grandparents grow old and die. You shouldn't cut yourself off from everyone."

"I don't think now is the right time to visit Wren. I know she's doing well and is busy with organising the community. I don't want to interrupt."

Vargus knew it was an excuse but he didn't press the issue. In time Danoph would seek out familiar people to keep him grounded. Being isolated for a long time created the kind of loneliness that would eat away at a person.

Without friends Danoph would begin to lose touch. If he wasn't careful months and then years would pass in the blink of an eye. Time would become unstuck and the world around him would fade away. Normally a family would help but their kind could not have children. Their bodies looked and felt human but they were not the same. It was a delicate subject Vargus expected he would have to discuss with Danoph at some point. It would probably become more important to him in the next few years as he grew into manhood and saw mortal friends getting married and having families of their own.

"Can I ask you something about Wren?" said Danoph, nervously licking his lips. On the other hand, perhaps it was a conversation they needed to have sooner than Vargus had anticipated.

"Ask me."

"Her community and what she's building. Why does it feel familiar?" said Danoph. "Has it happened before?"

"There was something similar a long time ago. If you focus, the details will become clear."

"Maybe later," said Danoph. He was still learning how to control his power. Vargus suspected his reluctance came from the possibility that he would discover more about Wren's past and her possible futures. "Tell me more about your meeting with our brethren. Who are they? What are they like?"

"That's a difficult question to answer. Some of their names will be familiar, but there are others you will not have heard. They come from every part of the world. Some exist because of a mania or a change in the way people live. Some rose to power as the mortal races evolved and others died with those who fell. Long ago people believed that storms were caused by a god, but he no longer exists. The Sun God is a distant memory and centuries ago there were darker gods, fed by blood sacrifice and gruesome rituals. They're gone as well, but a few of the oldest still exist."

"Because they've adapted over time," said Danoph, struggling to wrap his mind around it. "Like you, with the Brotherhood of the sword."

"Yes, although some of our kind are forces that simply exist, regardless of belief. Summer, Winter, the Weaver and maybe the Maker."

"The Maker. Is he still here?" said Danoph, gesturing at the world around them.

"We believe so."

"Even though no one has seen him in centuries."

"That's right," said Vargus, giving nothing away. Too much information could be as dangerous for Danoph as too little. At this time it was safer for him not to know the truth about the Maker. "It's his rule that we follow. We cannot interfere in the natural course of mortal events."

"I can feel it," said Danoph, squinting into the distance. He raised his right hand and his eyes became distant. "There's a disruption in the natural flow. It's far away, but it's steadily growing stronger as we ride north."

"I believe it's Akosh and her network of people that are causing it. They tried to steer events in Yerskania but those plans were thwarted. I think she's now in Zecorria. She will not give up another nation without a fight so we must stop her. Rise or fall, mortals must be allowed to make their own mistakes or else every victory will be hollow. For all that we are, it's not our place to control them and shape their future."

"And it's your job to keep the others in check." Danoph turned to face him in the saddle. His eyes were still distant and he'd said it as a statement. Vargus wondered how much the boy was seeing in him and how far back he travelled.

"Sometimes," he said with a shrug, trying to act casual. They all knew that he was called upon to investigate when one of their kind was under suspicion. But only a handful of his brethren knew about his other role. "We all vote and someone is sent to investigate the transgressor. Together you and I will unmake Akosh and stop her plans."

"How?" asked Danoph, coming back to the present.

"It's already begun, but I'll need your help when we reach the north. We cannot undo the past, but we can restore balance in the present. So you must learn to control your power by then."

"I will."

"Good. Then let's practise."

They had a long journey ahead but Vargus was confident that by the time they reached Herakion the boy would be ready. He needed him to be, as Akosh wasn't the only member of their family in the north that worried him.

CHAPTER 6

Deep shadows gathered in the mouth of the alley despite light coming from buildings on either side. In the inky blackness, wrapped in silence, Kai watched a building across the street. A short time later he saw one of Akosh's minions, a nondescript man, come out of the jeweller's and scuttle away. The man was one he'd seen several times before and appeared to be a favourite. Despite all of her talk Akosh still cared about those who served her and had a preference for certain individuals. It seemed as if the lesson he'd tried to teach her hadn't worked.

The minion paused halfway down the street where he pretended to look in a shop window. Kai could see he was scanning the street for people taking an interest in his business. His eyes passed over the mouth of the alley without stopping. Satisfied that he was unobserved he shuffled off. Kai waited until the minion had disappeared around a corner before gathering up the shadows and crossing the street.

The shop was not due to close for a couple of hours but it was already empty of customers. The bored-looking owner didn't look up at the sound of the bell above the door. He'd been paid handsomely not to care and would continue to do as he was told. Despite his appearance as a skilled craftsman and a respected member of the jewellery district, Kai knew the man was an addict. The only thing he really cared about was his next hit of black crystal, which Kai was happy to supply.

Like all mortals he was craven and pliable. All it took was finding his weakness. Money, sex, drugs, power, popularity. They all wanted something and he could give it to them. Love, family, honour, duty. All became smoke on the wind when you gave mortals their deepest and darkest desire. What they truly wanted wasn't what they talked about with friends and family. It was the secret they kept close to their heart. The one they couldn't risk sharing with others out of fear. But they told him and Kai turned their dream into a nasty reality.

Above the shop was a small apartment with a reinforced door. Kai could have broken it down but instead he knocked and politely waited. The bolts were disengaged and the door opened a fraction to reveal the bloody and bruised face of Akosh. Her fight with the mage had taken a severe toll on her resources.

"Lock the door," she said, heading into the other room. Kai ignored her and just closed it behind him. Anyone mortal who came through the door unannounced would not survive.

"What did your minion have to say?" he asked, helping himself to a glass of wine. It was a heavy red that was slightly sour and fizzy as if already spoiled. Apparently it had come from a vineyard in the volcanic mountains. It almost tasted like blood, which made him top up his glass. A poor substitute but it would have to do for now.

"That woman, she's still after me," said Akosh, flopping down into a chair like a stroppy child. "This is embarrassing, having to hide in my own city."

"You're right. It is," said Kai. "And to make matters worse, Vargus is on his way here to destroy you."

Akosh sat upright in her chair like a startled rabbit. Yesterday she would have felt the pull of a summons to meet with their brethren but had wisely chosen to ignore it. It was only fair to tell Akosh what she'd missed. "What are we going to do?"

"That's a very good question," said Kai, filling the room with his shadow. It crept across the floor, walls and ceiling, blacking out the windows until everything was shrouded in darkness. Slivers of light filtered in through the window but these too faded as the dark became absolute. His eyes glowed red allowing him to see Akosh scrambling away across the room.

"Wait! What are you doing?"

"You have a powerful mage hunting you and now Vargus is coming here as well. I've done what I can to hide you, but that protection is over. Your presence is disrupting my plans and I will not allow it."

"Tell me what you want. I can help!" pleaded Akosh. "I have a network of people here in the city and across Yerskania!"

Fumbling along in the dark she made it to the rear wall and was now crab-walking sideways until she found the corner. Kai stalked her in the dark, his mouth stretching wider and wider, the skin beginning to split.

"I should absorb you now, while you're still useful," he mused. "I could feast on you for years while the others bumble around the city, searching in vain. In fifty or sixty years all of your followers will be dead, but during that time you would be a nourishing meal."

Panting like a dog she tried to escape, falling over furniture, feeling around the edge of the room for the window or door. But they were coated in his shadow, black as pitch and hard as granite. Her nails began to bleed as she frantically clawed at the window like a trapped animal.

Akosh was more powerful than the others he'd consumed and some of them were almost spent. It would be a long time before she became an empty husk.

Kai watched with amusement as she brought her power to bear, trying to crack his shadow and escape. He relaxed, allowing a small amount of light into the room, giving her a glimpse of hope before he snatched it away. Her fear returned tenfold. His long purple tongue tasted the sweet stench of her rising terror. Scared meat always tasted better.

"I can help you," said Akosh, desperately searching for a way out. "Without me you won't be able to use my people across the west."

That wasn't true. He recognised a dozen of her people in the city and could use them to find the rest. If he applied a bit of pressure, or gave them what they truly desired, they would serve him as well as her. "You're still more useful to me as a meal."

"If Vargus comes here and I've disappeared, he'll keep digging. Sooner or later he'll focus on you and what you're doing in Herakion." Kai knew she was clutching at straws but she was partially right. Vargus was relentless. It might take him a little longer to find the truth, but he always got there in the end. If Kai was able to keep Vargus's search for Akosh focused on Zecorria, his plans elsewhere might go unnoticed. By the time Vargus and the others worked out what he was really doing it would be too late.

Keeping Akosh around might be a useful distraction. If she was seen on the streets of Herakion by the right people then all eyes would turn to the north.

With a grunt of effort Kai forced his hunger down and slowly, piece by piece, the shadows in the room receded. By the time they'd peeled away from the windows his human appearance had been fully restored. Akosh was huddled under a window, hugging herself with bloody fingers.

"I will keep our brethren at bay for a while longer," promised Kai, although that was a lie. It would take Vargus at least two weeks before he arrived in Herakion but Akosh didn't know that. "In return I need your followers to carry out a few tasks for me."

"I can't operate in the open," said Akosh bitterly, "as long as the mage is after me."

"Then take care of her."

"She's too powerful. I've never seen the like before. She nearly defeated me."

That made him pause. Such a powerful human would be a wonderful source of nourishment. On the other hand, apprehending her would require expending a considerable portion of his energy. Such a public display would also attract the wrong sort of attention. A shame, but this was one meal he would have to skip for the time being.

"I don't know how to beat her," said Akosh.

Kai sighed. Just like the others, she'd been living as a human for too long. "Then don't attack her from the front. Send an assassin, or poison her food. Mages need to eat like every other human. They're all sentimental and malleable. Kidnap her family and she'll keep her distance."

"I can't. She wants revenge for the murder of her family."

"Find her weakness. They all have one," said Kai, slurping his wine. It was a poor substitute for real blood or Akosh's power, but it would have to do. For now.

CHAPTER 7

As Tianne rode towards the mouth of the valley, her long journey from Zecorria to Shael finally coming to an end, a sense of calm washed over her.

On the ride south she'd experienced a range of emotions. Fear, that she'd be rejected by Wren and the others. Shame, that her grand adventure to her homeland had ended in defeat. She also felt guilty about leaving Kalina and the others behind where they would be at the mercy of the Regent and his brutal Royal Guards. But Kalina had chosen to stay and Tianne doubted the others would have left their home and a position of power based solely on her word. She wasn't responsible for their fate and the guilt she felt about leaving them ebbed away with every mile. However, that didn't stop her from feeling guilty about leaving Wren and the others in the first place.

Most nights she camped in the wilderness but every four or five days she stayed in a tavern, enjoying a bath and a decent meal. On those nights she overheard conversations about the raiders in western Shael. No one was exactly sure who had defeated them but the stories all agreed on one detail. The raiders were gone. The western road through Shael was safe once again. It sounded as if Wren had defeated Boros and all had gone well despite her absence.

Most often, with only her thoughts for company, Tianne found herself playing out events over and over in her mind. Looking for things she could have done or said differently. Clues she should have seen earlier that revealed the Regent had been manipulating her from the beginning. It made her wonder if he'd rescued any other young mages, as he'd done with her, in order to earn their loyalty. She was still angry with herself for being so naïve, but the past was done and could not be changed. Tianne was determined to learn from it and she would not be caught unawares again. Of course, believing that she had forgiven herself was much easier than actually letting go of her anger.

Oddly, she often found herself thinking of Garvey. His rage had been a constant, always bubbling away under the surface. It fuelled every word and deed. It isolated him and made people afraid of what he might do because he could snap at any time.

The event from his past must have been severe to injure him so badly. It had left a permanent wound that never healed. Or perhaps it was a hundred small things that had added up over time and he couldn't forgive or forget. Together their combined weight pressed down on him, scarring him within and without. After all that he'd done, going against the very principles of the Red Tower, murdering people and destroying whole communities, being blinded, captured and tortured, he'd remained defiant and unrepentant.

Tianne thought about what his actions had cost him and where he'd ended up. Blind, alone and locked in a filthy cell deep underground. Determined to be nothing like him, she worked on forgiving herself for the mistakes of the past. She wanted to let go of the anger, to look forward instead of back, and become a new person. She was determined never to be imprisoned against her will by someone like the Regent.

As she entered the familiar valley where they'd set up the new community, Tianne was surprised to see a small crowd had gathered to meet her. Wren was at the front and as Tianne dismounted her friend rushed forward to embrace her.

There were many familiar faces among the group but also many newcomers. She saw faces from across the west, but also a few young Seve teenagers, standing head and shoulders above the others. With the fall of the Red Tower it seemed as if young people with magic from across the world were finding their way to this safe haven.

"Welcome home," said Wren, wiping her eyes. Tianne was surprised to find she was crying too but didn't care. The relief was overwhelming. It felt like coming home.

"I have so much to tell you," said Wren.

"Me too," said Tianne.

There were more hugs, smiles and warm handshakes before Leonie the smith made it to the front of the crowd. "Good to see you again, girl. We'll talk later." Turning, she faced the crowd. "All right, everyone, get back to your duties. We'll celebrate tonight."

The group began to disperse, giving Tianne her first proper look at how much had changed since she'd left. Back then the skeleton of several houses had been erected. Now a dozen houses were finished and several more were in different stages of construction. The forge had been moved and in its place sat a long narrow building. There were also a couple of other peculiar structures she couldn't identify. She was about to ask about their purpose when she noticed Wren staring at her scar.

"What happened?" asked Wren, squeezing Tianne's hand.

"I'll tell you. Soon."

"Master Yettle could heal that for you," said Wren but Tianne shook her head.

"Not yet. I haven't earned it. For now it serves as a reminder of what I've been through." Tianne didn't remember Wren being so astute but she forced a smile, hoping her friend would change the subject.

"Let me show you around," said Wren.

The long narrow building turned out to be a brewery and beside it the cooperage. Every few weeks barrels of ale travelled out of the valley where they were traded at local villages for fresh supplies.

"You have real windows," said Tianne, noting that all of the finished houses had shutters but also panes of glass in the windows.

"A gift from Queen Olivia," said Wren, showing her to another new building where a glassblower was hard at work. On a raised platform they watched as the gaffer created a huge cone of glass, twice as tall as a man. The building was as hot and sweaty as the forge so they didn't linger.

The classroom was busy as ever with students learning to read and write, while outside others practised fighting with swords or empty hands. An aged Drassi Swordsmaster with a limp moved up and down the line of fighters adjusting stances and raising arms. Tianne was disappointed to see Choss wasn't teaching them which confirmed her worst fear about his fate.

On the far edge of the valley the farming had continued in her absence and the rows of crops were now at head height. On the near side a portion of the old wood had been cleared, more paddocks had been set up for cattle as well as a huge stable for the horses. She could just make out Morag, the old herbalist, leading a group of students through the edges of the wood, foraging for herbs with woven baskets tucked under their arms.

Everyone was busy and had a purpose. No one sat idle in the street. Even the few old people she saw were watching over small children at play or crafting something with their hands. It made her fingers twitch.

"What do you want me to do?" she asked, once her horse was stabled.

"I want you to get some rest," said Wren. "We can talk about it tomorrow."

"No. I've been idle on the road. I need to do something today."

"This isn't the Red Tower, Tianne, but it's up to you. What do you want to do?" asked Wren.

She had been thinking about that a great deal on her ride south. "I was unprepared. Tricked into a room where two unarmed men beat me unconscious." Her hand drifted towards her scar before she realised and quickly lowered it.

"Oh, Tianne," said Wren, but Tianne wasn't really listening. She was back in the room again, seeing the door close while her surprise turned to terror. Then she was back in the dank cell with the cold water and the rats. Despite her desire to learn from previous events and leave traumas in the past, it was her time in the cell that caused the most nightmares. Even now, in bright daylight, a shiver could pass through her whole body as she remembered losing feeling in her fingers and toes.

"I need to be able to defend myself, not just with a weapon," said Tianne, focusing on her friend's face. Staying in the present helped her keep the memories at bay. "I know we're not training to be Battlemages, or building an army, but I wasn't ready."

Tianne expected more sympathy and was prepared to shake it off but Wren surprised her again. "There are a few here who were attacked or chased from their homes. One was even hanged and left for dead." Wren's gaze drifted towards the line of students practising their throws and kicks with the Drassi master. Tianne noticed a tall, red-headed Seve girl among the group. There wasn't anything out of the ordinary about her at first glance. A second look showed she was wearing a wide black choker around her neck.

"Master Jan Ohre teaches a class three times a week," said Wren, gesturing at the group of students. "We also have a new teacher called Griswald. He's someone Master Yettle vouched for. Master Griswald teaches students how to protect themselves with magic. He has a class this afternoon if you want to take part."

"I'll be there," promised Tianne.

The next few days passed in a blur for Tianne as she settled back into the community. Part of her had been expecting lingering looks or people being uncomfortable around her, but despite many new faces she felt welcome. As an old friend of Wren, and someone who'd been on what the others thought was an adventure, she was treated with a mix of awe and respect. Even when she made mistakes in Griswald's class, or found herself on the ground during a sparring session, their opinion of her never changed.

Danoph's absence wasn't noticeable to others, but Tianne could see that Wren wasn't as calm without him. In both her and Danoph's absence Laila had stepped in and was helping to relieve some of the pressure, but as ever Wren was pushing herself harder than anyone else. She spent more time organising than training with her magic, making Tianne wonder how Wren's skills were progressing if she was always so busy.

It would have been so easy to offer Wren some help. To take on some of her duties and ease the pressure, but Tianne repressed her natural instinct. For once, she thought selfishly. She needed to focus on herself for the time being. Besides, if Wren was really stretched she could delegate as she'd done in the past. It seemed as if they both still had something to prove.

Tianne's first surprise was their growing community had been given a name, Corvin's Brow, to keep it consistent with other villages in the Rooke district.

Wren was determined to integrate their village with the

surrounding communities as much as possible. To that end every two or three days a wagon left their village to trade goods. Although the locals didn't know where Corvin's Brow was they soon became familiar with the names and faces of the traders. In time Wren hoped to be able to tell them the truth, but Tianne thought that was years away. If they told them now the villagers would drive the traders away, no matter how badly they needed supplies.

Despite defeating Boros and her raiders, regular patrols from their community kept watch on the road, protecting merchant trains and travellers heading in and out of Shael. Occasionally gifts were left and sometimes a child found their way to the stone marker. At the moment there was peace in the Rooke district but that only made Tianne train harder.

In every lesson, from herb craft to sword fighting, she pushed herself to the limit. As a member of the village she had a variety of duties which she attacked with equal vigour, whether it was cleaning out the stables or kneading dough. After one sleepless night of lambing she was sluggish the next day but didn't let it slow her down.

In her free time she went deep into the woods away from everyone to practise her magic. Sometimes she just needed to release the anger that started to build up inside. Garvey had taught her many lessons without realising. One was that she would not let anger define her.

Tianne still felt partially to blame for what had happened to her in Zecorria, despite knowing deep down that it wasn't her fault. Caught in a loop of guilt and anger she found release in blasting apart fallen trees for firewood. Her serenity would return for a time but frustration at her slow progress in class eroded it piece by piece.

After one of her sessions in the forest she found Wren waiting for her on the path back to the village. She was sitting on a stump in the middle of a clearing, basking in the sun like a cat. It was the first time Tianne had seen her sitting still since returning. A deep thrumming in Tianne's head told her Wren was channelling power from the Source but she didn't seem to be doing anything with it.

"I hear you've been working hard," said Wren, opening her eyes. Tianne felt her release the power and she sagged slightly. It was always like that for her too. The colours weren't as bright and her senses became dull.

Tianne shrugged. "I remember you had several nosebleeds at the Red Tower from pushing yourself too hard."

"It wasn't a criticism," said Wren, making room on the stump for both of them to sit.

Tianne forced herself to calm down. Wren wasn't to blame for what had happened. "I'm sorry. I'm still adjusting."

"Tell me what happened," said Wren, pointing at her scar.

"I can't."

"Why not?"

"Because I'll probably get angry, or start crying, and once I start talking I won't be able to stop."

"That's never stopped you in the past," said Wren with a wry smile.

"And they say Drassi don't have a sense of humour," noted Tianne. The tension eased and a comfortable silence settled between them.

Slowly, piece by piece, Tianne told Wren what had happened, starting with her journey north to Zecorria. Wren listened in silence, never interrupting to ask a question, but she did grip Tianne's hand and squeeze it. The physical contact kept her grounded in the present as her mind relived past events and their traumas. She listened to the birds, watched the trees swaying in the wind and as she spoke about her terror of dying in the water cell, it faded a little.

When she was finished they sat in silence, listening to the forest.

"You're safe now. It's over," said Wren.

Tianne shook her head. "No, it's not. That's why I need to be ready."

"Ready for what?" asked Wren. "The fighting is over here in Shael. I know it won't happen quickly, but we're going to rebuild people's faith in magic."

"That's here, but the rest of the world is still balanced on a knife. People hate magic, Wren. They're scared of anyone showing the signs. That's why you've got so many people showing up. Children are still being driven out or worse, murdered by their own friends and family. They don't see the beauty, only the destruction that magic has wrought. Then there's the Regent and his cadre. He says they exist to protect and serve the people, but that's a lie."

"What are you saying?"

A feeling had been creeping up on her, bubbling away inside, even before she'd fled south. This was just the calm before the storm.

"I think the attack on the Red Tower was only the beginning. We need to be ready to protect ourselves, because something is coming. Something much worse."

CHAPTER 8

Regent Choilan struggled to control his anger as he stared at the bruised and bloody faces of his six mages. It had been their first real challenge and they had proven to be utterly worthless. Even worse they were a laughing stock. Six mages against one and they had been summarily defeated. He knew they were young and lacked experience, but surely the odds should have been in their favour?

He wondered if it would have made any difference if the other six had still been in the capital. Currently they were in the city of Lorissa searching for more recruits. But if his mages weren't effective then it wouldn't matter how many were in his service. If Garvey returned to the city, or the mage who'd defeated them decided to walk into the palace and claim the throne, there was nothing his cadre could do to stop them. His Royal Guards would be equally useless against a mage. The war had shown everyone what one mage could do against an army. Despite everything Choilan found that he remained balanced on a knife edge, staring down at a pit full of sharpened stakes.

All of the young mages had their heads hung in shame except their new leader, Kalina. She was trying to put on a brave face in front of the others but avoided making eye contact. He took a deep breath, drummed his fingers on the arms of his chair and pondered what to do next.

Such a public defeat would send a clear message to his enemies that his mages were weak. Fear of magic had kept some of them at bay but not for much longer. He might have to start employing a food-taster and double the number of guards when he left the palace.

This had always been a gamble but it had also been his best chance of hanging on to the throne for at least another decade. The boy was still years away from being old enough to take over. However, there were other people waiting in the wings, ready to step forward when he fell, or was pushed, off the throne. Other, more faithful servants, who allegedly had the people's best interests at heart. That's what they would say to those who asked. They were nothing more than vultures, waiting to feast on his rotting corpse and seize control.

"Kalina, stay a moment. The rest of you, go and get your wounds treated." Choilan dismissed them with a wave, giving neither praise nor criticism. That would come later.

"My knowledge of magic is limited," he said when the others had left the room. "So, tell me what happened. What am I missing?"

"She was so strong. I've never felt anything like it," said Kalina, rubbing her arms as if cold. "It's difficult to explain."

"Try," he suggested, smiling through his teeth.

Kalina was about to argue until she saw his expression. Instead she took a deep breath and tried to find the right words. "Imagine standing outside on a freezing cold day for so long that your hands and feet go numb. It's a chill that goes right through your skin, right down to your bones. When she embraced the Source, just being close to her, it felt like that. It hurt."

"So, it's not about numbers?"

"No, it's more than that. Much more."

Choilan's fingers turned white on the edge of his glass of wine. "I'm beginning to lose my patience, Kalina. How do we beat her?"

"It isn't just that she's more powerful than us," said Kalina. "We only know how to move things with our magic because we were shown by Tianne. This mage conjured fire, ice and light. She's had years of training, probably at the Red Tower. It's not like milking a cow or riding a horse. There's no one to show us how it works."

She'd tried hard not to make it sound like an accusation, but Choilan clearly heard it in the tone of her voice.

"Get some rest. We'll discuss this later," he said, waving her out of the room. It was either that or he threw something at her head for such insolence.

The irony of the situation was not lost on him. He'd led the way with the banishment of all Seekers in Zecorria, which had ultimately led to the destruction of the Red Tower. After what they'd done, inaction against Seekers would have been worse. His people would have continued dying and he would've been blamed for not saving them from their children and rogue mages.

As far as the people knew Garvey had been imprisoned and then executed. Now, any reports about children with magic were prioritised and people were grateful to him for getting rid of them. From a distance everything had worked out for the best. But he could only maintain the illusion for so long. News about mages fighting in the city would soon begin to spread.

Choilan was disappointed that the adults they'd captured had not been more forthcoming. All of them had been self-taught amateurs with one or two magic abilities they used to trick others out of their money. None of them had been willing to serve and unfortunately their bodies had yielded no answers either.

Feeling despair starting to well up Choilan retired to his private rooms where he could vent his frustration away from prying eyes. The Royal Guards never said anything and were supposedly loyal to him, but lately he'd begun to wonder if some of them were taking money from his enemies. Every now and then he saw them exchanging looks or rolling their eyes at something he said.

He needed a solution, and quickly, or else he might be the one rotting in a water cell beneath the palace. An idea formed in the back of his mind and he sent a servant to find his first wife.

Selina arrived a short time later and found him nursing a glass of bitter kirsch. She glanced at what he was drinking and rolled her eyes.

"It's not that bad," she said, helping herself to some whisky.

"Not yet, but I have a plan."

"I'm listening," she said, eagerly leaning forward.

"My cadre is useless. They're bumbling around because they don't have any teachers." He held up a hand to stop her pointing out the obvious. "Yes, I know who's to blame for that. However, I don't think we've found every mage in the city."

"What makes you say that?"

Choilan smiled. "So far all of those we found were amateurs with only a few tricks. I don't believe that those with significant skill couldn't hide themselves from artless children. We need someone who's had real training. Someone to show my cadre what they can really do."

"And what part do I play in this plan?"

"Recently your agents have proven themselves to be very capable. I'm tasking you, and them, with finding me a skilled mage. Make sure the mage understands what I'm offering. They will live in luxury, here at the palace, and will be well paid for their efforts. I need a real teacher."

Selina heaved a long sigh. "After everything that's happened, it's not going to be easy."

"I thought you liked a challenge," he said. Selina didn't rise to the bait and just gave him a disparaging look. "Fine. What do you want?"

Her smile reminded him of a cat staring at a mouse. "In return you will give me control of all your agents."

It was the last thing Choilan had been expecting. It was one thing for her to play at being a spymaster, controlling a few people, but to run his whole network was totally different.

"You would have to forgo any other responsibilities as my first wife. How would I explain your absence?"

"You've two other wives to parade around at functions with visiting dignitaries and the like. Besides, they love those sorts of events and find you charming, whether you're drunk or sober."

Choilan downed the last of his kirsch in one gulp, enjoying the burning sensation in his throat. "Since you're speaking plainly, allow me to return the favour. You've had no formal training. Looking after a dozen loyal agents is very different to my entire network. There are a number of plans in progress, agents under-cover at home and abroad. To allow you to just take over would be dangerous and reckless."

Selina pursed her lips and he readied himself for another insult but she surprised him again. "You're right. But that still doesn't change what I want."

"Then what are you suggesting?" he said, folding his arms.

"I shadow the head of your network until such time as they think I'm ready to take over."

"That could take years," said Choilan but he recognised the stubborn set of her jaw. She must have known what he would say and the price. Apparently he'd become predictable to his first wife. "Fine. I agree to your terms."

"Done," she said, offering her hand, which he grimly shook. Somehow he felt as if he'd come out on the worse end of the deal.

"But first you have to find me a mage," he reminded her.

"I know," said Selina. "I've already got my people work-ing on it."

As Choilan watched her leave he recalled a brief time, years ago, when he'd enjoyed seeing his first wife. They'd been friends, lovers and allies. Now he found himself continually bargaining with her for support. Well, the final bitter laugh would be his if this plan failed.

If she, or his own agents, failed to secure a reliable mage to teach his cadre, then it would spell their doom and his as well. If Garvey, or any of the rogue mages, resurfaced and his cadre were unable to defeat them Choilan knew he wouldn't remain on the throne. At that point his arrogant first wife would suddenly find herself living a very different life.

It was a dangerous gamble but it was the only choice. In need of distraction for a little while, Choilan went in search of one of his other, more compliant, wives.

CHAPTER 9

Ben checked his gloves for a third time, pulled on his mask and slid down the tiled roof towards the edge.

It had been a long time since he'd crawled across rooftops for the Silent Order, but this current task required every available pair of hands. Those of the inner circle still able to climb a rope were not exempt. Baylor was almost seventy but she'd laughed when someone had suggested she stay at home. Only Hakari had declined as last year he'd lost the bottom half of his left leg and three fingers on his right hand to a bad infection.

The street below loomed towards Ben as he reached the edge of the roof. Just when it seemed as if he was about to slide to his death the rope went taut and he stopped. Half of his torso was hanging over the edge, giving him enough manoeuvrability to reach down and flick open the window latch. After squirting a mix of pig grease and water on the hinges he waited for it to soak in. It slid open without even a whisper.

Feeding more rope through the harness he slowly lowered himself over the edge of the roof and climbed in through the window. The apartment was in darkness. Light crept in from under a door across the room and through the open window. After securing the rope he closed the curtains and sat in darkness listening to the building.

On the ground floor a married couple were arguing, the wife angry at her husband for spending their money on beer instead of food. The argument sounded like one they'd had before, which suggested it would carry on for a while. Ben could hear a couple of people moving around in the apartment directly below, muttering to themselves in tired, annoyed voices. Being woken up yet again by their noisy neighbours was getting on their nerves.

Despite the candlelight leaking under the bedroom door the apartment around Ben was silent. It meant either the occupant had fallen asleep without putting out their light or something more sinister. It was possible they had left their apartment without extinguishing the candle, but given the careful nature of the occupant that was highly unlikely.

On silent feet Ben crept across the room and put his ear to the door. He thought he might hear deep breathing. Instead he heard a floorboard creak on the other side.

Instinct made him dive to his left, forgoing silence for speed. A second later the door flew open, falling off its hinges. A lithe man dressed in a pair of skin-tight trousers and a black shirt limped through the door, his arms raised in a defensive stance.

Light flooded the room and it took Ben a while for his eyes to adjust. When he saw who was waiting, his worst fears were proven right.

"Hakari," he said, inclining his head.

"Tomas," said his old friend. Hakari was one of only three people who knew his real name. "I wondered if you'd figure it out."

"We both know you can still climb a rope and get across rooftops. Then there's the story you've always told about not knowing your parents. None of us had any reason to believe you were telling the truth."

Hakari's smile showed perfect white teeth. "It's all true. My parents died when I was five and I was raised in an orphanage. The only lie I told was about the patron."

Ben briefly considered trying to reason with Hakari but deep down he knew it would be pointless. His friend would never tell him what he wanted to know about Akosh. Members of the inner circle were the elite of the Silent Order and each person had earned their position from long years of experience. No one was more deadly or determined. Only the best, or possibly the worst depending on where you were standing, became members of the inner circle.

While other followers of Akosh had killed themselves rather than be taken in for questioning, Ben knew Hakari would never make that choice. After so many years in death's service Hakari would not surrender to the black-hearted bitch without a fight.

The Khevassar had given Ben a long list of names to investigate, starting with those in regular contact with the Queen. It had been his idea to investigate members of the Silent Order. After all, only the inner circle knew who they really served. As such any member of the inner circle could ask for an audience with the Queen without raising any eyebrows. It was this niggling thought that had prompted Ben to triple check the stories of his closest friends.

Ben took a deep calming breath and tried to find his centre. Hakari waited as Ben took off his gloves and raised his arms in a defensive stance.

"You know, I've always wondered which of us was better," admitted Hakari.

"A foolish thought."

"We'll see, old man," said Hakari. With that he launched his first attack, a hooked hand towards Ben's face, going for his eyes.

Ben swayed out of the way and riposted with a jab to the throat, a kick to the shin and another to the stomach. Hakari was forced to shuffle backwards but miraculously didn't stumble. His wooden leg was securely attached and didn't seem to slow him down.

Hakari grinned and came forward, his fists blurring in a series of blows that Ben dodged or blocked with his raised arms. One or two jabs went under his guard, catching him on the ribs, but they were glancing blows and didn't slow him down. He hunched over slightly to catch his breath, raised his chin and retaliated. A series of kicks forced Hakari to dodge backwards in a hurry and he stumbled. A kick caught him in the ribs and Ben followed up with a knee to the groin. Twisting his right leg Hakari took the blow on his thigh. He grunted in pain and moved out of reach but was still ready to fight.

"Getting tired?" asked Hakari with a grin.

Ben didn't reply. Instead he went on the offensive, trying to blind or stun his opponent.

After a few minutes of battling back and forth it became clear that they were evenly matched. While Ben had more experience he was also older and a little slower. Hakari's speed made up for his injuries, which sometimes made him clumsy. Ben always fought with precision, his movements sharp, whereas Hakari was known for being more unpredictable.

Feigning a kick he rushed in close and grabbed Ben by the collar with both hands. As they grappled and tried to throw one another to the ground, a dangerous idea crossed Ben's mind.

When Hakari tried to sweep his legs Ben dodged and then fell backwards on purpose, still holding on tightly to his opponent. Caught off balance Hakari let go with one hand to brace his fall. Ben's thumb jabbed him in the throat three times before they hit the floor and rolled apart. Gasping for air Hakari scrambled backwards until he reached the wall and then forced himself upright. Before he had a chance to recover Ben picked up a chair and threw it at his old friend.

It caught Hakari a glancing blow on the face, gashing his forehead, blood running into one eye. As Hakari turned his face towards Ben a fist clubbed him on the temple. Hakari crumpled to the floor and didn't get up.

They had only been fighting for a few minutes but Ben's lungs were burning. With shaking legs he collapsed into a chair. His face was slick with sweat and he could feel more trickling down his back. Perhaps he was getting old. The irony of Hakari's defeat didn't escape Ben either. That the only way to win had been to use Hakari's erratic tactics against him.

When he could stand up again Ben made a cursory search of the apartment, looking for anything out of the ordinary. In the far corner of the bedroom was an old beer barrel and sat atop it one of Akosh's idols. The stone was scarred and pitted but its surface had been worn smooth from being handled over many years. With trembling hands Ben peered inside the barrel and felt his heart sink.

An hour later he was lurking in the palace waiting for the new Khevassar to finish her meeting with the Queen. The Old Man had been a relentless force for justice and from what he'd seen so far his successor seemed just as implacable. There was an inner strength to her that Ben admired. Perizzi was an open and friendly city but there had always been a dangerous undercurrent that most people never saw. As she waded further into those waters it would test the Khevassar. He would soon find out if she was tough enough to endure in the long term.

"Ben," said the Khevassar, looming over him as she came down the hallway. "You looked flushed. Is that a bruise on your face?"

"I need a word. It's urgent."

He followed her to the Queen's private sitting room where they sat down on either side of the cold fireplace.

"I take it you have news about the search?" she asked.

"Yes, and it's not good. Everyone in the palace has been cleared or removed." They had only found two servants with ties to Akosh and both of them knew very little. Neither had been in contact with anyone else or their patron. They no longer worked in the palace but beyond that Ben didn't know their fate. They probably had an appointment with the Smiling Chef, just to make sure they weren't hiding any secrets.

"Did we miss someone?"

"In a way," he said with a deep sigh. "One of the inner circle was loyal to Akosh."

The Khevassar sat back in her chair, her scarred hands tightening into fists. Her eyes became distant as she worked through the repercussions. A strand of her blonde hair had worked its way loose and she idly tucked it behind an ear.

"What happened?"

"I found a barrel full of idols in his home. Over one hundred."

There were at least one hundred followers of Akosh in the city. One hundred people that they couldn't identify any more because Hakari had warned them. That meant anyone on the streets could be one of Akosh's people.

"I will not live in fear," said the Khevassar. "It's what they want. To create a society that cowers behind its doors, that's always afraid. If this information were made public it would terrify some and others would form mobs. We saw it with the Seekers and I will not have that in my city."

"I admire your conviction, but what do you want to do in the meantime?" he asked.

"Most of Akosh's people are sleepers. They live normal lives until they receive an order. We need to monitor all messages coming into the city."

Ben whistled. "Perizzi is the busiest port in the world. Even if we somehow manage to keep an eye on all official channels, there are aviaries and then there are the Families. I don't see them following your orders."

Just as there were rumours about the origins of the Silent Order, some claimed the crime Families of Perizzi went back to the founding of the city. Ben didn't think they were actually that old but from what he knew they'd existed for over a hundred years. As well as running the underworld the Families had their own ways in and out of the city to smuggle goods past the authorities.

"We can't close every door."

"No, we can't," agreed the Khevassar. "But we can make it more difficult for Akosh to communicate with her people. It could also buy us some time to find out who they are."

"And the Families?"

The Khevassar grinned and much to Ben's surprise a shiver ran down his spine at her expression. "Leave them to me. I have an idea."

CHAPTER 10

Tahira, the rogue mage, thrashed against the restraints but her strength wasn't enough. No matter how hard she tried she couldn't break free. The gag prevented her from cursing or spitting, but she was still having a good try as drool leaked from her mouth. Balfruss shook his head sadly as he closed the cell door then activated the glyphs. The swirling runes came to life with a low audible hum. A moment later his restraints around the young mage were severed.

With a muffled cry of triumph Tahira scrambled up from the floor, ripped the cloth gag from around her mouth and reached for the Source. As energy coursed through her body she grinned at Balfruss and tried to unleash it against him. The black runes etched into both sides of the door glowed orange and then red in response, draining the energy. Tahira stumbled back looking disorientated, her whole body trembling. It was as if someone had slapped her hard across the face. She tried again, drawing more deeply from the Source, but the result was the same. The moment she tried to project anything the Red Tower absorbed the power, feeding the spells of protection that had kept the building standing, untouched by time, for hundreds of years.

Tahira could embrace the Source, draw as much power into

herself as she wanted, but she couldn't use it. She could bask in its majesty, listen to the very heart of creation and meditate upon it, but right now none of that crossed her mind. She just wanted to hurt someone.

When she realised she'd been hobbled Tahira slammed her hands against the door, screaming in frustration. Master Ottah slammed the food slot closed before she could spit through the narrow gap. A tirade of abuse and promises of what she would do followed Balfruss as he and the old librarian moved down the corridor.

"Are you sure about this, Master Ottah?"

"That's the fourth time you've asked me that question," snapped the librarian. "And you know I hate repeating myself."

"I just want to make sure you understand the enormity of what you're undertaking."

Master Ottah guffawed as he gripped the wooden handrail and slowly made his way down to the second floor of the tower. "Ha. I've kept plants watered and fed before. They're no different."

"They might try to hurt or kill you."

"Then they're even more stupid than they look," he said. "If they succeed, they'll starve to death in their cells. I couldn't open the doors even if I wanted to."

Ever since Garvey had asked him to take over his responsibilities and mantle of the Bane, Balfruss had been wrestling with the decision. From the start he'd been unwilling to murder any rogue mages, even the children like Tahira who had chosen to travel with Garvey. They were young and impressionable. There was the possibility of redemption for them, but not if he sent them to an early grave.

Tammy's cell beneath Unity Hall had been a temporary measure at best while he rounded them up and considered his next move. Eventually he'd realised there was no alternative but to bring them back to the Red Tower and return the former hospital back to its original purpose. Although he couldn't be certain who had built the Red Tower he believed it was the original Grey Council. What disappointed him most was the realisation that even back then some mages had sought to abuse their power and had to be imprisoned.

When they reached the second floor of the tower Master Ottah settled into his favourite chair and sighed with pleasure. He wasn't yet seventy but he moved at a sedate pace and Balfruss noticed he favoured his left leg over his right.

"Don't even think about healing my leg," said the librarian. "It's an old injury from when I was a boy. I didn't let that butcher Yettle try to heal it so I'm not going to let a bumbling amateur like you try to fix it."

Balfruss smiled at the old man's attitude. They both knew Master Yettle was the most skilled Healer in a hundred years. "I learned a few things across the Dead Sea that even he doesn't know," said Balfruss, letting a few sparks of energy dance across his fingers. "I could try straightening the bone."

"Don't you dare, boy," warned Master Ottah, raising a hefty book in one bony hand. "I will beat you about the head if you try."

They both knew he was lying. He'd never abuse a book in such a manner and risk damaging it. Of course he had no such concerns about Balfruss's skull.

"Yes, Master Ottah."

The librarian grunted and lowered the book. "Make yourself useful. Go and make me some tea."

Balfruss raised an eyebrow in surprise. No one was ever allowed to bring food or drinks into the library. To the librarian it was a sin worse than murder. "You want me to bring you a cup of tea here? In the library?"

"Of course not. I'll come to you upstairs."

Balfruss went up to the third floor which Master Ottah had made into his quarters. After drawing water from the pump he thought about using his magic to boil the water but changed his mind. Somehow the librarian would know the moment he tasted the tea as he always complained about it being bitter.

Many years ago Balfruss had been an eager young boy keen on reading every book in the library. Master Ottah had been no less strict but he had allowed Balfruss to continue with his impossible pursuit as long as he adhered to the rules. Back then he'd seemed old but thinking on it now Balfruss realised he would have been fairly young.

Balfruss set the kettle over the fire to boil, using a spark of magic to light the kindling, before feeding the flames with chunks of wood. The librarian would never know.

They had been determined to do things differently. To create a new Red Tower that was superior to those of the past. But once they realised Danoph was an Oracle their plans had changed.

Balfruss had worked tirelessly to stop the boy's vision from coming to pass but their worst fears had come true. In spite of all the preparations they'd made innocent lives had still been lost when the Red Tower fell. At least now, from the ashes of the school, he'd been able to salvage something of value. With him as the Bane the rogue mages had a chance at redemption. With Garvey all they received was an unmarked grave.

"The water is boiling," huffed Master Ottah, stumping into the room. "Can't you hear the whistle?"

"Sorry, I was lost in thought."

Balfruss filled the teapot with water, set out two glasses and delved into Master Ottah's vast larder for a fresh lemon. There were still a number of farmers in the surrounding area who remained loyal. They would keep the librarian and his charges fed for a long time.

"What's on your mind, boy?"

Given the number of problems, Balfruss couldn't help laughing. "Where do I start?"

"With what matters. With what you can change." Master Ottah sucked his teeth. "Sorcerer or homesick boy, you're still just one man."

"I'm not sure what I should do," admitted Balfruss. "Garvey asked that I become the Bane, and I have, but I know the job isn't done. It's never done."

"Then go out there and stop other rogue mages. That's your task. Focus on that."

"And ignore everything else?"

"Boy, are you the master of the world? Is it your job to fix everyone's problems? Did someone make you High King and ruler of every land from shore to shore?"

Balfruss didn't think Master Ottah actually expected him to answer, but when the old man glared at him he found himself smiling. "No, Sir."

"Are there other capable people out there trying to help?"

"Yes, Sir."

"Then maybe you should trust them a little more. The tea's brewed long enough, pour me a glass." Master Ottah put a slice of lemon in his mouth, not even wincing at the sharpness before sipping his tea through it. "Standing idly by is one thing. Running headlong into every fight is a sure way to get yourself killed. I thought you had more brains than that."

"Was that a compliment?" asked Balfruss, almost coaxing a smile out of the librarian.

"Your ears must be full of wax. I've got a syringe that can help with that."

"I'll pass," said Balfruss, crunching a sugared almond with his tea.

They sat in companionable silence for a while listening to the settling sounds of the Red Tower. Balfruss had rarely heard the building so quiet. Occasionally, late at night when all of the students were asleep, he'd pause in whatever he was doing and simply listen. Power, unlike any he'd ever known, hummed in the walls and deep beneath his feet in the wellspring. If he held perfectly still the vibrations almost sounded like music. A hidden language waiting to be unravelled by those with patience. Or perhaps it was simply a flight of fancy. The answer would be buried somewhere in one of the ancient books in the upper library.

"A time will come when they will need you," said Master Ottah, breaking the quiet.

Balfruss couldn't help ribbing the old man. "Are you an Oracle now, Master?"

"Boy," he said with a long sigh, "you're testing my patience."

"I apologise," said Balfruss, bowing in his seat. "Please continue."

Master Ottah waited until he was sure Balfruss wouldn't interrupt before speaking. "Killing is easy. You can do nothing and sometimes people still die. You can shove a bit of steel into someone's belly and they die. It happens every day. Most people don't want to talk about death, but it's there, waiting for us all. Why be afraid of the inevitable?" he asked rhetorically before picking up another slice of lemon. "Living. Now that's a difficult thing. Most people are too afraid to do that. It requires effort, sacrifice, blood, sweat and tears. It means that you stand up and get involved. It means being noticed instead of sitting quiet and just letting things happen then complaining about them afterwards. You've done a fair bit of living. But you're not done yet, so don't go racing towards your grave."

Balfruss waited until he was sure the librarian had finished speaking before asking a question. "Racing?"

"If you wade into the fight today, then it's likely you'll save a few lives. Maybe get yourself a hero's death. Earn yourself a big entry in someone's history book, maybe get a statue, but you won't change much. It's not the right time."

"And how will I know when it is the right time?"

Master Ottah raised an eyebrow. "You'll know, deep in your bones. Everyone faces a moment like that in life, more than one if they're unlucky. You've already faced a few. I can see it in your eyes."

Balfruss immediately thought of the war and his battle with the Warlock. He thought of the friends he'd lost in the fight and his exile from Seveldrom. He thought of his trials across the Dead Sea and instinctively traced the marriage tattoo around his wrist. He thought about Voechenka and the terror that had lurked in the heart of the decaying city. And he thought about the Red Tower in flames.

"Sleep, eat, and in a few days I'll be so sick of looking at your face, you'll have to leave." Master Ottah's smile was a rare and peculiar thing that looked as if it didn't belong on his weathered old face. "You've a long road ahead yet, boy."

Balfruss sat back, closed his eyes and decided to rest for a while.

CHAPTER 11

With a big smile Kai handed the package to the courier. "This is a very important mission," said Kai. "I'm trusting you."

"Yes, Sir. I appreciate it," said Farley, a stout Yerskani man.

A former member of the Watch, Farley had been kicked out for being drunk on duty once too often. There were also rumours that he'd looked the other way for a small fee on occasion, but that had never been proven. Mostly because he'd drunk away any evidence of his wrongdoing. Since then he'd drifted about as a mercenary and manual labourer. Despite his spotted history he still had a military bearing and responded well to orders. It also helped that he was one of Akosh's people and she'd told him to do exactly as he was told.

"To ensure you and the package arrive safely in Perizzi, two Drassi Fists will escort you south."

The masked Drassi warriors probably thought it was excessive to send ten men to protect one. Not that Kai would know because they never complained, barely spoke and never got drunk and gossiped in a bar. They were the perfect hired hands. They did exactly what they were told and didn't care about the job, as long as they were paid the agreed amount. Their fearsome reputation and weapons skill were renowned around the world. That alone would probably keep any bandits at bay on the journey south.

"Two Fists," said Farley, glancing again at the small package. It was a plain wooden box with a simple lock. Dropping it from a moderate height would break it open. Kai could see the wheels slowly turning in his tiny mind as Farley wondered what was so important that two Fists were being sent to protect the contents.

"When you arrive in Perizzi go to the Red Lion tavern. Someone will meet you there and give you final instructions." Farley was being paid a very generous amount of money to carry the box.

"And the other half of my payment," added Farley.

"Yes, and the rest of your gold," agreed Kai, smiling at the greed in his eyes. Farley hadn't questioned why he was needed with so many Drassi warriors and Kai knew he wouldn't ask. Given the amount of money he was being paid Farley just didn't care.

Farley's journey to Perizzi was long, boring and uneventful. His masked Drassi escorts were without a sense of humour and every night, when he suggested they play a hand of cards or game of Stones, they always refused. Trying a different approach he asked the leaders of both Fists to tell him stories about previous jobs they'd completed over the years. Again they politely refused and so Farley spent most of the journey muttering to himself, slightly tipsy from his flask, while he pondered on the box.

When he spotted the familiar sight of Perizzi on the horizon he heaved a huge sigh of relief. Once his business was concluded he intended to get drunk, visit a whorehouse, eat a decent meal and sleep in a real bed. And maybe not in that order.

The guards at the northern gate gave Farley and the others only a cursory glance, focusing their efforts on searching wagons for smuggled goods. A short ride brought them to the Red Lion and there, finally, Farley was free of his Drassi shadows. He thanked them for delivering him safely and offered to shake their hands. The leader of both Fists just looked at him and walked away.

With a shrug he put them from his mind and went inside for a drink. Farley bought himself two mugs of ale and had drained the first in seconds, barely tasting it. He found a table to savour the second and await his contact.

An hour later he was nursing his third mug and considering a fourth when a Drassi warrior came into the tavern. Masked like all of the others he could have been one of those who'd been travelling with him on the road. It was impossible to tell as they never took off the masks where other people could see them.

"Are you Farley?" asked the Drassi, his accent slightly distorting the words.

"Yes," he said, keeping one hand protectively on top of the box. The other moved under the table to rest on his dagger.

Instead of a weapon the Drassi produced a scroll and a bag of money which he set down on the table. "These are for you." With that he turned and walked out the front door.

Farley stared at the bag and tried to guess how much gold was inside. It looked fairly heavy. Breaking the wax seal on the small scroll he read the short message, his face crumpling up in surprise.

"Open the box and drink the flask. Then spend the money and enjoy yourself," he read. Farley turned the note over, expecting there to be more, but the other side was blank.

Inside the box he'd carried from Zecorria, nestled in layers of padded cotton, was a small flask. A quick sniff of the contents revealed it was some kind of brandy. Farley took a small sip and finding it to his liking finished the rest with another gulp. The brandy, together with the three mugs of ale, had blurred his senses a little, but more than anything he wanted a decent meal.

Peering inside the bag Farley's eyes widened in surprise. If he chose to live frugally the money would last him weeks, maybe even two months. Then there was the money he hadn't been able to spend on the road.

The note had instructed him to enjoy himself. Who was he to question orders? The Red Lion was not somewhere he'd normally stay, but with plenty of money in his pocket he paid for a comfortable room. Draining the last of his ale Farley left the empty box on the table and went in search of the finest meal in the city.

Normally the owner of the Tin Cup wouldn't have served the likes of Farley but it was amazing how a stack of gold could change someone's mind. Suddenly the muddy clothes, dusty boots and lack of noble heritage no longer seemed to matter.

Farley didn't care that he'd been tucked away in a private dining room so as not to upset the other patrons. In a way it made him feel even more special as he could order a drink without having to get up from his seat. All he had to do was ring a little bell and someone would appear to take his order.

Over the next two hours eight small plates of exquisite food were delivered to his table. Typically the chef selected a special glass of wine to accompany each course but after a bit of negotiation the wine was swapped for ale.

That evening Farley ate and drank like a king. He feasted on braised beef and black stout, blue-finned plaice and pale crisp beer, corn-fed chicken and a barley brew. With each plate of food he tried his best to savour all of the delicate flavours that were described, but most of the subtle tastes eluded his crude palate.

Feeling totally stuffed but somehow remarkably sober he wandered out in search of some fresh air and entertainment. Never lucky with cards, and conscious that the heavy purse hidden inside his clothing would make him a target for thieves, Farley only gambled a small amount of silver. Customers at the humble gambling den comprised of modest merchants, sailors and a few mercenaries. People with a little extra, although none of them could afford to lose much. Farley tried his best to double his money but ultimately lost everything. Disappointed, but secretly not worried, he left the dice table with empty pockets. The sly eyes of those with nimble fingers in the crowd ignored him and several other losers who left together in a group.

Farley was confident that he wasn't being followed but just in case he decided to stick with the others. They commiserated with each other over a drink at a seedy tavern not far from the docks then split up to go in search of their beds, their berth or some prettier company.

The money he'd been given enabled Farley to bend certain rules, but some doors would not open, no matter how much gold he offered. The Blue Lotus was the most elite and expensive brothel in the city. It catered to customers with vast amounts of wealth. The sort of person who never asked how much something cost. It was also frequented by individuals who required the utmost discretion and that also meant privacy from other patrons.

Even if he bought expensive clothes from the finest tailors they would turn him away at the door. Like many others Farley had heard stories about the women at the Blue Lotus. They were said to be the most beautiful in the world and some came from distant countries he couldn't even name.

With a sigh he put dreams of the Lotus to one side but still chose an establishment that was normally outside his price range. The armed guards at the front door of the Honey Pot looked at him with suspicion, as did the Madam inside, until he produced a stack of gold. Her frown faded with each coin he added to the pile until her predatory smile became unnerving.

The gold disappeared and in its place a parade of beautiful women appeared. Farley sipped on a glass of something sweet that made him cough in surprise. When he'd caught his breath he gulped down some water and focused on making his selection.

The next two hours were among the happiest in Farley's life. Her name was Giselle, at least for tonight, and rather than strip off and get straight down to it, she talked to him first. With delicate touches on his arms and face, he found himself entranced by her long brown hair and dusky skin.

She talked about her life before coming to Perizzi and he was hypnotised by the sound of her melodic voice. For once he didn't care that he was paying for her time and not making the best use of it.

At some point he found himself kissing her. The world melted away and what followed was both familiar and surprising. Much to his embarrassment Farley cried afterwards, but he blamed it on a night of strange food and drink.

Determined to get some sleep and put it from his mind, he found that somehow he was hungry again. Despite the hour he was still able to find a street vendor selling roasted meat on a spit. Even though he wasn't sure of its origin Farley devoured it with relish, dribbling meat juices all over his face and clothes. It didn't matter. Tomorrow he was planning to visit a tailor's shop and order some clothes that would be made for him. He imagined himself parading around the city in some colourful frippery, perhaps carrying a cane and wearing a large hat with a feather.

Before he reached the front door of the Red Lion his stomach began to churn and he dashed into an alley. Hot stinking vomit splashed all over his boots. His head swam and he felt feverish. Blaming it on the dubious meat he kept being sick until his stomach was totally empty. All of the fancy food and drink landed on the street, a feast for hungry rats. Perhaps they'd enjoy the delicate flavours more than him.

Hot, sweaty and suddenly tired, Farley realised it was quite late. He was very aware that in his current state he would make an ideal target for thieves. Clutching his dagger with one hand he wiped the spittle from his mouth and carefully made his way back to the Red Lion. On every corner he was alert for danger, peering into alleyways for watchers, confident that an attack was about to happen. Cold sweat continued to run down his face and his stomach turned over, but he blamed both on his nerves.

By the time the Red Lion came into view he was shaking and barely able to stand up without holding on to the wall with one hand. The stairs inside proved a challenge but eventually he made his way up them, pausing at the top to catch his breath before shuffling down the corridor to his room.

He managed to make it inside and close the door before vomiting again. This time all over the floor and himself. Unable to stand he collapsed on all fours and was both horrified and amazed that he had anything left inside. His stomach muscles ached from the strain and his throat was raw from bile. Tears ran from his eyes and the room felt stuffy and cloying from the stench.

Farley threw open the window, gulping in cool fresh air before another bout of spasms wracked his body. Time lost all meaning. Between the rounds of vomiting he gulped down all of the water in the pitcher beside the bed. Still feeling too hot he stripped off his jacket and shirt. Both of his arms were covered in red welts that itched and burned. He couldn't worry about them too much as his innards began to squirm again.

At some point he lost consciousness and awoke to find himself lying in a puddle of vomit on the bed. The skin across his whole body was on fire. The red welts had spread and his head was pounding. The room felt too bright, too hot and too noisy even though he was alone and in darkness. Brightly coloured lights flashed before his eyes and then his vision turned black but he could still hear himself breathing and smell the reek of vomit. Slowly that faded too until he fell into an empty and silent darkness.

The next morning Korle heard a woman screaming upstairs. Thinking one of his guests was getting too friendly with a member of staff he raced upstairs but before reaching the door a vicious smell hit him. Relle was stood in the corridor staring into the room with a horrified expression. Korle slowly approached, covering his nose and mouth with his sleeve, before peering inside.

The room was covered with vomit and blood. It was splashed all over the floor, the walls, the bed and even the fireplace. The occupant was still in bed, vacant eyes staring, his skin a mass of red blisters.

"Call for the Watch, now!" he said, ushering Relle down the stairs. He heard her running all the way down the street, sobbing as she went.

This wouldn't do. Not at all. He ran a clean business. The Red Lion had a good reputation that he intended to keep. This needed to be dealt with quickly and quietly.

Trying not to gag Korle hurried into the room, doing his best to avoid stepping in the mess. In a vain attempt to combat the stench he threw open the other window. After closing the door he fetched several buckets of water and lye which he lined up in the corridor. Once the Watch took away the body he would scrub the room from top to bottom. He'd have to replace the sheets, and probably the mattress, but that couldn't be helped.

Candles, that's what he would need. Lots of scented candles and incense.

In a day's time no one would ever know a man had died in the room and he would be able to rent it out again.

Idly scratching at a red rash on his forearm Korle wondered how much this was going to cost him to keep quiet.

CHAPTER 12

With a grunt of pain Tianne blocked Kimme's kick at her head on her forearms. Wasting no time she retaliated, catching her opponent in the stomach with her heel. The big girl huffed in surprise and walked backwards a few steps before dropping on to her arse.

"Are you all right?" asked Tianne.

"Just ... winded," said Kimme, gulping in deep breaths of air. "Give me a moment."

Tianne felt guilty about knocking her down but also a touch of pride. Physically the farm girl was one of the biggest and strongest in the village. Working long days for her father had made her tough, which meant most people avoided her as a sparring partner. Tianne picked her at every opportunity. If she could beat Kimme then she would be better prepared for whatever came next.

She offered Kimme a hand and pulled her upright with a grunt of effort. Not only did Kimme smell like a horse she weighed almost as much as one too. "I think you need a wash," said Tianne, wrinkling her nose. Kimme spoke her mind, regardless of other people's feelings, and she expected others to do the same. Tianne liked her a great deal but she did seem averse to bathing.

"Why? I had a bath a few days ago," said Kimme. She smelled her shirt and shrugged, finding nothing amiss.

"Excuse the interruption," said Wren, coming up behind them. "Kimme, Leonie was asking after you. She's in the smithy."

"This was fun. We should practise again tomorrow," said Kimme, slapping Tianne on the back so hard she knew there would be a bruise tomorrow.

"I think she likes you," said Wren, watching as people gave Kimme a wide berth on the street due to her pungent aroma.

"Did you want to see me about something?" asked Tianne, stripping off her damp shirt and drying herself before pulling on a clean one. Wren turned her back, allowing her some privacy even though they were alone in the practice area. Tianne smiled at her friend's back, amused by Wren's prudish attitude. After everything she'd endured Tianne found she cared less about the little things that would previously have kept her awake at night.

"We're sending out another group to visit one of the local villages. I thought you might want to accompany them," said Wren.

"You can turn around," said Tianne, gathering up her belongings. "I can't go with them today. I'm not ready."

Most of the time she knew exactly what Wren was thinking. She tried to hide her true feelings but had difficulty keeping them off her face. But every now and then she surprised Tianne. Today her eyes were unreadable.

"When will you be ready?" she asked.

Tianne shook her head, unwilling to name a precise time. "Soon."

"I was going to choose Bisse to lead the group, but I'd prefer you."

"Wren, stop."

They stood in silence while all around them the village continued to buzz with activity. Tianne could hear the ring of a hammer on the anvil in the smithy. In the distance the bleating of sheep was interspersed with an occasional whistle as they were herded to a new pasture for grazing. The clang of steel on steel rang out as mages and those without magic practised fighting with swords. These and many more sounds had become a familiar and soothing cacophony that spoke to Tianne of home.

"This isn't the Red Tower. We're not training for war," said Wren, breaking the silence between them. "And yet you seem to be."

"I told you why. Don't ask me again," said Tianne. "Not today."

"I won't, but I still think you should go. It's good to take a break and clear your head. Bisse can lead but you should go as his second. There's much to learn from watching and listening to others. Especially if they're using magic to heal."

"How would you know?" asked Tianne, struggling to control her irritation. "I know you've been neglecting your studies."

"You're right," said Wren, surprising her again. "I have, because I'm afraid."

Tianne's simmering anger faded at the anguish on her friend's face. They sat down together on a stack of logs waiting for the sawmill. Normally Tianne would have filled the air with pointless words, or offered her friend an empty platitude, but this time she waited in silence.

"We almost lost everything," said Wren, gesturing at the village around them.

"I've heard from others about what happened." At times it was as if Tianne had never left. Both those she'd known before and strangers seemed compelled to talk to her and divulge their secrets. Only a few days after her return she had in-depth knowledge of almost everyone's life and their concerns. There were a few minor gripes and complaints, as well as regrets about what had happened fighting Boros, but everyone was in agreement about Wren.

"No one blames you for what happened," said Tianne.

"They should. Six people died. Six." Wren shook her head in dismay. "I was trying to do everything. Train to be a healer as well as organise the village. When we found that girl and her mother, I tried to heal her for hours but it didn't work. If not for Master Yettle she would have died."

"No one expects you to be perfect."

"My mother would disagree," said Wren bitterly. "I could have killed that girl, Tianne."

"But you didn't. She's alive and so are many others because of what you did." Tianne pulled Wren into a fierce hug, squeezing her against her chest. She resisted at first but then held on just as tight. "I've spoken to a lot of people since I got back. No one blames you. They admire you."

"I've missed you," said Wren, wiping at her eyes. "Talking to people is really difficult!"

Tianne laughed and some of the pressure eased in her chest. Perhaps they'd both been holding on too tightly. "You should take your own advice. Let Laila, Rue and some of the others share more of your responsibilities. You need to practise your magic as well."

"I know. You're right. I should. I will," Wren promised, laughing at herself.

Boros was gone, but Tianne knew that in time there would be others and Wren needed to be ready. With so many mages being driven out of their homes, not all of them would find their way to Corvin's Brow and the safety of their community.

The Regent would snap up those in Zecorria but others across the west would fall through the cracks and disappear. There were worse masters out there who would exploit naïve young mages for their own gain. Even a competent beginner could become a dangerous member of the criminal underworld.

The next group of raiders who tried to move into the Rooke

district could even have a mage of their own. It made Tianne wonder why there hadn't been more rogue mages before Garvey and the others began their rampage.

"I will go with Bisse today, but only if you promise to spend more time on your studies," said Tianne.

"Agreed," said Wren, shaking her hand with a wry smile.

A few hours later Tianne was glad she'd made the deal, although those with her weren't as happy to be away from the village. For her a change of scenery and some exercise, other than training, was a welcome break.

After riding to Sour Crown, they'd set up camp within sight of the village. Bisse, a year older than her and from Yerskania, was a promising student of Master Yettle, whose ability to heal was bordering on being a Talent. He was handsome, kind and never made a joke at someone else's expense. If not for the fact that he'd nearly cut off one of his own feet during sword practice Tianne would have hated him for being so perfect.

"This is boring," complained Kimme, picking her nose with one grubby finger.

The others were frustrated and Tianne couldn't blame them. They'd been sat for almost two hours and so far no one from the village had approached them. A small group had gathered on the outskirts to stare but they'd quickly dispersed and not returned. The villagers were probably waiting for them to leave.

She wanted to blame them for their fear of magic, but couldn't do that either. Tianne didn't even hate them. To them magic was destructive and dangerous. It turned innocent children into weapons that could explode at any time. Their own flesh and blood poisoned against them.

It didn't matter that Wren and the others had saved them from Boros and her raiders. Some of the villagers probably thought they'd merely swapped one monster for another. Perhaps they were expecting Wren to ask for a tithe.

"I'm bored," said Kimme, earning a frown from Bisse.

"Let's go and gather some herbs for Morag," suggested Tianne. She'd spotted some in the woods that looked unusual on the ride in. Normally Kimme, who couldn't tell the difference between wolfsbane and chives, would have refused but she was so bored she quickly agreed. Bisse mouthed a silent thank-you as Tianne walked past with the farm girl in tow.

"How long do you think we'll stay out here?" asked Kimme, clomping through the trees.

"A few more hours. We'll probably leave before dark," said Tianne.

"This is pointless. They're never going to trust us. They hate mages."

"They don't know us," said Tianne, following a narrow trail. "For a long time mages were seen as mysterious and all-knowing."

"No one knows everything. Not even Master Yettle. Besides, most of us are still teenagers. Is this a herb?" asked Kimme, holding up a stinkweed plant.

"No. It's a weed. Here, look at this." She led Kimme to a small clearing where a tree had fallen and was beginning to rot. In the damp grass, deep in the shade, she found a clutch of tall white mushrooms which she gathered. "It's going to take a long time to earn their trust. Before that can happen, they need to see us as people."

Kimme looked at her askance. "Of course we're people. What else would we be?"

"Think of it this way," said Tianne, trying a different approach. "Did you train dogs on your parents' farm?"

"Yes. For herding sheep."

"And were they always trained from a pup?"

"Easiest way."

"What about if you get one that's been living wild since birth? How hard is it to train one of them?"

Kimme shook her head. "Almost impossible. Once they turn feral, it's hard to make them listen."

"To the villagers, we're all feral dogs. They need to see us doing normal, boring things, like cooking meals and gathering herbs, before they'll start to see us as people." Tianne dropped the mushrooms into her bag and moved on.

"One day is not going to change their minds."

"No, it could take years."

"Years!" said Kimme. "I'm not coming out here every day for years."

"I'm sure we'll take turns." Tianne spotted an unusual plant with small red and yellow flowers which she carefully dug up, including the roots. "But, it could be worse."

"How?"

Tianne's mind went back to the two men attacking her and the water cell. She forced herself to focus on it and not shy away from the memories.

"In Zecorria they round up people with magic and force them to serve the Regent. Anyone who refuses dies in a cell."

"Is that what happened to you?" asked Kimme, gesturing at the scar over her eye.

"Let's head back," said Tianne, dodging the question. "I'm sure Bisse has been missing you."

Her instincts proved correct when Kimme blushed. "Why would he miss me? Has he said something?"

"Not to me," said Tianne, hiding her smile behind a hand. As she'd suspected, Kimme was infatuated by Bisse. It was the reason she'd suddenly volunteered to go with them to Sour Crown.

"Do you really think they'll change their minds?" said Kimme, gesturing at the village in the distance.

"I heard your parents didn't care about your magic. In fact, they were pleased." Kimme's story was one of rare acceptance. It was only because of a nosy neighbour that she'd been forced to leave home.

"It made me stronger and I could do more than before." Kimme grunted. "Damn that Hogarth. If not for him I'd still be at home on the farm."

"Why weren't your parents scared?"

"Because they knew I'd never hurt them."

"And because you had control," added Tianne. "If we can prove to other people that magic can help them or even heal them, attitudes might change. How long would it take to convince Hogarth that magic wasn't a bad thing?"

Kimme nodded grimly. "A long while."

When they reached the others Kimme was quiet and lost in thought. The next few hours passed without any issues or further complaints. A few children from the village stared at them from the outskirts but they didn't venture any closer. Tianne took their curiosity, and the fact that the adults hadn't chased them away, as a good sign.

Bisse spent the remainder of the afternoon demonstrating healing to the others and Tianne paid close attention. Of all the things magic could do, healing was perhaps the most powerful they had to change minds. Somewhere, deep inside, her instincts told her it would be needed in the days ahead. Boros was gone but the Regent and his cadre remained and their numbers were growing.

CHAPTER 13

For most of her life Munroe would have said that meditation was a boring and pointless waste of time. The years she'd spent at the Red Tower had changed her mind as without finding an inner calm she would never have touched the Source. Her innate magic, her Talent, required no thought or a quiet mind. It was just like using a muscle.

Now, as Dox struggled to find even a few heartbeats of inner calm, Munroe felt sympathy for her old teachers.

"Maker's cock, this is boring," complained Dox.

They were kneeling across from each other on the floor of Munroe's room in the tavern. A candle sat between them and they were supposed to be concentrating on the flame. By emptying the mind of all distractions it became easier to hear and feel the Source at the edges of perception. At least that was the theory.

"Try again," said Munroe, working hard to swallow her irritation. "Clear your mind of everything but the candle."

"I've been trying for ages."

"You wanted to learn about magic. This is how I was taught. So, shut up and try again!" Munroe closed her eyes, ignoring the shock on Dox's face. When the silence in the room had reached a dozen heartbeats and the girl continued shuffling about, Munroe knew it wasn't working. "Let's try a different approach."

She snuffed out the candle and drew power from the Source, relishing the heightening of her senses as its energy flooded her body. Other mages could feel the innate connection between them. So far Dox had shown little sensitivity to being near other magic users. If not for the fact that Munroe could feel a faint pulse coming from the girl, she might have doubted Dox had a connection to the Source.

"Wait," said Dox, closing her eyes. Her face scrunched up in concentration as Munroe wove together a shield. The hairs stood up on the back of the girl's arms and a faint smile tugged at the corners of her mouth. "I can feel something. It's really weird."

"Try to describe it," said Munroe.

"It's like a heartbeat, but it's different. Louder and closer. There's a pressure against my ears. It's starting to hurt." Dox's eyes snapped open in surprise. "It's you."

Munroe cut her connection to the Source and Dox twitched in response, feeling the sudden change. "Listen for the sea. Close your eyes and focus on the sound of the waves."

Munroe watched Dox closely as she slowly extended her senses, desperately trying to feel for the Source. She was like a blind woman wearing thick gloves, fumbling around in a room trying to find the door. It was there. She just had to try really hard and it was a struggle not to be distracted.

For Munroe it felt as if she was permanently beside the docks in Perizzi, listening to the lapping waves. The Source was always there but if she didn't focus it would fade into the background. Now it thrummed in her veins, a bottomless ocean of power, calling to her. With it she could tear apart the fabric of the world, rip her enemy to pieces and have her vengeance.

Her hands involuntarily twitched, urging her to action. Munroe suppressed her need and tried to control her breathing but struggled to regain her calm. These days sitting still for too long always made her feel guilty. Sometimes Munroe worried that she couldn't see clearly the faces of her loved ones. With each passing day it became a little bit harder. If she had loved them so much, how could she forget what they looked like? At least once a day she forced herself to relive a memory of her husband and son. To bring it to the front of her mind and study every detail, focusing on their faces in that moment. The joy as well as the pain. To remind herself of all that had been taken. To stoke the coals of her rage. And to make sure she never forgot that the lives of her husband and son had been cut short by Akosh.

"That's enough for today," said Munroe, putting away the candle and grabbing her shoes. "Let's go. We have an appointment."

"Why does that make me nervous?" asked Dox.

"You're being paranoid," said Munroe, pulling on her jacket.

"Where are we going?"

"It's a surprise," said Munroe. "Don't worry, it's a nice one."

"Liar," said Dox.

An hour later as Dox was standing on the dressmaker's stool with her arms held out, Munroe couldn't help sniggering at her discomfort. The girl ground her teeth and there was pure hatred radiating from her eyes, but she couldn't say anything in front of the two tailors. One was measuring her from head to toe and the other was carefully recording the numbers in a notebook.

"Tell me again why I need a new dress ... Mother?" asked Dox. The word made them both uncomfortable but it was a necessary part of the deception if they wanted to remain unnoticed.

"Because you ripped holes in the last two," said Munroe, sharing a knowing smile with the tailor taking measurements.

"I have two girls myself," said the tailor, a mature lady with red cheeks and grey hair tied back in a neat plait. "One of mine was like your daughter at that age," she confided in a whisper to Munroe.

"What are you saying?" asked Dox, trying to twist around.

"Stay still, dear," said the other woman, turning Dox to face the front again.

"She was always climbing trees," said the tailor, smiling fondly at the memory.

"This one runs around like a street urchin. She's always filthy," said Munroe, earning a sympathetic smile from both women.

Unable to do anything Dox had to endure it in silence while she was no doubt plotting her revenge. She'd thought it was hilarious when Munroe had been measured for a dress but wasn't smiling now that it was her turn.

Eventually the tailors had everything they needed and retreated to the other room. "We'll be back soon. You can move a little, but stay up there, dear," said the tailor, smiling at Dox.

Dox's smile showed too many teeth but they didn't seem to notice. "Why, in the name of the Maker, are we doing this?" hissed the girl when they were alone.

"Because we can't just walk around the jewellery district dressed as we were. We'd attract too much attention."

"We could bribe people to talk," suggested Dox. "I know you've got plenty of money."

Last night Munroe had visited a few gambling dens, placed modest bets and steadily built up her winnings by using her Talent to manipulate the odds. Having spent years working in such places she knew exactly how much money to win before moving on without attracting attention.

"No one would believe you hadn't stolen the gold. Besides, if I start throwing money around for information it's not very conspicuous."

"Then why not just break some heads or follow people like before?" asked Dox.

"Because we don't have a name and this time she knows we're after her. If she sees me coming she'll run." Munroe's hands instinctively tightened on the arms of her chair and the wood creaked. Her knuckles turned white and she took a few deep breaths to calm down. "We need to hide in plain sight. All of her people are looking for me. They're not expecting some rich woman and her daughter shopping for jewellery."

As Dox mulled it over Munroe saw her eyes drifting over the colourful fabrics in the shop. Neither of them was particularly interested in fancy dresses, but she had to admit some of the material was beautiful. As a girl she'd imagined attending a ball at the Yerskani palace dressed in an expensive gown, her neck and hair glittering with jewellery. She wondered if Dox had similar fantasies or had they all been ground into the mud?

"I think the red suits you," said Munroe, nodding towards a bolt of fabric Dox had been eyeing up. The girl's secretive smile lasted only a moment but it reminded Munroe of her real age.

The tailors returned with several colourful pieces of cloth draped over them and the next hour was spent deciding on the fabric, colour, trim, the neckline and how fashionable to make it. Neither of them had any idea about the latest style so they went with the tailors' recommendation. It all seemed so frivolous, and more than a little tedious, but Munroe knew that blending in was vital.

The next time she fought Akosh it would be different. Munroe knew she had a form of magic and what to expect. She would not escape.

Once they'd decided on the details of two new dresses for each of them, the haggling began. There was a set price but Munroe wasn't prepared to wait around for weeks.

"Madam, we have a list of customers who are also waiting for their items," said the tailor.

"I'm sure that's true. You're both very talented, but I need our dresses as soon as possible." Munroe added two more coins to the generous stack on the counter.

The tailor stubbornly shook her head proving that she wasn't greedy. Besides she had a reputation to uphold. Even so, as Munroe added two more gold coins to the stack her eyes widened.

"Madam, really," she protested, trying to turn away but Munroe grabbed her hand.

"We chose your shop because of its reputation. We were told you've even supplied dresses to the palace. For the Regent's wives."

"That's true. His second wife is waiting for a new dress."

"I bet she has dozens of dresses. Would she even notice if you were a few days late? We have urgent business in the city that cannot wait," said Munroe, leaning forward. "Business that needs to be concluded in less than nine months."

The tailor and Munroe exchanged a look before they both glanced at Dox. She was busy inspecting another piece of fabric with the other tailor.

"Oh my," said the tailor.

"Someone was indiscreet. She won't tell me who it is, but I have a good idea. I need to find the one responsible and see that his father does the right thing, before it's too late." Munroe added two more gold coins to the pile but the tailor wasn't paying attention any more. "For your trouble."

"I can have one dress for each of you ready by the end of the week," the tailor promised. It wasn't as fast as she'd hoped but Munroe knew she couldn't push too hard.

"That would be wonderful, thank you."

Dox finished playing with the fabric and approached them at the counter. The tailor was staring at her sympathetically and the girl twitched.

"What?"

"You poor thing," said the tailor, dabbing at her eyes.

Before Dox could ask what she was talking about Munroe grabbed her hand and squeezed it tight. "Come along, dear. Let's leave these fine ladies to their work."

Munroe bustled her from the shop and kept hold of Dox's arm as they strolled down the street together like other mothers and daughters. Dox kept firing questions at her but Munroe wasn't really listening. She was staring at a small patch of blood in the mouth of a nearby alleyway. Someone had been attacked or murdered in the night and stepping closer a familiar and revolting smell assaulted her senses.

"Gauhh. What is that?" asked Dox, trying to pull away but Munroe held on to her. "What are you doing?" she asked as Munroe dragged her closer.

The narrow alley between the two rows of shops was barely wide enough for two people walking abreast and it was littered with rotting food, empty boxes, broken glass and puddles of stale water and probably piss.

Half a dozen paces down the alley was the body of a woman lying on her back. Her eyes were wide open, staring at the sky. Her trousers and shirt were covered in dried blood. The fingers on one hand were twisted and broken. The other had blood beneath the nails and there was blood on her chin. She'd fought hard against her attacker but the gaping stab wound in her side showed it hadn't been enough.

Dox's struggles only increased as she was dragged closer but Munroe didn't let go. They stared in silence at the woman and for a moment Munroe imagined it was Akosh lying at her feet.

"That could be you," said Munroe as Dox began to shake. "Those sweet grandmothers in the tailors' shop. They could be working for Akosh."

"You don't know that," whispered Dox. Perhaps she was afraid to disturb the dead. Either that or she didn't want to attract the attention of any rodents lingering in the filth surrounding the body.

"And if Akosh ordered it, they'd slit your throat and sleep well that night. I want you to understand the stakes." Munroe finally let go of her wrist but Dox didn't run. "For all the lies, the frippery and the games we're going to play, none of it matters. You can't trust a single person in this entire city, except me. If we're not careful, that will be us." As Munroe waved a hand at the dead woman a fly crawled out of her gaping mouth. Dox retched and ran from the alley.

All of Munroe's dreams of glittering balls and fancy dresses were gone. The only image that filled her mind at night was a river of blood flowing from the broken body of her enemy. Smiling at the thought Munroe left the alley and went in search of her fragile ward.

CHAPTER 14

Tammy had only just finished bowing to her Drassi teacher when she noticed they were being watched. Her teacher raised one eyebrow at the woman lurking in the doorway, his hand creeping towards his sword, but she shook her head. With a grunt, he pulled on his jacket and limped away, never once glancing at the newcomer. Faith cut a striking figure in her low-cut red dress and would normally turn heads wherever she went, just not here and not today.

"I must be losing my touch," said Faith, wrinkling her nose. The room stank of sweat, which she tried to dispel with a red lace fan. Through an open window Tammy could hear that it was still raining hard. The streets would be cold and damp but inside the small training room it was humid from their exertions. Her muscles ached and she already knew her left shoulder was going to hurt tomorrow, but it was worth it. Because for a time she could forget everything except the sword in her hand and her opponent.

"I wouldn't take it personally," said Tammy, wiping her sweaty face with a towel. "He's not that interested in people, men or women. I don't think he even likes me very much."

"Ah, and how about you?" asked Faith with a cheeky smile.

"I prefer men. You?"

"Professionally, I only work with men. Personally, I'm not picky," she said with an elaborate wink.

Tammy noticed Faith watching as she changed out of her sweaty vest into a fresh shirt but it didn't bother her. "I need you to deliver a message."

"To business, then," said Faith with a dramatic sigh. "Are you always so serious?"

Tammy shrugged as she pulled on her boots. "Only when there's an unknown number of religious maniacs hiding in my city."

Faith laughed and held open Tammy's Guardian jacket for her to step into. She had to stand on her tiptoes to do it so Tammy accommodated Faith by slightly bending her knees. "A fair point. So, who do you want me to visit?" asked Faith.

"The Families."

"Which one?"

"All of them," she said, strapping on her sword belt.

Dealing with the crime Families of Perizzi was something Tammy had hoped to avoid but perhaps it had been inevitable. They had been on different sides for a long time but even now she couldn't escape her history. After all, many years ago she'd worked for Don Lowell as an enforcer.

So far there had not been any repercussions for what she'd done to Don Lowell, but speaking directly to anyone in a Family was not a good idea. A few people might remember her, old memories might resurface and someone might connect the dots between Don Lowell's murder and her late husband. It was far safer to send a proxy in her stead.

"Call a meeting. Ask for all the Dons and Doñas to attend. They'll want to hear the news as it will affect them directly."

"If you're sure," said Faith uneasily, folding up her lace fan.

"I am. All four of them need to be there."

"That's not going to be easy," said Faith, biting her bottom lip as she mulled it over. "Someone murdered Don Lowell a few months ago and the person responsible was never found. As you can imagine, his successor, Doña Tarija, is more than a little paranoid."

"That's understandable. I've not heard much about her. What can you tell me?"

"Originally she's from the far east. She came here with her parents as a child so Perizzi is home. She's ambitious, but also sharp as a knife, so don't expect any turf wars. I suspect her strategies will be more subtle."

"That's good news. With everything that's going on with Akosh, it's the last thing we need."

The Watch Major had enough bodies to patrol the city and maintain the peace. A turf war between Families would be brutal and taxing for the Watch which she couldn't afford.

"I know about Don Jarrow and the Butcher. Who's the fourth? Who took over from the Duchess?"

Faith laughed. "You are out of touch. Her turf was claimed by Doña Chur. She looks a bit like you, only bald and ugly."

That meant Doña Chur also had at least one parent from Seveldrom. Despite having the pale skin of a Yerskani, the first thing people noticed with Tammy was her height. She'd lost count of the number of times people had commented on how tall she was.

"How long has she been here?"

"I know what you're thinking. Believe me, Chur isn't loyal to Akosh. We know exactly who her parents are. Sadly, both of them are still alive, as well as her five vicious brothers and sisters." Faith snapped open her red lace fan again. "Can we go somewhere less pungent? Perhaps get some breakfast?"

Tammy shook her head. "It's better if we're not seen together in public."

"Ah, so this is a clandestine tryst," said Faith with a grin. "The story of my life."

"You'll have to tell me about it another time," said Tammy.

She would grab something to eat on the way back to Unity Hall. Her first meeting was in less than an hour and the rest of the day would inevitably fill up in no time.

"So what am I offering the Families?" asked Faith.

"Do they know who you work for?" asked Tammy, dodging the question for a moment.

"Some of them. The rest could work it out if they tried."

"Tell them about Akosh and her cult. Stress that her people could be anywhere and anyone. Make sure they understand that her people are loyal only to their Mother. Tell them about what some of her followers have done. I want the Families to feel paranoid about their own people. I want them jumping at shadows and seeing potential betrayal in the faces of everyone they meet."

Faith raised an eyebrow. "Why?"

"Because in your next breath you're going to offer them a solution. Someone with a foolproof method of knowing if their people are loyal. They might not care about the rest of the city, but divided loyalty in their ranks isn't something they'll tolerate."

A long time ago, before she'd even met her husband, Tammy remembered what Don Lowell had done to someone he'd caught passing information to another Family. It had involved a lot of meat hooks and the thief had screamed for a very long time. Over the years it had become an urban legend that sent a clear message to anyone thinking of betraying their Family. Spying was one thing. They all did it to keep an eye on their rivals but every member of a Family only served one master. If it turned out anyone was secretly loyal to Akosh the repercussions would be very violent and messy.

Faith remained unconvinced. "That's still going to be a hard sell coming from me. They know who I am, but I'm not a member of any Family."

"That's all right. One of my people, Fray, will be going with you. He's the one with the gift."

"Are you sure that's a good idea? Sending a Guardian into Family territory?" asked Faith, which made Tammy grin. "What am I missing?"

"Talk to Don Jarrow first. He'll vouch for Fray."

Faith arched an eyebrow. "He will?"

Tammy checked the edge of her sword and finding it had been blunted a little, began to sharpen it on a whetstone. "They met a few years ago and Fray left quite an impression. We don't have time to screen all of their people, so tell the Families we'll focus on their Silver and Gold jackals."

Each Family had tiers of people working for them, starting with the lowest, paper jackals, right up to the most trusted, Silver and Gold. They had proven their loyalty over many years of service. If it turned out even one of them was devoted to Akosh it would have severe repercussions.

"It sounds like it's going to be quite the show," said Faith. "Are you sure you don't want to be there?"

Tammy shook her head and whisked her sword down the whetstone and then back. It kept her hands busy and her eyes averted so Faith didn't see how uncomfortable the conversation was making her. The Old Man had assured her only a few people knew about her history and she wanted to keep it that way. The last thing she needed was Faith prying into her background because she was curious. "Keep my name out of it. If they press, tell them all of this is coming from Queen Morganse."

"Hopefully it won't come to that," said Faith.

"In return for this generous favour, I want them to close certain doors, or at least, monitor them for messages from Akosh coming

into the city. Between that and investigating the rest of their jackals, I'm hoping it keeps them busy and not at each other's throats."

Happy that her blade was sharp enough Tammy wiped it clean
and moved on to her daggers. Even if all of the Families cooper-
ated she knew it would be impossible to intercept all information
flowing into Perizzi. However, the more barriers she could put
between Akosh and her people, the better it would be.

She still had the Silent Order, spies from Queen Morganse and
her own people trying to find the hundred or more people loyal to
Akosh in the city, but even with all those bodies helping it was
going to take time.

"We need the Families' cooperation," said Tammy. She didn't
need to scare Faith with stories of what could happen if they
didn't get it. The attempt on the Queen's life had failed but only
because of Morganse's actions. Everyone was feeling a little guilty
about not preventing it sooner. If there was a next time they
needed to stop it more quickly. Cooperation from the Families
was the only way.

Tammy had never considered that when she took on the mantle
of Khevassar she might be asked to work with the crime Families
to protect the city.

She needed this to work because if not her other plans were
even more risky and their outcomes uncertain. The Old Man had
warned her. Some days the only choices were bad or worse and it
all came down to what she could live with.

An hour later her secretary, Rummpoe, let Guardian Fray into her
office and Tammy gestured for him to take a seat. She finished
recording the latest entry in her private journal and then replaced
it on the shelf alongside the others. All but one of the shelves was
empty but over time the room would fill up with her account of
the city's history. The real one, written in blood.

"You wanted to see me, Sir?"

"I have another unusual request for you," she said. "But this isn't an order. You don't have to do it. Is that understood?"

"Yes, Sir."

"This is about Akosh and her network." She knew Fray had been involved in the house searches for her people. His magic and special Talent for talking to lingering spirits of the dead made him very useful. In addition he could study a place and dig into its history, searching for violence and murders, which left an impression. Unfortunately his abilities were still a closely guarded secret, even among his fellow Guardians.

"I need you to speak to the heads of the Families."

After explaining what was going to happen and what she needed from him Fray raised the most critical issue.

"But, Sir, I can't tell if someone is lying or not. My magic doesn't work that way."

"I know that, but they don't," said Tammy, fishing around in her drawer before producing one of Akosh's idols. "A bit of theatrics and misdirection is needed. Fear of magic has never been more powerful, so for once we're going to use that to our advantage. For some of them, fear of being discovered, especially when you show them one of these idols, will trigger a reaction."

Fray considered it for a moment before asking, "And for the others?"

"For those with more resilience I need you to dig into their past. Doesn't your Talent allow you to see their victims, who they killed and other details?"

"I can see that and more, but it's gruelling."

She could only imagine. Being forced to relive multiple murders, as well as talking to the restless dead, would test the sanity of anyone. "That's why this isn't an order, but we need the Families to cooperate."

Tammy knew she was manipulating him, with her position as his superior and with guilt over the potential repercussions if he didn't help, but it needed to be done.

"I'll do it," said Fray, nodding grimly.

"It's your choice," she said, knowing he'd already made up his mind.

"Who do I start with?"

"Don Jarrow. Let me know what you find," she said, handing him one of Akosh's idols.

After he'd left Tammy found she was staring at her office door. She was thinking about the personal cost to Fray, but also how useful magic was at times like these when she was out of options. Fear of magic was not going to ease for a long time but she needed a way to access those with special abilities.

It was a problem for another day. For now she turned to the next report on her desk from the city's chief coroner. It concerned three strange deaths at a tavern, the Red Lion, and another at a local brothel called the Honey Pot.

CHAPTER 15

The village of Tulan in Yerskania was an unremarkable place. According to Vargus nothing significant had ever happened here and no one of historical note had ever been born in the village. It was a place to rest while heading for somewhere more interesting rather than a final destination. Those with any ambition left as soon as they could and never came back.

Wedged between two larger towns which had several industries, Tulan had few local resources to generate money for its people. All of their gold was earned from the taverns, stables, brothels and blacksmiths that lined the main street. Almost every person in the village made their living from the travellers passing through. Beyond the one main street there were homes for local people and nothing else of note.

Travellers stopped in the village to sleep, eat, have fresh shoes put on their horses, perhaps find some company for the night, and move on. There was no reason to stay any longer than necessary.

As they rode down the main road Danoph noticed a variety of faces from across the west and beyond. On one side of the street a pair of tall Seve merchants were busy trading their famous

Sorensen beef with a pale-skinned local Yerskani. On the other side a Fist of Drassi warriors guarded a merchant train of five wagons driven by a horned Morrin. Caskets of exotic-smelling herbs and bolts of cloth were piled up on each wagon. A Drassi merchant, dressed in brightly coloured silk, was fiercely haggling with a Morrin woman. Both of them were on the verge of shouting at each other, but no one seemed to be paying attention, so Danoph assumed such screaming matches were normal. A moment later the two merchants came to an agreement, shook hands, and amicably went their separate ways.

"What am I looking for?" asked Danoph, turning to Vargus.

"Let's stop and stretch our legs first," he said, gesturing at one of the taverns. They stopped outside a place called the Drunken Duck and were immediately met by an eager boy who offered to tend to their horses. Although the boy was grimy and had straw in his hair, he was dressed in brown trousers and a white shirt adorned with a yellow duck. Vargus flipped the boy a small coin, which he snatched out of the air before making a renewed promise to take good care of their animals.

From the moment they stepped inside Danoph had the impression each tavern on the street was doing its best to outdo its neighbours. A serving girl in an outfit that matched the stable-hand met them at the door, guiding them to an empty table by the window. She took their drinks order and recited their food choices from memory, all accompanied with a warm smile. By the time they'd chosen what to eat someone else had already brought their drinks to the table. Finally the two barmaids withdrew, leaving them in peace to enjoy their ale.

Danoph sipped his slowly, making sure to avoid eye contact with any member of staff in case they raced over to ask if he needed anything.

"What do you want me to do?" he asked Vargus.

They could have ridden for a few more hours and made it to the next town but for some reason Vargus had insisted they stop here for the night.

"Pick someone at random on the street. Someone not too old."

Since Vargus had revealed the truth about his heritage Danoph had been practising his ability. Several times a day he focused on a place or a person and used them as an anchor to travel back in time. Before his eyes the history of the town or individual was revealed. It became a play on stage that only he could see and hear. Years passed before his eyes in the space of a few heartbeats. Cities he'd never heard of rose from nothing, sparkling in all their glory before they fell into ruin and vanished beneath the soil. People were born, grew to adulthood and then died old and wrinkled. Danoph had lost count of the number of people he'd studied. The twists and turns their lives took were sometimes remarkable. If someone had told him about the peculiar paths a life could take he wouldn't have believed them. Any city had an inevitable and final destination, dust upon the wind, but the unpredictability of a single person's journey through life fascinated him like nothing else.

"What about him?" said Danoph, gesturing at a middle-aged man with only one arm. He guessed the other had been lost in a war or perhaps an accident.

"No, find someone younger," suggested Vargus.

Danoph watched the street for a while and eventually spotted a gangly Seve teenager only a few years younger than himself. The boy had bright red hair, a bit of fluff on his top lip he was trying to cultivate into a moustache and was limping on his left. "How about him?"

"He'll do, but I want you to try something different this time," said Vargus. "I suspect there's little of note to see in his past. I want you to look into his futures."

"How?" asked Danoph.

"When you focus your power, when you open yourself to the weave of time, listen for the echoes."

Danoph was about to ask what Vargus meant when he remembered something from his time at the Red Tower. Like every other student he could feel the pulse within another mage which was their connection to the Source. It echoed in his mind like a heartbeat and some were louder than others depending on the strength of their bond. But there had been times when he'd sensed a dual echo within other people. A second pulse that lived between the beats. At one point he'd speculated about there being multiple beats, like musical notes, but had written it off because of his inexperience.

"I remember something," he said. "There were other pulses. It was like music."

"Those were pathways," said Vargus with a pleased smile. "Other possibilities in the future. Most people have hundreds of forks in the road but often there are only a handful of likely outcomes. Focus on the boy. Listen for the music and tell me what you see."

Danoph tried to calm his mind as he raised his right hand and focused his ability on the boy. Crisp white light glowed on his palm as he reached out, trying to find the discordant pulses connected to the teenager. At first there was nothing. Not even a pulse from the Source. The silence continued for a time and he worried that he couldn't do it.

"Let it flow towards you. Listen, don't try to pull it in," said Vargus.

Taking a deep breath he tried again, relaxing his muscles, unclenching his jaw and trying to feel for the boy's possible futures. And then he heard it. A single crisp note echoing in his mind like a silver bell. Behind it came another note, slightly lower, and then more still, combining with one another to create a unique orchestra of sound.

His eyes snapped open and a vast network of roads appeared in front of him. There were hundreds of crossroads that endlessly overlapped to create a monstrous weave that seemed without end. Every decision and conversation. Every meal and moment. There were too many to count and he started to panic.

"Focus on the pathways, not his immediate choices," said Vargus, trying to calm him. "Look beyond today and tomorrow. Where do all of those roads ultimately lead? What will the boy become?"

As if he were a bird taking flight Danoph felt his mind move away from the weave, drifting up from the ground to see beyond the minutiae. Slowly a pattern came into focus and five roads stretched into the distance. Three roads were long and two were much shorter. He focused on the first road.

In one future he saw the boy's mild limp becoming more pronounced. The local apothecarist told him it was only muscle strain and would go away in time. For several years he did his best to ignore it but the pain gradually became worse. By the time he was twenty his left leg was swollen and the boy could barely walk. His parents spent all their money trying to find a cure and eventually the only solution seemed to be amputation. Unable to work in the stables any more the boy, now a grown man of twenty-one, turned his hand to music. He played in every tavern in Tulan, earning enough for a modest life and for a time he was happy.

One day the pain returned, spreading faster than before, moving through his other leg into his chest. Six months after that he was bedridden, unable to work and without an appetite. No one could diagnose what was wrong with him or how to reverse the spreading pain and paralysis. Two months after that, emaciated and struggling for breath, he was dead.

Danoph recoiled from the images, turning his face away from the street. He didn't want to see any more. He'd felt the boy's suffering and the creeping pain as it spread through his body. The smell of rot and filth from the room where he'd died lingered in Danoph's nose. A ghost memory that made him feel physically sick.

"He's going to die young and alone after suffering for years," said Danoph, gulping down some ale in an attempt to settle his stomach.

"Was there only one road?" asked Vargus. "Or did you see more?"

"There were five roads that seemed the most prominent," said Danoph, looking into the street, but the boy was gone.

"Focus on one of the others. Tell me what you see," said Vargus but Danoph shook his head.

"I'm not sure I want to. I can still feel his suffering." Without realising what he was doing Danoph massaged the muscles in his left leg.

"I know it's difficult but you need to try again. It's important."

Danoph took a deep breath, shook off the memories of pain and extended his senses, searching for the boy again. He was only a street away and this time the roads beyond the network of choices were easier to find.

This time he chose one of the longer roads, hoping it was less miserable, as the details came into focus.

In this future, disgruntled with his life in Tulan, the boy left home when he was eighteen in search of adventure. Travelling north he made his way to the capital, Perizzi, where he was met with indifference and hostility from strangers. His ambitions became smaller and smaller as he searched for a true calling beyond the stables. After drifting from one job to another for a year he found himself back where he'd begun, working in stables.

Only this time it was in the capital city surrounded by strangers instead of at home where he knew everyone.

Forlorn and isolated he considered giving up and going home, but a chance encounter with a member of the Watch changed his life. He intercepted a thief trying to escape with someone's gold and after being thanked by the crowd, and a member of the Watch, he felt a glimmer of something he'd forgotten. Pride.

The next day he signed up to join the Watch and after enduring their gruelling tests he passed. What followed were some of the happiest years of his life, bonding with those in his squad, before rising up the ranks to command a squad of his own. Stopping a fight in a tavern brought him into contact with the owner who he later visited on his own time. Two years later they were married and a year after that their first child was born.

A run-in with one of the crime Families almost ended his life after which he spent several months in bed recuperating. With a second child on the way he considered leaving the Watch but instead was persuaded to try joining the Guardians of the Peace. He failed on his first application but persisted and a year later earned the famous red and black jacket. Many years later he retired to run the tavern with his wife before finally dying an old man surrounded by his children and grandchildren.

Danoph rocked backwards in his seat and it began to tip over. If Vargus hadn't grabbed his shirt Danoph would have fallen to the floor. Part of Danoph was in the tavern but the rest remained elsewhere. His eyes were wide and distant, his skin flushed and his mind whirling with a hundred emotions and memories that were not his own. The intensity of what he'd felt was incomparable. The love, the loss, the heartache and moments of joy. Even when he embraced power from the Source and felt connected to the world on a deeper level, it paled in comparison to this.

Unable to speak Danoph sat quietly as he tried to process

what he'd experienced. He drank his ale and then ate his meal in silence, awash with memories and emotions of a life yet to come. A life and a possible future that wasn't even his.

It was only much later, perhaps an hour after, that he dared look up from the table at Vargus. Slowly, piece by piece, he related what he'd seen.

"What you saw, and the emotions you felt, will stay with you," said Vargus, speaking from experience.

"What am I?" asked Danoph.

"You are the Weaver."

"But what does that mean?"

"Call it fate, luck, chance or destiny. Some even call it faith. They believe absolutely that something will happen. All of these names describe one force of nature. That is the Weaver."

"But why am I here?"

Vargus laughed, and after a moment Danoph had to smile at the enormity of his question. "Had anyone else asked me that, I would struggle, but with you it's fairly simple to answer. You need to understand your power, and how it works, so that you can prevent others from unravelling the skein of time."

The keen serving girl came to their table, a rigid smile in place. "Would you like another drink?"

Vargus stared at the girl for a long moment, until she became uncomfortable, before finally nodding. "Two more, please." She scurried away and he turned back to Danoph. "In that moment, there were two possible choices. The impact of ordering more ale or not was negligible. The world would continue much as before. But what if she'd not given me a choice? What if she'd simply put two more drinks on the table? Why do you think she would do something like that?"

"Because she thought it was what we needed."

"She had the best intentions, but she also removed our ability to choose." Vargus waited until the girl had delivered their drinks and withdrawn before speaking again. "The one rule, passed down from the Maker, is that we cannot interfere. All the mortal races are free to choose, to make their own mistakes, and each individual must be free to forge their own path. It is not for us to decide, even if we think we know better. Think of the boy. Think of the possible roads his life could take. Do you think it's right to nudge him towards becoming a member of the Watch?"

"It would mean less suffering and a longer life."

"But what if, as a musician, he inspired someone else to become a musician. Or more simply, to take a risk, setting them on a new path. Look again at both futures and in each you will see the boy touched countless other lives. The ripples from one path could change a hundred or a thousand other people in significant ways."

"You told me no one of note had ever come from Tulan," said Danoph. "Was that a lie?"

"No. But even in this nowhere place, it's impossible to say how one life here could affect another who goes on to greatness. Not even the Weaver can track all of those ripples."

"You're talking about Akosh," said Danoph, thinking of the disruption he'd been feeling. There was something wrong with the world. An underlying note of discord that was steadily growing louder the further north they went.

"I am. She's bending the weave to her will, ignorant of what may happen as a result in ten or a hundred years' time. Even our kind can be very short-sighted. Akosh may benefit now, but only you can see how many will suffer in the years to come. It is my task to stop her, but yours is more difficult."

The pieces started to fall into place in Danoph's mind. It wasn't a memory, not really, more of a feeling that had been steadily creeping up on him. The more he used his power the clearer it became.

"I have to unravel what she's done," he said. The thought of it was overwhelming and Danoph shied away from the enormity of what lay ahead.

"As best you can, and it will take a long time."

"What happens if we can't stop her?" asked Danoph.

"Humans have always been the most unpredictable of the mortal races. But they're also capable of remarkable kindness and grace, which can still surprise me. They are growing and changing. They need time to better themselves. If we do nothing to stop Akosh then it could spell out their doom at the hands of the other races, or themselves. A long time ago a race called the Necheye were driven to extinction. We cannot lose the humans as well."

He sensed there was more to the story that Vargus wanted to tell him, but he held back. Danoph needed time to process what he'd been told and to consider what lay ahead.

When he'd thought of himself as just another student at the Red Tower Danoph had wondered about his purpose. He'd often felt adrift as he had no real drive or ambition. Now, for the first time in his life, he knew exactly who he was and why he was here. It was a rare gift and not one that he intended to squander.

Chapter 16

No one had ever accused Regent Choilan of being particularly perceptive but even he picked up on the icy atmosphere as he entered the room. Selina, his first wife, and Bettina, his clerk, were sat on opposite sides of the short dining table where he regularly held informal meetings. The décor of the whole room was less sumptuous than the rest of the palace, with its polished wooden floor, bare stone walls and only one side table covered with bottles of whisky from across the world, but sometimes it was fun to play at being poor.

Bettina rose to her feet and bowed as he entered the room while Selina kept her seat and just glared at the other woman. If anything he would have expected them to get on well with each other as both were remarkably cold and calculating. Once again it showed how little he really understood women, even those closest to him.

"Be seated," he said, favouring Bettina with a smile because he knew it would annoy Selina. Deciding to continue with his fantasy of being a commoner he selected a harsh whisky from Seveldrom and poured himself a generous measure.

"Is there news?" he asked, arranging the cushions before sitting down at the head of the table.

"Yes. I've found a teacher for your mages," said Selina, looking pleased with herself. No doubt she was thinking ahead to the day when she ran his entire network of spies. "Marran Sedda."

On the other side of the table he saw Bettina twitch as if she'd been pinched. From her it was the equivalent of a scream.

"Do you have something to add, Bettina?" he asked, knowing she wouldn't directly contradict his first wife unless invited.

"I believe he's an unsuitable candidate and isn't up to the task. I'm confident we can find someone else."

"There is no one else," snapped Selina. "My people have been scouring the city for days and he's the only one."

"Perhaps, my lady, your people are not as well informed as my contacts," suggested Bettina, straining to remain impassive.

"Oh really?" said Selina. "Enlighten us."

"What about Torlen Kos?" asked Bettina.

"Dead," said Selina, crossing her arms. "Someone cut his head off a week ago with an axe."

"Helgan Loke."

"Dead. He drowned four days ago."

Bettina raised an eyebrow. "He was a ship's captain."

"I'm aware of that," came the tart response. "It was in the bath."

Choilan sat back and remained silent, happy to let them thrash it out. Sipping his whisky he waited to see who would come out on top.

Bettina's confident façade started to crack. "Roslin Sash," she tried.

Selina's smile showed a lot of teeth. "Dead. Someone eviscerated her last night." His first wife drew a line with a finger from her groin right up to her chest bone. Choilan shuddered at the grisly image but neither woman seemed affected.

Bettina consulted her papers on the table but his first wife was already shaking her head. "Don't bother. There's no one else. Every other mage in a hundred miles is a tin-pot amateur with no real skill."

A different kind of silence started to fill the room. When both women looked towards him with matching glares Choilan realised that was his cue to speak.

"So, it seems as if this Marran Sedda is our only choice."

"Nevertheless, I have grave concerns about him," said Bettina.

Much to his surprise Selina grunted in what sounded like agreement. "Something to add?" he asked.

"I don't believe so many accidents are a coincidence. Someone may be pushing Marran on to us. Besides, he has a colourful history," said Selina, gesturing at the papers in front of Bettina. A quick glance showed a list of crimes, dates and places going back several years.

"He's spent quite a bit of time in and out of the cells," said Bettina, ticking items off on her fingers. "Theft. Robbery. Attempted murder. Arson and bribery. He's a suspect in at least a dozen other crimes. Then there's the fact that he has some peculiar appetites."

Choilan glanced at his first wife and she grimaced. "He can be controlled. We just need to set firm boundaries. In addition he should be carefully watched, day and night."

"He sounds like a thoroughly revolting creature," said Choilan. "Are you certain there's no one else?"

The two women stared at each other in silence but eventually both shook their heads. "He's our last resort," admitted Bettina.

"Very well, but keep searching in the meantime. Scour the whole country if you have to," said Choilan. He was very aware of the tenuous position he was in and both women knew that their fates were intertwined with his. This could be his last chance to prove that his cadre of mages was a good thing and that magic could be controlled. Marran was a necessary evil until Selina and Bettina found a more suitable teacher.

If Marran was as grotesque as they were hinting at he would have to be kept away from any public functions. Choilan had started to trickle his mages into some small events, making them mingle with the crowd, but Marran would have to remain out of sight.

"Do you want to meet him?" asked Selina, startling him from his reverie.

"Not really, but I suppose I should."

A short time later a pair of Royal Guards entered the room with a small unctuous man walking between them. Marran was somewhere in his middling years with a pot belly and an untrustworthy face. He had watery eyes and a curtain of greasy, drab brown hair that hung to his shoulders. It did little to cover the growing bald spot but he'd attempted to compensate by growing a patchy beard. His clothes were rumpled, he smelled ripe and Choilan thought it was possible he had lice.

Marran was understandably nervous. As well as being a rogue mage who had been discovered hiding in the city, he was now standing in front of the Regent. From his petrified expression it was clear Selina hadn't told him why he'd been dragged to the palace.

"Bow," said one of the Royal Guards, elbowing Marran in the ribs.

With a squawk of pain he made a poor attempt and nearly toppled over on to his hands and knees. As he straightened up Choilan noticed how his eyes flicked across the front of Selina's dress, briefly lingering on her cleavage.

"I require a teacher for my cadre of mages," said Choilan. "You will teach them everything you know about magic. In return you will be well paid and well fed. You will live in the palace and enjoy a number of luxuries to make your stay more comfortable. Do you understand?"

"Yes, Regent," said Marran, although he was clearly surprised by this sudden turn of events. He straightened up slightly, no longer cowering, and a cunning look crossed his face. Ground rules would have to be set early.

"Captain, put your sword to his throat," said Choilan. Smiling, the Royal Guard drew his blade and tucked it under Marran's chin. The cunning was replaced with terror as Choilan leaned forward in his chair.

"Kalina is the leader of my mages. She will make regular reports on her progress under your tutelage. If I feel that you're holding anything back, or that you're dragging your feet to extend your stay, you'll be executed. Is that clear?"

"Yes. Yes, Regent," babbled Marran, wringing his hands as fresh sweat ran down the sides of his face.

"Do not test my patience or else you will have to deal with the Captain."

The Captain stared at the mage as if he were about to devour him and Marran visibly wilted. "I understand."

A few days later Choilan made an unannounced visit to the mages' training room. It was an old ballroom in the east wing, far away from other people, that had been cleared of furniture. Guards were posted at all of the doors and every palace servant knew to keep their distance.

Two Royal Guards pushed open the door and Choilan boldly strode into the room. The mages were standing in two long lines, their faces rapt with attention, as they all conjured something. Floating in front of several were glowing balls of light which created a kaleidoscope of rotating colours across the walls. Most were swirling orbs of blue but some glowed orange and one or two were red. Standing in front of them directing the class was Marran. At first glance Choilan almost didn't recognise him.

Someone had bathed him thoroughly, cut off his ridiculous hair and shaved his face clean. His bald head reflected some of the lights in the room and he was dressed in a smart palace uniform decorated with one blue star over the heart. He no longer smelled ripe but a bath and change of clothes did nothing about his untrustworthy features.

On more familiar ground, and without someone threatening his life, he was no longer cowering. He strode up and down the lines, gesturing and muttering to individual students who adjusted what they were doing. At first he didn't realise there were visitors in the room but eventually he noticed the distracted glances of his students.

The unctuous smile returned as he started to cross the ballroom but the Regent waved him back, gesturing instead for Kalina to approach. He took her to the far side of the hall away from prying ears.

"How are your lessons progressing? Is he proving useful?" asked Choilan, glancing significantly at the Royal Guards. One word from him and they would cut off Marran's head.

Kalina noticed where he was looking and with some reluctance nodded. "He knows a lot, but he's starting us with the basics. He said if we don't master those we could kill ourselves or someone else."

"Hmm," said Choilan, wondering how useful magical lights would be. "And how is he as a teacher?"

Kalina hugged herself and turned her back on Marran. "Fine."

"Has he done anything unsettling?"

She considered the question but eventually shook her head. Despite her denial Kalina was a lot more perceptive than she realised. Something about Marran was making her uncomfortable even though she'd not seen him do anything untoward.

Across the hall Choilan watched as Marran stepped closer to one of the students, helping to adjust her mage light. He whispered something in her ear and her frown deepened as she concentrated. The wobbling oval light between her outstretched hands started to solidify, becoming a globe full of swirling greys and blues. Marran's hands casually lingered on her shoulder and hip. It might have been innocent, and the girl didn't seem to notice, but Choilan saw something predatory in his eyes.

Kalina's instincts were right. After only a few days Marran was reverting to type and his true nature was rising to the surface. The threat of death had made him cower but it hadn't changed him.

Selina and Bettina were still searching for another teacher but so far all they had found was dead bodies. It could have been a coincidence but Choilan didn't think so. Someone was eliminating rogue mages. Three had been found dead in the city within a week. For the time being Marran remained his only choice.

Perhaps if he sent someone to the mage's quarters it would slake his lust. If not then he might have to sacrifice one of his mages to the deviant's desires. It might be the only way to keep him compliant. Choilan had twenty-one young mages now and all of them were at the same level of proficiency. Losing one at this early stage wouldn't make a huge difference. But he'd have to be discreet about how it was done. The other mages might become disheartened if they thought he'd sacrificed one of their friends to appease Marran.

"Keep a close eye on him," he told Kalina. "I will send for you in a few days for another report. Come directly to me if you see anything suspicious."

Once Marran had taught them everything he knew Choilan would have him beheaded. In the meantime his cadre of mages would just have to be uncomfortable. There was too much riding on them. He needed this to work or else it could be his head that ended up on the chopping block.

CHAPTER 17

It was the end of another long and boring day of pretending to be interested in jewellery. Munroe's search of the area was slow by necessity to avoid arousing suspicion, but the worst thing about the experience was the fake smiles. After three days her face ached from maintaining a near-rictus grin as she pretended to get excited about different rings and necklaces. But in comparison to the jewellers she was an amateur.

Their smiles were so perfect it was difficult to see through the cracks. If Munroe concentrated long enough she caught a glimpse of their real opinions. But those sneers and eye rolls could disappear between one blink and the next. In every shop the wealthy of Zecorria browsed the glass cases for gaudy and overpriced decoration to drape on their sagging flesh. And in every shop a smiling shopkeeper was happy to find them something that would separate them from their money.

Some customers were there to buy an item to celebrate a special occasion, but many seemed to be wealthy individuals who wanted to be noticed. Munroe was surprised by the level of desperation in their eyes. They had a fervent need for people to stop and stare at them in admiration. They had what many Zecorrans wanted, enough money not to worry about the future, and yet they were hollow imitations of people.

Much to her credit Dox played the role of her daughter with aplomb. In every shop she cooed and giggled over rings and necklaces, admiring herself in the mirror while she modelled them. At times it was a struggle for Munroe to recognise her as the same scrawny teenage girl she'd met in Rojenne. With regular meals she'd put on a little weight and was starting to grow out of that awkward phase where she'd been all knees and elbows. The tailor-made dress, make-up and artful styling of her hair had transformed her into a young lady that turned heads.

Normally both of them would never wear such clothing but without the frippery they couldn't blend in with the wealthy clientele. And while the shopkeepers tried to impress her and Dox with their wares they talked. Sometimes it was about their families. Sometimes it was about the business and sometimes about other customers. It was all designed to impress and lull them into feeling comfortable in the hope that they would return in the future.

The words came tumbling out and together they sifted them for useful nuggets in their search for Akosh and her people. A couple of shopkeepers had heard rumours about a religious cult operating in the city but sadly didn't know anyone involved. Munroe had swallowed her disappointment and moved on to the next shop.

Much of the gossip and political manoeuvring didn't interest her but she heard many stories expressing concern with the Regent. His new stance on magic and his cadre of mages was a topic everyone danced around. People in the city were gradually becoming used to seeing them patrolling the city with Royal Guards but they were still nervous of magic. Many were struggling with the Regent's sudden change of attitude from banning all Seekers and labelling children as dangerous to recruiting them.

While some people were happy for the Regent to have such powerful servants under his control, others remembered their history. After all it had been the previous ruler of Zecorria, dubbed the Mad King, and his pet wizard the Warlock who were responsible for starting the war ten years ago. Seeing so much power in the hands of someone on the throne again made a lot of people very nervous.

The wealthy in the city could hire countless guards and build walls around their homes but none of that mattered to a mage. Although none of the shopkeepers said it, Munroe had the impression that several customers were making plans to eliminate the cadre of mages, and perhaps knock the Regent off the throne. Such political upheaval didn't concern her as long as it didn't interfere with her plan. However, if the city was thrown into chaos by a coup it would be a different matter. Her hunt was already difficult enough.

Desperate to get out of her corset Munroe decided this would be the last shop they visited for the day. There were only a handful left and they would tackle them tomorrow.

The current shop was a reasonably modest place and so far the owner hadn't managed to annoy her, which was a first. Also he wasn't as oily as some of the others who pushed hard for a sale from the moment she set foot inside the door. If anything he seemed distracted. As if there was something more important on his mind.

With sunken cheeks and slightly wild hair he appeared intimidating at first glance. But he was softly spoken and didn't seem to mind helping Dox make a selection. Munroe was about to suggest they leave when Dox became particularly excited by a rather plain necklace.

"Mother, you must look at this," she said with a big grin. Munroe pasted on a fake smile of her own and approached the pair.

"What is it, dear?"

"Don't you think it looks gorgeous?"

Munroe stared at the plain silver necklace that was adorned with half a dozen small red stones. Compared to what she'd seen over the last few days the work was neither intricate nor particularly skilled. It had a certain rustic charm but Dox seemed overly enthused by it, so she decided to play along.

"Korell was just telling me he has something similar with sapphires. Can I try that one on, please?" said Dox in a wheedling voice.

Munroe turned to the shopkeeper and raised an enquiring eyebrow. "It's in the back room. I'll just be a moment, Milady," he said with a faint smile.

Dox's smile stayed in place until Korell went into the stockroom and closed the door behind him.

"Did you notice his eyes?" whispered Dox.

"He seems a bit dazed."

"It's more than that. He's addicted to black crystal. I've seen it before. It eats away at a person's body over time."

It had been many years since Munroe had mixed with the underworld but Dox had more recent experience from her time in Rojenne. Venthe was the most common drug sold across the west. It was an addictive high that left blue stains around the mouth. Black crystal was much more lethal. It left addicts hungry no matter how much they ate while it slowly consumed their body. It explained the shopkeeper's hollow cheeks and distracted manner.

"So he's an addict. It doesn't mean he's involved with Akosh."

"There's something else," said Dox. "He kept staring at the ceiling, so I asked him if someone was upstairs. He lied and said no."

"And?" asked Munroe, knowing there had to be more.

"I mentioned the story others have told us about a new cult in the city. I threw in her name and asked if he'd ever heard it before." Dox's eyes drifted towards the ceiling and Munroe's pulse quickened. "He lied," she whispered.

Munroe's hands clenched into tight fists and she instinctively started to reach for the Source. Its glorious power flooded her body, awakening her senses and changing her whole view of the world. The drab little shop was transformed as every gemstone sparkled with majesty.

Akosh would not escape this time. She would tear down the whole street if necessary. Unleash the full force of her magic and rip her enemy limb from limb. She might be able to heal from some wounds but Munroe wanted to see how she coped with no head.

Even as she considered it Munroe remembered those who hadn't escaped the orphanage. She'd given them a warning but it hadn't been enough to clear the whole building. Those deaths were partially her fault but mostly she blamed Akosh.

It would be so easy to keep drawing power from the Source until it felt as if her skin was about to burst. She could release it all at once and turn every stone in the building to dust and anyone inside would be burned to ash. But that was the problem. She didn't know who else was here and she had no definitive proof that Akosh was hiding upstairs. Perhaps it was simply another of her minions. Perhaps Korell himself was loyal to her. She had to be sure.

Forcing herself to breathe slowly, Munroe released her grip on the Source, letting the power trickle away. Her fists uncurled and she focused on studying the intricate pattern on a solid gold bangle as a distraction.

Korell returned empty-handed from the back room. "I'm sorry, we must have sold that one. I'm so forgetful," he said with a distracted smile.

"Never mind, we'll try somewhere else," said Dox. "Come

along, Mother." She looped her arm through Munroe's and had to practically drag her out of the shop. Once they were back on the street it was a little easier to repress the urge to scream or destroy the building. She needed a distraction to focus on while the rage ebbed away.

Dox guided her to a public square where a group of travelling entertainers had set up their brightly coloured wagon. A small crowd had gathered to watch a pair of jugglers and a fire-breather, whose ability wasn't magical in nature and therefore acceptable. Even so, a pair of city guards were watching the crowd. Another squad walked past, exchanging terse nods with their colleagues, hands resting on weapons. There was a growing tension in the city wherever she looked, in the hunch of people's shoulders and their clenched jaws. Only the children seemed immune, whooping and clapping in delight as the fire-breather swallowed another flaming baton without apparent injury.

"I remember the first time I saw someone do that," said Dox. "I thought it was real magic."

"How old were you?"

"Five or six. I'm not sure." Dox shrugged as if it didn't matter, but Munroe could hear the pain in her voice. So far they'd talked very little about her life before she'd worked for Cannok, the former crime lord of Rojenne.

"What happened to your parents?" asked Munroe.

It was a long time before Dox answered. She was watching the children clap and laugh with abandon. Her eyes were full of regret and perhaps longing for an earlier time in her life. Suddenly she seemed so much older than her sixteen years.

"Dad died at sea when I was eight. The whole ship went down in a storm. I remember a lot of shouting after that. Moving from one place to another. Always living in small, stinking rooms. Mum always came home late at night, tired, and just fell asleep.

The next morning she was gone before I'd properly woken up. We were living in Perizzi and during the day I ran wild in the streets. Almost joined one of the Families as a paper jackal, but somehow my mother found out. She dragged me away from all my friends to Rojenne in the south. I was miserable, alone, and I started acting out. Going to the worst parts of the city. Listening on corners where I shouldn't. My Talent developed and a year later, Mum was dead from a wasting disease and I was working for Cannok."

Dox shrugged again, as if none of it mattered. As if talking about it didn't hurt and that's all there was to her story. There was more she hadn't said but Munroe didn't push. The story explained her resentment towards adults. Dox was used to looking after herself as life had taught her that eventually everyone left.

This time Munroe tugged on her arm and together they walked back towards their tavern. They left the entertainers and the smiling children behind, turning their backs on happier times to focus on more grim events in the present.

"Tonight, I'm going to go back to the jeweller's shop and find out who is staying in the apartment upstairs," said Munroe. "Do I need to tell you to stay at the tavern this time?"

"No, it's fine. I'll stay."

"Good."

"I wanted to ask you something," said Dox, unwilling to meet her eye. "What happens after?"

It wasn't really something Munroe had considered. All of her thoughts were focused on finding Akosh and then destroying her. She had no other plans. Her old life was gone. Any dreams she'd had with her family had become meaningless. There was no tomorrow, only today.

"I have no idea," admitted Munroe. "Ask me again when she's dead."

Dox looked as if she wanted to say something but she changed her mind. Perhaps she understood that making plans for the future was foolish. It was so easy for them to be ripped apart. But some things felt inevitable. That no matter how much people tried to change them the outcome was always the same.

Deep in her heart Munroe knew that no matter what, one day she would kill Akosh. It was only a matter of when.

Akosh sighed with relief as Munroe and a girl walked away down the street. She pulled the curtains closed and flopped into a chair. Wiping the sweat from her brow, her hands began to shake as the adrenaline wore off.

She'd come close to throwing herself out of the window to escape. If she'd heard even one footstep on the stairs Akosh would have fled. Hate and self-loathing warred inside. Hiding in a tiny apartment like a trapped rat. Afraid of a mortal and ready to run rather than stand and fight. Fear was for the weak. It made Akosh sick to her stomach to think how far she'd fallen.

She still had a network of people in the city but there was little they could do about Munroe in the short term. Her people had helped find a teacher for the Regent's mages, but it would be a long time before they were a serious threat to Munroe. Her strength was unparalleled. It harkened back to a time before she had existed, when there had been more than a handful of Sorcerers in the world. If only one of her orphans had been a mage of comparable strength. She had a few with minor abilities but none of them were in Zecorria. The Regent and his mages had made sure there were no other magic users in the city.

As much as she hated to admit it Akosh needed help but so far Kai had been ignoring her. She'd not seen him in days, ever since she'd recommended one of her people, Farley, for a special task in Yerskania. Other than regular visits from Doggett and one or two others, Akosh received little news. She couldn't even risk going into the city by herself any more in case Munroe sensed her presence. When Munroe had been downstairs Akosh had felt her drawing energy from the Source. The echo of power had drummed Akosh's temples as if someone were beating her about the head. Her feet had been moving towards the window before she'd even realised.

The sound of footsteps on the stairs brought her back to the present. Akosh drew a dagger and prepared herself for a fight. If this was to be the end she would face her enemy on her feet with a blade in her hand. The shuffling steps continued towards her, prolonging the torture just a little longer. Burning sweat ran into her eyes and she irritably wiped it away.

Oddly there was a polite knock at the door. "May I come in?" said Korell.

Akosh's legs trembled with relief and she had to hold on to a chair to stop from falling over. Annoyed at her own weakness she sheathed her dagger and poured a drink before yanking open the door, startling the shopkeeper.

He stared up at her with fevered eyes. "I was wondering—"

"I've told you, I don't have any black crystal."

"Yes. I see." Korell licked his lips and slowly bobbed his head. "Well, I'll leave you alone."

"Wait," said Akosh, hoping she didn't sound desperate. "I need you to deliver a message to him. Tell him I want to see him. Soon."

There was no need to say who he was. Kai was the most important figure in both their lives.

Korell considered her order as if it were a request. "I don't close the shop for another two hours. Send someone else."

He was so numb Akosh wondered if he would even notice if she cut off one of his arms. "There isn't anyone else. Close the shop and find him. I need to see him. Now!"

"Um," said the shopkeeper, taking his time, "well, it is quiet today. I suppose I could close early."

Akosh gritted her teeth to stop herself ripping out his throat. "He'll give you some more crystal if you deliver my message," she promised.

That caught his attention. "Well, I should deliver that message. I must be going."

He shuffled away, leaving the door open, and trotted down the stairs and out the front door. Peering down the stairs Akosh realised he hadn't closed the shop up or even locked the front door. Moving about as if she belonged she checked the shop was empty before locking the door and turning over the sign. There were a few people on the street but no one seemed to be paying attention to her.

An hour passed as she paced about in the apartment, occasionally glancing out of the window for signs of the shopkeeper. After another hour she realised he wasn't going to come back. Either he'd found Kai and had delivered the message or he had simply forgotten and was high on black crystal staring at the ceiling.

She couldn't rely on Kai and her people couldn't help her deal with him or Munroe. At best they could find a new safe house but she wouldn't be able to hide there from him for long. With Kai lurking in the city and Vargus on his way, Akosh was almost out of time. If she didn't find a way to escape the noose that was tightening around her neck she'd end up being destroyed or worse, slowly consumed by Kai. Out of options and allies Akosh decided to take the biggest risk of her life.

Chapter 18

Tammy turned her neck to the left and it cracked loudly releasing some of the tension in her shoulders. She'd been hunching forward again without realising, her head dipping closer and closer to the page as darkness fell. She stood up to light a few lanterns and her back adjusted itself making her groan.

She'd underestimated the number of hours she would spend in this office reading reports. Sometimes when a really interesting case came across her desk it was a struggle not to pull on her jacket and head out the door to investigate. Instead she had to assign it to someone else.

Today had been particularly challenging. It was the first time she'd interviewed several novices in training. It was a formal part of the process in applying to be a Guardian of the Peace and a rite of passage for the applicants. Her predecessor, the Old Man, had dug into each person's psyche with his searching and brutal questions, unravelling their self-image, stripping them down to the core.

The Guardians were the elite group of investigators called upon by rulers from across the world to investigate unusual cases. The role required not only intelligence, intuition and being an excellent study of people, but great internal fortitude. Coming face to face with horrific crimes and the perpetrators responsible day after day took a toll on each Guardian.

One of the Khevassar's responsibilities was to make sure each novice understood themselves and the challenges that lay ahead. Before they could begin to question the motives of others they needed to know who they really were and why they wanted to be a Guardian. When the truth was laid bare, and their real self was revealed, some novices couldn't cope. Others took the blow on the chin and went on to become outstanding Guardians. It was better to separate the wheat from the chaff rather than have a Guardian snap under pressure.

All these years later she still remembered her interview with the Old Man. None of the novices she'd interviewed this morning had started crying in her office but all of them had been shocked. Tomorrow she would see how many came back for another day of training.

There was a knock on the door and Guardian Fray came into her office. He was out of uniform and his plain clothes were worn and cheap. He didn't have a military bearing like some who'd spent years in the Watch as he'd lived on the fringes of society before joining. With no unusual features it made him the perfect Guardian for undercover work. As Tammy gestured for him to sit down she wondered how long it had been before the Old Man saw his people as assets first and individuals second. It crept up on her at times and Tammy didn't even realise she was doing it. It was ruthless. However, she couldn't do this job by herself and she needed to use the right people at the right time.

"Report," she said, noting the shadows under his eyes from late nights. There was mud on his boots and his clothes smelled of stale beer.

"I met with Don Jarrow. He remembered me," said Fray with a wry smile. It probably hadn't been a pleasant experience for Don

Jarrow given their previous meeting. Much like her interviews with the novices, Fray had brought up some old and unsettling memories for Don Jarrow that he wanted to forget. "It took some persuading but he called a meeting and the heads of all the Families attended. Once I explained the situation, and the potential of disloyalty within their own organisations, they were quickly on board."

"Did you find anyone loyal to Akosh?"

Fray nodded grimly. "Three. Two Silver jackals and, believe it or not, one Gold working for Doña Tarija. She had the jackal disembowelled on the spot. I think that scared the others more than my magic. I had to dig into the past of a few others, but I couldn't find any connections to Akosh."

From his expression Fray must have been forced to relive some disturbing memories. No one in any of the crime Families rose to the upper tiers without spilling a lot of blood. Tammy could see that he was exhausted, and part of her wanted to apologise for what he'd endured, but she held her tongue. Now that she was the Khevassar and his superior she couldn't be his friend any more.

"They're still ferreting through the rest of their ranks for others that might be disloyal," he said.

"It doesn't matter. Those further down the chain don't have as much influence to be disruptive. Did the Families agree to your deal?" asked Tammy.

"Yes. They're not going to stop any information coming into the city, but they've agreed to monitor all messages. Any that look suspicious will disappear."

"You've done well. Get some rest," she said, dismissing him.

It wasn't a perfect solution but it was the best she could manage for the time being. There would still be ways to get messages into the city that not even the Families knew about but the flow of information to Akosh's people would slow. This way if they were planning something one of her Guardians might find out about it before it was too late. It would also buy her some more time for her people to dig into the hundred operatives who had dumped their stone idols.

An hour later there was a frantic knocking and sounds of an argument in the outer office. Tammy yanked open her door to find Rummpoe trying to prevent a vaguely familiar man from entering her office. He was stocky, like all Yerskani, with strangely hairless doughy arms and a clean-shaven head. Dressed in black clothing and a white apron there was a strong smell of chemicals on his skin but she didn't think he worked in an apothecary. An air of authority clung to him as he eyeballed Rummpoe. Unusually his hands were also hairless and his skin's pallor was that of someone who spent little time in direct sunlight.

"Khevassar, I must speak with you. It's urgent!"

"He doesn't have an appointment," said Rummpoe.

"Girl, do you understand the meaning of the word 'urgent'?" snapped the man. "There's no time to make an appointment."

Rummpoe drew herself up to her full height as if he'd just slapped her across the face. "There is always time to make an appointment."

"Who are you?" asked Tammy, glaring down at him.

"Chief Coroner Lugano, Sir," he said with a slight bow. She vaguely remembered meeting him on a previous occasion, but it wasn't often she saw the chief death doctor. For him to have come in person and left the gloomy confines of his dungeon, as they all called it, meant it was serious.

"It's all right, Rummpoe, let him in," she said. "See that we're not disturbed."

Her secretary grudgingly stepped aside and Lugano swept into her office. The chubby man remained standing after she'd taken a seat and he refused her offer, preferring to pace the room.

"I apologise for barging in while you're working. I hate it when people do that to me." He glanced at the closed door behind him with a faint smile. "She's tough. Reminds me of my granddaughter."

Tammy raised an eyebrow and reassessed her estimate of his age, increasing it by another twenty years. There were a few lines around his eyes but little else to give her any clue.

"What can I do for you?" she asked.

"Did you see the report my office sent you about the deaths at the Red Lion?"

"Three suspicious deaths. The owner and two others."

Lugano bobbed his head. "It was a nasty virus, but it seemed self-contained. A red rash on the skin, vomiting and swelling of the organs, followed by death within a few days. Then I saw another report about a body found down by the river. The victim, a Yerskani man, had died somewhere else and been dumped there. I didn't realise there was a connection until I saw the body. It was the same virus."

"Was he a fourth victim from the Red Lion or is it a second outbreak?" asked Tammy.

Lugano continued to pace back and forth. "I had an old friend, Guardian Faulk, look into that. Apparently the owner of the Red Lion paid the Watch to look elsewhere after one of his guests died in the night. Rather than scare his other customers the body was dumped and he tried to cover it up. But the virus had already spread. It killed him five days later."

Tammy felt a cold prickle of fear run down her spine. "Why do I get the feeling that's not the end of the story?"

Lugano's smile held little mirth. "Because another body was brought in two days after that. The same red rash, swollen organs and vomiting. This time it was a woman from a fairly expensive brothel called the Honey Pot."

"Is there more?" she asked, hoping for the best.

"Yes. You should come and see," said Lugano.

Tammy pulled on her jacket and followed him through the corridors of Unity Hall before they stepped out on to the street. There was an annoying drizzle coming down that clung to her clothing, gradually seeping into the material. Rather than getting irritated by the weather Lugano was invigorated by the rain. He wet his hands and ran them over his scalp then stared up at the moon, squinting at its brightness.

The streets were busy with people heading home after a day at work or at the beginning of the night out. Squads of the Watch kept an eye on rowdy groups while music and an array of smells from taverns tried to entice people out of the rain.

Since becoming Khevassar she tried to avoid going out at night as much as possible unless required for work. It left her feeling lonely as it reminded her of what and who she'd sacrificed for the job. But it was the only way to keep them safe. She had to remain nameless and beyond reproach.

A short walk took them to a plain squat building with no upper floor. The only unusual features were a large set of wide doors and long narrow windows like arrow slits set at intervals on each wall. Most people who walked past every day probably had no idea what went on inside or that it was the city's largest mortuary.

Lugano led her to a small side door which he unlocked with a stout key before locking it behind them. They passed through a locked gate, guarded by two members of the Watch, and another door before reaching the main entry hall. Perizzi was home to followers from a dozen religions and had visitors from across the world, each with their own beliefs. For all of their differences the one thing they had in common was the benevolent treatment of their dead. Security at all mortuaries in the city was almost as tight as Unity Hall.

Lugano lit a pair of lanterns, driving back the thick shadows that were starting to gather. The building was silent and cold like a grave. This image was reinforced in her mind as they descended several flights of stairs, going deeper into the earth. Their lanterns were the only source of light and the darkness seemed to press down on her from all sides.

On the lowest floor Tammy could see her breath frosting on the air and was glad she'd pulled on her jacket. Lugano seemed immune as he bustled down the corridor, sweeping past a dozen closed doors. Tammy glanced into one through the window and immediately wished she'd repressed the urge. A dead man lay on a cold stone slab, his chest cavity open to the air. One woman was carefully removing his organs and weighing them while another was recording the details.

During the day sunlight was channelled through the narrow windows with mirrors, ensuring even the lowest rooms were brightly lit for delicate work. Tonight the corridors were rich with shadows, lanterns providing small oases of yellow against the impenetrable black. The two coroners had several lanterns in the room but the light made their skin look as pale and sickly as the corpse on the table.

At the far end of the corridor was a large black iron door which Lugano unlocked with another key from his belt. Inside was a huge room with a ribbed ceiling giving her the impression they were standing inside the belly of a huge beast. Lanterns were spaced around the room at regular intervals but they offered no heat to chase away the cold that was seeping into her bones.

One wall was taken up with row after row of small doors which she assumed housed bodies in cold storage. They would be held here until they were released to the family or a local temple. If nobody claimed a body they would be consumed by fire and blessed by a priest of the Maker.

There were ten stone slabs spaced down the centre of the room, all of which were occupied with bodies covered up to the neck with a white cloth. A pair of coroners sat at the far end of the room, eating a meal between shifts, ignoring the dead bodies around them. Guardian Faulk sat with them, chatting and laughing, although Tammy noticed he was wearing gloves and a scarf. The coroners were dressed in loose cotton clothing and seemed immune to the cold.

"I asked Guardian Faulk to meet us here," said Lugano as the Guardian joined them. Lugano approached the first body and then glanced up at Tammy. "You're not going to be sick, are you?"

"I'm fine. Who is he?"

"The man we found down at the river," said Faulk. "Lugano thinks he was our first victim."

Lugano pulled back the sheet, revealing the cold grey flesh of a Yerskani man. The Y-shaped incision showed he'd been opened up at some point but the puckered flesh had been sewn together with thick black cord. Red sores mottled the flesh of his arms, shoulders and upper chest. There was more of it on his neck and face.

"It's far worse than any other victim we've seen. It's extended down his legs as well," said Lugano, pulling on a tight pair of black gloves that stretched to his elbows. "I think he was the first victim and the carrier."

"Who is he?" asked Tammy.

"I'm still digging into his background, but from what I can tell he only arrived in Perizzi a few days ago," said Faulk, consulting his notebook. "Guards at the northern gate remembered him because he was accompanied by two Fists of Drassi but they weren't protecting any cargo."

"He was the cargo," she said.

"It seems that way," said Faulk, "but as far as I know, he's not a member of nobility or anyone of importance. I'm tracing his path through the city."

"Is this what you wanted to show me?" she said, turning to Lugano.

"Sadly no." He gestured at the other nine bodies. "All of them died from the same virus. It's definitely an outbreak."

"How virulent is it?"

"There's good news," said Lugano, forcing a smile. "You have to be fairly intimate with a person to catch it. I think it's spread by prolonged physical contact or fluids."

"That's good news?" said Tammy.

"If it was in the water or the air, we'd all be in trouble," said Lugano.

This wasn't something she'd anticipated or had any experience with. Once again the city of Perizzi was proving to be full of unpleasant surprises. "Has anything like this happened before?" she asked, turning to Faulk. He'd been investigating crimes as a Guardian for over twenty-five years.

"Yes. There was a ship."

"What do you suggest we do?"

"Trace the path of the virus through the city. We've got victims in a few specific areas. It could be our carrier was responsible, or there could be another hot spot," he said.

"We need to isolate it to stop it spreading," said Lugano.

"What about a cure?" she asked.

Lugano shook his head. "I don't know. Too early to say. Find me a live victim and a good doctor, then we'll see. Right now containment is our best hope."

"Who else knows about this?" asked Tammy. If word spread about the virus before she had a strategy in place there would be panic in the streets. People would try to flee the city, potentially making matters worse by spreading it beyond the walls of Perizzi.

"Only a few of my people and Faulk," said Lugano, a note of warning in his voice. "But it won't last. Word will spread quickly."

"Then we need to move fast. Faulk, take as many bodies as you need to run down leads. Get me some answers. Find out how far it's spread."

As ever there was a huge amount to be done and little time. Someone with symptoms may have visited an apothecary or doctor, so they would all have to be interviewed, starting with where the victims had been found and working outwards. It was possible one of the doctors had already treated and cured someone. If so they would be a critical resource in the days ahead. It was also possible one or more of them had been infected. All guards on the gates would have to be put on alert and down at the docks to watch for anyone with symptoms. Ideally she would close the city gates, but she had neither the authority nor enough evidence to convince the Queen. The moment that happened there would be widespread panic.

Lugano was right. Even limiting information about the virus to only those who needed to know, it was inevitable that word would begin to spread.

For a moment Tammy wondered if this was an attack by one of Akosh's people. The timing could be a coincidence but she believed in those less every day. Ultimately it didn't matter. There was a plague in her city which she needed to eradicate before it was too late.

CHAPTER 19

Vargus and Danoph brought their horses to a stop in the middle of what had once been the village of Garrion's Folly. All that remained above ground were piles of tumbled stone along the main street, broken timbers, cold grey ash and a sea of freshly dug graves.

Surveying the wreckage Danoph hoped to see some spark of life in the ruins but there was nothing. Not even a stray dog looking for scraps. After spending time in western Shael, he'd seen abandoned villages before but never this level of destruction and not in northern Yerskania. In Shael the raiders would sometime squat in the ruins of abandoned villages, but every building in Garrion's Folly had been flattened. Even more worrying was the lack of mould or rot. Until very recently the village had been a living, breathing community.

Beside the main road a section of land had been cleared and someone had carefully dug the graves. Danoph stopped counting at sixty. None of them were marked with a stone or any kind of identification but from the size Danoph could see some of them belonged to children.

"What happened?" asked Danoph, his voice thick with emotion. "Was this the work of Akosh?"

Vargus was staring up at the forest-covered hills with a puzzled expression but he turned away to survey the village. "No. This was the work of humans."

"Who dug the graves?"

"I don't know. Perhaps Queen Morganse sent soldiers after the massacre."

"You know who was responsible for this, don't you?"

"I do, but that's not why we're here," said Vargus.

Even though Vargus hadn't told him why they'd come to this village a part of Danoph already knew. They were close to the Zecorran border and after a few more days of travel they would reach the capital city, Herakion. Akosh had last been sighted there and he knew Vargus would need his help when they arrived.

Danoph was still learning about his powers but he was running out of time. Akosh wouldn't be patient or give him a second chance. If he was to be of use he needed to deepen his understanding.

"What do you want me to do?" he asked, looking around for clues.

"Everyone who lived here is dead. Not a single person escaped." Even though Vargus had given up the mantle of the Weaver long ago his intuition still bordered on the supernatural. Or perhaps it was simply a product of his unnaturally long life. Danoph was slowly beginning to realise his ideas about time needed to change. The only clue Vargus had given about his age was a vague reply about witnessing the birth of all five mortal races. Danoph could only name three.

"If all of the villagers are dead, can I still see their individual futures?" asked Danoph.

"No. The pathways would have faded by now. If you used your power to search for them you'd only find an absence."

"Then what am I looking for?"

"The ripples spreading out from this void," he said, gesturing at the utter destruction. "In Tulan you saw how one person could affect countless others. Here, because everyone died, those echoes will never spread. Imagine dropping a pebble into the middle of a still pond. You can't see the people in Garrion's Folly and their individual futures any more, but you should be able to intuit the combined impact of the whole village. Those ripples will only extend so far. Close your eyes and try," he added, seeing Danoph's confusion.

Danoph took a deep breath and then reached out with his senses, focusing on the village around him. As light blossomed in his right hand he tried to concentrate on the echoes as before. Just as Vargus had warned it felt as if he had been struck deaf and blind. For half a mile or more in every direction there was nothing. An absence of light, sound, touch and even smell. There should have been dozens of people with hundreds of potential pathways but there was only silence and the endless dark. Perhaps it was his imagination but it felt cold. There was also no way to tell the passage of time. Part of him was terrified that if he screamed no sound would emerge from his throat and he might be trapped in the void for ever.

With a jolt Danoph's eyes snapped open. His heart was pounding and he stared at his surroundings, soaking in all of the colours, inhaling the smells of the forest and freshly turned earth. He stumbled and would have fallen if Vargus hadn't caught him by the elbow.

"Try again, but focus on the land beyond the village," said Vargus, keeping him steady with a hand on his arm.

Part of Danoph was loath to close his eyes in case he found himself back in the void, but he summoned his courage and tried again.

The void was still there, waiting, but he stretched his senses and tried to look beyond it. Slowly he became aware of faint pathways stretching out into the distance. They were like worn tracks in a forest that were slowly being reclaimed by the undergrowth. Some of them were there for a few heartbeats and then gone only to reappear a short time later. They were the remnants of pathways leading outwards from the village.

"I can see pathways but they're fading," said Danoph.

"Those are events that would've been directly affected by people in this village. Push beyond them and move further away," suggested Vargus. "What can you see?"

"Three strong pathways. Others flicker and change but they seemed fixed in place. They extend away from the village for miles."

"Three. I had hoped there would be less," said Vargus.

"What are they?"

"Three major events that should happen. Now, they will never come to pass."

"Should I follow the pathways?" asked Danoph, feeling them pull at him. It was like an insistent dog on a leash, tugging him forward.

"We should know what's been lost. Follow them, but be careful. You could become lost in the tangle of what will be and may not want to come back," warned Vargus. Danoph felt him grip one of his hands. The old warrior's hand was calloused and rough. "Use me as an anchor. If you start to drift, think of this place and focus on my hand."

Danoph reached towards the nearest glowing pathway with his magic. It stretched out towards the horizon, shimmering with promise. The moment he made contact he was swept away like a cork falling into a fast river.

Hundreds of unfamiliar faces and many that he recognised flashed past his mind's eye in a whirlwind of colour. Laughter merged with screams and a hundred conversations to create a cacophony of sound so intense he immediately tried to pull away. Powerless he continued to rush forward before suddenly snapping to a halt so abruptly he felt a sharp pain in his joints.

Standing in the corner of a small room Danoph played silent witness to a woman giving birth to twin sons. Her husband was at her side, crying and laughing at the same time as a second boy came into the world. Danoph could feel the mother's intense exhaustion and her relief at seeing two healthy children. The babies were wrapped up and presented to the parents who laughed and cried at their twins. Danoph had a moment to share in their joy before something grabbed him by the back of his neck. Unable to scream he was pulled away, fell into the flowing stream and was carried forward again.

He stopped again with another jolt, staring out at a scene of utter devastation. Fire rained from the sky on to a bloody battlefield that was already a blackened nightmare of ash and ruin. Two armies clashed beneath a lead-coloured sky, grinding into each other with mud-spattered steel. A rain of arrows came down, bouncing off armour, digging into joints, slipping under shields. Screams of warriors and metal on metal overlapped until the two were indistinguishable. Mud was churned underfoot, which changed colour from black to grey to dark red as blood and bile soaked the ground. A flaming comet struck one group of warriors. The lucky ones were killed by the impact or incinerated while those who survived were slowly roasted alive in their armour. Their screams were lost in the din. Their deaths meaningless among the widespread carnage.

Desperate to be anywhere else it was a relief when Danoph was yanked into the stream of events again. Part of him was aware that he had become unstuck in time and he couldn't feel his body any more. A kaleidoscope of colour flashed in front of his eyes, full of images that went by too quickly for him to identify. Sounds merged together into a tidal wave of chaos that threatened to deafen him from the intensity. Somewhere in the maelstrom he heard a voice calling his name.

The flow of events began to move backwards. Repeating what he'd seen before he was travelling at speed until all images began to stretch and blur into a white wall of light and sound.

As before he stopped suddenly with a jolt. At first Danoph thought he was back in the present but glancing around he saw Garrion's Folly of the past. Small, with only a dozen buildings in total, he saw locals clearing an area of trees that would become the main street upon which he stood. For some reason his eyes were drawn to the hills beside the village. Another area had been cleared of trees around a monument that seemed incomplete. He saw what looked like half a bridge before someone was shouting his name.

A sharp pull on Danoph's arm brought him back to the present, ripping him from the river of time. He stumbled to his knees, coughing and spluttering, heart pounding in his chest. Through bleary eyes he saw the ruined village around him and his hands on the ground. He relished the feeling of gravel digging into his knees, the burn of air in his lungs, the trickle of hot sweat down his back.

Slowly the real world took shape around him. As he regained control of his breathing Danoph tried to sort through the images.

"Tell me what did you see?" asked Vargus.

"There was a birth. Twin boys. I don't know who they were."

Vargus rocked back on his heels. "There's no way to know what has been lost. Now, I suspect they'll never be born. What else?"

"I saw a war," said Danoph remembering the blackened landscape and widespread carnage. "A vicious and bloody war with fire falling from the sky."

Vargus grunted. "Hopefully that won't come to pass. And the third?"

"I don't know. I think I was turned around. I saw this village many years ago. There weren't many houses but I could see a ruin in the hills." Danoph looked towards where he'd seen the clearing but the hillside above was an endless canopy of green. "Why did you bring me here?"

Vargus sat down beside him on the road and his face became sombre. "To show you what has been lost. The good and the bad."

"Those children."

"They're gone. For ever. You witnessed their birth and felt the indescribable joy of that moment. Now it will never come to be."

"Why did you do this?" asked Danoph, when he could speak.

"To make you understand. Akosh, and many others before her, have manipulated events in order to extend their existence. They're afraid of the future. But it will be far worse for you than all of our brethren, because you've seen and felt what will be. The joy and sorrow. The pain and wonder. You've lived it." Danoph began to understand that Vargus was speaking from experience. The depth of sorrow in his eyes was unlike any Danoph had ever seen. "Without knowing what may come, they're willing to risk everything, even though it goes against the one rule. In twenty or thirty years, after experiencing so much suffering, how do you think you will fare?"

Vargus's words rained down on Danoph like blows from a hammer. Even now if he closed his eyes Danoph knew he would hear again the first cry of twins being born. He tried to imagine living with the knowledge that thousands of people he'd seen and touched would never be born. Year upon year. Memory stacked on top of memory. The emotional weight of not only knowing so much but also feeling it all would be crippling.

With his knowledge of future events it wouldn't take much

to nudge a few people in one direction to stop a war or make sure a special child was born. The ripples could be monitored to minimise the impact in years to come. But if he did it once and got away with it, why would he stop there? Why not save someone else?

And so it would go. Building over time until he was the perpetrator being hunted down by Vargus for changing the natural flow of events.

"That's why you gave up the mantle of the Weaver," said Danoph. "The weight of all that you'd seen was too much to bear."

A heavy silence fell on them both as Danoph contemplated the task that lay ahead for him. "Were you ever tempted," he asked, "to change events?"

Vargus nodded. "To save the Necheye."

"What stopped you?"

"Older and wiser friends. One day, many years from now, you will find yourself in a similar situation. You will be emotionally wrung out, drowning in sorrow and bitterness. Angry at everyone and uncaring of the consequences. You will be desperate to change events and save a live. Just one life. Because surely saving one person won't change anything. And when that day comes, call on me before you do something you will regret. Otherwise, I will be forced to hunt you down, as I've done with many others."

For the briefest of moments Danoph felt the full weight of Vargus's will and he recoiled at its immensity. On the outside he resembled a grizzled middle-aged Seve warrior. But on the inside he was old beyond any traditional measure of time. He was as relentless as the tide and as implacable an enemy as had ever existed. And since the beginning he had hunted down and destroyed countless others who had broken the Maker's one rule.

Danoph struggled to swallow the lump in his throat and was relieved when Vargus went to retrieve the horses. If the time came when he considered changing events he would strive to remember this moment and the inevitable cost of his actions. He wanted to be better, but a small part of Danoph wondered how many of those who'd been destroyed had started out with the best intentions?

Despite the loss of his eyes Garvey's remaining senses had never been more acute. It wasn't just that his hearing and sense of smell had dramatically improved. It was that he had a more profound understanding of his connection to the world and his place within it.

A few months ago he would have scoffed at the idea. He knew there wasn't a grand plan. Everyone wasn't born for a specific reason and the future wasn't set. But since becoming blind Garvey had experienced things he would previously have thought impossible and had spoken to beings beyond his realm of understanding. The world was both more terrifying and exciting in ways he'd not felt since he was a child.

Different layers of the world were being peeled back and exposed one after another, revealing their secrets, and all he had to do was listen.

From where he was standing Garvey knew he was in a forest surrounded by trees. Despite not being able to see he could feel them in a multitude of ways. The gentle breeze made the branches sway, their shadows dancing across his face, exposing and revealing sunlight which he could feel on his skin. The sighing of the boughs and the endless rustling of the leaves overhead sounded like the tide. Far above birds and squirrels moved through the branches giving him the impression of their height. Laying a hand on one trunk the tree felt immovable and eternal. Extending his senses with magic Garvey could feel its roots digging down into the earth. At least a century old it had seen and weathered far more than him and yet it remained strong and proud.

Deep in the earth the trees were connected. Their roots intertwined and although they often fought for the same precious water they also sheltered one another against violent storms that tried to rip them up from the earth. Thus the blended roots of one tree tied its fate to those around it creating a symbiotic relationship.

So it was with him. His actions as the Bane were supposed to create room so that those who wielded magic in a positive light could thrive. But since returning to the Red Tower the public's perception of magic had declined, ultimately leading to people uniting in their hatred against him for the terrible things he'd done. But rather than suffer for his deeds events had led him back here, to Garrion's Folly, the scene of his worst crime. He'd dug graves for all of those who'd been murdered but Garvey had no illusions about such an act balancing the scales. There could be no forgiveness for what he'd done. Down below on what used to be the main street many restless spirits still wandered, caught in peculiar loops, performing chores and going to work.

The village was gone but it too would serve another purpose, if only he could reach a new level of understanding.

Five paces to his left the trees stopped, the soil was bare and beneath the ground the tree roots refused to stretch. Reaching out with one hand Garvey ran his fingers over the cool surface of the half-finished bridge. Although he couldn't see them, Garvey knew the black stones were unmarked by time or local fauna. Birds and other creatures avoided the ruin as it made them distinctly uneasy.

The longer he touched the stones the more Garvey was able to sense the strange aura surrounding the bridge. It wasn't alive. But deep within there was the presence of ancient magic that was both alien and familiar. He'd felt something similar many times when in proximity to the Red Tower, but at the school it had been active and engaged. Here, the magic was buried deep as if asleep and waiting to be woken up.

Stretching his senses with his magic, Garvey dug tendrils of energy across and then deep into the stones. Hours passed unnoticed as he stood immobile with both hands resting gently on the bridge. Darkness fell without him realising as he searched. Eventually hunger forced him to stop, seek shelter and food. Sleep washed over him the moment he lay down but the next morning he started again, examining the bridge in minute detail. Days passed but time and everything else beyond his search became meaningless.

One day, when the sun was high and warm on his face, Garvey found something buried deep within the bridge. It was contradictory because it felt both connected to the stones and separate. The more he focused on it the more it created a very specific feeling within. Anticipation.

Garvey struggled to understand what he'd discovered. It was a part of the world in front of him and yet not really there at all. It took him several more days before he was able to describe it in a way that made sense.

The bridge was a lock, waiting to be opened, and somehow he needed to fashion a key.

CHAPTER 20

Normally Regent Choilan would have been idly lounging with a drink as he listened to one of Bettina's reports. Today he sat upright in his chair, hands gripping the armrests as she described in her emotionless tones what the whore, Celeste, had told her.

"I questioned her myself, and apparently, Marran was completely normal in every way during her visit. He seemed genuinely surprised when she appeared at his door and was polite and accommodating. Celeste described him as a little nervous." Bettina's tone of voice never wavered, giving nothing away about how she felt about letting a prostitute into the palace. "However, it wasn't his first time paying for it. She was certain of that. He knew exactly why she was there."

"Did he?" he asked, wondering if Marran was smart enough to know the real reason they'd sent Celeste to his room. Choilan still remembered the way Marran had looked at some of his students. Just thinking about it made his skin crawl.

Bettina had warned him that Marran was unsuitable for the job but wasn't so petty as to point out that she'd been right. With people waiting to see Choilan fall from the throne the odious mage appeared to be his last hope of turning the cadre of mages into a success.

It hadn't escaped his notice that all of the other mages in the city, who potentially could have been a suitable teacher, had recently been found murdered or had died in suspicious circumstances. While he didn't think Marran himself was responsible, Choilan suspected someone else had orchestrated it. Half a dozen of his agents were investigating what had happened. So far they hadn't come up with any names about who was responsible. His spies had also yet to determine why someone wanted Marran inside the palace. He didn't think it was something his enemies would do as their hatred of magic was so intense. So if Marran was not in the palace to assassinate him, why was he here? And who had sent him?

Bettina lifted one shoulder. "Marran may suspect we sent Celeste to keep him calm. Shall I continue?"

Wishing he'd not sent away all the servants Choilan was forced to get up and pour himself a drink. "What else did she say?"

"She reported that everything proceeded as expected when she disrobed." Bettina made it sound clinical and cold, like a procedure that had to be endured rather than a pleasurable indulgence between two people. "He made no peculiar requests and everything of his worked as normal. He wasn't abusive or angry and thanked her after the inevitable conclusion. He tried to pay and when she explained it had already been taken care of he didn't become upset. She left and that was the end."

Choilan doubted that was the end. A person didn't change overnight. Marran had been clever enough to hide from his cadre when they'd been scouring the city for recruits. Devious. That was the word Choilan most often used when he pictured Marran. That or grotesque. Something about the man unsettled him right down to his bones. There was an inherent sliminess that made Choilan want to scrub his skin with a coarse brush.

Every few days Kalina reported on their progress and what they were learning from Marran. So far there had only been one incident where one of the girls had felt uncomfortable after a lesson. When questioned she couldn't say why but the following day had been shaking and in tears. She'd had screaming nightmares for two nights after that until she was moved into a bedroom with another student. Just as suddenly her night terrors stopped and her fear ebbed away.

There was no proof Marran had done anything, since he was watched day and night, but everyone had suspicions. Now the mages, especially the women, were told to travel everywhere in pairs and they shared rooms as well. Choilan drained his glass, barely tasting it, and poured himself another.

"I think he knows," said Choilan, voicing his thoughts. "He's pretending for our benefit, but deep down he's the same creature."

Bettina exhaled a long breath through her nose and finally nodded. "Shall I have him put to death?"

He could order something to be slipped into Marran's food which was brought to his room every night by the same Royal Guard. Something tasteless that would settle into his body and when he fell asleep that night he'd sink deeper and deeper until he was dead. It was tempting. Very tempting.

As much as it sickened him, until Selina and her people came up with a viable alternative, he was stuck with Marran.

"No. Not yet," said the Regent, offering Bettina a thin smile.

She left without another word and Choilan found himself by the window staring out at the city. The weight of what he was doing gnawed at him but he kept reminding the little voice in his head that it was necessary.

Magic wasn't going to go away. Habreel had been right about that. Children were going to keep being born with it. Prayers and the bad old days of killing any child showing the signs wouldn't stop it from happening. Something new was needed.

He would remake Zecorria as a nation that had a firm grip on magic. Other countries blamed his people for the war, because of the Warlock and his influence over the Mad King, but that was the past. He was in charge of the mages and they were loyal to him. They would become a powerful force in the future.

The doubters would have to face the truth and find a way to cope. His cadre was just the beginning. He would create an army of patriots who bowed their heads to him and prayed to the Blessed Mother. People would begin to change their minds when they saw what the mages could do and how hard they fought to protect ordinary people.

Getting there would take time and sacrifices would have to be made. A few losses along the way were inevitable. In the meantime he could shoulder the burden of Marran and his unsettling proclivities. Soon his mages would become teachers themselves and the miscreant would be rotting in an unmarked grave.

Feeling reinvigorated Choilan smiled as Selina entered the room, which seemed to unnerve her.

"Would you like a drink?" he said, gesturing at the selection of bottles.

"No, thank you," said Selina, raising one puzzled eyebrow. "I have a report on Marran from my people. I thought you should hear it."

Choilan's sudden good mood threatened to disappear but he forced the smile to stay in place. He didn't really want it but he poured himself another drink and sat down opposite his first wife.

"What's happened now?"

"They've been listening to him in his rooms—"

"I thought there were no spy holes or secret passages in that part of the palace," he said. Maybe that was how Marran was getting out of his rooms at night without being seen by the guards on his door. They'd have to move him to another part of the palace. But how could they do that without it looking suspicious?

"There aren't any," said Selina, intruding on his thoughts.

"What?"

"There are no secret ways out. My people have taken up residence in the adjoining room. When Marran was training his students they drilled a listening channel into the wall. Don't worry," said Selina, holding up her hands as he started to protest, "it's very small and undetectable. You can't see it from his side. It only allows them to listen."

Choilan wiped at his forehead and was surprised to find it dry. "What did they hear?" he asked, taking a big gulp of his whisky and wishing it burned more.

"He's been talking to someone in his rooms."

"Who?"

"We're not sure," said Selina.

He couldn't help laughing at the situation. Were it anyone else they'd be dangling by their heels in a dungeon having the truth cut out of their flesh by a torturer. This situation with Marran was going to hang around his neck like a millstone, wearing him down every day.

"Then what can you tell me?"

"I don't appreciate your tone of voice," said Selina, fussing with the hem of her dress.

Choilan laughed again. "And I don't appreciate your mediocre attempt at spy craft." Not for the first time he reconsidered his promise to Selina. He should have left the head of his network in charge of observing Marran.

"I think he's communicating with someone using magic," said Selina. "And I think he's their puppet."

"What?"

A sly smile crept across Selina's face, pleased at having recaptured his interest. "He's subservient and scared when he talks. At first they thought he was mad, as he seemed to be rambling, but my people eventually realised it was one half of a conversation."

Taking a moment to consider, Choilan put down his glass and closed his eyes. The room briefly swam from drinking so much on an empty stomach but he ignored it. Until they knew why Marran was in the palace it made little real difference to whom he was reporting. Although, if they were able to find his master, it might give them some insight.

He considered doubling the number of guards, just to be safe. Although if Marran was half as talented as he pretended Choilan wasn't sure it would make a difference. Perhaps he should start carrying a poisoned blade again.

"Are they transcribing his conversations?" he asked, opening his eyes.

"Yes. I've brought you a copy," said Selina, offering him a stack of papers.

"Give them to Bettina. She'll take care of it."

Selina pursed her lips. "I will find out who he's working for."

"Have you considered the alternative?" he asked.

"Which is?"

"That he's mad and is conversing with a voice in his head."

His first wife looked as if he'd slapped her across the face. Her eyes drifted to the bottles on the far side of the room and he could see she was suddenly reconsidering his offer of a drink. Part of him hoped Marran was insane and talking to himself as it would put his prideful wife in her place. It would also prove that she was as fallible as everyone else.

"I will keep that in mind as well," she finally said. "One final thing. We've been digging into his history. We've found stories of at least seven girls that have gone missing in the city."

"Girls?" he asked, swallowing the lump in his throat.

"Yes," said Selina. "Some of them were of a similar age to your cadre."

"We need him. We must suffer for just a little bit longer."

Selina didn't reply but her expression was enough. He was thinking the same. How long before Marran became too much of a liability? And what was he willing to sacrifice to maintain his position as Regent?

After another tiring day of training the students Marran plodded along the corridors of the palace towards his rooms. The familiar pair of Royal Guards shadowed him the entire way. He'd not tried to talk to them. Not even once. Their uniform expressions of disgust told him enough not to even bother asking their names.

Wielding power from the Source for hours on end was a glorious way to spend the day, but it was so exhausting that sometimes his bones ached. In the moment, when he was creating fire or weaving together a shield, it made him feel like a god. Every part of his body hummed with raw and pure energy that filled him up more than food, sleep or sex.

He was connected to the world in a way that few could understand. When he stared out of the window at the city below Marran saw an enormous hive filled with thousands of glowing beings like ants in a huge nest. It was only when he cut his connection to the Source that the mundane world crept back in. Then it became just a collection of stone buildings, dirty streets and a crowd of sweaty people. If he accomplished anything from his lessons Marran wanted to impart some of that joy to his students.

Marran's door was unlocked and he went inside. The two guards then took up their posts on either side. In exactly one hour there would be a knock on the door. One of them would watch him with a hand resting on their sword while the other held out a tray of food. In the morning they would repeat the process for breakfast before walking him to his lessons. The rest of the time he was expected to stay in his rooms.

As far as prisons went it was very comfortable with a soft bed, a small collection of books, three hot meals a day and armed guards. He knew they weren't there for his protection but in a strange way they were a reassuring presence. He'd been in places that were a lot worse and at least in here he was protected from a number of threats outside the palace walls. But, sadly, not everything. Some could reach him even in here.

Marran extinguished all of the candles in his room and pulled the curtains tight. Fumbling along in the darkness he moved to the further corner of the room and sat down in front of the darkened mirror. Drawing power into his body from the Source enhanced his senses, but he closed his eyes. Sometimes it was better not to see.

Using a small knife he sliced open the palm of his hand and smeared blood across the glass. Moments after gripping the surface he had the sensation of something huge within rushing towards him. Its presence seemed to fill the room, driving out all the air, choking the breath from his chest. Its weight pressed down, compressing his spine, making his joints creak. A gasp of pain escaped his lips and then somewhere deep in the darkness he heard a monstrous voice.

"Is it done?"

"No, Master."

Even though Marran couldn't see his Master he could feel his disappointment radiating through their connection. Fresh pain blossomed behind his eyes. It felt as if someone were driving a spike up his nose into his brain.

"You're running out of time. Get it done."

"It's become more difficult, Master. The mages all share rooms at night. Even during the day they walk around in pairs."

"You were sloppy. Someone saw you."

"No."

As the silence stretched on Marran felt blood trickle down his face from one nostril. He wanted to scream but couldn't.

"What did you do?" asked his Master.

A small part of him was tempted to lie, but he quickly changed his mind. Somehow his Master always knew. "There's a girl. The light inside her is so bright. I haven't done anything, not yet. I just told her she was special but she became frightened."

Even with his eyes closed he felt the presence in the mirror draw closer. Every fibre of his being was screaming at him to let go of the glass that had started to freeze against his skin. Blood was freely running down his chin, dripping on to his chest.

"You will control yourself until this is done. Afterwards you can indulge as much as you want. Fail me and I will make your agony last for an eternity."

Marran wanted to argue but his Master's voice brooked no argument. He also knew the price of disobedience. "As you command, Master," said Marran but he was speaking to an empty room. The moment he severed his connection to the Source the pain in his head and body faded to a dull ache.

With a groan Marran slumped to the floor, finally wiping the blood off his face. He needed to finish his task otherwise his Master, Kai, the Eater of Souls, the Pestilent Watcher, would make sure his suffering lasted for years.

CHAPTER 21

A little after midnight, when the tavern finally closed, Munroe knew it was almost time. The last of the customers had left an hour before, but since then the owner and his staff had been tidying up and preparing for tomorrow.

She paced the bedroom while they bustled around downstairs, willing them to move faster, holding back her rage. She had to be certain. If it was Akosh then she would hit her with every drop of energy she could channel from the Source. She would burn her with fire and keep pouring it on until the flesh melted from her bones faster than she could regenerate.

Munroe was also preparing herself for disappointment. It was possible that the person hiding above the jeweller's shop was another minion from Akosh's network. At least it would be a step in the right direction. That was what she kept telling herself.

More worrying, although she'd not said it aloud, was that her rage was waning. Now, when she thought about her murdered family, sorrow threatened to smother her anger. She pictured their faces as they'd been and then imagined how they'd looked when the light behind their eyes was gone. Their flesh icy cold. Their bodies rotting in the ground. New fire surged through her veins, stirring the coals, making her feel powerful, focusing her mind on the task ahead.

Eventually she grew bored of pacing and tried to relax by helping Dox, who was practising her magic. So far she'd not accomplished much but Munroe couldn't fault her persistence. Every day she sat and meditated, trying to calm her racing mind long enough to feel and hear the Source. She'd come close a few times, and could now sense a magical connection in others, but had yet to embrace any power.

"It's like the tide is constantly too far away," complained Dox, opening her eyes. "I can finally hear the damn waves, but I can't get in the water."

Downstairs Munroe heard the owner bid his staff goodnight and lock the back door. If he followed his normal routine he would head to his bedroom and shortly be asleep. With a little time to spare she sat down cross-legged on the floor in front of Dox.

"Think of it like this," said Munroe. "The Source is the biggest and deepest ocean in the world. If you try to wade into it, you'll drown. You need to siphon off a small amount. Create a little stream that runs from it into your body. But the energy has to flow towards you."

Dox listened attentively and tried again, closing her eyes and concentrating on her breath. They'd given up meditating with the candle after she'd fallen asleep and nearly set the room on fire.

When she'd first become a student at the Red Tower, Munroe had struggled in the same way. Using her Talent to manipulate the odds was easy and she didn't need to think about it. It was instinctive, just like breathing. Reaching towards the Source and drawing its energy into her felt like a step backwards and Dox was probably feeling the same. When she and Dox used their Talents it was more of a sixth sense. This required focus and a mind clear of distraction.

Closing her eyes to blot out the room Munroe stretched out with her senses to see how her student was progressing. A smile quirked her lips at the idea of her being someone's teacher, but it soon faded. It made her think of the school at the Red Tower, now a burned-out ruin, and those who had died.

Focusing on the present she was pleased to see Dox had listened to her. Instead of trying to wade into the Source, she was stretching out towards it, while trying to draw off some of its energy.

"What is ...?" said Dox, a second before a trickle of energy flowed from the Source into her body. It was barely a whisper. There and then gone when she lost concentration, but in that moment her face was transformed. Her eyes widened, her whole body trembled and her expression was euphoric. "Oh my," she said, biting her lip in pleasure. "That was amazing."

Munroe knew exactly how she felt. The first time she'd embraced the Source it had only lasted for a few heartbeats but it had almost been orgasmic. In that moment every part of her body had felt more alive than ever before in her life.

"I did it," said Dox. "I need to do it again."

Munroe put a hand out. "Wait."

"What?" asked the girl.

"You worked for Cannok for a while, right?"

Dox's elation began to fade. "So?"

"I'm guessing he sold venthe and black crystal. That's how you knew the jeweller was an addict." When Dox didn't disagree she pressed on. "Have you ever seen an addict desperate for another fix?"

"Lots of times," said Dox with a shrug.

"And how many of those addicts lived to be old?"

"None."

"Tell me again, how did it feel drawing power into your body?"

asked Munroe. Dox didn't need her to drive the point home but she needed to understand the repercussions. "Embracing power from the Source is a more powerful high than any other. If the Families could bottle and sell it they'd live in palaces. Draw too much energy into yourself and it will burn you up from the inside out. You'll love every second of it as the flesh melts from your bones like hot wax. You won't even notice when your head explodes as you'll be alive with pleasure."

"So what do I do?" asked Dox after an uncomfortable silence.

"Think of yourself like a water-skin. You can only draw so much power before it starts to hurt. Reach for any more and you'll split apart and die." It wasn't strictly true, of course. It was one of the first things she'd been taught at the Red Tower. A mage's strength could change over time, but right now Dox was struggling with the basics. "Try again. But do it slowly. Just a sip at a time, as if you're drinking whisky."

Dox looked worried, which was a good thing. She needed to take this seriously. If she drank too much whisky the worst that could happen was a bad hangover. If she tried to draw more power than she could manage she'd kill herself. There were no second chances.

More cautiously this time Dox reached for the Source and drew a small trickle of energy into herself. Munroe saw a shudder run through her body but this time it was controlled, her face screwed up in concentration as she fought to manage the euphoria.

"Slowly, open your eyes, and look around the room," said Munroe.

Dox opened one eye slowly and then the other. All of her senses would be more acute than ever and the world awash with colours she'd never seen before. She'd be able to hear what people were saying in every room in the tavern and even across the street if she concentrated. It would feel as if she'd been looking at the world through a keyhole and suddenly someone had opened the door. It would take days of practice to become accustomed to the changes.

After she embraced the Source Munroe focused on the tavern owner and finally heard him beginning to snore in bed. Outside the street was empty and a quick peek out of the window showed darkness in every visible window.

"Stay here," she whispered. Dox winced at the sound of her voice, which probably felt like a shout. "Practise for a while, but don't overdo it. It will sap your strength." Munroe waited until Dox agreed before pushing open the window.

The main reason she'd chosen this tavern, and picked a room at the end of the corridor, was the window wasn't overlooked from the building across the street. The bank had only a few small windows on street level and narrow slits at irregular intervals on the upper two floors.

Digging her fingers into the pitted stone wall Munroe scrambled down to the street. With a little time she could have tried to pick the lock on the front door, but there was less chance of being seen if she came and went the same way.

Flitting from shadow to shadow, sticking to quiet streets and alleyways, Munroe made her way back to the jewellery district. Several times she had to duck into doorways as patrols went by, but they were too busy to notice her, dealing with drunks or looking for troublemakers. There were few people walking the streets at this hour so it wouldn't do for her to be stopped and questioned.

It took almost an hour for her to reach Korell's shop, by which time her nerves were taut with listening for footsteps. From a secluded spot Munroe carefully watched the street. All of the shops were closed and the surrounding windows in darkness. With her heightened senses she could hear a few people sleeping, snoring or having sex in some of the apartments above the shops, but all of the buildings downstairs were empty. She tried focusing on the apartment above the jeweller's shop but couldn't hear anything from this distance. After taking a deep breath she sprinted across the street and down the side of the building towards the rear of the shop. The back door was sturdy and the lock impressive. Peering through the small window she also noticed a heavy steel bar sealing it tight. Even in a modest jewellery shop like Korell's there were many expensive items inside that he couldn't afford to lose to thieves. Traditionally it would be impossible for anyone to break in through the back door, but she wasn't anyone.

It was a risk that using her magic might alert whoever was upstairs, but she couldn't afford to be seen breaking in from the street. It would take her too long to pick the lock and she didn't want to attract any undue attention. Working as fast as she could Munroe drew power from the Source and crafted it into a fiery dagger, focusing energy on the blade until it glowed white hot. The dagger cut through the steel bar like warm butter. As it started to fall to the ground she carved out the lock and shoved open the door.

There was a loud clang that rang around the shop as the melted steel bar hit the floor and she froze, eyes trained on the ceiling.

Silence. No sudden footsteps. No panicked flight. Keeping an eye on the dark interior of the shop Munroe stood in the doorway and peered up at the back of the building. The window above was still closed. She'd expected to see a pair of feet appear above her head as someone tried to make their escape. After a while she realised either the person upstairs hadn't noticed or the apartment was empty. Or they were laying in wait.

Throwing caution to the wind Munroe drew power from the Source, wove a dense shield around herself like a flexible cocoon and stormed up the stairs. The apartment door was locked but she cut out the lock with her fiery blade and kicked it open.

In the first room she found Korell lying on his back on the

floor, fast asleep. Despite all the noise he hadn't woken up so she left him and quickly searched the other rooms, which were empty. She saw the scattered remains of several meals, an unmade bed, a few empty bottles of wine and more evidence that someone had been living in the apartment. Before shaking the shopkeeper Munroe tied a scarf around the bottom half of her face. It wasn't perfect but when she smelled his sickly sweet breath Munroe realised it wouldn't matter.

"Korell, wake up," she said, slapping him across the face, but he barely stirred. His eyes were still rolled up in his head and even shaking didn't jolt him awake. She slapped him a few more times and yet a smile still tugged at the corners of his mouth. That and the smell confirmed it. He was high on black crystal.

After filling a bucket with water Munroe pulled Korell into a sitting position and then dunked his head under the surface. At first he didn't notice, but after a while something filtered through his addled senses as he began to twitch and thrash about. When his hands scrabbled about for purchase on the floor she pulled him up, coughing and spluttering.

"Wait!" he said, a heartbeat before she dunked him again, forcing his head as far as it would go into the water. She repeated this process another half-dozen times before releasing him. He lay in a soaking wet mess on the floor, gasping for air, coughing weakly and struggling for breath. She gave him a little while to recover before summoning fire. Iron shackles formed of nothing more than her will clamped him to the floor. He was about to scream until she created a glowing sword of flame, at which point he tried to flee. Struggling against the invisible bonds was pointless but it didn't stop him trying. Munroe let him squirm around for a while, keening like an animal caught in a trap. Eventually, even in his addled state, Korell realised he couldn't escape.

"Do I have your attention?" she asked, raising the blade of fire which filled the room with light, casting shadows that danced across the walls.

"What do you want?" croaked Korell.

"Who was living here?" asked Munroe.

A furtive look crept into Korell's gaze and she sighed, knowing he was about to lie. Munroe touched the edge of the blade to his clothes which smouldered and he squeaked like a child.

"I won't ask again. If you lie it will cost both of your hands. Then I'll take your feet. After that I get creative," she said, moving the blade towards his groin.

"Please stop," he gasped and she knew it was enough. Whatever loyalty he had it didn't extend as deeply as others in Akosh's network, which suggested he wasn't one of her people. "It was a woman. She was hiding here from someone. I wasn't supposed to know anything, but I saw some of her people coming and going." Munroe's heart started to pound. Her hands curled up into fists and she instinctively reached for more power from the Source until her skin was tingling with a mix of pain and pleasure.

"What was her name?"

"Akosh," said Korell, his eyes locked on to her glowing sword.

"Last question. Where is she now?"

"She left a few hours ago. I don't know if she's coming back."

Munroe dispelled the blade but held on to the energy coursing through her a moment longer. All she wanted to do was scream. To unleash the fire inside her. To burn down the building and let its heat consume everything. But she had to wait. Just a little longer.

"Then why don't we sit and wait together," suggested Munroe. Korell turned pale at the idea but he nodded, unwilling to disagree with anything she said. "While we wait, is there anything to drink around here?"

*

After practising her magic for a few hours Dox had fallen into a deep sleep brought on by exhaustion. Her pleasure at finally being able to channel power from the Source had been tempered by Munroe's warning. Without magic running through her body the world felt so mundane and bleak by comparison. However, she could see that it would be easy to become addicted to wielding magic. For the first time she also understood why some junkies preferred living in a fantasy world to a harsh reality.

She'd expected to sleep through until morning but something disturbed her. It must have been Munroe, stumbling into furniture, as she heard someone moving around the room.

"Did you find her?" she asked, trying to lift her head off the pillow. Through the open curtains she could see it was still dark outside. Dawn was hours away. "Munroe?"

Dox forced herself upright and in the gloom could just make out a figure sitting in a chair across the room. With little natural light she reached for the Source, drawing a small amount of energy into herself. The shadows peeled back and objects in the room became more distinct. A thrill ran through her body and she couldn't stop from smiling.

"Was she there?" asked Dox, suppressing a yawn. "Was it her at the jeweller's?"

Still, Munroe said nothing. Fearing the worst she slowly approached the chair, expecting to see tears or the more-familiar anger. As her eyes adjusted to the dark Dox realised the woman sitting in the chair wasn't Munroe. It was Akosh.

CHAPTER 22

Tammy was led by a Royal Guard to a part of the palace she'd never visited and for once she found herself pleasantly surprised. The sunroom was an enormous area filled with unusual-looking plants and trees she knew weren't natural to Yerskania. At ground level the plants created a lawn of green, red, brown and dark purple. Some plants were nothing more than stumpy green shoots with a few leaves. Others grew up to her waist, resplendent with small pink and white flowers.

She followed the guard along a narrow winding path of small round stones, being careful not to step on any of the unusual specimens thriving in the warm black soil. Far above her head large glass windows funnelled heat and light into the room making her sweat beneath her uniform.

They found Queen Morganse resting on a bench surrounded by pungent purple and red plants that were vaguely familiar. The Queen's head was tilted back and her eyes closed, her face bathed in sunlight, but she woke at their approach. She was less pale than the last time Tammy had seen her but she was still a long way from being fully recovered. Even in this heat there was a thick blanket on her lap and her dress was lumpy and unflattering, although Tammy guessed that was because of the bandages beneath.

"I can see from your expression that it's not good news," said the Queen, gesturing at a space beside her on the bench. Tammy was about to refuse when she saw how Morganse was craning her neck.

"The infection is starting to become a serious problem." Tammy knew what needed to be done but she didn't have the authority. She'd been keeping the Queen appraised of the situation ever since her meeting with the chief coroner three days ago. That it had come to this so quickly was what truly alarmed her.

"Apothecarists and herbalists across the city are trying their best, working with coroners to find a cure, but so far nothing they've tried has worked. It's spreading quickly and we need to take decisive action. We can't wait any longer."

Despite her best attempts, news of the infection had started to trickle out to the population. There was a general feeling that something was wrong, and a few people had said the word plague, but for the most part the city was carrying on as normal. The Yerskani people were not known for panicking and they tended to take most things in their stride. Tammy felt they were approaching a tipping point where people would soon be unable to pretend the problem didn't exist.

So far no public declarations had been made but she knew that would have to change. Until a cure was found drastic changes were needed to protect the city.

"How decisive?"

It was something she'd thought about a great deal. She'd also talked it through with the Old Man as he'd faced something similar during his time as the Khevassar.

"We have to isolate the city and lock it down."

It was easy to say, but she knew that controlling the flow of information out of the city had been difficult. By comparison stopping people coming and going would be almost impossible.

The city relied on trade and was a focal point for it across the west. They couldn't completely seal everyone inside its limits, not only because they would riot, but because they'd also starve to death in a few weeks. Still, once people realised they were unable to leave by traditional means they would look for alternatives.

"I know something like this has happened before," said Tammy. "The Old Man told me all about it."

Morganse grunted. "I'd barely been married six months, but I can still remember it. The smell. The dead lying in the streets. The silence. It was so loud. In a city of so many people, I couldn't understand why it was so quiet." The Queen's eyes became distant and troubled. "I'll need to bring in part of the army."

It would be an unpopular move—soldiers on the roads to stop people from leaving the city—but it was better than the alternative. If they didn't stop the infection here, it could spread to other towns and cities in Yerskania and from there to other nations in the west.

"We need to identify those infected, send them to hospitals, and set up an isolation zone."

A royal declaration would also have to be made with posters being nailed up across the city. Rumours would only make things worse. People needed to know about the infection, the symptoms, where to go if they became ill and how it was spread. It wouldn't stop widespread fear and panic, but it was better that people had the right information rather than leaving them guessing. Rumours and lies could create as much damage as the truth.

City authorities needed to identify those infected and limit their exposure by sending them to an isolation zone. It would be seen as cruel and there would be violence when they had to separate families, but she kept reminding herself of the alternative. Hopefully it wouldn't mean house-to-house searches, but she expected if it continued to spread they might be needed.

Tammy tried not to think about her family and what she would do if one of them became ill. The nobility and those with money would stay behind closed doors and wait for it to be over while everyone else suffered around them. Most people needed to work to put food on the table and that wouldn't stop, not even for this.

"Is there any good news?" asked Morganse.

"A little," she said. "So far only humans are being affected. Morrin merchants seem completely immune and nothing touches the few Vorga in the city. Even so, I think we need to create merchant barriers outside the city limits and at the docks."

"Agreed. And they'll need to be heavily guarded," said the Queen. They would still need supplies during this time but no outsiders would be allowed within the city limits and no sailors allowed off their ships. If those kept inside the city thought they were going to starve to death they would attack the merchant trains. All thoughts of who was responsible for this had been pushed to the back of her mind as she focused on how best to tackle it.

Morganse rang a small bell and a servant appeared. She sent him to bring pen and ink, as well as a map of the city. Over the next hour they scanned the city for suitable areas to set up temporary hospitals, places to house soldiers while they were stationed in the city and finally an isolation zone. More than once Morganse sighed and rubbed her temples. Tammy suspected she'd probably been working more than her doctor had advised, but in these circumstances there was little choice. Tammy didn't think she'd get a full night's sleep in the foreseeable future.

Finally they decided on a location close to the meat district where all of the abattoirs were located. It consisted of run-down businesses and low-rent housing. Its main source of income came from peripheral enterprises set up by the Families. Gambling dens, whorehouses and drinking holes. Marching into that part of the city with anything less than an army would be suicide. It would require some careful negotiation. They would also need the Families to agree not to smuggle anyone out of the city. There were more ways out than through the gates or on board a ship.

Tammy knew even with permission from the Queen, it was not a meeting to which she could send a proxy. They would need to see someone in a position of authority before they would seriously consider any deals. It was something she'd been avoiding but now seemed inevitable. She would have to sit down with the heads of the crime Families.

Dressed in her Guardian uniform, but without the familiar and comforting weight of a sword on her hip, Tammy entered the warehouse. The two armed jackals at the door didn't recognise her but that didn't ease the growing tension in her shoulders. It was inevitable that someone would know her. She hoped it wouldn't lead them to look too deeply into her history with Don Lowell. With all the trouble that lay ahead with the spreading infection she hoped they'd be too busy to investigate.

In the middle of the warehouse a space had been cleared of boxes and in the centre was a large round table. Five identical chairs had been placed around it and four of them were occupied by people she knew by reputation.

The Butcher was perhaps the most mysterious. There were many unconfirmed rumours about his history but the only fact she had was that for the last eight years he had ruled his part of the city with an iron fist. Brutal, intolerant of stupidity or disloyalty, he had carved out his domain from the bones of those who had fallen before him.

Don Jarrow was a familiar face who'd been new to his seat at the table when she'd worked for Don Lowell. He was still a big man with broad shoulders, but the black in his hair and thick beard was now dominated by grey. She remembered him as a verbose man who enjoyed the best things in life. The man in front of her was quiet, watchful and there was deep sorrow behind his distrustful eyes. Being betrayed by your wife would do that to a man.

Doña Chur was as described. A thick-necked woman with a shaven head, meaty arms and a permanent sneer on her wide Seve face. Guardian reports indicated she was brutish and coarse, but Chur wouldn't be running a Family if that's all there was to her. Behind her greedy little eyes Tammy saw a sly, cruel intelligence. The nearly identical-looking man standing over her shoulder, who was busy glaring at Tammy, had to be one of her brothers. The only difference between them was the enforcer's face was criss-crossed with faded scars and someone had broken his nose at least once.

Finally there was Doña Tarija, a dusky-skinned woman whose ancestry came from the desert. Whereas Chur was big, ugly and mean, Tarija was beautiful, elegant and petite. She was actually the one person at the table who made Tammy the most nervous as she'd taken over when Don Lowell had been murdered. If anyone was going to come after her for Lowell's murder it would be Tarija.

Standing behind each person at the table was an enforcer. She had been offered the chance to bring someone but had decided to come alone. Fighting was the last thing she needed or wanted today.

"I must say," said Doña Tarija as Tammy sat down, "this is a pleasant surprise. I never thought we'd be sat across a table from one another."

"Neither did I," admitted Tammy, earning a smile from the deadly woman.

"To be honest, I didn't believe you'd show up," admitted the Butcher. "I just came because I was curious."

"I thought you came to see me," said Doña Tarija, fluttering her eyelashes at the tattooed Don.

"You are beautiful," admitted the Butcher, "and as deadly as a pit viper."

"Enough of this horseshit," snapped Doña Chur. "What do you want?"

"You don't know?" asked Tammy, taunting the big woman but also testing her.

"She's here about the plague," said Don Jarrow, speaking for the first time. His voice had a harsh rasp that was new. Probably a side effect from drinking coarse spirits judging by the broken veins across his nose and cheeks.

"That's right, although it's not a plague yet. It's just an infection," she said.

"What's the difference?" asked Chur.

"The number of dead bodies," said Doña Tarija with a friendly smile at her opposition.

"I'm here because there are two dozen dead bodies in the morgue and it's only going to get worse." Tammy looked at each of the leaders in turn. "I'm here because I need your help."

A strange silence fell on the room. The enforcers, perhaps not known for their intelligence, looked confused. Don Jarrow and the Butcher sat back in their chairs and exchanged looks. They had a tangled history but if Tammy had to guess she expected they would both agree to help. Doña Tarija pursed her lips in thought while she tapped her painted nails on the table. Only Doña Chur seemed lost.

"Is this a joke?" she asked. "Our help with what?"

"If the infection spreads and it becomes a real plague, hundreds or even thousands of people could die," explained Tammy.

Doña Chur shrugged. "And?"

"If we don't stop it here, in Perizzi, then it could reach other parts of Yerskania and then other countries."

"That's not my problem," insisted Chur. She seemed to be waiting for something. Tammy had the distinct impression Chur was testing her as well.

"It will become your problem if all of your people die."

"I'll just hire more," said Chur with a shrug.

"But what if all your customers die as well? How will you stay in business?" asked Tammy.

"Stop playing the idiot, Chur," said Doña Tarija. "You know what's at stake."

"Fuck you, desert whore," sneered Chur. "Don't tell me what to do."

"What do you need from us?" asked Don Jarrow, steering the conversation back on track.

"The city is going into lockdown. No one gets in or out via the port or the gates. I need you all to make sure there are no other ways out of the city."

Tammy knew what she was asking. There were a number of people in Perizzi with a lot of money, some of whom might approach one of the Families about being smuggled out. Then they'd ride out the plague on their country estate. Such a breach was also the most likely way for the infection to spread. She was asking them to potentially give up a lot of money.

These weren't good people. They didn't care about their neighbours. Appealing to their humanity was pointless as most of them lacked empathy. But they did care about the city. Perizzi was the trading heart of the west and the busiest city in the world. If its population was decimated by plague, then the rest of the country could follow, leaving them with no customers and no business.

"What are you offering in return?" asked the Butcher, folding his arms.

"Until the infection is dealt with, there will be no patrols by the Watch in certain areas of the city."

She wasn't giving them free rein. It was more an easing of the rules for a short time. Besides, the Watch and all of the soldiers brought in would have bigger problems to deal with.

Tammy leaned forward, resting her forearms on the table. "To be clear, I'm still watching. So if the sewers start running red I'll ask the Queen to bring the rest of the army into the city. After that there will be squads on every street corner."

In times of stress people sought relief in a variety of ways, all of which were available from one of the Families. Such an imposition on their businesses at such a profitable time would be painful. Despite stopping the infection from spreading Tammy knew she had to give them something. She just hoped it would be enough.

"Do we have an agreement?" she asked.

"Yes," said the Butcher, glancing at the others expectantly.

Don Jarrow nodded slowly. "Until it's done."

"What about you, Doña Tarija?" asked Tammy.

"I appreciate that you came here in person to make this offer."

"It seemed appropriate when dealing with people of such esteem."

Doña Tarija's laugh was warm and genuine, completely at odds with the stories of what she'd done to people who crossed her. "You are a delight. I will agree to your terms."

"Doña Chur?" asked Tammy.

"I've got a different idea," said the burly woman. "Why don't I just kill you? You're already a pain in my arse. In the long run you're gonna be as bad as the Old Man—if not worse. I know your Guardians don't have the numbers to come here for revenge. Besides, they're going to be busy dealing with the plague."

Over Doña Chur's shoulder her brother grinned and cracked his knuckles.

"I would advise against trying that," said Tammy. "I don't want to spend the next month butchering one member of your inbred family after another because of a blood debt."

"You won't leave this building alive," promised Chur's brother.

"Shush. The adults are talking," said Tammy, ignoring his bluster as she turned back to address his sister. "Keep your dog on a leash."

"Ugh, must you do this?" said Doña Tarija, trying to appeal to Chur who was also glaring at Tammy now. "It's so tedious."

"Kill her, Rom," said Doña Chur, ignoring her.

As Rom started to move around the table towards her, Tammy took off her Guardian jacket and readied herself. Rom was as tall as her and more heavily muscled and his scars indicated he'd been in a few fights. He moved well for such a big man but Tammy knew she needed to make an example of him to send a clear message.

For the first couple of minutes they tested each other, looking for weaknesses, as they traded blows and dodged around the room. Long before Tammy had been a Guardian she'd been an enforcer and a pit fighter. Her time in the ring had given her the skills and endurance, but it was being a Guardian that had taught her patience. Rom had the same reach and was stronger, but he was also overconfident and quick to anger.

"So, how does it work, being your sister's brother and her lover?"

With a snarl of rage Rom swung at her but Tammy easily dodged to the side, elbowing him in the head on his way past, which sent him reeling. When he turned around a hard left slammed into his face breaking his nose. Rom grunted in pain but didn't back down so she followed up with two blows to the ribs. He hunched over to protect his sides and came back at her with an uppercut which she barely dodged.

Focusing on her breathing Tammy shifted her weight to her

back leg and waited. Rom inched forward believing he was still out of reach. Tammy's front foot cracked against his shin and then his stomach in quick succession. As he stumbled forward she hit him with a series of blows, rocking his head one way and then the other. He swung blindly, trying to catch her but she nimbly avoided his fists, swatting them aside with ease. As blood ran into his left eye she dropped to her right and kicked out, sweeping his legs. The sound of Rom's head impacting on the stone floor echoed around the warehouse.

Dazed and bruised, with a broken nose and blood running into one eye, it took Rom a while to get up. His eyes were glazed but he refused to give up.

"Tell me, Rom, if your sister is also your boss, does that mean you're never on top?"

Rom charged towards her with both hands outstretched. When he tried to strangle her she grabbed him by the wrists and yanked him forward off balance. As he stumbled she tried to knee him in the stomach but caught him in the groin instead. Before he had a chance to recover she twisted one arm behind his back, forcing him first to his knees and then face down on the ground. With both hands on his wrist and her foot on his shoulder she kept him there. Tammy waited a moment, to make sure he understood that she was completely in control before she wrenched his shoulder, popping it out of joint while breaking his wrist with both hands. As he writhed on the floor in agony she calmly pulled on her Guardian jacket and sat back down at the table.

The other enforcers were now staring at her with a mix of fear and awe. Everyone was doing their best not to look at Rom. "Anyone else?" asked Tammy, checking with each head of Family, but none took up the offer.

"I'm going to kill you," said Rom, stumbling to his feet, one arm dangling at his side.

"No, you're not," said Doña Chur. "You lost. Suck it up. Or do I have to break your other arm?" The siblings glared at one another but eventually Rom backed down, proving why his sister was in charge and not him.

"You have a deal," said Chur.

"I take it you can adequately control your lapdog?" Tammy asked.

"He won't come after you for revenge."

"Then our business here is done."

The head of each Family stood up when Tammy did, perhaps as a small nod of respect. Only Doña Tarija came around the table to shake her hand. "This is going to be fun," promised the petite woman.

Tammy didn't know if she meant the next few weeks or the two of them being at odds in the coming years and months. It was a problem for another day. She'd deal with it, and Doña Tarija, if the city survived the growing infection.

CHAPTER 23

Waking up in a soft bed was proving to be an alarming experience for Tianne. Most mornings she awoke in a panic thinking she was back in the palace in her comfy prison cell. It was only as her heart started to slow that she took in the familiar surroundings of the room she shared with Wren. The slightly wonky table they'd made together which rocked on three legs. The repurposed sheets turned into thick curtains to keep out the light. The woollen blanket made from their newly shorn flock. She was in Corvin's Brow, their flourishing community. She was safe.

The cool wooden floorboards beneath her bare feet were a welcome shock. They helped shake off the last remnants of sleep. After getting dressed and eating a modest breakfast of porridge she joined the other students for another lesson with Master Jan Ohre, their Drassi teacher. Soon the sweat was pouring off her forehead as she tried to wrestle or flip her opponent, Resne, to the ground. He was taller and stronger but Tianne used his weight against him, ducked under his arms and after tangling his legs, knocked him forward on to his face. The moment Resne started to fall she scrambled on to his back, pinning him down with one arm wrapped around his neck and a knee on his back. With his free hand Resne tapped the ground in surrender. Tianne released him and stood before offering a hand up which he accepted.

"Much improved," said Master Jan as he walked past, earning a grin from Tianne. From him it was high praise. Resne surreptitiously rubbed his sore neck.

"That kind of hurt," he said, swallowing hard. She'd left a mark but didn't think it would bruise.

"You're a big boy. I'm sure you'll be fine."

"I might be, if you kissed it better," he suggested. Tianne turned away and sought a different sparring partner. Resne wasn't the first who'd made such an offer. Some had been less obvious, but she'd ignored them all.

Since coming back to the community Tianne's priorities had changed. For some reason the boys seemed more attracted to her than before. At first she'd dismissed it as ego and her imagination. Then she thought it was merely excitement of the new, but soon she noticed that people were looking at her differently. At the Red Tower she'd mocked Wren for pushing herself in lessons. Now she made her friend seem lazy by comparison. But it was more than that. Beyond the scar, the time in Zecorria had marked her.

It wasn't that she'd lost interest in boys. When she'd rebuffed one boy he'd suggested it was because she preferred girls. Tianne had considered it, but after rolling the thought around for a day, she realised it wasn't that either. It was just at the moment boys weren't a priority. She wouldn't be caught unawares again. She had to be ready.

Tianne wasn't naïve enough to think she could train for every eventuality, but when she'd left for Zecorria she'd been ill prepared. Now she had a solid grounding with a sword, was excelling in unarmed combat, and her magic skills were much improved. Most importantly she had gained a rudimentary ability to heal. It didn't always work but every day she was getting better.

The day after she defeated Resne, news reached the settlement from a merchant who'd passed through Yerskania. Tianne instinctively knew it was what she'd been waiting for.

"Plague?" said Wren, later that day as they ate lunch together.

"That's what the merchant said," said Kimme, shovelling food into her mouth. "He tried to say it wasn't bad, but the capital city is sealed up tight. Apparently it's been like that for almost ten days now. No one goes in or out. Trading is slow, with it all being done outside the gates under heavy guard, but people are still getting paid. A couple of nobles tried to buy their way out of the city. I heard they're rotting in cells with the rats."

Tianne suspected the last part was Kimme's imagination but this was the second story about the plague they'd heard in as many days. A dangerous and powerful infection was sweeping through the streets of Perizzi. The doctors, herbalists and apothecarists were doing their best to halt its progress, but so far they were losing. Nothing stopped it once someone was infected. Within two weeks anyone who showed the symptoms was dead. Bodies were being burned day and night, the Yerskani army had created a cordon around the city, and an isolation area had been set up inside the walls for the infected.

While the others talked about the plague and how it was being contained Tianne's thoughts strayed to those who'd been infected. It must be terrifying. First, to realise you had it and then be forced to make an impossible decision. If a person stayed at home it put those they loved at risk. Or they could voluntarily leave everyone behind and walk into the isolation zone knowing it was unlikely they'd ever come out.

"If you only had ten days to live, what would you do?" asked Tianne, startling the others. The question caught them off guard but she saw how deeply it hit.

"Go and visit my folks on the farm," said Kimme. "I wouldn't care what the neighbours said if I was dying. I'd want to see my parents before the end."

"What about you, Wren?" asked Tianne. "Would you visit your parents?"

"No," said Wren, which wasn't surprising. Late at night, just before they fell asleep, she and Wren often voiced truths in the dark they wouldn't speak about in the light of day. If Wren never saw her mother again it wouldn't upset her. Her father was a different story. She knew Wren wanted to see him again, but death was handled in a strange way in Drassia. To visit someone, knowing you were about to die, was seen as putting a great burden upon them. The dead were honoured and treated with respect by their family and community, but not the dying. There was no honour in screaming, weeping and suffering for days. Better to simply end it so the family could take care of the body and begin the ritual process of mourning. That was the Drassi way.

"Then what would you do?" asked Tianne.

Wren was silent for a long time before finally shaking her head. "I don't know."

"Kind of morbid, thinking about death," said Kimme, scraping her plate clean. Nothing put her off food. Not shovelling horse shit in the stables or carving up sheep in the butcher's yard.

"You asked the question, so I assume you have an answer," said Wren, turning towards her with a knowing look.

"I do."

Kimme looked between them with a confused expression. "So what is it?"

"If my days were numbered I'd want to help people," said Tianne. "I wouldn't want to die knowing there was something I could've done but didn't, because I was too afraid."

She'd been afraid many times in her life. For herself. For Wren and Danoph. But all of those paled in comparison when she thought about the people trapped inside Perizzi, waiting to die, with no hope.

"Are you sure?" asked Wren.

"I'm going to Perizzi." Tianne didn't mean to make it sound like a challenge, but it came out that way, as if she was daring her friend to say she couldn't. Wren still ran their community with help from others, but she wasn't their ruler.

"Why?" asked Kimme.

"Because people hate magic. Because it's going to take years before they trust mages again." She knew Wren dreamed of having a village Wise in every community like she and Queen Olivia had discussed, but reaching that point would take a long time. Every week different groups of young mages made a trip to villagers across the district. And every week the local people ignored them.

The fear of Seekers. Dangerous children with magic. The wounds were too fresh. A few months wouldn't make a difference. But this was something they could help with today.

"If we don't do something, what is all this for?" said Tianne, gesturing at the community around them. "If we sit here, we'll be safe, but it will also mean we're no better than the Red Tower."

"This plague is deadly. You don't know if you'll be able to cure it," said Wren. "What happens if you become infected? Do you think you'll be immune?"

Tianne shook her head. "I don't know the answer to either of those questions. But sitting here talking about it isn't going to answer them. People are suffering and there's a chance I can help them. What would you have me do?"

Wren couldn't answer and even Kimme fell silent.

She knew what Wren was thinking. This was the same as when she'd travelled home to Zecorria. Her trip north had been for all the wrong reasons. She'd wanted to prove something to her family and former friends. To show them she was special and that magic was a good thing. To become a beacon and, if she was honest with herself, a national hero. For a brief moment she'd been so proud to be the first of the Regent's cadre of mages. It was everything she'd ever wanted. Power, prestige and respect. None of it had been real.

This time she didn't care what people thought. She wasn't going to impress anyone and she knew this wouldn't change their minds about magic. They wouldn't trust her or want her there. None of that mattered either. She had to try.

Garvey had been wrong about so many things, but Tianne did agree with him on one subject. Magic was a gift and it shouldn't be squandered. He'd refused to run and hide. If she stayed here there was no risk. Nothing would change and life would continue. But in her heart, Tianne knew it was cowardice to hide.

"When will you leave?" asked Wren.

"Tomorrow." She needed the rest of the day to gather supplies and herbs. "Will you come with me?"

"I can't," said Wren. "There's still so much to do here."

It was the truth and yet they both heard the whisper of a lie in her words. Although Wren had finally delegated more work, many people still came to her with their problems. In spite of that she was trying harder than before in her studies which she'd been neglecting. More proficient than Tianne with a sword, but less in unarmed fighting, Wren also had a long way to go. Her skill with healing was excellent, although it was still basic in comparison to their teacher, but every now and then she seemed to make a sudden leap in her ability. A few speculated she had a Talent for it but Master Yettle had dismissed that. Wren merely had a unique way of looking at the weaves.

With over a hundred people in Corvin's Brow the work was now more evenly spread. Wagons left three times a week to trade goods in the district. The roads were patrolled for bandits, and groups travelled to villages every week to offer them help. There were still problems to deal with each day, big and small, but now Wren was merely one voice on the newly formed Council of Eight.

Sometimes, before they went to sleep, Wren spoke about her nightmares of being crushed to death. A large part of her still felt the success of the community was solely her responsibility.

"Are you really going to go by yourself?" asked Kimme. She was staring at Tianne as if she was mad.

"If I must."

Tianne tried to stay busy for the rest of the day and not dwell on her decision. It scared her but not in the same way as when she'd returned home. Word must have spread about her plans because people were staring again.

That evening she ate a quick meal, kept her head down and tried not to make eye contact with anyone. She'd expected one of the former teachers to try to talk her out of it. To tell her she was being foolish, childish and stupid. Instead everyone just stared and whispered when they thought she wasn't watching. Part of her wanted to take back what she'd said, but to silence the frightened voice within she only had to think of those who were suffering. The doubt faded and she started making eye contact again, unafraid of being judged.

When she went to the stables to discuss borrowing a horse for the journey one had already been prepared. It was the same story when she went to their stores for provisions. With time to spare Tianne carefully sorted through her meagre belongings. In the end she settled on taking a few sets of clean clothing, a spare pair of sturdy boots and nothing else. Where she was planning to go people had very little. She considered taking a sword but in the end decided against it. It might be seen as threatening and if anyone attacked her she had a dagger and her magic.

Feeling restless and not sure what to do Tianne took a long

walk through the woods to clear her head. By the time she got back it was already dark and she used a mage light to avoid tripping over obstacles. She undressed and slipped into bed beneath her cool blanket, noting that Wren was already asleep. Her body was exhausted from the walk but her mind wouldn't stop racing. Fear about what lay ahead kept her awake for hours before she finally dropped off.

Tianne had hoped to just say goodbye to Wren and then sneak away. To ride out without anyone noticing, but when she woke up Wren's bed was already empty. At breakfast there was no sign of her friend and she noticed a few familiar faces were missing from the crowd. There had probably been a crisis of some kind and Wren had been called in to deal with it.

Tianne waited for her friend to return but after a while it seemed as if Wren would be gone for some time. In the end she left a note on Wren's bed.

The morning was cool and crisp. Her breath frosted slightly and there was the promise of rain to come in the air. When she reached the stables Tianne was surprised to see six horses had been saddled for a journey. Each was laden with supplies and a large crowd had gathered. A low hum of conversation hung over the group which abruptly faded as she approached. Wren emerged from within the crowd, stepping forward to hug Tianne.

"What's happening?" asked Tianne.

"We're coming with you," said Wren. For the first time Tianne noticed Wren and four others were dressed for a journey. Some of those in the crowd were crying while others were making tearful farewells.

"I thought you couldn't leave. Who will look after Corvin's Brow?"

"You were right. If this place can't survive without me then it's in trouble," said Wren with a wry smile. "Besides, we left the Red

Tower behind to choose a new path, one where we help others. It was never meant to be limited to people in Shael."

Tianne was surprised to see Kimme among the group preparing to leave. Yesterday the farm girl had been aghast at the idea but now she seemed at peace. "Are the others sure about this? Do they understand the risks?"

"Several of the Council have spoken to each individual," said Wren, giving Tianne's shoulder a squeeze. "They know what this means."

"Do you?" asked Tianne. "We might not return."

"I know, but you're my friend, and as Danoph once said, my path lies with you."

CHAPTER 24

Time was running out for Marran. He felt as if he'd been backed up against a wall and forced into a corner.

If his Master didn't torture him for years or just kill him outright, the Regent would have him beheaded the moment he stopped being useful. So far he'd been able to keep his head because he had something to teach and there was no one to replace him. That was also thanks to his Master who had killed off the other mages.

Another concern was that his students were quickly soaking up everything he taught them. It had taken him years to master some of his skills but they were fast learners. He estimated he had another three or four months at most before they knew everything he did. It might take them years to perfect everything but once they understood the principles he would have outlived his usefulness.

Even if he somehow managed to make it out of the palace someone was waiting for him beyond the relative safety of its walls. He was now three ways dead.

It was time to do something drastic.

After washing the blood off his face from his latest talk with his Master, Marran embraced the Source. Normally channelling power calmed him down, allowing him to think clearly, but not tonight. He couldn't stop focusing on the likelihood that in the next few days someone was going to murder him. Various images of his bloody corpse appeared in his mind. His body bent and broken, dismembered, beheaded and drowned. Opening his eyes didn't help. The images were still there every time he blinked, lurking in the dark.

As Marran's senses became enhanced by the Source he heard a faint scraping as if someone were moving around in the next room. This was the third night in a row he'd heard something but the room was supposed to be empty. But as he sat there listening a strained silence developed. The person in the next room had become utterly still. It was possible they'd just fallen asleep but Marran's intuition told him they were waiting for something.

Focusing on his magic, he started to weave together something he'd not shown his students. It was not a construct he would ever share with them. It was the most powerful and dangerous kind of magic that he knew. Once it was ready he held it up between his hands for inspection. It was a crude mesh like the cat's cradle game that children played with string. He would have to be quick and if it didn't work he'd be dead.

Marran pretended to choke and then cough, holding his hands against his chest as if he couldn't breathe. It kept them immobile and the weave intact as long as he didn't lose focus and move around too much. With a loud gurgle he kicked the door to his room and then fell backwards on to the floor, arching his back as spittle ran from the corners of his mouth.

The door flew open and one of his two guards came into the room with his sword ready.

"Maker's cock, he's choking," said the man, sheathing his weapon before rushing forward. He pulled Marran into a sitting position and started to thump him on the back while the other guard lurked in the doorway. They hated and despised him but they also knew how important he was to the Regent. Despite the guard's efforts Marran continue to gasp for air as if his throat were blocked. "Go and get some help!" shouted the guard. His friend hesitated for a moment but eventually relented and left his post.

Ignoring the attempt at soothing words from the man beside him, Marran closed his eyes and listened. When the second guard's frantic footsteps had receded he concentrated on the weave held between his hands. With a sigh of relief he discovered that it was still in one piece.

"That's it, breathe normally," said the guard as Marran relaxed and opened his eyes. "Did something get stuck?"

Marran smiled and launched himself at the man, gripping the guard on either side of his head. As he started to protest Marran fed energy into the weave and the guard's eyes widened in terror. With a squawk he tried to push Marran away then lashed out with his fists but the mage doggedly held on. Now it was the guard's breathing that had become laboured. He started keening like a wounded animal and his arms flopped about as they had lost all strength.

It was taking too long. Any moment now the other guard would come racing into the room and stab him in the back. Finally the guard fell silent, his breathing returned to normal and he relaxed as if on the verge of sleep. With drowsy eyes he stared at Marran and smiled.

"You will tell no one about this and do exactly as I say. Do you understand?" said Marran.

"Yes," said the guard, surprised at his own response. Marran still wasn't sure if the compulsion weave had taken hold but he was out of time. Releasing the Source he scrambled backwards and moved to the far side of the room. The guard on the floor shook his head and slowly got to his feet.

"What happened?" he asked.

"I was choking and you helped me."

There was some lingering confusion in his eyes but it disappeared as the other guard returned. "I couldn't find anyone," he said, stepping into the room.

"I'm fine. A piece of meat was caught in my throat," explained Marran.

The returning guard sensed that something had happened in his absence. He slowly moved one hand to his sword and was on the verge of drawing it when his friend spoke.

"It was just like he said. It's over."

Marran turned his back on them both and pretended to admire the view out the window. Summoning power from the Source again he started pulling together a second identical weave. The two guards were talking amongst themselves, the second making sure that nothing untoward had happened. He ignored them until it was ready and then turned around. They glanced at him but didn't react as they couldn't see or feel the magic held between his hands.

Marran addressed his first thrall. "Hold him still and keep him quiet."

The second guard was about to ask a question when his friend leapt on him. They rolled around on the floor, kicking and punching each other, completely ignoring Marran. At first glance he thought his servant was going to lose the fight. If that happened he was dead. He was about to intervene when his servant kneed the other man in the groin. The fight immediately stopped and both men stared at each other, one surprised by his actions, the other with a dawning sense of dread. Then the pain hit him and the guard curled up into a foetal ball.

"Hold him steady," said Marran, kneeling down beside the man. His servant clamped one hand over his friend's mouth and pinned him to the floor with a knee on his chest. It made it difficult to breathe but it allowed Marran to grip his head and feed power into the weave.

This time it took more easily and a short time later both of them were calm again. Their uniforms were dishevelled and each had cuts and bruises on their face. Not for the first time Marran wished he had some ability to heal with magic to cover up their minor injuries. Instead he ordered them to clean themselves up as best they could and then resume their posts outside his door.

What he'd done to them was brutal and unsophisticated. It bent them to his will, forcing them to ignore all of their own instincts. The mage who'd taught him this form of mind control had described it as taking an axe to the mind. Suppressing a person's willpower and making them go against the grain caused permanent damage to their brain.

For the time being he had two slaves that were bonded to him. Asking them to lie wouldn't hurt much but if he forced them to do something abhorrent, something completely against their nature, they would still comply, but the damage would be more severe. To begin with there would be no outward signs, apart from the occasional nosebleed, but eventually the damage would build up and they'd die. For that reason Marran intended to use his bond as infrequently as possible, but with so many people planning to kill him he thought it might become necessary.

As Marran was contemplating what to do next he heard more scraping coming from the next room. Summoning his guards Marran ordered them to find and detain whoever was in there. After what sounded like a vicious fight the two guards dragged in a nondescript man.

"Who are you? Who do you work for?" he asked but the man refused to answer. It looked as if they would have to do this the hard way.

"Close the door and hold him still," said Marran, building a mind-altering weave yet again. The man thrashed about and tried to break free but the two guards were far too strong. A short time later he was a lot more forthcoming, revealing that his name was Doggett and that he was a spy.

"Who do you work for?"

"Selina, the Regent's first wife. She's been spying on you since your first day in the palace. Everything she learns from us is fed to the Regent," said Doggett with a smile that seemed out of place. Marran had the impression that he never smiled or showed much emotion on his blank face. It was the first sign that something was wrong with him. The magic was working hard against his nature and it also spoke of a disciplined and strong mind. Even without giving him any commands Marran thought that Doggett would die in only a few days' time.

If Marran was going to survive his time in the palace he needed to keep the Regent happy, but more importantly he had to please his Master. All of which led back to the cadre of mages.

"Doggett, continue with your duties as normal, but from now on you will be compelled to speak with me before making any reports to Selina. Understood?"

"Of course," said Doggett, as if it was something he'd always intended. He returned to the room next door and Marran heard him take up his position again.

"You," he said, addressing one of the guards. "Go and fetch the young mage, Kalina. Tell her the Regent needs to speak to her urgently. Then bring her to the training room."

The guard left without saying a word while Marran and his other guard made their way there as quickly as possible. Performing the weave three times had already drained most of his stamina but Marran wasn't done. Exhaustion was making his limbs feel leaden, but he'd come this far in one night. Just one more step and then he would be on the right path to keeping his head attached to his neck.

The following night a pair of Royal Guards brought Kalina to a private room where Regent Choilan sat waiting. The tension that he'd previously seen in her posture was gone. She strode into the room full of confidence, giving him a glimmer of hope that perhaps his cadre of mages could work.

"Has something happened?" he asked, forgoing his usual approach of easing into the conversation. He tried to give the impression that he cared by making her feel comfortable. Tonight she didn't seem to notice or be offended by his blunt approach.

"Something clicked in my mind," said Kalina, her eyes alight with pleasure. "I was struggling with my magic, but now I'm beginning to understand. I think even Marran was surprised, and a little worried at my progress."

That was good news. If she could learn everything from him quickly then perhaps she could become the new teacher. It wasn't a perfect solution but there were currently no other alternatives. Someone had been very thorough about that. His agents were still struggling to find out who was responsible.

"That's good news. What about Marran? Has he been acting strangely at all? Any problems with the other students?"

Kalina shook her head. "No. He's been completely focused on the lessons. Everyone seems more relaxed now. We're all getting comfortable with our magic."

Choilan remained unconvinced. "And what about your roommate? Is she still having nightmares?"

"All gone. She's happy," said the girl, wiping her nose.

Marran hadn't changed. Predators were cautious and patient. He was merely biding his time, waiting for the opportune moment.

"Keep an eye on your friend, in case there's a relapse," he said, pretending to care about the other girl's wellbeing. Kalina's progress was encouraging but there were still his enemies to worry about. They wanted him off the throne and every mage locked up or dead as soon as possible. His network of agents was keeping an eye on them but they too had suddenly gone very quiet. It made him nervous.

Choilan noticed a trickle of blood coming from Kalina's nose but even this didn't seem to alarm her. "Marran said this could happen if we push ourselves too hard."

"Be careful," he said, thinking that he couldn't afford to lose her. She was the most loyal of his mages and all of the others looked up to her. If she died it would be an inconvenience and he didn't have the time to start pandering to another mage, pretending they were favoured.

For the time being he'd halted the search for more young mages in other cities. He needed a strong foundation on which to build before he could create a new kind of army. His enemies would soon slope off into the shadows and his place on the throne would be secure. Perhaps the young heir could even have an accident at that point.

But as with everything, one step at a time.

CHAPTER 25

At first Dox didn't believe what she was seeing. She was still asleep and this was a nightmare. As the beating of her heart quickened and sweat trickled down the small of her back, Dox realised she was wide awake. Her mouth stretched open and somewhere deep inside a scream started to build.

"Don't make a sound," said Akosh. Dox's cry died in her chest before it could fully emerge. She managed only a soft whimper of terror. "If I wanted you dead I'd have cut your throat while you slept."

It wasn't cold in the room but Dox found she was hugging herself for warmth, shifting from foot to foot, while desperately hoping this was just a really elaborate nightmare. Any moment she'd wake up. Any moment. Maybe if she pinched her skin. Didn't pain wake you from a bad dream?

"Sit down," said Akosh, gesturing at the other chair. Dox glanced at the door, barely a flick of her eyes, but somehow Akosh saw her do it. The knowing smile didn't reach her eyes and the slight shake of her head made Dox hug herself tighter. With slow shuffling steps she moved to the other chair and climbed into it, bringing her knees to her chest, making herself small.

For a while Akosh said nothing. She just stared into the cold ashes of the fire. Perhaps she was waiting for Dox to light it. Perhaps she was prolonging the moment while she decided how to kill her.

"I came here to talk," Akosh said eventually. Dox waited for her to say something else but when the silence stretched on she realised Akosh was waiting for her to speak.

"Why?" she managed to stammer. Her teeth were rattling together from the shock.

Akosh's face twisted in pain as if someone had just stabbed her through the chest. The anguish reached her eyes and at first Dox thought she was being attacked. "I need your help."

The words floated around the room and then landed like a lead weight. It took a while for Dox to process them and believe what she was hearing. At first she thought it was another lie. This was all part of a complex game where she was just another small piece in someone else's plan. Then she realised what Akosh had said and, more importantly, what she hadn't felt.

The lie.

Whenever someone lied she felt it. Once, as a young girl, she'd stumbled into a knot of nettles with bare legs. At first there was no pain. Then came a burning sensation across her skin, the itchiness, the swelling red welts and finally the pain coursing through her legs. A lie hurt. Not as intensely as the nettles but she felt it every single time. It was as if someone had pinched the skin on her arms hard enough to leave a bruise.

Akosh was telling the truth.

Once she realised that the tense silence in the room became something different. Her fear ebbed away and a laugh bubbled up until it burst out of her mouth in a rush. Her body unfolded and Dox began to cackle, pounding the arms of her chair as tears of relief ran down her cheeks. Akosh bore it all in stony silence for a while, even though she was seething with rage. Dox knew

Akosh was tempted to strangle her to stop the laughter but she couldn't because she needed their help.

Even when Akosh kicked her in the leg it wasn't enough to quash her amusement. She'd been so frightened of Akosh it was hard to bring the two versions together. One was a calculating and murderous cult-leader and the other was someone who'd been forced to sneak into the bedroom of her enemy late at night. Dox could see it was causing her pain to ask for help which helped keep the smile on her face.

"Understand, worm, normally I'd stamp on your neck and not think about it."

"But today isn't a normal day," said Dox, delighted at Akosh's suffering. "So, why do you need my help?"

"I need your Master's help."

Dox's smile faded. "Munroe isn't my master."

"Really?" said Akosh with a sneer. "I've been watching you. I know she's your teacher and you do as you're told, like a good little pet."

"What do you want with Munroe?" asked Dox, refusing to play games with her. Akosh was already trying to get under her skin. It was a tactic Dox had used a few times when she'd been overwhelmed.

"You're scared," she said, expecting Akosh to deny it. Instead she averted her eyes.

"I'm being corralled like cattle," said Akosh, shaking her head in dismay. "I've never been someone else's prey."

"Prey?"

"Girl, you need to understand something. To me you're nothing. All of you. You're just ants, or worms crawling through the mud. Here for a little while and then gone. Forgotten. You don't matter to me at all."

The words were the truth and Akosh meant them to be

painful—to make her realise how small and insignificant she was. To a certain degree they hit the mark, and yet Dox found herself smiling. Her reaction infuriated Akosh, which made her grin widen, but that wasn't the only reason.

She was important.

However old or powerful, or whatever Akosh really was, in her darkest hour she had turned to a couple of humans for help.

"What is hunting you?"

"A being far more powerful than I. He's terrifying," said Akosh. Dox had been expecting more deception but the truth made her smile falter and then fade away. "Yes, girl," said Akosh with a vicious smile. "You're right to be scared. You should be pissing yourself. I've never met a creature more malicious and dangerous."

She wanted to believe Akosh was being overly dramatic to scare her but her Talent told her otherwise.

"So, your Master," said Akosh and this time Dox let it pass. "I need her help to fight my enemy."

In spite of her fear Dox couldn't help laughing at the absurdity of that request. "And why, by the Maker's cock, would she help you?"

Dox was surprised when Akosh winced at her blasphemy. "Because even if she managed to kill me, it wouldn't make any difference."

"I think it would," said Dox. "I think she'd be happy at getting her revenge and find some peace. Then she could move on with her life."

"Girl, you don't understand. I might look the same as you, but I'm not human. I'm like nothing you've ever seen before."

As far as Akosh believed she was telling the truth. Then again Dox had once met a man who thought he was a goose and regularly tried to lay eggs. "Convince me that anything you've said is the truth."

"Insolent child," said Akosh, ramping up towards another rant.

"Maybe I am, but I know for a fact the moment Munroe sees you, she will try to rip off your head. So unless you can convince me, you've no chance with her."

"Didn't you see some of our fight at the orphanage?" asked Akosh. "You saw my wounds heal."

Dox folded her arms. "Powerful mages and Sorcerers can heal themselves."

"Then what about the orphanages? They're all devoted to me. They're my children."

"Your grandmother could have started those and you share her name. Try harder."

Akosh was grinding her teeth so hard Dox heard them squeak but she didn't back down. She knew the next time Munroe saw Akosh she wouldn't hesitate to try her best to kill her. She would need a very convincing reason not to try.

Slowly Akosh's anger eased away and an unnerving smile spread across her face. "Remember, girl, you asked for this," she said, leaning forward.

"What are you doing?" said Dox, moving out of reach.

"I need to touch your face, that's all," said Akosh, holding up one empty hand. "It won't hurt."

"Liar," said Dox, even before she felt confirmation from her Talent.

"It won't cause any lasting damage," said Akosh. Dox's magic told her it wasn't a lie but she was still unsettled. However, it seemed to be the only way to find the truth about why Akosh had taken such a risk by sneaking into her room.

"Hold still," said Akosh, extending her hand again. She pressed two fingers to Dox's forehead above her right eye and muttered something quietly.

Dox was expecting a flash of pain but nothing happened.

"Now what?" she asked.

The second the words left her mouth she felt a presence racing towards her. Something monstrous. It overwhelmed her senses, pressing her deep into the chair. She was unable to move, barely able to breathe. Darkness raced in and she was swallowed by an empty void.

There was nothing to see or hear. Nothing to feel. Just empty space and she was without a body, without senses, and yet she still felt like herself.

Had it all been part of an elaborate trap? Was she merely bait for Munroe? Cursing herself for a fool Dox tried to break free of the black but she had no hands or feet. No body at all and no way to move through the space around her.

Time passed. How much she couldn't tell but somewhere in the darkness she became aware of a subtle change. Suddenly there was grey. Far away was a tiny pinprick of light. Only its most distant echoes reached her but without form she had no way to move towards it.

Suddenly Dox experienced a sense of movement, of space rushing past her, but there was no sound, no wind on her face. The light drew closer. It became so bright that it filled the horizon, filled every part of her and she was born into the world.

Somewhere in a dark room a man named Lore bowed his head in prayer, muttering under his breath as he knelt on a dirt floor. Painted on the wall of his crude shack was a hooded figure holding a bloody knife. Her name and the idea for the painting had come to him in a dream. He was her first disciple.

The scruffy man finished the prayer and rose to his feet before hurrying out into the night. Lore was separate from Dox and yet a part of her rode inside his head, resting somewhere behind his eyes. Lore skirted the edge of the village before settling down against a wall behind the tavern. He tried to squat down before giving up and just flopping into the mud on his backside. At least it hadn't rained.

His movements were clumsy. He had no grace and lacked finesse. Without her blessing he was doomed to failure.

Tomorrow he would have enough money for new shoes and several pairs of trousers. Enough to buy food for weeks. And all he had to do was kill a man. The reason didn't matter to him. Lore had nothing left to lose. No family. No friends. No home beside the rickety hovel that was no better than a cattle shed. If Akosh guided his hand and kept his aim true, the blade would go into the victim's heart before he could scream.

The night wore on. A crowd came down the street, filling the tavern with noise and song. A fiddle played, someone tapped out a rhythm on a drum and the singing became loud and raucous. There was laughter and joy but Lore felt nothing. The music didn't stir him. It didn't excite him. The prospect of the kill gave him no pleasure. He merely waited. In the darkness. In the cold.

After two hours the back door opened and a man stumbled out in desperate need of a piss. He crossed the muddy track, stepped into the outhouse and groaned in pleasure. Lore relaxed his grip on his knife. It wasn't him. This one was fat and smelled like horses. Three more came out the back to empty their bladders and each time Lore tensed up, ready to strike, but it wasn't him.

Finally, after another hour, his target stumbled out the back door, unsteady on his feet. He almost missed the latrine, walked into the door then wrenched it open. Lore waited. Getting warm piss on him wasn't something he wanted. It seemed to go on for ever, a steaming torrent, but eventually the man was done.

With grace he'd never before possessed, Lore moved as quietly as a shadow across the muddy track. At the last moment the victim saw him coming and smiled, thinking he was another customer bursting at the seams. The dagger slid into the victim's chest and at first he didn't notice. He thought Lore had just bumped into him. Then something warm seeped from the victim's body, splashing on to Lore's hand. The victim's knees buckled, his smile faded and Lore stepped back holding the gory knife aloft.

The victim fell face first into the mud and was dead. Lore returned home and later that night collected his reward. It was the first of many. He thanked Akosh for her guidance, for her strength and true aim. In time the old shack became a house and Lore took on an apprentice who taught others about the life, the prayer and the blessings they received. In time they met other assassins who envied the wealth that Lore possessed. In time her name began to spread. The number of disciples swelled and she grew in power.

Years passed in what seemed like the blink of an eye and Lore died as a fat, rich old man. Then his young apprentice died of old age. Then more died and yet she remained. Walking the earth. Enjoying all of its pleasures.

She met others like her who were far older, wiser and more powerful. Nethun. Vargus. The Blessed Mother.

The ebbing was barely noticeable at first. One or two fell away and their prayers stopped. Then the trickle became a flood as more fell silent. Soon she heard few prayers. Her followers had gained much and now believed all of it was because of their own skill. Only a handful uttered her name and she was brought low, reduced to little more than a human shell. That which had never mattered before became vital. Time. Akosh could feel the grains of sand trickling through the hourglass and hers was nearly empty.

Desperate, in search of guidance, she wandered the city and saw a group of hungry children begging on the street. They became the first of her new children, devoted from an early age. Soon after they taught others, opened more orphanages and once

more the passage of time became less important. Fear of oblivion
ebbed away.

The back of Dox's head cracked against the floor as her chair
toppled over. Black stars danced in front of her eyes but her disorientation wasn't only from the fall. She'd been sweating and her
nightshirt was soaked through. She started to shiver and tried to
stand up but her legs didn't work. The world threatened to fade
away until she felt a strong hand on her arm. She was pulled
upright, the chair straightened and unceremoniously dumped
into it. A blanket landed on her head and she quickly unfolded
it and covered herself.

"Drink this," said a voice, pressing a glass into her hands. Dox
instinctively took a big gulp and instantly regretted it as the harsh
alcohol scorched her throat. It created a fire in her belly, giving
the illusion of warmth but thankfully her head started to clear.
When her heart had finally slowed and the glass was empty the
room came back into focus.

Akosh was sipping her whisky, one leg dangling over the arm
of her chair, staring into a roaring fire. Dox hadn't noticed her
lighting it but, then again, she had been elsewhere.

"So, when I say that you're like a speck of dirt on my boot, it's
nothing personal," said Akosh. "I've seen tens of thousands just
like you die over the years."

"You're facing the threat of that emptiness again." Dox's voice
had acquired a rasp from the whisky.

"The Void," muttered Akosh. "Now you understand why I
need Munroe's help. I will not go back there, to that nothingness."

"She won't care."

"Then think about this. If she kills me and destroys this body,
then as long as I have a single follower anywhere in the world, I
will be reborn. I will come into this world like every other human,
a fat, pink, squalling baby. In time I'll learn who I really am but

by then Munroe will be fat and old. She could kill me again, but then she'd be dead and I'll still be here."

"I heard you'd lost a large number of orphanages," said Dox, trying to smother her fear. What she'd seen weighed heavily on her mind and it threatened to turn her into a screaming lunatic. Dox had seen people shouting at clouds or talking to their invisible friends and she didn't want to become one of them. She needed time alone to come to terms with it.

"That was a blow," conceded Akosh. "But it doesn't matter. I still have hundreds of followers out there who are adults. The only way to stop me coming back would be to kill all of them and then me, one final time. Do you really think she'd do that?"

At the moment Dox wasn't sure. She was struggling to remember her own name. The memories Akosh had shared were overwhelming.

"Tell her everything. Make her understand."

"I'm not sure I can." Even after everything she'd seen, Dox still had doubts.

"You know what I am. Now imagine something far worse. Something enormously powerful that wouldn't hesitate to kill you, me and every person in this city. Something so horrific, that if I showed you its real face, it would destroy your mind."

Dox hoped for a lie but was left wanting. The bottle of whisky beckoned. She wanted to disappear into oblivion and forget everything about this night.

Akosh sat forward on her chair and Dox instinctively tried to move away but she was already pressed into the back. "Girl, there's something worse than dying, worse than the Void, and I've seen it. Our common enemy will consume everyone unless he's stopped. I don't have the power, but working together with Munroe, there's a chance. It's slim, but I'll take it over the alternative. Make her understand," she said.

"I'll try," said Dox.

Akosh grunted and moved to the door. "Try hard, girl. All of our lives depend on it. If she agrees, meet me in two days' time, at midday, in the Karshall market."

After she was gone Dox remained frozen in her chair for a long time. Her limbs cramped from not moving but she couldn't help it. All of it threatened to overwhelm her. Thoughts about what was to come. The memories Akosh had shared and the scale of what she'd seen. Most of all her thoughts lingered on the infinite darkness of the Void. All of it left her feeling so drained that despite her fear she fell asleep.

She awoke to the sound of the front door opening. Unattended the fire had burned down to glowing red coals and the heat was stifling. Munroe flopped into the other chair and Dox jumped, thinking that Akosh had returned.

"She wasn't there," said Munroe, gripping the arms of her chair until her knuckles turned white. "We were so close."

Dox tried to speak several times but her voice kept failing. Eventually she managed to just blurt it out.

"I had a visitor."

Munroe looked around the room. "Who?"

She couldn't say it. She tried but every time she formed the name in her mind it reminded her of everything she'd seen. Akosh's history as a figure of worship and near-immortal being. Something far beyond anything she'd thought was possible.

"What happened?" asked Munroe. Dox felt her embrace power from the Source until the echo of it started to throb against her temples. "Who was it?" she demanded, although Dox thought a part of her already knew.

"It was Akosh."

Chapter 26

Tammy reread the note for the sixth time even though she'd memorised the words.

"As you did something nice for me I thought I should return the favour." Like the rest of the note the author's signature was in a flowing script. Doña Tarija.

It made her wonder how much Doña Tarija knew. The two people sat across from her were talking but Tammy had tuned out their voices and was ignoring them. They were rich, entitled and thought the law didn't apply to them. Doña Tarija's people had caught them trying to escape the city. For the last six hours they'd been stewing in a cell and were now venting but her mind remained elsewhere.

Maybe Doña Tarija was merely thanking her for putting Doña Chur and her idiot brother in their place. Maybe she'd wanted to do something like that herself but the opportunity hadn't come up. Or maybe, just maybe, Doña Tarija was thanking her for killing Don Lowell. After all she'd inherited his territory and taken over the running of his operations.

Perhaps she'd been waiting for the old Don to die for years but he'd stubbornly held on. Only recently Tammy had learned that Don Lowell was an accomplished liar who cared nothing for his people. All of his people saw him as a kindly grandfather figure who thought of them as family. If Doña Tarija had ordered his death it might have turned the whole Family against her. Instead she'd been able to pretend that she too had been affected by his tragic murder, while quickly taking over without any issues, all thanks to Tammy getting revenge.

Or perhaps Doña Tarija meant something else entirely. There was no way to know and after a short time thinking about it Tammy knew any more would be a waste of effort. She had more pressing matters to deal with. In the back of her mind she was aware that the list of problems to be tackled another day was growing exponentially. But every day brought new challenges and some had to be addressed before they festered while others, like Doña Tarija, could be delayed.

"Are you even listening to a word I've said?" demanded Lord Norcross, as she finally tuned in the sound of his voice.

"No, I wasn't. Now let me be very clear about your situation," said Tammy, making sure she had their attention. "You were caught attempting to flee the city after the Queen issued a decree that placed Perizzi under quarantine. You also attempted to bribe several members of a crime Family into letting you out." She noticed Doña Tarija's people hadn't returned the money. They cared about the survival of Perizzi but weren't altruists. They would line their pockets while the city fell apart, especially if it meant betraying idiots like the pair sat in front of her.

"That was just a misunderstanding," tried Lady Norcross. Tammy raised an eyebrow and the woman wilted, turning to her husband.

"I demand to speak to whoever is in charge," he said, puffing out his chest.

"I'm in charge. I'm the Khevassar."

"Oh," he said, less sure of himself. "Well, who is your superior?"

"The Queen. And she gave me the authority to detain, imprison or hang anyone who went against her orders."

Even Lord Norcross fell silent at that. He sagged in his chair, tried to wipe some of the filth off his expensive coat and grimaced as it only smeared it further. She'd made sure the cell they'd been locked up in was particularly ripe, decorated with old and new patches of vomit.

"Surely you wouldn't hang us for this," he tried in a meek voice.

"We just wanted to get away from this awful place until it was over," said Lady Norcross, holding a handkerchief to her nose. Unfortunately some of the unpleasant smells in the room were coming from her vomit-splattered dress. "We have an estate in the country. I swear we were going straight there."

Much like other wealthy nobles in the city, Lord and Lady Norcross had several homes. This included a modest ten-bedroom country home where they liked to rough it and pretend to be common folk while servants tended to their every whim. They were not the only ones who had attempted to flee the city after the Queen's declaration, but they had been the most daring. An example was needed to dissuade others.

"Technically you broke the law by going against the Queen's decree," said Tammy, pretending to consider their fate. Tears welled up in Lady Norcross's eyes and the blood drained from her husband's face. "And in this case I think the punishment should suit the crime."

"No," Lady Norcross whispered. "Do something!" she demanded of her husband but he'd become mute.

"However, on this occasion you may consider yourselves lucky," said Tammy, deciding that they'd suffered enough, for now at least. She was confident Queen Morganse would speak to them once the crisis was over and demand a favour for such leniency. "Normally I'd be tempted to lock you in a cell and leave you there, but I can't afford you taking up valuable space. So instead you'll be escorted home, where you are to remain, until this is over."

Since the quarantine had begun looting and random acts of violence had significantly increased across the city. People were attacking each other under false pretences. Sometimes in a panic about being infected and sometimes just to settle old scores. For some reason they thought now was the right time to chance it despite soldiers patrolling the streets at all hours.

The city wasn't completely out of control, not yet, but she felt that it was getting a little worse every day.

"We're free to go?" said Lord Norcross, not quite believing it.

"Yes. A pair of soldiers are waiting outside to escort you home." She dismissed them with a wave but Rummpoe had to help Lady Norcross out of the office. Fear, and perhaps six hours of being locked up in a cell, had robbed her of all strength in her legs.

Tammy pushed thoughts of them aside and focused on what needed addressing next. She had a stack of reports describing what her Guardians had seen in the city. Normally she would make a list of recommendations but right now she was tired of staring at the same four walls. Seeing a situation with her own two eyes was often better than reading about it.

The wise thing would be to walk to the room at the end of the corridor, lock the door and get a minimum of six hours' sleep. It had been several days since Tammy had slept for more than a few hours at a time. It felt as if her head was stuffed full of wool and her eyes were coated with sand. But she needed some fresh air and an opportunity to stretch her legs. Her gurgling stomach was a reminder that it had been a long time since her last meal.

In the outer office she found Rummpoe dozing at her desk. Tammy ordered her to go home, get at least six hours' sleep and a hot meal before coming back. Her secretary grumbled but eventually agreed to go.

She stopped off at the tavern nearest Unity Hall, often frequented by Guardians, but today it was almost deserted. All of her people were either catching up on their sleep or out on patrol. A handful of Guardians sat together in one corner stuffing their mouths with some kind of stew and warm bread. Their faces were gaunt, eyes ringed with shadows, and they were eating as if starving. Tammy thought about joining them but knew from recent experience it would only make them uncomfortable. Instead she sat alone on the other side of the room.

The owner brought her a big plate of stew, a huge chunk of bread, butter and a thick wedge of cheese. The meal was rich, filling, and it gave her a temporary boost of energy. It wasn't the same as six hours of sleep and a hot bath but it would have to do.

As the other Guardians left the tavern they all gave her a nod but didn't stop to chat. They knew what they had to do. A few minutes later Tammy went out the door after them. Only a few streets away she came across a mob trying to stone two people to death.

A squad of the Watch was trying to hold back about a dozen people but were having some difficulty. The two people lying in the street were being pelted by a hail of stones and the Watch were caught in the middle. They were armed with bucklers and swords, but these were proving ineffective for non-lethal crowd control. A couple of soldiers already had cuts and bruises from stray rocks. Although none of them had drawn their swords she could see their patience wouldn't last much longer as talking to the crowd wasn't working.

Tammy drew the walnut baton from the inside of her jacket and charged into the mob. Using her full weight she knocked down four people who then stumbled into others. Before they had a chance to recover she started clubbing knees and elbows, forcing people back as they cried out in pain. The Watch charged in behind her, slamming their shields into people's faces, bloodying noses and tangling legs with sheathed swords. Rocks fell to the street from broken fingers and the mob dispersed, carrying their injured away.

"Send for a doctor," said Tammy, grabbing the nearest member of the Watch.

"Can't. He's infected," said the man, pointing at the two people in the street. One was a priest of the Maker, a burly Seve woman with a shaven head in a plain grey robe. The other was a middle-aged man with a grey beard. One side of his face was covered with lesions similar to those she'd seen on others.

"We were on our way to the isolation zone when they attacked," said the priest, dusting herself off. There was blood on her scalp, one of her eyes was swollen and she had cuts on her face and arms. Remarkably the infected man had few wounds. The priest had shielded him with her body throughout the ordeal.

"Make sure they get there," said Tammy to the squad leader. He gestured for the priest to walk ahead while he and the rest of the squad maintained their distance. Since the start she had received numerous requests from priests asking to be let into the isolation zone to look after the infected. At first she'd intended to refuse. It was a death sentence and they knew it, but in the end she relented. So far the doctors and apothecarists hadn't found a cure and in such dire circumstances people needed hope.

A short time later she rounded a corner and saw a plume of smoke coming from a building a few streets away. By the time she arrived a human chain had already formed with people passing buckets of water to tackle the blaze. One of the buildings in the middle of the street had smoke pouring out of the upper windows but she could see fire flickering around the edges of the front door.

Guardians and members of the Watch were keeping a crowd

back while a mix of soldiers and local people tried to put out the fire.

"What happened?" shouted Tammy, grabbing the nearest Guardian.

"Someone painted the front door with a skull. Claimed the owner had the plague. When he wouldn't leave they tried to burn him out," said the Guardian, shaking her head.

The two people closest to the fire stumbled back gasping for fresh air. Soldiers dragged them clear of the blaze where a doctor tended to them as best as she could. Other people rushed in to plug the gap and Tammy joined the chain, passing full buckets of water from left to right. After a few minutes her eyes were streaming with tears, her lungs were burning and she'd developed a racking cough. Her arms and shoulders burned from the repetitive motions but she ignored it like those around her. The smoke seemed to be getting worse but a ragged cheer went up from the crowd. The people on either side of her stumbled away to collapse in heaps, gasping for air.

The fire was out. Smoke still poured out of the windows but for now it was over. Moving clear of the smoke she took deep lungfuls of air until it was easier to breathe. A young boy offered her a ladle of water which she accepted, washing her face and hands before checking with the other Guardians that everything was under control.

It could have been much worse. If there had been any wind one of the neighbouring buildings could have caught fire. Putting out one flaming house was difficult enough. Two was almost impossible. At that point the only way to contain it would have been to evacuate the street and tear down buildings to create a fire break. Tammy wished Balfruss was here. Any competent mage would do. Fray was out on the streets but his abilities were limited and had to be kept a secret. No help from any magic user was coming. They were on their own.

After taking a short rest she moved on, leaving behind the soot-smeared crowd. Her clothes reeked of smoke and her eyes were raw but gradually her breathing became less painful.

It was the noise that made Tammy quicken her pace. The sound of breaking glass. The barking of orders and screams of pain. When she entered the square the first thing she saw was a Yerskani soldier on the ground with blood on her face. She lay between two groups of people. A seemingly peaceful group of onlookers and a violent mob battling with several soldiers who were trying to keep them back.

In the last ten years the Yerskani army had been vastly improved by Queen Morganse. While not poorly trained in the past they were now exceptional and every soldier had been schooled in several weapons and unarmed combat. Each carried the traditional Yerskani blade, a slightly curved cleaver, but they were also armed with spears which they were now putting to good use. Using the shafts they were forcing people backwards, tapping the knees and ankles of those who refused or were on the brink of violence. Gradually the unruly group was being forced backwards out of the square.

On one side of the mob was a row of shops. All of them were closed except a bakery. The windows had been smashed and the front door hung askew on one hinge.

"What happened?" said Tammy, helping the injured soldier to her feet.

"A mob broke into the bakery. Someone started a panic about there not being enough food. A group tried to steal everything, and when the baker refused, someone killed him."

"Did anyone see who was responsible?" she asked, inspecting the soldier's wound. It was a long but shallow cut diagonally across her forehead.

"We all did. Two soldiers are holding him in the shop. We were trying to take him to Unity Hall when the others got in the way."

"Show me," said Tammy.

The inside of the bakery was a mess. The shelves had been torn off the walls. The floor was covered with broken loaves of bread, splashes of blood and a dusting of flour. In one corner of the room lay the baker, the left side of his head caved in from something heavy. His right eye stared at her, the other was gone, turned into a red pulp. Two soldiers were standing over a third man kneeling on the floor, his hands secured behind his back.

"Sir," said one of the Yerskani soldiers, saluting out of habit, even though he didn't report to her.

"Did you see him kill the baker?"

"Yes, Sir. All three of us and two more out there," he said, gesturing at the square. Food shipments were still coming into the city on a regular basis. As she'd expected trade at the city gates was difficult but not impossible and no one in the city was starving. But it didn't stop people panicking or being afraid. Every day she read reports about attacks on the infected, or even on those who looked a little unwell.

Break-ins like this one had been infrequent at the start of the quarantine but there were more every day. People were brazenly breaking the law in a way they would never have dared in the past. But this was the first murder in the city over food. A line needed to be drawn. She went into the storeroom at the back of the shop, found what she was looking for and marched back into the square.

"Bring him with you," she said to the soldiers.

The jeering from the angry crowd had mostly faded but now it rose in volume again. The murderer smiled and even gave a little bow to his friends as if what he'd done was a noble thing. The group of onlookers on the other side of the square were right to be scared. This wasn't the norm and Tammy was determined that it never would be. Not in her city.

"Who here saw this man murder the baker?" she asked in a loud voice that normally would have silenced the crowd. Instead some people were still cheering and talking.

Five of the soldiers stepped forward and raised their hands. Tammy studied each soldier and then ran her eyes across the crowd. "And would you be willing to swear to that during his trial?"

"Aye," said all five soldiers in unison. The laughter was starting to fade as even the slowest person in the square realised something was happening. The mood among the crowd began to change.

"Would you all swear a blood oath?" asked Tammy.

A deathly silence swept the crowd.

A blood oath was an old custom built on centuries of lore that wasn't used these days. It had no weight in the law but everyone, from all parts of the world, knew about them. Swearing a blood oath was the deepest and most powerful way to bind someone to the truth. Breaking such an oath wasn't just considered bad luck. It was seen as a death sentence. It wasn't a game that even the most daring children played for fun.

Tammy knew a blood oath normally involved a ritual but the five soldiers had made a public declaration in front of a large group. Time was short and she needed to set a clear example that people could not flaunt the law in her city.

Every face in the crowd was watching her closely, including the five soldiers.

"Would you all swear?" she asked again.

"Aye," they said, more hesitantly this time.

"Then I declare this man a murderer and his sentence will now be passed."

While the soldiers had been deciding she'd kept her hands busy, knotting the rope. With everyone watching she looped the noose over the murderer's head, cinched it tight about his neck and dragged him across the square. That was when he finally started babbling and pleading for his life. Next came apologies for what he'd done, as if he'd just stolen a loaf of bread and not bludgeoned a man to death. As if his words would resurrect the baker and stop the grief that would follow.

She threw the rope over a high branch of a tree, grabbed the dangling edge and hoisted the murderer into the air. After looping the rope around the trunk she stood directly beneath looking up at his face.

The only sound in the world became his final choking breaths. His legs kicked at the air, trying to find purchase. He gagged and thrashed in desperation, swaying this way and that, trying to escape, but the rope around his neck didn't break. The skin on his face turned pink and then purple as his eyes bulged and red spittle ran from his mouth. The struggling subsided, his eyes drifted closed and his legs hung towards the ground. Tammy kept watching until the murderer choked out his final breath. When she was sure he was dead she turned around to face the crowd.

No one dared look her in the eye. Not one person. A clear message had been sent.

No one flaunted the law in her city.

The story would quickly spread. By the end of the day she expected most people would have heard about it. Some of them wouldn't believe it and would want to see proof with their own eyes.

"Leave him there for two days," she said to the nearest soldier. "Then cut him down and burn the body."

"Yes, Sir," said the soldier.

Chaos was spreading throughout Perizzi but here, today, people had been reminded of the price of breaking the law. The Guardians had never been figures that inspired fear, but perhaps for a while, it was better if they were.

CHAPTER 27

As Danoph passed through the city gates into Herakion a wave of energy swept through him. Even with his magic held firmly in check he rocked in his saddle as if drunk. Vargus steadied him with one hand until he was able to regain his balance.

Despite being told this would happen he was amazed at the physical impact. He'd never experienced anything like it before. They were riding into the centre of a huge web of divergence because of the actions of Akosh and her people. The entire city felt slightly askew, as if every building was on a slant that was just discernible. Danoph felt himself tilting his head to one side to try to correct it.

The air also felt alive, as if it were crawling with biting insects. As well as being slightly dizzy he felt a little nauseous, as if he might vomit at any moment and not be able to stop.

Everyone else was completely immune to the effects. They couldn't feel that something was terribly wrong in the city. For them life continued to unfold as normal but he knew the natural course of countless lives had been spun in new directions. Unfortunately, with each passing day, they were led further astray. He tried not to think about the number of people or how much work lay ahead to correct it.

To take his mind off what was awaiting him Danoph studied his surroundings. It was his first trip to Zecorria and at first glance the capital city seemed much like any other, with shops and businesses, taverns and temples, merchants and travellers. His second impression was that it was a city balanced on a knife edge that had nothing to do with Akosh.

It was there, in the face of every person. Sometimes out in the open and sometimes well hidden. It was in the deeply etched ridges between their eyebrows. In the furtive looks. In the way they tightly gripped their belongings.

Fear.

A gut-wrenching, bone-deep fear. At first he thought it might be xenophobia as there were fewer foreigners than when they'd passed through Yerskania. But both visitors and locals seemed unusually nervous, as if they were expecting trouble to erupt at any time. The slightest loud noise drew every eye on the street.

As they rode further into the city Danoph saw merchants from Seveldrom, Shael and Yerskania, most of whom were shadowed by Drassi bodyguards. An air of calm surrounded the masked warriors who seemed untouched by the anxiety among the population. There were no Vorga this far north but plenty of Morrin who lived in the neighbouring country, Morrinow. Every time he saw a pair of horns sticking out above the crowd it reminded him of the torturer from the camps. After all this time, and everything he understood, Danoph was amazed that something so everyday could make him feel fragile.

When a group of Zecorran Royal Guards, resplendent in their colourful jackets and polished breastplates, walked past, he understood why everyone was afraid. At the head of the squad was a young Zecorran teenager, dressed in a uniform with a blue star over his heart. He was young to be leading soldiers but even more peculiar was the tattoo running down one side of his face.

"Did you see?" asked Danoph when the guards were out of earshot.

"He's one of them," confirmed Vargus.

They'd heard the stories on the road. The Regent had his own cadre of mages. It was ridiculous, given that he'd banned all Seekers in Zecorria and had seemed intent on banning all magic. To move from one extreme to the other spoke of desperation or a fickle mind.

Magic. It was the cause of everyone's discomfort and it all went back to the war. A nation led astray by the Mad King and the Warlock. Thousands dead and a black mark left on an entire nation. As much as seeing a Morrin made him feel uncomfortable, Danoph knew Tianne and others like her had it much worse. Even though it had been ten years people would still stare if they saw the dark eyes and pale skin. As if every Zecorran had been complicit in the Mad King's plans and was somehow to blame for his actions.

With that kind of legacy hanging over them Zecorrans were right to be wary of magic. And now the Regent was creating his own private army of mages. His promise that the cadre were there to protect the people was falling on deaf ears, despite the capture of Garvey. It was still one of the most talked about stories on the road. The other was the plague in Perizzi.

They had bypassed the capital on their journey north, a route which now seemed fortuitous as they could have been trapped within its walls, preventing them from coming to Zecorria. Vargus was particularly worried about the plague, and would listen intently to every conversation when people spoke about it.

"We need to find somewhere for the night," said Vargus, leading him away from the main street towards a less affluent area. The buildings were a little more worn and the shops in need of fresh paint, but the staff at the Cooper's Arms were no less friendly. After a filling lunch of rabbit stew, black bread and ale, Danoph felt ready for whatever came next.

"Where do we start?" he asked.

"I've been thinking about that a great deal," said Vargus, wiping the last of the gravy off his plate with a piece of bread. "If I were in her position, I'd place my people as close to the Regent as possible. After all, she did the same in Yerskania."

"Do we need to get into the palace?"

"No. Somewhere close by should be enough. But you'll need to be careful," warned Vargus. "I saw how you were buffeted when we entered the city. Opening yourself up to everything will be overwhelming."

They left their horses stabled at the tavern and went on foot, giving Danoph another chance to look at his surroundings. A common misconception was that Zecorrans were cold and dispassionate people whose devotion to the Lady of Light made them intolerant of other beliefs. Although there were many churches of the Holy Light he didn't see any preachers standing on street corners berating strangers for their sinful ways. The icy stereotype was also quickly disproven when he heard much laughter.

Like any other city he witnessed first-hand both the good and the bad. The genuine warmth of two old friends meeting in the street. The callous nature of a mugger who tried to rob an old man of his money. Vargus's foot repeatedly found its way into the thief's face, knocking out three teeth, before he was taken away by a passing city patrol. A couple who had witnessed the attack walked the victim home while another witness offered to buy Vargus a beer. He politely refused and they carried on their way towards a small public park close to the palace.

There were a few elderly couples out for a stroll but for the most part they had the place to themselves. After finding a secluded bench Danoph took a deep breath and braced himself.

"This will hurt," said Vargus, pulling no punches. "The only way for you to survive will be to focus on why you're doing this. Think of someone you care about and hold on to a good memory. Something to act as an anchor. You're going to experience hundreds, maybe thousands of lives askew of their natural path. It will all seem like so much chaos and noise. But as you've done in the past, you need to step back and trace the source of the disturbances. Find Akosh."

Danoph remembered how he'd almost become lost in the minutiae. It had been a challenge before. This would be infinitely more difficult.

"I know you're scared," said Vargus, reading his mind—or perhaps it was the terror on his face. "But this is your purpose. This is why you are here. Trust in that. Trust that you were meant for this."

Danoph nodded and took a deep calming breath, trying to find an anchor. The last few years had been challenging but the memory came quickly, making him smile despite the fear knotting his stomach. It was shortly after they'd arrived in the valley which became their new community, Corvin's Brow. The first few weeks with his friends had been a blur of activity, building primitive houses, hunting for food in the day and cold nights huddled together in the caves.

His grounding memory was the day when they'd completed the first building and then celebrated that night. Warm, dry and with a full belly, he'd felt a sense of accomplishment like never before. He was surrounded by friends, building a new life, literally with his own two hands, and he was free. Free to make mistakes but also free to live his life however he wanted. The nightmares from his childhood that sometimes haunted him had felt so far away.

Holding on to that memory Danoph closed his eyes and slowly opened himself up to the city.

Something like a stampeding horse slammed into him, knocking him backwards off the bench. Before he had a chance to catch his breath he was hit again and again. It felt as if a rampaging herd was intent on smashing him to pieces. As well as the physical assault thousands of memories washed over him, pulling him in a hundred directions, threatening to tear him apart. His mind was flooded with intense emotions that made him want to laugh and cry at the same time. Murders. Joyous births. Vicious crimes and bloody wars. Intense sweaty sex and fear so terrifying his heart skipped a beat. There was just too much. Too much to see. Too much to experience. Too much noise.

Somewhere in the distance Danoph heard an indistinct voice. It could have been Vargus or Wren. As the assault continued and he was buffeted about Danoph tried to focus on the memory of better times. A golden time so full of promise. Slowly, bit by bit, he weathered the storm, like a stubborn pebble that refused to be washed away by a river. The tide of memories and emotions flowed around and over him, but he dug in and refused to move. The pressure was still there but he wasn't swept away.

Danoph was aware of his body in the park, but a part of him drifted free of his flesh until he was floating above the city. Untethered he rose higher and higher into the sky until everyone below became nothing more than pinpricks of light. They drifted around, seemingly at random, but even at this distance be could feel a presence pulling many of them astray from their natural rhythms.

Keeping the memory from his past firmly in mind, Danoph started to drift closer to the city, trying to locate the source of the disturbance. The emotional barrage started to increase, buffeting against him like a strong wind, but rather than try to block them, he let the feelings pass through him. Instead of reliving every memory he was only exposed to brief flashes. Between one heartbeat and the next he felt an intense emotion and caught a glimpse of someone's life, but it was only one frozen image. Before he had time to process it another took its place and then another. And all the while he drifted closer to the source.

As Vargus had predicted a lot of the disturbances were centred around the palace, but he noticed there were also other hot-spots in the city. As Danoph tried to pinpoint Akosh's location amidst the swirling lights something passed in front of his eyes like a shadow. It was there for a moment and then gone only to reappear somewhere else. Even though a part of him was separate from his body Danoph felt a shiver run down his spine.

The shadow wasn't just a spot of darkness in the city. It was an absence. Staring into it he felt as if it were a bottomless void, and even worse, he could see its corruption spreading across the city. Tendrils, like the arms of some huge creature, were snaking around buildings, crawling along streets and swallowing whole groups of people. Whatever fell under the shadow simply disappeared. Without realising Danoph had drifted closer to one of these inky black threads. His mouth fell open in shock as he realised the shadow was alive and, worse, it was aware. It blindly reached out towards Danoph but he quickly backpedalled and withdrew to a safe distance. As large as the shadow was becoming he sensed the bulk of it was elsewhere. He had no intention of tracing its point of origin. He was here for Akosh.

He'd become so used to drifting about the city Danoph was surprised when he felt something coming towards him. Intense pain raced through his body as something grabbed him by the ankle. Searing fire ran up his spine and across the back of his head as agonising needles of pain dug into his brain.

Danoph was aware of his body thrashing about on the ground somewhere far below. Staring down he saw part of the shadow had coiled itself around a tall building and it had stretched itself upwards to reach him. He tried to pull away but the shadowy tendril held on tight and was slowly pulling him down towards it. Somewhere in the endless void he saw an opening that coalesced into the wide beak of a monstrous creature.

With every ounce of energy Danoph tried to escape from the thing that held him but it had no effect. He tried to focus on the golden memory, using it like a shield, but nothing happened. He tried to return to his body but something was blocking him. The pain in his head became more intense as another tentacle gripped his left arm.

He was being torn apart. Whatever had him in its clutches intended to consume him. In desperation he focused on the tendrils and summoned his power, trying to understand its nature.

Danoph caught a brief glimpse of an ancient ziggurat, a stone altar with a naked woman bent backwards and a priest holding a bloody knife. People were chanting, and looming over them all was a huge malevolent statue of a tentacled creature with dozens of eyes.

His invasion of its past shocked the creature enough for it to loosen its grip. He used its hesitation to pull free, hurling himself across the city towards his body.

Danoph jumped up from the ground, gasping for air as if he'd been running for miles. His heart was pounding and fear sweat had soaked his clothes. Vargus was talking to him but he couldn't hear the words. The danger felt so real but gradually he realised he'd escaped the creature's grasp.

Slowly the soothing tone of Vargus's voice penetrated the fog of terror and he returned to the present. The fear was still there in the back of his mind but for now the monster couldn't touch him.

"What happened?"

"There's something worse than Akosh in the city," he gasped, wiping his damp forehead. "Something huge and ancient. I saw a temple with a woman being sacrificed."

"Ah," was all Vargus said, filling that one brief sound with intense disappointment and sorrow. But he was not surprised by Danoph's revelation.

"You knew it was here?"

"Yes, but I didn't know if he was involved."

"What is it?"

"I think it's time you met someone. An old friend of mine," said Vargus, ignoring his question.

Danoph experienced a moment of disorientation and then he was standing inside the banqueting hall again. The walls were plainly fashioned from stone. The fireplaces large enough to walk into but they held nothing but cold grey ash. Only the massive table at the centre of the room held a spark of life. All of the chairs along both sides looked identical but now that he was more familiar with his power Danoph sensed that each one was unique. Like musical notes each had its own pitch and they all vibrated at different levels and strengths. The largest and loudest was the huge chair at the head of the table but he was trying his best not to stare. The very idea of who sat in the chair terrified him without looking beneath the surface.

As he looked around for a distraction Danoph noticed that in this place Vargus was different. Normally he hid behind the human guise of a veteran, and although he still looked the same, the nature of his mask had never seemed so flimsy. Without trying he sensed a deep and ancient well of power within Vargus that stretched back centuries. There was blood in his past, a river of it, but Danoph didn't sense the malevolence or glory in causing pain that he'd felt from the shadowy creature. Vargus was a warrior who had fought on every battlefield in history, shoulder to shoulder with men and women from every nation and every race. He was their shield brother who led from the front, inspiring warriors to surround themselves with family who would die for them.

He also noticed Vargus was standing towards the head of the table behind his unique chair. Those closest to the Maker were the oldest and most powerful, making him wonder who Vargus had been before the Brotherhood and the Weaver? How far back did his legacy really go?

The air beside Vargus rippled like water and a moment later a swarthy sailor appeared. Barefoot and bald, with broad shoulders, thick arms and a hawk nose, the sailor wasn't someone Danoph recognised. He had an easy smile and thick calloused hands which he used to slap Vargus on the shoulder. He nearly pulled off Danoph's arm when he shook his hand.

"Good to see you, boy," said the sailor.

"This is Nethun," said Vargus, introducing his friend.

It took a while for the words to sink in at which point Danoph's knees gave way. Part of him could accept that he was standing in a banqueting hall that only existed between heartbeats. Part of him could even cope with the idea of an ancient table at which a gathering of gods met to discuss events. Such ideas were vague and without any proof. There would be no way for him to convince another person that any of it was real. They'd just think he was drunk. But now, holding him upright, was a god so old he'd been around almost since the dawn of Mordana. A god who had shaped the earliest Vorga tribes and been their deity for thousands of years. A god of storms and the sea. A god to whom every sailor, regardless of nationality, fervently prayed for a safe voyage.

"Take a moment," said Nethun, guiding him towards a specific chair. Some time later, it was hard to measure in this place, Danoph realised the chair was his and that it fit him perfectly. It felt as if it had been made for him as when he leaned his head backwards it rested on a high back.

Vargus and Nethun were talking in hushed tones and from the concern on both their faces he could guess the topic.

"Are you sure?"

"He felt it," said Vargus, gesturing towards where Danoph was recovering. "A vast shadow spreading across the city. It seems as if Akosh is nothing more than his puppet."

"What do we do about it?" asked Danoph, forcing himself to stand. He still felt as if he might throw up or faint, but he was a part of this. No matter how terrifying or overwhelming it felt, he was meant to be here. "What was that?"

"It's an old god. A god of hunger, plague and pestilence. One that should have died a long time ago," said Nethun with a smile. "But Kai is wily."

"Did you hear about the plague in Perizzi?" asked Vargus.

"Of course. Many of my people are unloading goods in port, but they're not allowed into the city."

"I don't think it's a coincidence," said Vargus.

"He's feeding off it and growing strong."

Vargus shook his head. "I should have just let him die."

Nethun grunted. "We all have regrets."

"So what do we do?" asked Danoph.

"That's a good question, boy," said Nethun as he approached. "When one of our brethren steps out of line they are eliminated. Vargus breaks their human shell apart and scatters their essence. Then their power is eroded until they cease to exist. Akosh was the target but now you will have to find a way to tackle Kai as well."

"Me?" asked Danoph, struggling to swallow the lump in his throat.

"Don't worry," he said with a laugh. "I'm not asking you to do it alone."

"He will not be easy to defeat," said Vargus. It was the first time since they'd met that Danoph thought he sounded worried. "He's grown powerful in the last few years."

"I'm sure you'll find a way," said Nethun, glancing briefly at Danoph. A silent message passed between them and the old warrior nodded. "I'll tell the others. Good hunting."

The sailor gave him a wave and then disappeared, lifting a weight from Danoph's shoulders. It was as if the air in the room had been heavier with Nethun's presence.

"What did he mean?" asked Danoph. "Find a way?"

If Vargus's smile was meant to be encouraging it didn't work as Danoph could see he was still worried. "He meant that working together, you and I must unravel what has been done."

"How?"

"Your power is the key. It's why I've been pushing you so hard."

"He said you'd done this before. Destroyed other gods. Is that true?" asked Danoph. A small part of him wanted to know the answer but the rest was telling him to be quiet. He'd never killed anyone before and the idea of it filled him with dread. Erasing someone completely from the world went beyond murder. It meant uprooting them from the mind of every follower until even their name ceased to exist.

"Yes. Many times," admitted Vargus. "And each time I hope it's the last, but some of our brethren seem incapable of learning."

Fresh sweat ran down his back at the thought of seeking out Kai. The terror rising up inside threatened to overwhelm him but he refused to give in.

"Where do we start?" asked Danoph.

CHAPTER 28

Tianne's hope of getting into Perizzi without being noticed fell apart when she saw the line of wagons waiting on the road ahead. A quick conversation with the merchant in front confirmed her fears. The infection had spread, a quarantine order had been given, and now the city was closed to all travellers. No one was allowed in or out and all trading was being done outside the city walls.

From their position on the road she could just make out the low surrounding wall that ringed the city and the tops of spires and churches rising up above. Several districts were spread out on the surrounding hillsides. It had outgrown its original boundaries many times, giving it a haphazard appearance. It looked as if the outer wall had been shored up and repaired in places but it would pose more of a deterrent than a real barrier to an invading army. Right now it served as an effective way of keeping the population inside the city.

In addition to the wall she could see several camps of Yerskani soldiers stationed outside, creating another layer of defence in case someone made it over the wall.

With little to do but wait their turn she and the others took some time to stretch their legs and eat a meal. They didn't know when they would have time for another.

"You should go and talk to people," suggested Wren.

"Why me?" asked Tianne.

"Because people like talking to you."

After a week of living on the road with seven other people it meant there was very little Tianne didn't know about them. In search of news, and not because she was a gossip, she walked up and down the line chatting to people for the next two hours. By the time she returned to her group she had a better idea of what to expect if they were allowed inside the city.

"So, what did they say?" asked Wren.

"It's quite bleak," said Tianne, trying not to scare them but they needed to have a better idea of what they were facing. "One of the merchants has a brother trapped inside who's been sending him letters. There's an isolation area where they send all the sick and the streets are constantly being patrolled by soldiers and the Watch."

"That doesn't sound too bad," said Kimme, stuffing her face with food.

"The herbalists and apothecarists are still trying to find a cure, but haven't had any luck. There have also been murders, mob attacks, buildings being burned down and some looting, mostly people breaking into shops for food."

Wren and the others looked suitably worried but it was too late to turn back now. They'd come this far and Tianne had no intention of going home.

"Well, it doesn't really change anything," said Kimme. "Once we're in the isolation zone we'll be safe."

Tianne was about to point out that it was probably much worse where people were dying and had nothing to lose, but Wren shook her head. She'd already scared them enough for today.

"The Queen recently brought more soldiers into the city, so I'm sure it will make the streets safer," said Tianne, trying to sound positive. The merchant had also told her about a dozen people who'd been caught trying to escape and had been hanged. There were also the nightly bonfires for the dead. Clouds of foul black smoke spread across the city until dawn. The only good news she'd discovered was that so far the plague had not spread beyond Perizzi.

It was another hour before they reached the front of the line, by which time all of the merchants ahead of them had unloaded their goods. The nearest village with taverns was a couple of hours away and it was a race to see who could get there first for a room.

As they approached the gates Tianne saw a series of carts had been positioned in an arch to create a barricade. There were two rings and each cart had been stripped of its wheels to make it immobile. It meant anyone going in or out of the city had to weave between the obstacles, which were only wide enough for two people abreast. It also explained why it had taken so long for the goods to get into the city. Each had to be unloaded by hand and carried to a cart waiting inside the gates. While merchants were still making money from selling their goods Tianne imagined they could make a fortune if they smuggled someone out in the back of their cart. The authorities were not taking any chances with the plague.

Eight members of the Watch and a dozen Yerskani soldiers were waiting for them at the barrier.

"That's far enough," said the leader, a burly Yerskani Watch Captain with a bushy moustache. "What's your business?"

"We're here to help the sick," said Wren who, after some persuasion from the others, had agreed to take the lead.

"You're too young to be priests," said the Captain. Tianne could see that he was tired and under a lot of pressure, but he was still trying to treat them fairly. She also noticed he was favouring his left leg over his right.

"We're healers," said Wren.

"We've got enough herbalists and apothecarists in the city," he said, dismissing them. "Come back another time."

"How long has your right leg been hurting you?" asked Tianne, embracing the Source. Moving slowly and carefully, just as Master Yettle had taught them, she extended tendrils of energy towards the Captain. "It's your knee."

All of the soldiers and members of the Watch were now staring at her. "How did you know that?" he asked. Tianne was suddenly reminded of when she'd approached the palace in Herakion. The clerk hadn't believed her either.

"I can heal your knee, if you let me," said Tianne, holding up one hand. Blue balls of light danced across her knuckles like coins.

The Captain remained sceptical. He'd probably seen other sleight-of-hand tricks before, but he nodded, giving her permission. Closing her eyes made it easier to focus, allowing her to block out everything except his injury. By slowly extending her senses towards his knee Tianne quickly found the problem. It wasn't as severe as she'd anticipated with only a small muscle tear.

Just as Master Yettle had shown them she started to weave together a golden net, building it up one layer at a time. A muscle injury only required a small weave, which she wrapped around his knee. If she wasn't careful the weave could do more harm than good to the surrounding healthy tissue. Once she was sure it was properly in place Tianne trickled a little more energy into the weave. On the periphery of her senses she was vaguely aware that the Captain was speaking as the magic started to work. In less than a minute it was done and she carefully removed the weave before letting it dissipate.

When she opened her eyes Tianne saw the Captain stretching his knee and walking back and forth. The limp was completely gone.

"Will you let us inside?" asked Wren.

"No, but I'll send a runner for someone who can make that decision."

One of the soldiers set off at a jog so they were forced to sit and wait. A short time later she returned, walking next to a tall Seve woman with the pale skin of a Yerskani. She was dressed differently to the others, in a long red and black jacket, and Tianne noticed they all deferred to her, even the soldiers. She and the Captain had a brief conversation in hushed tones before she approached the barricade.

"I'm the Khevassar. I'm in charge of the Guardians. The Captain tells me you're healers."

"We want to help with the plague," said Wren.

"Do you think you can cure it?" asked the Guardian.

Wren shrugged. "We won't know unless we try."

"Did you come here by yourself?"

"We're survivors from the Red Tower," said Tianne, stepping forward. Once again she found everyone's attention was suddenly focused on her but she didn't care. "We were chased from the school by an angry mob."

"Tianne—" said Wren, but she ignored her friend.

"In spite of that we've chosen to come here, to help people. No one forced us to do this. We might be able to cure the plague, but not from out here."

Tianne thought she might have gone too far. The others didn't bother her but there was something unnerving about the Khevassar's stare. As well as towering over everyone she had an air of danger. Tianne's fear ebbed away when a faint smile lifted the corners of the Guardian's mouth.

"You've got courage, girl, I'll give you that," she said. "But do you understand what you're asking?"

"What do you mean?" asked Wren.

"If I let you inside the isolation zone, you can't come back out again. Not until the plague has been cured or everyone inside is dead."

Tianne had considered it but from the expression of those around her they hadn't thought it through. This was most likely a one-way trip. To their credit her friends recovered quickly and stepped forward.

"We're ready," said Kimme, speaking for the others.

"This is your last chance to turn back," said the Khevassar.

Tianne gripped Wren's hand and squeezed it tight. "Let us inside."

The Guardian gestured for the Captain to let them pass. "You'll have to leave your horses here. We'll take good care of them."

They stripped their saddlebags of all their belongings, which mostly consisted of food, clothing and herbs, before following the Khevassar through the barrier into the city.

As they walked through the streets of Perizzi, famed for being open to everyone, Tianne found it difficult not to stare at her surroundings. After spending so many years in Shael, and even after her trip back to Zecorria, she wasn't used to seeing so many people from all over the world.

Burly Seves and horned Morrin stood out most in the crowd because of their height but she even spotted a blue-skinned Vorga bartering with a merchant. The Vorga towered over the stout Yerskani merchant but that didn't stop him from firmly shaking his head at the latest bid. Reaching some sort of impasse the Vorga spat something in its own language and then stormed off.

"She'll be back," Tianne heard the merchant muttering to himself. "Where else can she go?"

Despite the plague and the isolation zone, people were trying their best to carry on with their lives as normal. A fair amount of strain showed on their faces, but the alternative was to lock themselves indoors and wait for it to be over.

In Zecorria the capital city had been carefully built and then expanded over time. Here it was more haphazard with an old decaying church sat next to a row of modern shops. Winding streets that looked as if they would continue suddenly came to a dead end. Twice they were forced to cross the river that split the city in two, walking across narrow footbridges.

The other thing she noticed, which Wren had also spotted, was the soldiers patrolling throughout the city. Squads of the Watch were to be expected, but she also saw soldiers stationed in squads of ten at regular intervals. All of them were armed with the local curved Yerskani cleavers, but each also had a shield and spear.

The pretence of normal life was disrupted every now and then by the shell of a burned-out building, a fresh splash of blood on the street and sometimes the sounds of a fight in the distance. Twice the noise of a clash became so loud they paused to see if it would cross their path but it faded as more soldiers ran towards the danger. Finally they reached the edge of what had to be the isolation zone.

A ring of heavily armed soldiers, each carrying a loaded cross-bow, stood in front of a high stone wall that was topped with shards of broken glass. What would normally be a wide street had been blocked off apart from a postern gate that was barred on the outside. The message was clear. You could go in but you couldn't come out on your feet.

Other gaps had been boarded up or blocked with new walls and more soldiers patrolled the edge. For the first time since they'd arrived in Perizzi Tianne felt a flutter of fear grip her stomach. She swallowed hard, ignored the taste of bile and reminded herself of why she'd come.

People were in desperate need and it was possible she and the others could cure them. It was an easy thing to say but she knew it was going to be the biggest challenge any of them had ever faced. There were no guarantees they'd be able to find a cure. It was likely they'd all get infected and die.

At the very least they could use their magic to relieve the suffering of those in pain. It wasn't much, but right now Tianne was willing to bet people would take it. Even if it meant their reprieve came from magic. When death was close, people changed their minds about all sorts of things.

"Are you sure?" asked the Khevassar, perhaps sensing that some of them were reluctant.

"I'm going," said Tianne, not wanting to speak for the others. They had to make up their own minds. They'd come this far but she'd not force anyone to go in there with her. Wren stepped forward as well, followed shortly by Kimme and then the others.

"All right, open it up," said the Guardian, gesturing at the gate. The soldiers formed a tight ring in front of Tianne and the others, perhaps expecting those inside to rush out. The soldier in charge unlocked the gate and then quickly pulled aside the thick bar.

A terrible silence filled the empty street beyond. No one was making a desperate attempt to escape. Six corpses lay further down the road, three sitting against walls on either side as if they'd paused there to rest. But their eyes never blinked and flies crawled all over them.

Reaching deep inside herself Tianne drew power from the Source as she stepped through the gate, channelling it into fire which she poured on to the bodies. The buzzing of flies grew louder, as a hidden host lifted off the dead, but then they were instantly burned to ash. Wren added her own fire and together the combined heat made short work of the bodies, melting the flesh and scouring them down to bones which soon crumbled and folded in on themselves. When Tianne was sure there was no chance of the plague spreading from the remains she released the Source. Grey motes of ash rained down and the air was rank with the stench of burned hair and flesh.

The shadows of six people had been etched on to the walls where the bodies had fallen. As she stared at the outlines Tianne hoped it wasn't an omen for the six of them going into the isolation zone. Dismissing it as a childish fantasy she walked down the abandoned street, barely noticing when the gate was sealed behind them.

CHAPTER 29

The Karshall market was a busy square filled with stalls selling a range of goods from around the world. Spices, fruit, silk and carved religious figurines dominated the stalls, but there were also a few selling carved wooden handicrafts, leather-bound books and exotic garments.

Dox marvelled at the array of brightly coloured powders that the dye merchant, a dark-skinned man from the desert, had available. He and a local Zecorran woman had been haggling over something for a while, taunting each other with outlandish insults. It was obvious they were enjoying themselves and took pleasure in shocking the other with the inventiveness of their curses. The crowd in the market ebbed and flowed but as they built towards midday the numbers increased.

Half of the space in the square was taken up by tables that were reserved for a tiny tea room and bakery. The shop could fit half a dozen people inside at most but such was its reputation that they had commandeered half of the outdoor space. The stallholders didn't seem to mind as whenever people flocked to sample the pastry chef's latest creation many stayed to browse the stalls.

When Dox and Munroe arrived, an hour before they were due to meet with Akosh, most of the tables were empty. A queue normally formed at the door of the bakery a little after dawn in order to sample the first batch. The chef's second batch was due at midday. As they sat there sipping tea and watching the crowd begin to grow Dox could see why Akosh had chosen it.

By midday they wouldn't be able to move for bodies. Every chair would be taken. The stalls would be heaving and a long snaking queue of people would form at the door. It had already started and at least two dozen people were patiently waiting in line even though they were half an hour early.

On the other side of the table Munroe said nothing. She merely crunched her sugared almonds and gulped her tea. Her eyes never stopped moving, flitting from one face in the crowd to the next, frantically searching for Akosh. It was likely she'd arrive a little early, or send one of her people to check the area for an ambush, before showing her face.

Every day Dox became more sensitive to the Source and her ability to recognise magic in others was growing. Now, as the two of them waited, she could hear and even feel a constant drumbeat in her head. It was so powerful it hurt being close to Munroe. It was as if someone were tapping a finger on the inside of her skull, over and over. When they were busy it wasn't really noticeable, but the longer they sat the louder it became. And this was without Munroe embracing the Source. It felt as if Dox's skin was on fire when Munroe was angry and started throwing things around with her magic.

"We're just here to talk," said Dox. "You agreed to that."

"No, I didn't. I agreed to meet her," said Munroe, glancing at Dox briefly before resuming her study of the crowd. "Who can say what happens after that?"

As midday approached the chairs in the square filled up, the stalls became busy and the queue of people waiting for pastries stretched around two sides of the square. And still there was no sign of Akosh. A wall of people blocked Dox's view in most directions and every time someone nudged Munroe's chair she winced, expecting a violent outburst. The fact that it never came somehow made it worse. It meant Munroe was saving up her anger for one person.

A dark idea took root in the back of Dox's mind. What if all this was just an elaborate trap? What if Akosh had set it up so that she could kill both of them? It was obvious she didn't care about people. After all, it was her followers who had been stirring up trouble against the Seekers and anyone connected with magic. Akosh had arranged this meeting in a busy space knowing that she would be relatively safe as Munroe would never risk harming bystanders. But she had no such compunctions about murdering innocent people.

How could she have been so naïve?

"I don't like this," said Dox, frantically studying the crowd.

"It's too late," said Munroe, gesturing with her chin.

On the edge of the crowd, only a short distance away, was Akosh. She was dressed conservatively in black trousers and a grey shirt, but Dox noticed a knife sticking out the top of each boot. There was another on her hip and Dox was willing to bet there were others hidden about her person.

Instead of immediately approaching their table Akosh kept her distance. She seemed to be waiting for something and a short time later a plain-faced man appeared at her shoulder. He whispered something into her ear and then disappeared into the crowd. He must have been looking for a trap. Despite having made the arrangements she clearly didn't trust them.

Satisfied that they were alone Akosh sauntered over and sat down on the only free chair in the entire square. Several times people at other tables had attempted to claim it but had been stopped by Munroe's glare. The weight of her gaze made even the bravest turn pale and back away. This, more than anything, terrified Dox. She knew Munroe had nothing to live for except revenge. She had been denied it once and Dox didn't think she would let an opportunity slip away again. Perhaps she was beyond caring. Perhaps she would kill everyone in the square just to get to Akosh.

A small cheer went up from the crowd as the pastry chef appeared in the doorway to the tea room. He bowed to the line of waiting people, made a small announcement and then went back inside. The queue shuffled forward as excited conversation and tantalising smells washed over Dox.

The square was busy and noisy, making their conversation completely private.

For a while the two women merely stared at one another. Dox could see the muscles jumping in the side of Munroe's face as she clenched her jaw over and over. Akosh was no less tense and kept moving one hand to the knife at her waist, as if to check it was still there.

"I'm going to kill you," said Munroe, which wasn't the friendliest of opening gambits. "Today, tomorrow, next week. It doesn't matter. One day it will happen."

"You're welcome to try," said Akosh with a smile that bordered on a grimace. Dox thought she was putting on a brave face but underneath was genuinely scared. "Besides, it wouldn't make any difference. I'd just be reborn."

"So you said, but I have my doubts," said Munroe.

"Then do it," said Akosh, inviting Munroe to attack. "Kill me, and in twenty years' time, when you're fat and old, I'll find you and snap your neck."

"You're so full of shit," said Munroe. "You're scared out of your mind. I can see it in your eyes."

"Murdering each other is for another day," said Dox, trying

to get them to focus on the more immediate problem. "There's something worse out there in the city. Remember?"

"I'm not sure why it's our problem," said Munroe with a shrug. "If this thing kills her it makes no difference to me."

Dox felt her embrace the Source. The pressure against her senses grew more intense until it felt as if she were deep underwater. Her chest became tight and it was difficult to breathe. Black stars danced in front of her eyes and sounds became distorted.

"Then do it," said Akosh, taunting her. "Avenge your family. Right now, maggot."

"I will make you beg," promised Munroe.

"Shut up!" shouted Dox. Both women were startled by her outburst but apart from one or two people nearby no one else really noticed. Her words were swallowed by the noise of the crowd. "You," said Dox, jabbing a finger at Akosh. "You came to me. You need our help. Is that true?"

"I don't need—"

"Yes, you do," said Dox. She didn't even need to use her Talent. "You wouldn't be here otherwise. You wouldn't risk exposing yourself like this unless you were in real danger."

Munroe chuckled at the other woman's discomfort at being dressed down by a teenage girl. Akosh was about to make a bitter retort when Dox cut her off. "And you," she said, pointing at Munroe. "Stop pretending you don't care about anyone else. If that were true you wouldn't have saved the orphans when the building collapsed. Also, you'd have killed Akosh and everyone in the square the moment she sat down. Both of you, stop fucking lying and have an adult conversation."

Dox's outburst proved to be draining as she flopped back in her chair, suddenly tired and hungry. Lying didn't normally have an effect on her but being wedged between two people who hated each other with a passion was taking its toll.

To fill the uncomfortable silence Munroe ordered another pot of tea and some sweetcakes. The tea arrived quickly but judging by the number of people racing out of the bakery she thought their food might take a while. Determined not to break the silence Dox sat back and closed her eyes. For a long time neither woman spoke, even when the small diamond-shaped pastries arrived.

Dox quickly gobbled down two of them, savouring the sweetness of the honey and the crunch of the chopped nuts. It was gooey and delicious and both women made similar noises of approval.

"Is she your daughter?" asked Akosh, gesturing at Dox.

"Gods, no," said Munroe. Dox tried not to take it personally but was also grateful Munroe hadn't mentioned her family. It would have sent her into another rage spiral that would have led to more threats. And at least they were talking about something other than killing each other.

"She swears like you."

One corner of Munroe's mouth lifted. "Yes, she does." She almost sounded proud.

"Did she tell you about what is hunting me?" asked Akosh.

"A little," admitted Munroe. "She said it was something dangerous and powerful."

"Imagine your worst childhood nightmare made flesh. A horror of mangled limbs, tentacles and a hundred eyes. Something devious, monstrous and without mercy that lives and thrives in the shadows. Now imagine it was a thousand years old and more powerful than any Sorcerer." Dox could hear the fear in Akosh's voice and knew it was genuine. Munroe must have noticed it too because she was taken aback.

"What does it want?" she asked.

"What do any of us want?" said Akosh rhetorically. "Power. He wants every single mortal to pray to him and no one else. He wants to swallow up every one of my brethren until we're all slaves to his will. He's already eaten a few."

"Eaten?" said Dox, her glass rattling against its saucer. She hadn't even noticed her hands were shaking.

"He's absorbed at least half a dozen and is feeding off their energy," said Akosh with a shiver. "You can only die once. If he catches me I'll be slowly consumed over decades. I'll wish for oblivion long before it finds me."

"I'm still struggling to see why this is my problem," said Munroe.

Dox expected another angry outburst from Akosh but she just shook her head. "Then let me make it clear. For every one of my brethren that he absorbs and every mortal that pays him tribute he grows stronger. Can you imagine the entire world in his control? Do you know what that would be like?"

"It doesn't sound too bad," said Munroe with a shrug, but Dox's Talent told her she was lying.

"In the old days, long before I existed, your ancestors prayed to the sun, the Maker and old bloody gods whose names have been forgotten. He comes from that time and was called Khai'yegha, the Eater of Souls, the Pestilent Watcher." Akosh's voice sent a chill through Dox despite the warm glass of tea she was clutching. "They captured slaves from opposing tribes and sacrificed them, cutting out their hearts on an altar. But this wasn't just once in a while. It was every day. Later, as the number of mortals increased and towns grew into cities, it was disease and rot that fed him. If Kai becomes the dominant power it will mean constant war, famine and suffering, which breeds infection and misery. It means chaos simply because he likes it. A world at peace doesn't nourish him. Would you want to go back to that? Entire nations bending their knee and praying to him, where disobedience means death. No warnings. No discussion. Just a bloody knife and an altar."

"Wait, you said he feeds on disease?" said Dox.

"Yes, before you ask, the plague in Perizzi is because of him. He's feeding on the victims and their suffering."

Dox gulped down her tea, savouring the burn against the back of her throat, although it didn't warm her through. Her entire body was flushed with terror because she knew every word Akosh said was the truth. If they lost this fight that was the future awaiting them. It was clear Akosh didn't really care about mortals, not even those who followed her, but she needed them for her survival. And she knew they couldn't stand idly by and do nothing, leaving the world to be enslaved.

Munroe said nothing for a while. She just stared at the table, sipped her tea and ate a couple of small pastries. Dox gobbled up another three in quick succession but the sugar failed to give her any new energy. It felt as if she'd been awake for days.

"What, exactly, are you proposing?" asked Munroe.

"An alliance, albeit briefly, to fight him," said Akosh. "You need to understand it might not make the slightest bit of difference. In which case you'll be dead and I'll be in constant agony, being fed upon for years."

Munroe's smile showed what she thought of that idea. "Either way, it sounds like I win."

"Won't he just come back?" asked Dox. "If we somehow manage to kill him."

"He'll be reborn, but it will take years before he can try again. That gives us time, which we don't have right now. He's been backed into a corner and will fight for his survival." Dox knew that Akosh was also speaking for herself. She had nowhere else to turn and this was her last chance.

"What do we need to do?" asked Dox, trying to avoid another round of insults.

"Draw him out and then attack him."

"That's it?" said Dox.

"He likes to stick to the shadows. Getting him to show his face is not going to be easy," admitted Akosh.

"Then I think we need some bait," said Munroe. "By now he's probably worked out that you're no longer his lackey."

Akosh took a deep breath, perhaps swallowing an insult, before speaking. "I've been sneaking around and hiding from him for days. He knows."

"What would happen if you were suddenly seen in public?" asked Munroe.

Akosh was already shaking her head. "He'll just send one of his people with a message."

"Are you sure? Won't he be upset with you for ignoring him?" asked Munroe.

"No," said Akosh and Dox heard the lie. She glanced at Munroe and shook her head.

"What if you were seen trying to leave the city? Would that upset him?"

It was slowly becoming apparent to both women that if this was going to work each had to compromise. Munroe would have to temporarily put aside her vendetta and in return Akosh would have to put herself at risk. She was already in danger but this would be far worse.

When he came for Akosh they would be laying in wait, ready to strike. Dox hoped that it would be enough and that Munroe would go through with the plan. It was possible she would hold back in order to see Akosh suffer or let her be destroyed.

"If I make a few public enquiries about leaving the city, maybe hiring a carriage, that could draw him out," said Akosh.

"If you were leaving late at night, it would mean a smaller crowd," said Dox, thinking that other people might get caught in the middle of a battle. From the matching expression on both women's faces neither of them had considered it. "It would also mean fewer witnesses, which he might believe if you were trying to sneak away."

"That's true," conceded Akosh. "He has spies in the city and I only know a few of them."

"When?" asked Munroe, which was the next obvious question. Their tenuous alliance wouldn't last for long.

"The sooner the better," said Akosh, mirroring Dox's thoughts. "I'll make enquiries today and plan to leave the city tomorrow at midnight via the southern gate."

"We'll be there," promised Dox, before Akosh could threaten Munroe if she didn't turn up. With their business concluded Akosh got up from the table and walked away. The plain-faced man appeared in the crowd beside her and together they vanished into the flow of bodies.

It was only then Dox noticed Munroe's knuckles were white on the arms of her chair. When Akosh had disappeared Munroe struggled to unclench her fingers. It made Dox wonder how close she, and everyone else in the square, had come to dying at Munroe's hands.

As Kai stared at the prostrate man on the floor he struggled to repress the urge to smash his head against the wall until it was nothing more than a soggy red pulp. Without realising what he was doing the shadows in the room stretched until they blocked out all natural light. His eyes adjusted to the absolute darkness while the man on the floor whimpered in terror.

After taking a series of long slow breaths he slowly regained a semblance of calm. The darkness receded and natural daylight flooded the room through the open windows.

"Stand up," said Kai, and the man jumped to do as he was told. "What was your name again?" he asked, having already forgotten.

"Doggett."

He knew the man was one of Akosh's people but recently Doggett had joined the growing ranks of those who'd been enslaved by his servant, Marran. It was this compulsion to tell Marran the truth at all times, even if it meant betraying his Mother, which had led to this revelation.

"They're planning an alliance, against me?" said Kai, making sure he'd heard the man correctly.

"Yes. The mage, Munroe, a girl and Akosh are going to ambush you." Doggett spoke without hesitation but blood was now trickling from both nostrils. He was being forced to turn against Akosh, someone who he held in the highest regard. Such disloyalty would be causing irreparable damage to his brain. He might only have a few days to live.

"Do you know where?" asked Kai.

"I have all the details," said Doggett, coughing up a wad of bloody phlegm. Maybe Kai had been generous with his estimate. It looked as if Doggett had only a few hours.

"Tell me everything," said Kai, his eyes gleaming with malice.

CHAPTER 30

The bodies of the dead had barely turned to ash when Wren and the other mages were confronted by a group of strangers. Six men and women, all infected, approached them carrying an array of crude weapons. Their leader, a bearded man wielding a pickaxe handle, looked them up and down.

"Who are you?" he asked, visibly disappointed. Perhaps he'd been expecting another delivery of provisions.

Wren was about to tell him the truth when she saw Tianne shake her head. "New arrivals," she said instead.

"You don't look sick." The man had red lesions on his forearms and down one side of his neck.

"We're all infected," said Tianne.

Rolling his neck from one side to the other the man didn't seem to hear. "Turn out your pockets."

"We don't have any food," said Wren, holding open her pack to show him the bandages and packs of herbs inside. Lying hadn't worked so she decided to try the truth instead. "We're here to help."

Tianne hissed through her teeth and Wren felt her embrace the Source. On her other side Kimme did the same, clenching her fists and readying herself for a fight.

"Let us through," said Kimme, stepping forward.

The thug laughed at her bravado but behind him the others were aware that something was amiss. A mismatched group arriving in the isolation zone probably wasn't uncommon but six uninfected teenagers posing as healers must have been rare.

"I like 'em big," said the man, licking his lips as he eyed Kimme up and down.

She didn't even wait for him to attack. With a roar Kimme unleashed the brute force of her will, lifting the man off the ground and smashing him sideways into the nearest building. The impact knocked the wind from his body and he stumbled to one knee. Unwilling to give up he scrambled to his feet using his club for support. He straightened up just in time for Kimme's fist to connect with his jaw, spinning him around.

One of the mob tried to grab her from behind but Tianne whipped her away, hooking the infected woman with her magic. The woman was dragged across the street on her stomach into the nearest building where the front door slammed closed behind her. The others realised they were facing mages and quickly scattered but their leader wasn't done. Kimme had turned away to stare down the others when he swung his club at her head. Wren had been watching and stopped it in mid-air. He stubbornly tried to pull it free but it wouldn't move. With a snarl Kimme lifted the man off the ground and made a twisting motion with her fist.

Wren heard something pop and the man screamed in pain.

"That's enough," said Wren but Kimme wasn't done. "Stop it now!" she shouted, pulling on the big girl's arm. Finally she released the thug.

He dropped to the ground, whimpering in pain and cradling his left arm. The skin was broken and Wren could see bones protruding from the wound.

"Let me help," said Wren, moving towards him. With a feral

cry he ran before she had a chance to heal him. Kimme stared after him and Wren felt her pull forward. "Let him go."

It was not the most auspicious start and although she hadn't expected a warm welcome Wren was still disappointed. Even here, at the end of the world where everyone was living on borrowed time, the worst of humanity was still apparent.

The street was deserted but Wren felt they were being watched from nearby buildings. Word of what they'd done would spread. She didn't think the man would come after them for revenge but she couldn't be certain.

They chose a direction at random, aware that soon enough they'd reach the edge of the cordon as the isolation zone was only a few streets wide. Their priorities were to find shelter and somewhere secure for the night, then they could try to help the infected. Many of the doors and ground-floor windows on the street were boarded up but even so the stench of rot and filth from inside was intense.

Between buildings the alleyways were piled high with stacks of rubbish that had been discarded by the new occupants. Wren spotted several expensive and flimsy gowns, piles of broken glass from unwanted mirrors, a metal table with twisted legs and the fly-ridden bodies of several dogs. Anything made of wood was being hoarded for fuel to stay warm. Amidst the refuse she heard the squeak of rats and scurrying of little feet.

"Hello," said a voice, startling the group. Wren felt the others embrace the Source but they didn't attack. A portly man in a grey robe cautiously moved towards them. He was bald with a tidy red beard and his ears comically stuck out from his head. The grin on his broad face was out of place in such desolate surroundings.

"I'm Andras, a priest of the Maker." Kimme instantly relaxed but Tianne remained alert, scanning the streets as if expecting an ambush. Since she'd returned from Zecorria Wren had noticed

Tianne had difficulty trusting other people. Given what had happened to her she couldn't blame Tianne but not every stranger was an enemy.

"Can we help you?" said Wren as he approached. Sensing their apprehension he paused a short distance away.

"Perhaps. I work at one of the hospitals. There are three," he offered, gesturing vaguely to his left and again to his right. "The third one is back this way," he said, jerking a thumb over his shoulder.

He made no demands and said nothing else but his intent was clear. If they were really here to help they would have to choose one of them. "Thank you."

"I saw what you did," said Andras. "I will pray to the Maker that you can truly help these people in their darkest hour."

Walking carefully the priest backed away. Even when he'd disappeared from sight Tianne didn't relax. Perhaps she couldn't until this was over, one way or the other.

"We need to choose," said Wren. "We can't stay out in the open. It makes sense to speak with other healers and find out what they know about the plague."

"I don't trust him," said Tianne.

"I know, but that doesn't change the facts. Do we follow him or head to one of the other hospitals?"

Kimme shrugged and the others looked to Wren to decide. "We should head to one of the others," said Tianne.

In less than an hour of being in the isolation zone they'd been attacked. She had to believe there were some good people worth saving and that not all were like the thugs they'd encountered.

"We follow the priest," said Wren. Tianne pursed her lips but didn't disagree. She didn't need to. Wren knew exactly what she was thinking. She also hoped it wasn't a decision they would come to regret.

A short walk brought them to a narrow street and beyond it an old battered church. The spire had fallen off at some point leaving a jagged stump. The roof was full of holes with birds nesting in the rafters and the once grand windows had been broken. Only a few jagged pieces of coloured glass still clung to the metal frames. Warm orange light glowed in all of the windows and as they approached Wren saw the first of the infected.

A woman and a young boy had collapsed on the stairs leading up to the church. She looked to be in the late stages as her face was a mass of swollen welts. Her hands were mangled claws and there was blood on her clothing. The boy was trying to pull her upright but he was too small. With no regard for his own health Andras picked up the woman as if she weighed nothing and carried her inside. A priest of the Holy Light, dressed in a blood-spattered robe, ushered the boy inside after his mother.

"Come inside," Andras called over his shoulder.

The thick front doors were still intact, providing an effective barrier against the cold and damp. The inside of the church had been gutted of all furniture and stripped back to the bare stone walls to provide more floor space. At least fifty infected people lay on worn beds, straw pallets and blankets spread on the floor. It wasn't crowded yet but Wren knew it would only get worse.

Half a dozen braziers spread around the room provided heat while above their heads someone had temporarily patched the holes with old wooden planks to try and keep them dry. Despite that at least a dozen leaks trickled from the rafters into buckets. Heat was escaping through the gaps in the roof and the broken windows made the church draughty but it was still warmer than outside.

A dozen priests and healers moved around the room giving comfort to the sick and the dying. Wren saw Andras lay the woman down on an empty pallet which had just been vacated.

The former occupant was a dead man who had been wrapped in a blood-stained sheet and carried through the back door.

Everywhere people were crying, moaning, being sick and weeping in pain. The air was rank with the smell of blood, vomit, shit and death.

"Are you here to help or just stand there?" said one priest, a ragged woman with short blonde hair. Wren noticed all of the priests had short hair and she suspected it was to prevent lice.

The others behind her hadn't moved and judging from their horrified expressions they were reconsidering their decision. But it was far too late. Tianne recovered more quickly than the others and a steely gleam entered her eyes.

"To help," said Wren, watching as Tianne moved to the bedside of a middle-aged woman. "Kimme, can you do something about the ceiling and the windows?" she asked.

The farm girl glanced up and grunted. "I'll need to scavenge some materials."

"Take Baedan with you," she said, gesturing at the stout Yerskani boy. He wasn't particularly adept at healing but his connection to the Source was almost as strong as Kimme's. Together the two of them would make a fearsome team if anyone tried to tackle them outside the church. "Try not to hurt anyone."

"No promises," said Kimme, clenching her jaw.

"Rue, see if you can help Andras." The petite girl from Shael had a delicate touch, making her the ideal candidate to be a healer. Her skills were progressing but none of them had anticipated such a difficult challenge so early. "Valmor, see what they're doing with the dead."

The tall girl from Seveldrom was almost a mute even though she could speak. She always wore a black scarf or choker around her neck to cover up the scar where people from her village had tried to hang her. Despite her ordeal she was still incredibly determined and Wren knew dealing with the dead wouldn't upset her.

Now the only task that remained was the most difficult and the one she'd been putting off. Trying to find a cure.

Out of excuses Wren moved to Tianne's side where she was inspecting an infected woman. She was in the early stages and still breathing comfortably, unlike many of those around her who were vomiting or choking for air.

Closing her eyes to the misery Wren embraced the Source and all of her fears ebbed away. Reaching out with her senses she inspected the sick woman, getting her first real look at the infection.

It had been three days since they'd arrived at the church and Wren was no closer to finding a cure. She'd barely slept, ate sparingly and spent most of her time studying the infection. She'd spoken to all of the other healers and priests but they were also at a loss. All of their combined skills and knowledge came to nothing. The best they could do was give patients kammra root to ease their suffering towards the end when the pain was intense.

After studying several patients Wren knew that the infection typically started in the stomach and lungs, before spreading to other organs. From there it ate the person alive, digging into each organ to make them suffer. It caused vomiting, red painful welts on the skin, a high temperature and finally death from blood loss, dehydration and internal damage. A simple healing weave had no effect. To fight such a complex structure she needed to build something from multiple layers which she'd accomplished in the past.

More people had been brought into the church, which was now a lot warmer than when they had arrived. She hadn't asked and Kimme hadn't told her how but she'd found enough wood to seal all of the holes in the roof to make it watertight. Thick curtains covered the windows to keep out the wind and yet they allowed some of the stench to escape. Many of the patients were now complaining about being too warm with some casting off their blankets as they thrashed about on their beds.

Locarr, the man in front of her, was a local and only a few years older than Wren. From talking to him over the last two days she'd learned he was an apprentice candlemaker. His mother was still alive, and thankfully healthy, but his father had died when he was a young boy. When it happened he'd been forced to find work and had been doing well until he'd been infected. He still didn't know how it had happened, although he'd been quite vague about a recent birthday celebration. Wren had suspicions about how he'd caught the plague but she wasn't there to judge him.

"It must be bad," said Locarr. "You're scrunching up your eyes."

Wren forced herself to relax as she released the Source. In less than a week the infection had reached his kidneys, which meant he only had a few days left. The plague moved faster through some people than others. "Get some rest," she said, having quickly learned not to make promises or offer false hope about a cure.

So far all of their efforts with magic had come to naught. Every day people were carried out the back door in bedsheets never to be seen again. The priests had been burning the bodies but had been using up valuable wood to fuel the fire. Now, once a day when it was dark, Valmor and usually Tianne consumed the bodies with magic fire. The flames were more intense and the blaze hotter so that in only a short time nothing remained but ash. Sometimes Wren went outside to watch the fire as the blaze dried her tears making it difficult for others to tell that she'd been crying.

She moved to Andras's side where he was tending to a young boy. He'd arrived at the church at the same time as them three days ago. The boy's mother had little time left but the boy was doing better. The only symptom he had was a small rash on one arm.

"It's barely noticeable," said Andras, ruffling the boy's hair. Wren thought the infection had spread a little but she made sure it didn't show on her face.

She was enormously relieved that Tianne had been wrong about the priest. He was one of the most caring and genuine people she'd ever met. In some ways he reminded her of Master Yettle, the Healer.

"They've been gone a long time," said Wren.

"It's normal," said Andras, accepting a hand to get up from the floor. He was older than she'd guessed, approaching sixty, and sometimes his hips were a little stiff.

Every five days the city delivered a new shipment of supplies for those inside the isolation zone consisting of food, bandages, sheets, clothes and herbs for the healers. Until their arrival there had been a constant battle between the different groups to grab as many supplies as possible. There was plenty to go around but once again Wren had been let down by the selfish nature of some people. To her there was little point trying to stockpile food as no one who was infected survived for more than two weeks. But groups and communities still formed and habits started by one person were passed on to the rest of the group. Andras had tried talking to them but they didn't want to listen and had chased him away.

To ensure that everyone received a fair portion Kimme, Baedan and Tianne were on hand for the delivery. If any group tried to take more than their share Kimme and the others would stop them, hopefully without casualties. There was enough death and pain without them causing more. The visit to the gate also gave them an opportunity to speak, at a distance, to the Khevassar and inform her of their progress, or lack thereof.

While she, Tianne, Valmor and Rue were focused on healing, Kimme and Baedan had become informal guards, keeping the peace in the hospital and the surrounding area. Both of them lacked the necessary subtlety for such complex healing and were better suited to the task. It also gave them something on which to focus and occupy their minds. Wren had seen Kimme's face when the dead bodies of small children were carried out to be burned. The farm girl was as tough as they came but Wren knew she felt helpless in the face of such a relentless disease. At least she now had a role that made a difference to the lives of the people around her.

Healing had always seemed impossible and totally impenetrable to Wren. Her knowledge of the body was excellent but it meant little if her magic refused to work. It was only recently, because of practice or intuition, that she'd had a moment of clarity. After that, while never easy, she was able to create healing weaves with three layers. The others said her skill was remarkable but she knew they were just being kind. It was rudimentary but she was getting better every day.

"You look tired," said Andras, startling Wren from her reverie. She'd been drifting, almost asleep on her feet. "Get some rest."

"I will, I promise," she said, knowing that if she didn't sleep soon she would collapse. Then she'd be no good to anyone. She'd been making sure the others took regular breaks but so far hadn't been following her own advice.

Valmor was tending to one patient while Rue was taking a break. From where she was standing Wren could hear Val talking in a quiet but soothing voice to the woman. She only had a little time left. Sometimes the patient didn't want to hear any more prayers, but they could offer companionship and a friendly face. No one wanted to die alone. Val held the woman's hand and wiped a damp cloth across her fevered brow.

When someone cried out in pain Wren instinctively moved towards the sound. It was amazing how quickly she'd adapted. Normally such a sound would send her running or looking for others to help. As it happened she reached the dying man first, eased him back into his bed and accepted a damp cloth from Andras. The old priest's expression told her everything she needed to know. The man had little time left.

"Will you remember me?" he asked deliriously. Several times he'd mistaken Wren for his daughter. She'd died of the plague before they'd arrived but he'd already forgotten.

"Of course," she said, holding on to his grasping hand. Another spasm of pain wracked his body, causing his spine to lift off the bed. Embracing the Source she reached out with her senses to make another attempt at curing the plague, or at the least relieve his pain.

In her mind she could see the infection as it spread through the body like a mass of thorny tendrils that dug into each organ. Every time she attempted to cut off one of the limbs another sprouted in its place. There was no heart to the infection. It fed off the host and used that energy to replicate itself while causing agonising pain. As she delved deeper, following the black threads twined around the man's organs, she was aware that he'd fallen silent. This often happened but it wasn't a solution, merely a distraction. The infection had reached several parts of his brain. She could see black veins growing through the tissue. He would be dead in moments.

Wren made one last desperate attempt. She was exhausted, didn't really understand what she was doing, but had to try. She was her last hope. Channelling power from the Source she started to create a lattice weave, building it up slowly and meticulously in layers. The first to treat the skin, calm the sores and drain the infection. A second to unravel the coils around his kidneys to help pump clean blood around the body. A third to ease the heart infection and keep him alive. She knew that he needed a fourth, to sever the infection in his brain to stop it getting worse. Repairing the damage was impossible but she tried not to focus on that.

Wren tried to add a fourth layer but she almost lost control and the weave threatened to fall apart. Sticking with three layers for the time being seemed wise. Eventually she managed to stabilise the weave but her grip threatened to slip at any moment.

Sweat was running down the sides of her face. She was aware of her own heavy breathing but she persisted, laying the weave across his body.

For the briefest of moments it seemed to be working. The heart relaxed, his kidneys began to work normally and the infection contracted. All too quickly it sprouted new limbs, digging into his lungs, making him gasp for air. A second thread burrowed into his brain and he screamed. Wren's weave collapsed and she fell back, also struggling for breath. By the time she'd recovered and the black spots had faded from her eyes the man was dead.

She'd failed.

"We'll take care of him," promised Andras, helping her up. Despair threatened to engulf her but more powerful than her misery was the need for sleep. Her body was already physically drained and now she'd taxed her reserves even further. There would be time enough for tears once she'd slept.

As Wren was shuffling towards the stone cellar, where she and the other healers rested, she saw Valmor returning from outside. She was stumbling and blood was running from the corner of her mouth. Val slumped sideways and Wren managed to catch her before she hit the ground.

"Help. We need help!" shouted Wren.

"I was looking for Rue," whispered Val. "There was a group of them. They hit me from behind and dragged her away. They've taken her."

CHAPTER 31

Tammy hissed in pain as her teacher's wooden sword rapped her on the knuckles. Before she had a chance to complain his follow-up caught her on the elbow. With a grunt of pain her sword fell from numb fingers to the floor.

"Pick it up," he said, clearly disappointed.

"I think I'm done," said Tammy. She'd been weary even before the training session had started. Getting a full night's sleep wasn't possible at the moment. She snatched a few hours, here and there, but it was never enough. Some nights, instead of going home, she dozed off in one of the storage rooms at Unity Hall but there was always another crisis that needed her attention.

"We are not finished," he insisted.

"Let's just leave it for today."

He hated to repeat himself so instead just pointed at the fallen sword. Sometimes, in a rare idle moment, she wondered why at his age he was a teacher in Perizzi. He had given up wearing the Drassi mask of service many years ago but for some reason had not returned home afterwards. Knowing nothing about him usually made their lessons easier. He became a nameless opponent, not a friend, allowing her to focus on nothing but her sword. All other thoughts were driven from her mind because she was facing a Drassi Swordsmaster whose skill far surpassed hers. It would take her another twenty years of practice before she had a chance of beating him.

Today she regretted having never asked about his family or background. Did he have anyone he cared about in the city? Did he know anyone who'd been sent into the isolation zone? How many of his friends had died in there?

"Why are you here?" she asked.

Instead of answering he lowered his sword and gave her the smallest of bows. "Do you wish to continue with our sparring sessions?"

"Perhaps when this is over," she said with a vague gesture. He knew she was the Khevassar but nothing else. He obviously preferred it that way as well.

"As you wish."

He left without another word while she tidied up the room and changed out of her sweaty clothing. Tammy had hoped a sparring session would clear away the cobwebs and give her some clarity of thought but she was still struggling to concentrate.

She was aware that in the last week she'd become short tempered but she wasn't the only one. Everyone was on edge and having sleepless nights. Even so other Guardians quickly moved out of the way when they saw her coming in the corridors of Unity Hall. Some of it was undoubtedly due to her position but it was also because of what she'd done to the murderer. Hanging him in public had sent a message but now everyone, strangers and Guardians alike, were afraid of her. Without her family, and anyone to really call a friend beyond the Old Man, she'd never felt so lonely.

As she crossed the city heading for Unity Hall her feelings of isolation blossomed into despair. A pallor of smoke constantly drifted above the city from the nightly fires in the isolation zone.

Depending on the direction of the wind every morning a different part of the city awoke to a grey sheet covering the buildings and roads. Everyone knew what it meant and did their best to ignore it. They just swept it into the gutters and tried to carry on as normal.

Since the quarantine began the main streets of the city had become quiet, lacking the usual crowds of locals and visitors. At times Tammy was the only person walking down some of the side streets making them feel eerie, even in broad daylight.

Many of the businesses had decided to close until the plague had passed making some parts of the city seem abandoned. The butchers, bakers and other food sellers were still open, but anything non-essential was silent and dark. Some people stayed in their homes and only ventured out in search of food when necessary.

Others had decided to handle the crisis in a different way. Almost every tavern in the city remained open and they continued to serve drinks from early morning to late at night despite the obvious risks. Everyone needed an outlet to deal with their pain and while some had turned to violence, which she and the Guardians were tackling, the majority sought to numb it with beer, wine and whisky.

People flocked to the taverns that remained open but instead of being noisy inside each was wrapped in a peculiar strained silence. People muttered into their beers, spoke in whispered tones and eyeballed each other for symptoms. Every time someone coughed a mild panic ran through the crowd.

The Watch was keeping a close eye on all of the taverns and regular patrols from the army helped to maintain the peace. But it was all balanced on a knife edge and each day they squashed angry mobs or arrested people for horrific acts of violence and sometimes murder. Normally peaceful people, those who'd never been in trouble before, were finding themselves in a cell with no real knowledge of what they'd done or why. Day by day a peculiar form of madness was slithering into the city.

Even at this early hour, when most people were asleep, there were a dozen people sitting outside one of the taverns. The Captain of the Watch keeping an eye on them inclined his head as she passed. All of the drinkers also tracked her progress down the street.

The only good news was that the number of people being infected was falling. The isolation zone and precautions they'd insisted upon were slowly working but that was small comfort to any family who had watched a loved one dragged away by the army because they were infected. As well as trying to find a cure every doctor and apothecarist in the city was busy tending to injuries from the daily scuffles.

In addition to the plague there were still a number of serious problems to deal with. At least a dozen times a day she heard about children going missing from home only to be found hours later. With the schools closed they were being kept indoors and many were too young to understand the danger. Sneaking out to play with their friends seemed like a fun game until they were brought home by a Yerskani soldier. It was even worse when they couldn't locate the child or they were found with an infection.

A rumour had begun to circulate that someone was using the plague to abduct children but so far none of her Guardians had found any truth to the story. Tammy did nothing to quash the rumour, letting it spread in the hope that it would serve as a deterrent for any child thinking of going out to play.

The entire city was holding its breath, just waiting for the next outbreak. Every day she saw the strain on her own people getting worse. Yesterday she'd stepped in to break up a fight between two Guardians. When questioned neither could really tell her why they'd been fighting.

Guardians were problem solvers. They had no way to fight the plague. Frustration in the face of an enemy they couldn't fix was seeping into all her people.

The best they could do was try to contain it. Once they'd traced the origin of the plague, at the Red Lion tavern, and how it was being spread the only thing left to investigate were new outbreaks. But even when they located the infected there was no feeling of pride. Having someone taken away to face certain death among strangers was difficult to swallow day after day.

By the time she reached Unity Hall Tammy was struggling to throw off her melancholy, knowing that the day had only just begun and was likely to get worse. When she stepped into her outer office and Rummpoe rose to her feet Tammy knew something was wrong. These days her secretary was always pale-faced and tense, hunching her shoulders and dry washing her hands, but today she was particularly anxious. Her eyes were red-rimmed from crying and she kept sniffing.

A sliver of ice traced its way down Tammy's spine as her mind conjured up the worst possible scenarios. Her secretary wasn't prone to tears so that meant it was someone close to her. Perhaps someone close to them both.

Fear tightened her throat but eventually she managed to ask, "What's happened? Is it the Old Man?"

Rummpoe shook her head. "No, he's fine."

Her secretary knew her name and a little about her background, but she didn't know about her sister and family. The Old Man had kept that to himself to protect them.

"Then who?"

"My father," said Rummpoe, quickly wiping the tears that ran down her face. "He had a rash on one arm . . ."

She didn't need to say any more. They both knew what it meant.

"When?" asked Tammy.

"Last night. He's already inside. I didn't get a chance to say goodbye."

Despite their difficult first meeting and often strained relationship she did care about Rummpoe. They weren't exactly friends so Tammy wasn't sure if she needed sympathy or something else.

"If you need to be at home with your mother—"

"No," said Rummpoe. "I need to work. I need to make sure this doesn't happen to other people."

Tammy gave Rummpoe's shoulder a brief squeeze which she seemed to appreciate.

Barely an hour after sitting down there was a frantic knocking at her door. Rummpoe burst in looking distraught, but the focus of her grief had shifted.

"What's happened?"

"There's a man. He's asking for you," said Rummpoe.

"Who is he?"

"I don't know. A group of soldiers picked him up. There was a fight and ... " She struggled to find the right words.

"Is he here? Show him in," said Tammy.

Rummpoe shook her head. "He's infected. They're outside."

Normally anyone with symptoms was immediately escorted to the isolation zone. Then again this was the first time that someone had asked to see her. Pulling on her coat and adopting a neutral expression that was fast becoming her everyday mask Tammy made her way to the front of Unity Hall.

Stepping outside she glanced at the lead-grey sky and noted it wasn't yet midday. A light annoying rain was drifting down that meant eventually water seeped into every nook and cranny. Tiny rivulets were forming around her collar, running down the back of her neck, soaking the inside of her shirt.

Across the square a squad of Yerskani soldiers were keeping

a close eye on one man. Three of them had unsheathed their swords as if expecting trouble although their prisoner appeared to be unarmed. One of the squad held the prisoner's blade in her hand, its surface awash with blood. Uncaring of the weather the prisoner was sat on the ground with his face towards the sky, tasting the rain on his tongue as it washed blood from his face. Even at this distance she recognised the shaggy beard and curve of his jaw. She'd spent many nights staring at his features in the dark.

It was Kovac.

Her uncaring mask cracked but no one noticed. By the time she'd crossed the square she was back in control.

As she approached Tammy noticed blood on Kovac's hands and splashes on his armour. A small red pool was slowly forming around him on the ground.

"We didn't touch him," said the squad leader, noting her expression. "We found him like that, covered in blood, surrounded by dead bodies."

Kovac lowered his head and opened his eyes. They were exactly as she remembered. For a second time she almost lost control, especially when she noticed the red lesion on one side of his face.

"I had a disagreement with someone," said Kovac with a lopsided smile.

"Who?"

"Tars Lohan."

Tammy rocked back on her heels but none of the soldiers twitched at the name. Tars was a suspected murderer, known wife-beater and vicious loan shark. When someone fell behind on their payments he didn't hire someone else to dole out punishment. He did it himself because he enjoyed the work.

Several times his wife had turned up at a doctor's or an apothecary after falling down the stairs or walking into a door. Tammy knew of at least six people, four men and two women, that had vanished only to turn up dead in an alley after being viciously beaten to death. Their skin had been so badly bruised they'd barely looked human. Everyone knew who had done it and why but no one dared come forward.

She was about to ask Kovac if he'd done it because he owed money when she saw his expression. He'd done it for her and for the others who'd suffered.

"I'll escort him to the isolation zone," said Tammy, holding out a hand for his sword.

The soldier complied, happy to be away from her and the blood-covered man. She waited until they'd retreated down the street before turning to face Kovac.

"Do you know what they call you?" he asked, a wry smile on his face. "The Steel Giant."

She grunted. "I thought as much. Still, there are worse nicknames."

Standing in the rain together, on an abandoned street, Tammy was briefly reminded of their time together in Voechenka. Kovac must have been thinking the same thing because he muttered something about the Forsaken which, in spite of everything, made her smile.

"How long?" she asked, gesturing at the red rash on his neck.

"Spotted it yesterday."

"We need to go this way," she said, pointing down the street. Walking a few paces apart the two of them made their way across the city towards the isolation zone. "Why kill Tars?"

Kovac shrugged. "Why not? I've nothing to lose and he was filth. A friend of mine was a day late and Tars cut off one of his fingers. A day."

"Who were the others?" she asked. "The soldiers said you were surrounded by dead bodies."

"They were exaggerating. There were only five," he said with a wink. "They were some of Tars' cronies. No one will mourn them."

A heavy silence settled. With every step it felt as if she were walking him towards the headsman.

"Why did you come back?" she asked, desperate to touch him but unwilling to take the risk.

"I tried to stay away—went on a few jobs here and there—but in the west all roads lead to Perizzi. I didn't plan this," he said, gesturing at himself. "I didn't tell anyone about you. Not a single word. I'd never betray you."

Tammy sighed. "I know." His loyalty had never been in question.

"I just wanted to see you one last time."

A response caught in her throat. For a time the only sound in the world was the gentle patter of the rain.

As the gate to the isolation zone drew closer a desperate thread of hope surfaced in her mind.

"I need you to do me a favour," she said, choosing her words carefully.

"Name it."

"A few days ago a group of young mages went inside."

Kovac raised an eyebrow. "Mages? From the Red Tower?"

"It's a long story. They're trying to find a cure. There's no guarantee it will work, but at this point, we've nothing to lose."

"What do you want me to do?"

"Protect them," she said. "They're young and naïve. Inside there, I can only imagine what desperate people with nothing to lose would do to them."

As the gate came into view the soldiers guarding it saw them approaching and came to attention. Even at this distance Tammy was easily recognisable.

"I will help them, for as long as I'm able," he promised.

She desperately wanted to say something. But now they were being watched. In a few moments the soldiers would be within earshot. She was running out of time.

"My feelings haven't changed," she whispered and in spite of everything he smiled.

When they reached the soldiers she explained the situation and they readied themselves to open the gate. Several took up their crossbows while others gathered spears. So far no one had tried to escape but in this situation they couldn't take any risks.

Tammy returned Kovac's sword, earning a raised eyebrow from one of the soldiers. They did not send armed people into the zone. Kovac would be the first.

They were out of time and out of words. This was not the place for sweet partings or tears of regret. She was the Khevassar and he was a mercenary.

They stared at each other for a long moment, trying to say so much with their eyes. She tried to remember every detail of his face as this was the last time she'd ever see him.

"Sir," said one of the soldiers, awaiting her signal.

"Open the gate," she said, without breaking eye contact.

Kovac gave her a smile and without hesitation walked past the soldiers, through the gate and into certain death. When it closed behind him, with a hollow thud, it felt as if the last part of her that could feel hope had died.

Chapter 32

The southern gate of Herakion was the busiest in the city but at this late hour there were only a handful of people roaming about. Two pairs of guards were trying their best not to laugh as a merchant struggled with a stubborn mule.

Ahead of the struggling merchant on the road another merchant train had just begun the long journey south. Three flat-bed carts were protected by a Fist of masked Drassi whose keen eyes scanned the land around them for trouble.

Eventually the merchant managed to shift his beast and the guards cheered him on. Akosh stood off to one side, trying her best to look inconspicuous and bored. As agreed she'd made a number of not so subtle enquiries about leaving the city and travelling south in a hurry. After securing a luxury carriage to take her to Perizzi, and paying half of the extortionate fee up front, she'd spent the day in hiding.

It still galled her that despite the number of followers in Herakion the city had become a prison. She could send every one of her people against Kai and it wouldn't make a difference. He was just too strong. In a foul mood she'd lurked in a run-down tavern all day drinking wine and counting the hours until it was time to spring the trap.

There was a good chance it would all go horribly wrong but with Kai breathing down her neck and Vargus due to arrive any day, her chances of survival were already slim. Surrounded by enemies who wanted to either kill or feast on her, Akosh could almost feel the noose tightening around her neck.

Not far away she could feel a strong pulse from the Source, so she knew that the mage was watching. It had occurred to her that Munroe might only have shown up to watch her die. The girl, Dox, had promised they would help but when the moment came revenge might be all that mattered. If Kai took the bait and came in person then he would make short work of her so at least Munroe would be happy.

The loud clatter of hooves startled Akosh from her reverie as a black carriage pulled by four white horses drew to a halt at the gate. The driver hopped down, stretched his back and looked around for his fare.

The time for hiding was over. After taking a deep breath to calm her nerves Akosh moved out of the shadows towards the driver. She couldn't sense if Kai was close by but there was no way to tell. Her brethren often walked among the mortals and they could conceal their true identity from everyone. She would know he was here when he wanted her to, and not a moment sooner.

"Did you think I'd let you run?" said a voice. Akosh looked around for the source but couldn't see Kai until he stepped out of the carriage. As usual he resembled a handsome and healthy man that many women found attractive. If only they knew what was lurking under the mask of skin. They'd be driven insane by the sight of his true face.

He was at ease so she tried to match it. "It was worth a try. I didn't want to end up as just another meal."

Kai made a dismissive gesture towards the carriage. The driver took the hint, turned the horses around and drove it away, leaving the two of them alone on the street. The guards suddenly made themselves scarce and anyone who'd been lurking faded away.

She didn't know if it was something Munroe had planned to limit the number of casualties, or an effect that Kai was having on the bystanders. While the gesture might have soothed Munroe's mind it had the opposite effect on Akosh. Being alone with Kai terrified her more than time in the Void or a final end. Without witnesses he had no need to hide what he was and even wearing a human mask his true nature was starting to leak out. His eyes glowed red and the skin on his face rippled as something beneath it moved.

Munroe needed to hit him hard and fast. It would be the only way. Once she'd distracted him Akosh would draw on her reserves and attack on a second front. It was likely he'd brought some of his servants with him but anyone caught in the middle of such a battle would be torn to shreds.

"You are mine," said Kai with a sibilant hiss. "My tool, my meat." His jaw cracked open, the skin splitting across his face as something started to emerge from the depths of his throat.

If Munroe didn't hit him soon it would all be over.

"You're nothing but an arrogant old fool." Akosh was playing for time, hoping that Munroe was as good as her word. Her insult caught Kai's attention and the human mask began to repair itself. The skin across his face knitted itself back together until he could speak again.

"A fool, am I? Do you really think so?" Kai made a beckoning gesture and someone began to walk towards them from the mouth of a nearby alley. At first glance the man was unfamiliar as he walked with an unsteady gait. As he drew closer Akosh caught sight of his face and her eyes widened in surprise.

It was Doggett.

Dried blood stained the bottom half of his face like a brown beard and two fresh rivulets ran from his nostrils. He kept walking forward like a puppet whose strings had been cut. Behind him came a group of people she didn't recognise.

"I'm sorry, Mother," he managed to gasp.

"Be silent," said a scruffy-looking man in a palace uniform. Beside him were a group of teenagers with matching facial tattoos.

"It's a trap," said Doggett, forcing each word out from between his clenched jaw. The effort cost him greatly as he collapsed on to his side and started convulsing. It took only a few seconds and then he was dead, blood running from the corner of his mouth. Akosh was about to curse him when she looked again at the group standing behind Doggett. The scruffy man was a mage and with him were perhaps eight or ten young people. All of them wore the same uniform, which made them members of the Regent's cadre. Even more worrying was the way they were all staring at her. There was something wrong with them.

"What have you done?" said Akosh.

Kai misinterpreted her question, smiling down at Doggett's corpse. "I told you not to get attached to them. It's your own fault."

"Not him. Them," she said, pointing a finger at the mages. She could see narrow black wires extending from the scruffy mage towards the others. They'd been enslaved to his will. Even worse she could see the impact it was having.

They were dying.

Every day, as they fought against their mental prison, their bodies were being destroyed piece by piece. Such dangerous and ruthless magic had not been used since the war.

Kai merely shrugged. "They're servants, nothing else."

To him there was no difference. One mortal was exactly the same as another. All of them were there to serve his will. For a long time she'd believed it too, but then a mortal had thrown her through a building. One with enough power to unmake her. One single mage.

And now Kai had nine mages in his control all under the direction of a tenth. If she could explain to Munroe what had been done Akosh was confident the mage would fly into a frenzy. It was exactly what she needed. A distraction that might buy her enough time to escape in the chaos.

Munroe probably thought she was facing a disparate group of inexperienced mages. Instead she was facing one with the power of many. Against such odds even her prodigious strength would be tested.

She turned to warn Munroe but Kai closed the distance between them with unnatural speed, clamping her jaw shut with one hand.

"This is a trap," said Kai with a broad smile. "Only now, it's my trap for you."

Munroe stared at the ten mages with surprise. Nine of them were Zecorran teenagers, many of whom she'd seen before. The tenth was an older, scruffy man, with a seedy leer that made her skin crawl. He was also a mage of moderate strength, which was unexpected. From what she'd heard the Regent had killed or chased away all mages except the youngest. Seeing an older mage leading them made her wary but her grin didn't slip. Those she'd humiliated before were trying their best to look mean but she could see they were nervous about facing her again.

Akosh tried to say something, perhaps offer a warning, but the one she'd called Kai stopped her speaking. As they began to grapple it became apparent that Akosh was in trouble. Kai threw her around like a small child and Munroe's smile stretched even wider.

"Don't you remember what happened last time?" said Munroe,

turning to address the young mages. She left Akosh to her beating. She could take it for a while.

"It's different now," said one of the young mages, a surly teenage girl. Their leader gestured for the girl to be silent. To Munroe's surprise the girl did as she was told but continued to glare. In fact all of them were looking at her with the same expression, one of genuine hatred.

"It is different now," repeated the older man.

"Who are you?" asked Munroe.

"Marran. Their teacher," he said, licking his lips.

"I don't like this," said Dox. "Something's wrong with them."

Munroe agreed but said nothing, waiting to see what they did next.

"You are under arrest," said Marran.

"Why?" she asked, playing for time. So far none of them had embraced the Source, which was weird. They'd come in force, expecting a fight, and yet weren't ready. Besides, how much could they really have learned in a few weeks?

"You're an unregistered mage." He said it as if he were speaking to a simpleton. "But the Regent is a lenient ruler. If you come with us quietly then you won't be injured. You'll be held until you can be judged."

She didn't need Dox to tell her that he was lying. She also wondered who would be judging her. Garvey had been maimed and then executed by the Regent, or so the stories claimed. She wasn't confident that their judicial system was fair and balanced.

"And if I refuse?" she asked.

"Munroe," said Dox, pulling at her sleeve. But it was too late to run.

"I told you," said the same teenage girl in a knowing voice. Marran made a cutting motion with one hand and the girl winced as if she'd been slapped.

"Dox," said Munroe, turning slightly so they couldn't see her face, "when it starts, run and hide."

She thought the girl would argue, as she often did, but for once Dox said nothing. Munroe knew she could feel it now. The sudden change in the air.

Marran raised one hand and all of the young mages drew power from the Source. Munroe did the same, drinking deeply until every part of her body came awake as if from a deep sleep. Her senses sharpened until she could hear everyone's heartbeat. Her eyesight deepened until the darkest shadows were peeled back. Every part of her skin was so sensitive that the feeling of her clothes was almost unbearable. Even her sense of smell dramatically improved until Dox's fear sweat became apparent.

Marran was terrified as well, although she didn't think it was because of her. His eyes kept darting to where Kai was holding Akosh off the ground with one hand. She was struggling to break free but her attempts to loosen his hand made no difference. Kai was enjoying himself, playing with her like a cat toying with a desperate mouse. Munroe thought she saw the skin on his face begin to split in two across the mouth.

"What is your decision?" asked Marran, although they both already knew her answer.

A huge wave of force rolled out from Munroe towards the mages. She intended to scatter the children and then focus on Marran. Much to her surprise, instead of flinging the children in all directions, a barrier of equal force appeared, moving towards her at speed. The two forces collided with a loud crack like a snap of thunder. The aftershock made everyone stumble but Munroe managed to remain upright.

Her ears were ringing and everyone else seemed to be suffering as well. The only people immune were Kai and Akosh as their one-sided battle hadn't stopped. Dox had fallen but quickly scrambled to her feet and ran for her life. It was one less thing to worry about.

As Munroe planned her next move she saw Marran raise both arms then mutter something to the mages. In unison they all wove fireballs in exactly the same way. Some commonality was expected, being taught by the same person, but this was something else. Something unnatural.

When she'd been at the Red Tower most pupils waved their arms about as it helped them visualise the weaves. A rare few could do it all in their heads but everyone had a distinct style.

Everything the cadre did was identical and without personality. It was then that she realised the young mages were puppets for Marran.

Changing tack Munroe started pulling together a dense shield, adding layer upon layer to create a hard barrier. She'd barely finished it when the first fireball struck. She was shielded from the heat, but it felt as if someone had clubbed her on the arm with an iron bar. Gritting her teeth she channelled more power into her shield as fire streaked through the air. Munroe felt each impact like a physical blow and just as the first barrage was done a second began. Marran was directing them so that she had no time to retaliate.

Heat from the fire began to seep through her shield and Munroe started to sweat. The air was full of smoke and glowing embers, making her eyes water. Soon she couldn't see them but the barrage continued, over and over, battering her shield.

When she'd been a pupil at the Red Tower there'd been many days when her teachers had despaired. They'd thought she'd never learn. In a fit of frustration one of her teachers had commented that if all else failed she could rely on brute force and stubbornness to see her through. No one doubted her strength, only her skill to put it to good use. Battlemages were weapons, designed to fight and protect, but she'd never been given the honorary rank, mostly because they didn't know what to do with her.

With a fierce grin Munroe kept weaving her shield while focusing her Talent on the nearest building behind the cadre. She heard the loud crack but it was quickly lost in the din of fireballs striking her shield. At first no one noticed and she was hit three more times before the barrage abruptly ended. A section of the building had fallen into the street forcing the young mages to run for cover. As they scattered Munroe dropped her shield and flung two of the mages wide with a burst of pure will. One collided with a nearby wall, bounced off and collapsed on the street. Another slammed face first into a cart. She didn't know if the girl was dead or unconscious.

Marran was trying to marshal his troops but she didn't give him a reprieve. She returned the favour, drawing heat from the air to send a ball of fire at his head. Instead of deflecting it himself he ordered two of those nearest to do it for him, which was a mistake. He was relying too much on them.

While they dithered Munroe focused on a teenage boy who was independently starting to pull something together. Instead of using magic she marched towards the boy, which sent him into a panic. He rushed backwards, tripping over his own feet.

Munroe kicked him in the face and once in the stomach, leaving him on the ground in a weeping ball. A screech behind made Munroe drop to her knees and raise a quick shield. The surly teenage girl who'd been mouthing off landed on the shield, blunting her raised dagger and knocking the wind from her chest. As she fell to her knees Munroe stamped on her hand, breaking her fingers.

"Focus!" screamed Marran, waving both arms. Like puppets dancing to a tune all of those young mages still able to fight moved in unison. They turned to face Munroe with blank eyes and each started to pull together something lethal.

Marran seemed unable to split his focus so she decided to test her theory. While controlling all of the young mages made him stronger it also robbed them of independent thought. Every attack had to be directed, leaving him with little focus to use his own magic.

Lifting a section of the fallen building from the street she sent it high into the air. Marran saw it immediately but the young mages were so focused on their task they hadn't noticed.

With a snarl he had to change tack, ordering them to run moments before the slab of stone hit the street. One of the young mages wasn't fast enough and it clipped him on the shoulder, breaking bone and almost ripping his arm off. Another one down. Marran was down to five puppets now and one of them already looked fairly unsteady on her feet. Blood was running from one nostril and when he ordered them to attack the girl collapsed.

His smug arrogance evaporated as Munroe stalked towards him, brushing off anything they threw at her. It was time to end this.

Akosh felt her spine break as Kai smashed her into the stone wall surrounding the city gate. There was an audible crunch, a spike of pain that pierced the back of her brain and then darkness crept in. Akosh tried to rush into the oblivious warmth of unconsciousness. After that it wouldn't matter what he did to her body. She wouldn't feel it any more.

"Ah ah," chided Kai, dropping her to the ground. Her power immediately asserted itself, fusing bone, popping discs back into place between the vertebrae. The skin across her back sewed itself together and gradually the darkness receded until she was awake.

Only then did Kai pick her up, hoist her into the air again with both hands this time and begin to choke her to death.

This was merely a taster of what he had planned. Her torment would last for decades, possibly longer, as she was slowly eaten alive while being drained of every drop of power she'd accumulated over the years. Her struggles made him grin as they both felt how weak she was in comparison.

"Yes," he said, almost purring. "That's it. Fight back. It makes this fun!"

Flailing around in the air Akosh managed to kick Kai in his smug face, knocking out one of his teeth. She split his bottom lip as well and a small trickle of blood ran down his face. The kick gave him pause and he dropped her to the ground, checking his face. Akosh gulped fresh air into her lungs as she tried to crawl away.

It had all gone horribly wrong. The trap had turned out to be one of Kai's making. Doggett had died trying to warn her but it was too little too late. She was no match for Kai and Munroe couldn't help as she was busy fighting the Regent's mages. A quick glance showed that she was actually winning, which was both surprising and terrifying. Akosh had never seen so much raw power in the hands of one mortal. It gave her a brief glimmer of hope that perhaps if she joined forces with Munroe they might stand a chance against Kai.

The ember was crushed as Kai's injury vanished almost immediately. A new tooth grew in to replace the old. The split lip healed and then he was glaring at her with eyes that had turned completely red.

She was on her own facing an enemy she couldn't defeat. There was only one way out. Akosh drew two daggers and stood, readying herself for battle. Kai was briefly taken aback but then he grinned, amused at her defiance.

"Yes, keep fighting," he urged her. With a flick of her wrists she flung both daggers at his stupid, handsome face. With an equally casual flick of his hands he brushed them away, but it was exactly what she needed. Drawing another dagger from her baldric she placed it against her throat and slashed open the skin. She would rather die and go into the Void, waiting to be reborn, than live another moment as his plaything. Feeling nothing, being nothing was preferable to being eaten alive.

"No!" shouted Kai, rushing towards her. She tried to laugh at his panic even as the hot blood ran down her skin, soaking into her clothes. Her knees hit the street and the world turned sideways. Unfortunately she fell into his arms rather than hitting the road. The creeping cold that had been seeping into her extremities started to recede and panic flooded her mind. It should have been the end.

Instead she felt warmth enveloping her as the glow of his power seeped into her body. Beneath the healing energy was a layer of misery, pain and sickness; the foundation for his power. Its stench flooded Akosh's senses even as she felt it rebuilding her.

She tried to struggle. She wanted to choke to death but instead she could feel her severed throat being repaired. The bleeding stopped, tissue regrew, the skin reformed and then she was breathing normally, staring up with clear eyes into the face of her monstrous saviour.

Kai's savage grin was worse than any before. "You don't get away from me that easily," he cooed, rocking her like a child as his arms tightened until it became painful and then unbearable. She was being crushed against his chest, her chin on his shoulder. In a desperate attempt she tried to turn her head and bite his neck but the breath was driven from her body. Akosh just wanted to die but even that was denied.

A sob wracked her body and unseen tears dripped down her face. She'd made no sound and yet Kai knew.

"There, there," he said, patting her on the back while also strangling her, driving his shoulder into her throat.

He'd won.

All of her work over the decades meant nothing. Akosh tried to think of something to offer him. Some juicy morsel with which to bargain, but he had everything he needed. The Regent's cadre of mages and now her. She was just another meal to him.

Even as she thought about what lay ahead Kai opened one side of his coat. The colourful lining faded away to reveal the infinite space within. A swirling universe of alien stars, inside which tormented gods suffered in agony until they were drained of their power.

"Wait," she pleaded, but Kai just shook his head. It was too late to talk her way out of this.

The membrane of the space within began to change, becoming porous as he prepared to consume her. Akosh struggled but he held her one-handed with ease.

"Stop!" said a commanding voice. It was so loud her ears rang and everyone paused to see who had spoken. Kai flinched and Akosh thought she saw something flash across his face. Something she didn't think he experienced. Fear.

Turning her head slightly Akosh saw her saviour standing beside a teenage boy from Shael.

It was Vargus.

Munroe was pressing Marran and his cadre, forcing them back, when the stranger's voice rang out. She paused but maintained her hold on the Source just in case he tried something while she was distracted.

Glancing over her shoulder Munroe was surprised to see a student she recognised from the Red Tower and a face from her past. Vargus.

In her old life, as a member of the Perizzi underworld, she'd worked for Don Jarrow and his wife. Vargus had been one of their Naibs. As one of their personal bodyguards he'd known almost as much about the Family business as those in charge. He'd been one of their most loyal with a history that spanned decades. As far as she knew he was just a soldier who'd become a bodyguard, but Akosh and Kai's reactions made her wonder if any of that was true.

It had been at least a dozen years since she'd seen him and yet, somehow, Vargus looked younger. There was colour in his hair where once it had been a uniform lead grey and he was leaner with heavy muscle across his chest and arms. He still had a sword over one shoulder but no one was worried about his blade. It was his eyes that had captured everyone's attention. They had always been a rich blue but now they were pale and cold as the heart of winter.

"What have you done?" he demanded. Kai was frozen with indecision. Munroe didn't know if he was about to attack or apologise. It was then she noticed something strange about the inside of his coat. She could see a swirling emptiness within as if it had become a window to another place. For a moment Munroe thought she saw tormented faces swimming around inside. From the look of it Kai had been about to shove Akosh inside. Perhaps her story about being eaten alive was true. With a sigh Kai seemed to deflate and the glow faded, returning the coat to cotton and silk. He let go of Akosh and she collapsed face down on the street.

"I thought you knew," said Kai. "Admit it. Deep down, some small part of you knew the truth."

"I suspected," admitted Vargus. "I didn't want it to be true."

Kai shrugged. "We are what we are. It's my nature."

"But this?" said Vargus, gesturing at the prostrate form of Akosh. "Consuming your own kind?"

Red flashed behind Kai's eyes. "I am nothing like you. It's been that way since the beginning. I embrace my nature while the rest of you have become soft and compliant. You're almost human. Sentimental." Kai calmed down and his eyes returned to their normal colour. "I was on the brink of extinction and it was you that helped bring me back."

"A decision I deeply regret," said Vargus.

Munroe glanced at Marran and his mages but those still upright were exhausted and in no position to fight.

"How many?" asked Vargus.

Kai shrugged, as if it didn't matter. "As many as I need to survive. Because that's all it's about for our kind. Survival. The mortals play games, scheme and fight each other for dirt. We endure. We watch and listen and we continue. That's our only drive because that's all He allowed."

Munroe wasn't sure who they were talking about but it sounded like they answered to someone. The thought of who that might be made her skin clammy. She quickly brushed the idea aside, afraid of where it might lead.

"What else should we do? Help the mortals? Guide them to a better future?" asked Vargus. "Or do you want to rule them?"

Kai laughed in his face. "Of course not. Don't be absurd. A whole world bending the knee in unity. Such dreams are for smaller beings," he said, nudging Akosh with his boot. She stirred a little but didn't try to crawl away. Having seen how quickly he moved earlier Munroe knew it would be easy for him to bend down and snap Akosh's neck before they reached him.

Power from the Source continued to thrum in her veins and it was perhaps because of that she noticed something different about the three of them. They all looked human but there was also a distinct absence as if they lacked something vital. She couldn't put her finger on it but the longer Munroe studied them the more apparent it became. The faces and bodies they wore were nothing but masks. Probing with her magic she wondered what lay beneath.

"You know how this must end," Vargus was saying. "There can be only one outcome."

"Perhaps," said Kai. A sly smile tugged at the corners of his mouth as if he had a dangerous secret.

"Don't do this," said Vargus. "They've already seen too much. Come with me."

"The time for hiding in the shadows is over," said Kai. His smile turned a little sad, as if he regretted what he was about to do.

"The hard way, then," said Vargus.

Staring at him now Munroe wondered how she could ever have thought he was just a bodyguard. There was something timeless and utterly terrifying in his gaze. An agelessness that made her think of the mountains. Every year they became a little more ragged but they endured regardless of wars and weather. His grizzled face gave her the same impression. That he'd seen much, suffered greatly, and yet had survived to tell the tale. Curiosity wasn't something she considered a risk, but in this case she knew different. Nevertheless she needed to know and turned her attention to Kai.

While he and Vargus talked she reached out with tendrils of magic towards him. Almost immediately she wanted to take it back as Kai's head snapped around. He was aware of what she was doing. His smile stretched wider and wider until the skin split across his cheeks. His eyes glowed red and for a brief moment she caught a glimpse of the creature within.

It was vast, old beyond her understanding of time and malicious on a scale she couldn't comprehend. It had caused endless suffering, tortured thousands and demanded human sacrifices in its name for generations. An ocean of blood, disease and pain were its nourishment. It had feasted on mortals from every race and every part of the world. It was the rot. A pestilent creature that had seen the downfall of empires, the eradication of entire races and yet it felt nothing. No compassion. No sympathy and no regret. Its only concern was its own survival and that meant more conflict, anguish and pain to feed its hunger.

Munroe was aware that someone was keening like a trapped animal. Vargus was shouting at Kai but he didn't seem to be listening.

Something was happening to Kai's face and body. He was beginning to change into something.

"Do you really want to see, little mage?" he said, pulling at the skin on his face, which sloughed off like hot wax. She caught a glimpse of something underneath that wasn't human. While her mind tried to work out what she was seeing another part of her was trying to scramble away.

Munroe didn't want to know any more. There was a growing pressure inside her chest that was squeezing her heart. She gasped but couldn't catch her breath. Her lungs were aching and her head felt light.

Akosh must have been pretending as she scrambled to her feet and tried to run. One of Kai's arms shot out to grab her. The bones and muscles stretched far longer than humanly possible, transforming it into a fleshy noose that coiled around her ankle. With a scream Akosh lashed out with a dagger, severing the arm-shaped tentacle.

Munroe was struggling to breathe, but she pushed at Kai with her innate Talent, trying to summon the worst possible thing to befall him. Black spots were starting to dance in front of her eyes and she knew he was going to kill her.

Her magic lashed out and with a bone-sickening crunch Kai's

head twisted around to face in the opposite direction, snapping his neck.

But the body didn't fall.

Akosh ran until she reached Vargus's side before keeping him in front like a shield.

The pressure on Munroe's chest disappeared and she fell to one knee, gulping in fresh air. Someone helped her up and she found Vargus was beside her now. Akosh was lurking a few steps behind, her eyes wide with terror. Beside her was the boy from Shael and, much to Munroe's surprise, Dox. She was gripping the boy's hand and Munroe could see she was trembling. But she was here, facing down the nightmare.

Grabbing his head with both hands Kai twisted it around. There was a wrenching sound and a grisly pop before it settled forward on his neck. The skin on his face was full of holes, exposing something bony and inhuman beneath. One of his arms was a mangled knot of ropey flesh that trailed on the ground. His right eye had fallen out or dissolved but instead of an empty socket Munroe saw a glowing red orb. It was fixed on her and the malevolence was unlike anything she'd experienced.

"Steady," murmured Vargus, sensing her rising terror. Taking a deep breath she fought hard to repress her urge to run screaming.

Marran and his mages were beaten. Kai was physically in a bad way but despite what they'd done to him she didn't think he was seriously injured. If anything he seemed angry rather than hurt. She also noticed there wasn't a single drop of blood anywhere.

"Soon," hissed Kai, in a grisly voice.

Waving his one good hand he gestured for Marran to withdraw. As he and the other mages shuffled away, Munroe's attention remained focused on Kai. He was staring at Vargus and a silent message passed between them. Dragging his arm behind him the monstrous thing turned and walked away. Munroe only relaxed when he moved out of sight.

A huge weight dropped on to her shoulders and she would have fallen if someone hadn't held her upright.

Kai was gone but it wasn't over. They still had to find a way to fight that thing.

Chapter 33

The number of infected in the hospital had grown to the point where they were running out of space. When Wren had first arrived the situation had been desperate. Now, as she tried to focus on healing the infected woman lying in front of her, the cries from many others disrupted her concentration. She hadn't become immune, and didn't want to ignore them, but unless she found a way to cure one person she couldn't help the rest.

At the moment the only comfort she could offer was the same as the priests and herbalists. A kind word. A gentle touch. A damp cloth to cool the burning skin. And later, when the pain inside transformed into unbearable agony, something to numb their senses. They weren't curing anyone, just tending to the dying.

So far all of Wren's attempts to stunt the growth of the infection had failed. It continued to spread throughout the body no matter what she tried. The other reason for her lack of focus was that Rue was still missing. It was now two days since she'd been abducted.

The first night without her had been the worst. Wondering where she'd been taken and if she was still alive. Wren believed Rue had been abducted because they knew she was a mage.

They were desperate people with nothing to lose. People who would do anything in the hope of obtaining a cure. Since their arrival in the isolation zone they'd created a few waves. Mostly by getting involved at the gate to make sure everyone received a fair share of the supplies. Twice Kimme and Baedan had been forced to use their magic to stop people fighting over food. No one had been seriously injured but since then word of their presence had spread.

On the first morning Kimme and Baedan had left at first light to find Rue and only returned when it was dark. It should have been easy to find her in such a small area but they'd come back empty-handed. They'd been angry at their failure and everyone feared the worst. Not knowing what had happened to their friend hurt all of them.

No one really slept during the night and Wren woke the next morning with sandy eyes and heavy limbs. The second day was painful. By now the people who'd abducted Rue would know that she couldn't cure the plague. It made Wren wonder if they'd panic and kill her or keep pressing her for a cure.

Tianne thought the abductors were evil and she'd set out with Kimme to find and punish them. Wren knew they were just desperate people who'd become reckless. The worst that could happen to them was death but they were already living on borrowed time. Once infected no one survived for more than two weeks.

The second night had passed as slowly and painfully as the first. Today was the third day and despite their past failure Kimme and Tianne had set out again. They had wanted to take Valmor with them but Wren refused. Val was needed at the hospital. Kimme started to argue but then her eyes were drawn to a woman dying on a nearby bed. Only then did she seem to remember why they had travelled all this way.

There was also the fact that if left alone at the hospital Wren wouldn't be able to focus on healing and protecting herself. The idea of a guard at a hospital was ridiculous but now they were all a little afraid of being abducted. She'd insisted a minimum of two mages stayed at the hospital at all times.

Thankfully there had also been some relief from an unexpected source. On the morning after Rue's abduction a man named Kovac had turned up at the hospital. Wren's first impression was that he'd been a soldier because of the way he carried himself. She'd been suspicious, even when he claimed that the Khevassar had sent him and they were old friends. She changed her mind when he showed Wren his sword. No one was allowed into the isolation zone with a weapon. Also the Khevassar herself had escorted him to the gate, which put Wren's mind at rest.

She knew her trust in Kovac was not misplaced and so far he'd proved to be a valuable ally. Although he was infected his condition was in the very early stages so he wasn't bedridden yet. Instead he spent the day patrolling outside or standing guard at the door. So while Tianne and Kimme hunted for Rue, Kovac and Baedan provided protection.

With the matter of their safety pushed to the back of her mind, Wren was able to focus on the challenge in front of her. Healing the sick might be beyond Kimme but she and Val still had a chance, no matter how slim. She couldn't give up. She wouldn't.

Wren hoped Rue was still alive and murmured a brief prayer. Perhaps her delicate touch with magic would flourish under pressure. If she was making progress towards a cure then her captors would keep her alive. Even if she wasn't then Rue was smart enough to fake it. She would know they were searching for her and Wren hoped that Rue could keep herself alive long enough for the others to find her.

Returning her attention to the woman lying on the straw pallet Wren drew power from the Source and closed her eyes. As its joyous majesty filled her body, setting her skin and nerves alight, she began to pull together a single-layered weave. After days of practice this first stage had become relatively easy. It was what she did next that was the real challenge.

In what felt like a lifetime ago at the Red Tower Master Yettle had drilled it into them that strength wasn't required to be a skilled healer. Up to now she'd been trying to trap the infection. She attempted to cut off new tendrils whenever they sprouted, but the infection could replicate itself faster than she could pin it down. A different approach was needed.

In the past Wren had used a knack she'd developed to look into the heart of a magical weave. It gave her a better understanding of how something was built. The first time had been by accident. Shortly after arriving at the Red Tower she'd looked into one of the magical lanterns fixed to the wall of the dormitory. Peering within she'd discovered a single glowing strip of nodes that endlessly rotated in a ring, enabling the mage light to glow without constantly feeding it energy. She'd never thought of it as a Talent, as it didn't always work, but perhaps it could help her understand the nature of the disease.

Stretching out with tendrils of energy Wren sank them deep into her patient's body. They passed through the skin without noticing and she made sure to avoid interfering with the natural flow of the woman's body. She exerted no influence, merely observed the normal functions while trying to locate the infection. It didn't take her long to find a cluster. In her mind it was a black, oily globule deep in the woman's lungs. Wren could see ruptures in the lungs. There was ongoing damage that was causing the woman's shortness of breath. Her hacking cough had become so bad that she often spat blood.

Focusing on the disease Wren tried to use her knack to look beneath the surface. She experienced a moment of disorientation as the room swam but she maintained her grip on the Source.

Wren took a moment to try and understand what had happened. It was almost as if there had been some resistance. Moving slowly she focused on the infection in the woman's lungs again and tried to apply her knack to it. Her vision blurred and then resettled but instead of seeing an ugly black cluster there was a vast network of fibrous pathways. The only thing Wren could compare it to was the busy streets of a city, thriving with people, with hundreds of crisscrossing roads. Tiny glowing nodules shaped like grains of rice were whizzing around the network. With nothing to lose she reached into the cluster and interrupted the flow, imagining a blockade at one crossroads. There was a moment of resistance and then the tiny travellers redirected themselves around the blockade. The disease cluster swelled and she felt it grow, stretching its tendrils even deeper into the woman's lungs. Her hacking cough returned and Wren pulled back, afraid she might have caused serious damage.

Wren held the woman's head steady as she coughed into a cloth. When she was done she flopped back in exhaustion, blood trickling from the corner of her mouth. With her mind on what she'd seen Wren absently wiped the woman's face and applied a fresh cloth to her forehead.

"That feels good," murmured the woman. A cold cloth or some fresh air outside sounded like a good idea to Wren. The hospital was always warm now that they'd patched all of the holes in the walls and ceiling.

Wren smiled at Kovac as she stepped outside to stretch her legs. He was perched on a barrel, keeping one eye on the street as he honed the edge of his blade on a whetstone.

She'd had no idea something like that was possible. To see

inside the infection itself. She needed to better understand her knack. To know if it really was a Talent or not, but more importantly, Wren had to find out if what she'd done had made it worse.

Taking a deep breath she tried to ignore her fear, her fatigue, her concern for her friends and the gnawing hunger inside. The only thing that mattered was the plague. Back inside Wren embraced the Source again, bowed her head and slowly reached out with her senses towards the dying woman.

Tianne had lost count of the number of buildings they'd searched. A few of them were empty but most were occupied by groups of people who had clustered together for protection and warmth. And even here, at the end of the world, a hierarchy had developed where the strong stole from the weak. She and the other mages were doing their best to prevent it but they couldn't be everywhere at once and those who preyed on others knew that.

Predatory groups followed the weak from the gate back to their temporary homes where they fought over supplies. She and Kimme had already burned over a dozen bodies that had died from stab wounds or being clubbed to death. Ultimately it was all so pointless. Having more food than someone else with the plague made no difference to how long they lived.

It sickened Tianne and made her so angry but on the outside she remained calm, channelling that rage into her magic. Kimme had no such restraint. She spat, swore and manhandled anyone who tried to stop them finding Rue.

Tianne suspected some of her friend's anger was directed towards herself for letting them abduct Rue from right under their noses. After all, she and Baedan had taken on the role of protectors and he was also raging about what had happened.

With every door they broke down and every person they questioned Tianne hoped they were getting closer to finding Rue, but by the end of the second day doubt had begun to set in. At that point she came to a conclusion. Rue's captors never stayed in the same place. It was the only explanation after they'd thoroughly searched the entire area. It was possible they'd missed her but Tianne didn't believe one person was holding Rue. It had to be a group as she could easily overpower one person with her magic.

The one advantage they had, which only mages knew about, was their ability to sense one another. It was how Seekers had tested children for centuries and it would give them a clue to Rue's location if she was nearby. Kimme's echo had become a constant on the periphery of Tianne's senses. A loud second pulse that spoke to the strength of the farm girl's connection to the Source. Rue's was more subtle but it would be no less apparent in an area with so few mages.

They'd visited this street on the previous day but Tianne had a hunch. There were several groups occupying the run-down buildings. She'd spoken to all of them at least once and none of them made her suspicious. But as Tianne had learned in the past, first impressions could be deceiving.

In the first building they spoke to a devout group who said they had nothing to hide and willingly let Kimme search every room. As one of the smaller groups they had been suffering until the arrival of the mages so they were happy to help. As followers of the Blessed Mother they believed that their faith would help them to survive. Tianne encouraged them to visit one of the hospitals but they politely refused. Even before Kimme had finished with her search Tianne knew they wouldn't find anything.

The next two buildings were empty but they searched them anyway, looking for hidden doors or evidence that someone had been living there. In a basement of the next empty building they found a splash of fresh blood. Beside it someone had started scratching a message into the stone. Tianne didn't know if it was

Rue or a lost soul wanting someone to remember them once they were gone.

Kimme's frustration was growing and when the next group started acting belligerently at the intrusion Tianne said nothing to calm her down. The leader, a middle-aged woman from Shael, spat at Tianne, called her a black-eyed bitch and blamed her kind for the plague. When she turned to curse Kimme the farm girl punched the woman in the face, breaking her nose.

There were a dozen men and women in the group, but as they surged forward to defend their friend Tianne wasn't worried. Roaring like a wounded bear Kimme threw them around the room like ragdolls. Picking up two or three at a time she slammed them into walls, bounced them off the ceiling and then let them drop to the floor. It wasn't long before all of them were bruised, bloody and battered.

Once they might have been physically strong people but the plague had sapped their bodies of its strength and stamina. They didn't have the energy for even a short fight any more. Not that it would have mattered. Their numbers meant nothing when stacked against Kimme's will and her rage. She threw one man so hard against a door that it snapped off its hinges and both landed in the next room.

"That's enough," said Tianne, tapping Kimme on the shoulder.

The other reason she'd let it continue was the furtive way their leader had been looking at them. She was hiding something.

Tianne knelt down beside the woman who now had a broken arm to go with her broken nose. "Talk." The woman pursed her lips and Tianne clamped her jaw shut with her magic before she was spat on. "Or you can talk to her some more."

On cue Kimme loomed over Tianne's shoulder. The woman reconsidered and swallowed instead, nodding slowly that she was willing to talk. Tianne released her but remained alert.

"She was here," said the woman. "That girl you're after."

"When?" asked Tianne, holding up a hand to keep Kimme at bay.

"Yesterday."

"Was she alone?"

"No. She's being held by a man named Blaine ... or Glaine? He's a local, not like you," she said, glancing at Tianne's dark eyes.

"Where is he?"

"I don't know," said the woman, spitting blood on the floor. She touched her broken nose and winced in pain. Her right forearm was bent at a peculiar angle.

"Kimme, are you convinced?" asked Tianne. She didn't even need to look over her shoulder for an answer. Kimme actually growled.

"I don't know where," insisted the woman.

"But you know something. Why else would our friend stay with this man? How many people does he have in his group?"

"If I tell you, will you kill them?" she asked. It was more of a request than a question. Her callous attitude sickened Tianne and she didn't hide her disgust.

"What does it matter? You'll all be dead soon enough." The woman sneered and Tianne thought she was about to curse her when she felt Kimme looming again.

"He had seven with him. They wanted to sleep in our building for a share of their food. I refused so they moved on. That's everything. I swear by the Maker."

Her hunch has been right about why they'd been unable to find Rue. They left the battered group and went back on to the street where a steady rain was falling. The water quickly soaked into their clothes making them tight and sticky but nothing was going to deter her. The next two groups were no help but as they entered the next building Tianne heard the sound of running feet racing down the corridor away from her.

"Go around," she yelled at Kimme. Tianne set off in pursuit, glancing into the main room as she raced past. A man was holding a family hostage with a handmade knife fashioned from scrap metal. As she processed what she'd seen Tianne's pace slowed and then stopped as she reached the back door. Peering outside she saw the young boy was already a good distance away down the alley, his legs flying along as he ran for his life. He paused and looked back over his shoulder, even going so far as to give Tianne a little wave. It was meant to enrage her and guarantee she'd follow him. Kimme came skidding around the corner and was about to race after him when she saw Tianne.

"What are you doing?"

"Let him go and come inside," she said quietly, retracing her steps to the main room. Kimme was about to ask what was going on when she saw why Tianne had stopped.

As they entered the room the Yerskani man, a scruffy, rotund sort with wispy hair, pulled the woman against his chest. He pressed the crude dagger to her throat while two children cried and screamed. The woman was torn between trying to reassure her children and trying not to anger her captor.

All of them were infected, of course, but the woman was the worst. She was already having trouble breathing and the sores on her skin looked incredibly painful. In spite of it all she was trying to comfort her children. It should have been uplifting. That even when her own life was in danger she was thinking of others.

"Are you Blaine?" asked Tianne. The man twitched but didn't reply.

Tianne was just so tired. Tired of people hurting each other for petty reasons. Tired of people looking no further than the end of their noses. She just wanted to curl up in a ball and sleep for a week.

It was at that moment Tianne knew her hunch was right. There was something peculiar about the tableau in front of her. The children were pleading and crying. The woman looked suitably scared and Blaine was angry and wild-eyed, but his eyes gave it away. They were a peculiar shade of green, much like those of the younger child and the boy who'd run from the building. It was all meant as a distraction. To keep her focused on the woman's peril. Even the children were designed to keep her off balance.

Closing her eyes for a long breath she double-checked her suspicion.

"Put the knife down," said Tianne.

"I'll kill her. I will!" promised Blaine. Tianne felt Kimme embrace the Source, readying herself for a fight, but she waved the farm girl back.

"Why would you kill your own wife? Or your children?"

"I'll do it!" he said with equal enthusiasm, even going so far as to press the edge of the metal to the woman's throat. She pretended to be suitably scared by the threat.

"Tianne," said Kimme, a warning in her voice.

"Just stop. It won't work," said Tianne, ignoring them all. "Where's Rue?"

"Who?" he asked.

"I can feel that she's nearby. Where is she?" If she ignored the half-hearted threats, the crying children and Kimme's steady echo, Tianne could feel another pulse. It was slow and steady but loud enough to tell her that Rue was somewhere in the building.

Blaine exchanged a brief glance with his wife. They were probably trying to decide whether or not to continue with their charade. Tianne rushed forward and he instinctively moved back, pulling his wife out of reach. But she'd not been aiming for them. The little boy squealed as Tianne yanked him across the room by his arm. Drawing deeply on the Source she pulled heat from the room until a churning ball of fire had gathered in her open palm. Everyone's breath frosted on the air and shadows flickered across the walls from the dancing fire. The boy was squirming around but she held on tightly, digging her fingers into his arm.

"Tell me where to find Rue."

"I don't know," said the man.

"You have to the count of three. Then I will burn your son alive," said Tianne. The boy looked at the fire and this time he started to cry for real.

"What?" asked Blaine, easing his grip on the woman. Of course she made no attempt to flee her captor despite him barely holding on to her any more.

"One."

"Tell her," said the wife, shrugging off her husband's arm, effectively ending the pretence.

"She won't do it," he said, confident in his assessment of Tianne's character. A year ago he would have been right about her. Now, after all that she'd endured, Tianne didn't know if she would actually go through with it or not.

"Two."

Tianne drew more power from the Source and fed it into the fire which glowed white. The boy's struggles were frantic as she brought him closer to the flames. He was flailing around so much it singed his shirt. The heat briefly touched his skin because he screamed as if he were dying.

"Tell her!" pleaded the wife.

"Wait!" said Blaine. "Stop! She's here. Right here," he said, pointing at the ground beneath their feet.

"Where?" asked Tianne.

"There's a trapdoor." He moved to the far side of the room and with a grunt of effort pushed the heavy wooden cupboard aside. Beneath a ratty old rug was a thick trapdoor with an iron ring. With a heave he yanked it open, revealing the edge of a ladder that descended into the dark. "Bring her up," he shouted into the hole.

"Are you sure?"

"Just do as I say, boy!" he shouted.

A short time later a gangly teenager with the same green eyes as his father came up the ladder with Rue over his shoulder. Her eyes were closed and her body was limp.

"Check on her," said Tianne, maintaining a solid grip on the boy's arm. Kimme shoved the teenager aside and easily lifted Rue out of the hole. After laying her gently on the floor she checked Rue's heart and peeled back her eyelids.

"She's alive, but there's something wrong," said Kimme.

"What have you done to her?" asked Tianne.

"We needed her to help us. To make us better," said Blaine, nervously licking his cracked lips. Tianne pulled the boy towards the fire in her other hand to encourage him to speak. "We gave her some venthe to stay with us."

Venthe was a destructive drug that gradually rotted a person's mind and body. Unfortunately venthe was highly addictive even after just one taste. She'd heard rumours about girls being hooked on venthe and forced into prostitution but never something like this. Enslaving someone in the hope that they would heal your family. If Rue had left Blaine and returned to the hospital it was possible the withdrawal would have killed her.

Tianne was so numb she let go of the boy's arm and he flopped to the floor in a heap. Blaine rushed forward and scooped up his son, cradling the boy in his arms. She was horrified that he could justify kidnapping and drugging Rue because he cared so much about his children. She'd heard parents say they would do anything for their children but she wondered how many would actually go this far.

Her concentration trickled away and the ball of fire vanished. The other boy appeared from the back door and quickly went to his mother's side but it was far from a happy reunion.

"I'm sorry," said Blaine. "We just needed her to heal us. I'd already lost my brother and my eldest daughter. I couldn't lose anyone else."

There was always a reason. An excuse they told themselves to justify their actions, but she just didn't care any more. Kimme's simmering anger began to boil over and Tianne felt no inclination to stop whatever happened next.

As she turned away to leave the room Blaine realised he was still in danger. "Please. Please help us!" he begged.

"If you'd come to the hospital we would've tried our hardest," said Tianne from the doorway.

"What are you going to do?" asked Blaine.

"Nothing. She's the one you need to worry about," said Tianne, gesturing at Kimme.

Tianne slung Rue over one shoulder, braced herself on the wall and slowly stood upright. She could have used magic to help her but right now she didn't want to heighten her senses. It would only give her a clearer image of their scared faces and sharpen the stench of human filth. She wanted to forget this place and everyone in the room. She wanted to walk out and never think about any of it again.

"Don't go!" said the wife, but it was too late.

As Tianne walked out she felt Kimme drawing power from the Source. By the time she reached the front door the pleas of the family were deafening.

They deserved whatever happened next. It wasn't Tianne's job to stop it. Part of her knew it was cruel, especially for the children. They probably didn't even understand why they'd been taken from their home and locked up in this awful part of the city. She tried to picture herself ten years ago, to see the world through their eyes. At their age she'd not even thought of her parents as human. They were special people and never wrong. It was only years later she realised they were as fallible as everyone else.

Once again Tianne found herself thinking about Garvey. About his brutality, his lies and manipulation. He had insisted that magic was a good thing, and yet he had used it to hurt others while pursuing his own twisted goals. He always justified his actions no matter how horrific. She'd walked away from him, and the Regent who'd sought to enslave mages for his own twisted ideals. She came to a decision and retraced her steps.

"Stop," said Tianne, gripping Kimme by the shoulder.

The farm girl had been pulling together something black and vicious between her hands, a nightmarish ball of agony swirling with threads of fire. The whole family were huddled together in one corner of the room. Blaine was shielding the others with as much of his body as possible. It was a noble but vain attempt to save them from injury. Whatever Kimme was summoning would have destroyed all of them. "Leave them."

"Why?" asked Kimme. She was clenching her jaw so tightly the muscles were jumping on the sides of her face. "They deserve it."

"They're already dying," she said in a quiet voice. Adding more misery to their suffering wouldn't make a difference. In some ways if she let Kimme kill them now then it would be a mercy. They wouldn't have to suffer days of agonising pain and they wouldn't have to watch members of their family die. But she wasn't Garvey.

Tianne wondered if there would ever come a time when people saw a mage and their first thought was positive. It might happen one day but she doubted it would be in her lifetime. Nevertheless she wouldn't add to the list of crimes committed by mages.

"Leave them. Let's just go."

The fire behind Kimme's eyes faded and her grip of the Source evaporated. Tianne could see that she was also just so tired. They picked up Rue from where Tianne had left her and set off towards the hospital leaving the family to their fate.

Wren's smile was short-lived at seeing Tianne before nightfall as Kimme was a step behind with Rue slung over one shoulder. Her head was lolling to one side and her limbs flopped about. Andras guided them to an empty space on the floor where Kimme gently set her down. With some trepidation she approached the others as the priest inspected Rue. Wren knew what he was looking for. They did it every day with all of their patients. Lesions on the arms and face were usually the first signs of infection.

After a short time Andras stood up and shook his head. "She doesn't have the plague, but something is wrong."

Wren listened with growing horror as Tianne explained what had happened to Rue. It was only then she noticed the faint blue stains at the corner of her mouth. Andras knelt down again and peeled back Rue's eyelids, checking for something. He put his head to her chest and listened to her heart for a long time.

"Is she going to die?" asked Kimme. Her whole body was trembling with rage or fear.

"No, she's not." Andras sounded confident.

"Are you sure?" asked Tianne, scratching at her arm. "I thought the withdrawal would kill her."

"It can, but there are ways to lessen the impact."

"You've dealt with addicts before?" said Wren and the priest nodded. "What can we do to help?"

"Tend to the others, I will look after Rue. In time she will recover, but she won't be able to heal anyone for a while."

"I'm sorry," said Kimme, curling her hands up into fists. "I'm sorry we couldn't do more."

"She's alive," said Wren. "You found her and I'm very grateful." Normally Kimme's refusal to bathe deterred others from making any physical contact with her, but Wren could see she was barely holding on. She pulled the farm girl into a tight hug and felt her whole body was shaking.

"You both saved her," she said, looking over Kimme's shoulder. Tianne was distracted and was staring into the distance. It had been her idea to come to Perizzi and now she wondered if, for the first time, Tianne was regretting it. All of the others had expressed doubts, at one point, but she'd always seemed so sure.

"I'm going to get some air," said Kimme, wiping her face and quickly turning away so they couldn't see her tears. "Thank you." She briefly clasped Tianne's hand on the way out. Her friend smiled but it was merely a shadow on her face, there for a moment and then gone. It made Wren wonder if Tianne had told them the whole story about their encounter with Blaine and his family.

Baedan went outside to keep Kimme company and a moment later Wren heard him repeating one of his dirty jokes that Kimme found amusing. In time the farm girl would recover but right now Wren was more concerned about Tianne.

"What happened? What is it?" she asked, trying to move Tianne to one side for some privacy but her friend pulled her hand out of reach.

"Back home in Zecorria I was never deeply religious," said Tianne. "In the north it's expected that you go to church. If you don't they think there's something wrong with you. So I did it in order to fit in with everyone. I mouthed the hymns, said prayers and went through the motions, but I never felt it. That thing people speak about. That inner glow."

"What do you mean?" asked Wren.

"Have you ever felt it? That there's something out there.

Something greater than us. A benevolent god that watches over us all."

Wren didn't know where this was going but she decided that honesty would be the best approach. "No. I've never experienced it either. Why do you ask?"

"I think it would be nice, don't you?" said Tianne. "Just once, I would like to have felt something like that."

"Tianne, you're scaring me. What's wrong?"

Tianne rolled up the right sleeve of her shirt exposing her arm. A small red lesion had formed in the crook of her elbow. She'd been infected.

CHAPTER 34

Normally Kai would have just marched into the room and butchered any mortal who didn't instantly obey him. Today wasn't a normal day. Today found him sat in a corner of the Zecorran throne room, drinking wine and eating fruit while Marran explained the new status quo to the Regent's first wife, Selina.

Last night his plan to absorb Akosh and kill her friends had been going well until Vargus had shown up. In some ways a confrontation between them had been inevitable for a long time.

For years Kai had been hiding in the shadows, feasting and growing strong by absorbing smaller beings. At the same time the number of humans praying to him for help with their sick and dying patients had changed from a trickle to a flood. And during those years he'd gobbled up a host of nasty viruses, toxic poisons and vicious blights. He'd wolfed down miles of pestilent flesh and gorged himself on countless diseased organs. And with every apparent miracle, every remarkable recovery, their belief had grown stronger.

Kai hadn't expected to go unnoticed for ever but he'd hoped for a few more years. Vargus had been there at the beginning, when he'd first been born as a deity to the primitive human race.

But unlike Nethun and the Blessed Mother he'd been forced to reinvent himself to extend his life.

Since the beginning Kai had known he was different from the others but that didn't make him immune. As the number of his followers, the Eaters, had dwindled down the centuries he'd been arrogant and ignored the warning signs. He would have faded from existence if not for Vargus's actions but that didn't matter now. They were brethren, of a sort, but still enemies. The real question became, after all this time, and all that Kai had done in recent years, which of them was stronger?

Something had been niggling at the back of his mind since Vargus had appeared. For some reason he'd been accompanied by a teenage boy from Shael. Kai didn't think he'd ever seen the boy before and yet there was something oddly familiar about him. He knew that from time to time Vargus travelled with mortal companions, but why this one and why now? Why bring him to such a dangerous fight? It wasn't by chance. Vargus wouldn't risk one of his precious mortals. So who was the boy?

As he gulped down wine with his one good hand Kai assessed the damage to his physical shell. The flesh was torn and many of the bones were broken or ground to a fine powder. One of the hands was completely gone and the skin on his face was marked by gaping wounds. Several times Selina had glanced at him with a mix of horror and fear. If he didn't repair the body soon it would collapse and then he would have to expend even more energy to rebuild it.

"I don't understand," Selina was saying for the fifth time as Marran explained who was in charge. A little display of power would make things easier.

Kai knocked the fruit bowl aside and picked up the metal tray. Staring into its mirrored surface he watched as the flesh on his face started to rebuild itself.

"He is our Master," Marran was saying. "Watch and learn."

Torn flaps were all that was left of his cheeks but the remaining skin stretched downwards until it covered his jaw, hiding what lurked beneath. The wet blood turned brown and then flaked off leaving pink skin in its wake. With a grinding sound pieces of bone in his damaged spine burst out of his back and new nodules grew in their place. The skin on his broken arm contracted while the bones realigned themselves until all he was missing was a hand. New bones started to grow from the stump, were quickly wrapped in muscles and veins, until fresh skin covered his fingertips. Piece by piece the skin regenerated as if he were slowly pulling on a glove until it joined with the flesh at his wrist. He felt a slight pinch and then fresh blood pumped into his new hand which he flexed. There was no lingering pain and with a quick brush of his hands any remaining dried blood came away from his face.

"You are the Regent's first wife, yes?" said Kai, striding towards the tall woman. She was an imposing figure, used to intimidating others, but now she cowered with child-like fear. Selina swallowed hard and tried her best to look him in the eye but couldn't manage it for long.

"Yes, but I have other duties as well," she said, as if it mattered.

"Marran and all of the mages work for me. We also have a few Royal Guards and one or two others, here and there," he said, waving a hand vaguely. The more Selina thought she was being watched the easier it would be. "Some of them follow me willingly, others had to be persuaded. Marran, show her."

"Fetch one of your friends," he said to the Royal Guard stationed at the door. A short time later two guards dragged in a third between them. The struggling woman had a cut on her left temple but was still putting up a good fight.

"Hold her steady," said Marran as he approached the little

group. Last time one of the guards had kicked him in the crotch and he'd spent an hour curled up in a ball.

The guards held their former friend tightly, using their combined body weight to pin her arms back while she knelt on the floor.

Kai felt Marran summon magic from the Source while he waved his hands about in front of his face. When he was ready he approached the struggling guard and laid his mind trap over her head. At first she screamed and thrashed about but that quickly faded until her eyes turned glassy and compliant. It was all over before he'd even finished his second glass of wine.

The guards released their new friend, gave her back her weapons and she took up her post inside the throne room.

"What have you done?" asked Selina, aghast at Marran. She'd been suspicious of him since the beginning, but Kai had left them with no other choices for a teacher. Her attempt to satisfy his unusual proclivities in a safe way barely scraped the surface of what was lurking within. Kai suspected if he allowed Marran to indulge his every desire it might make for an entertaining week or two. Unfortunately such distractions would have to wait.

"Tell her," said Kai, gesturing at the seedy mage.

"I've bound her mind to my will. She's—"

"A slave. They're all slaves," said Kai impatiently. "My slaves. You can work for me and have free will or end up like her." The new Royal Guard was still at her post and hadn't moved a muscle. She would do exactly as she was told until given a new command or her brain turned to sludge from internal damage.

"Why is he bleeding?" asked Selina, pointing at one of the other guards. Blood was trickling from both of his nostrils but he remained oblivious.

"The more they fight against it the sooner they die," said Kai with a shrug. Selina stared expectantly at the newly enslaved

Royal Guard. "It doesn't happen that quickly, but it will to all of them eventually."

"I see," she said. Fresh fear sweat burst from her pores and to Kai it was sweeter than any perfume.

"Choose quickly," he suggested, tiring of their conversation.

"How can I serve you, Master?" she said with an elaborate bow.

"Decisive. I like it. Marran tells me you have your husband's ear."

"I do," she said but he heard the lie. "He will listen to me once I explain the situation," she clarified, sensing his disapproval.

"Good. I need his Royal Guards and any soldiers in the city to aid me. Make it clear what will happen if he refuses." Kai gestured at the dying guard who was now bleeding from his mouth but still remained stoically at his post.

Marran, his mages and plenty of armed idiots with swords would be enough to take care of Vargus's mortal allies. That would leave Akosh and Vargus for him to deal with. The time for hiding in the shadows was over. What the people in Herakion would see in the next few days would be spoken about for a long time. A long time to them, at least.

The woman was talking again, intruding on his thoughts despite Marran's protests. "What?" said Kai, having missed the question.

"Can I ask for something in return?" she said again.

"Are you trying to bargain with me?" She knew Marran could enslave her mind, making her a willing accomplice, and yet she was still trying to make a deal. "I'm not in the habit of bartering with servants."

"Then think of it as a favour," she suggested. If nothing else he had to admire her spirit. Marran hadn't dared ask for anything in all the time he'd served Kai. In fact Selina was the first. The rest were too terrified even to consider it. Perhaps he was being too lenient with her.

"What do you want?"

"Zecorria."

"You want the whole country for yourself?" he asked, surprised at her ambition.

"In return for helping with your war," she said. "I want you to leave my country."

Sometimes it was just easier to hold them down and break into their mind. To muzzle their righteous anger and turn that energy inwards. So the more they raged the more damage they did to themselves. It stopped the complaints and most of all it stopped them asking questions. It was also a lot quieter.

But sometimes by letting them keep their free will, and by giving them the illusion of hope, they still did everything he wanted. In the front of their minds they convinced themselves that it would all work out in the end. They completely ignored the little quiet voice in the back that told them they would still die.

"Do you want to rule? To sit on the throne and have a nation of your own?" asked Selina. Her narrow and short-sighted thoughts mirrored those of Akosh. She'd spent so long playing at human that she now thought like one.

"Absolutely not."

"Then why stay?"

He pretended to consider it, to give her hope that she was getting through to him. His mind was already made up but she seemed full of ideas. She might prove useful and if he enslaved her she'd never willingly offer any suggestions.

"Fine," said Kai, feigning acceptance. "Once my business is concluded I will leave Zecorria."

Selina smiled and bowed again. Even if he left it wouldn't make any difference. Once the war with Vargus was over his people would still be here, in apothecary shops and surgeries, healing the sick and praying to him. He didn't need to be here in person to benefit.

"It's time to prove your loyalty," he said and immediately she was nervous again. "Speak to your husband. I want him to make a public speech and issue a list of names with sketches. These people are highly dangerous enemies of Zecorria and are to be killed on sight. A generous reward for any reliable information should also be offered. Make up whatever crimes you need," he said, negligently waving a hand. It didn't really matter, so long as Vargus and the others couldn't move freely about the city without someone informing the authorities.

"I will see to it immediately," said Selina, waiting for his permission before leaving the room.

"Go with her," he said to Marran who scuttled away. He also sent a couple of Royal Guards to keep watch, just in case the Regent tried to run. Normally Kai preferred it when they ran. There was nothing more exciting than the chase. Hunting animals was boring as their minds were simple, but mortals, they were so unpredictable. A pleasure for another time. For now the Regent would bend the knee or they'd break his mind too, although that would be a last resort as he was the one mortal Kai couldn't easily replace.

It was late in the afternoon and Regent Choilan was lounging in bed. The sheets were tangled and he felt tired enough to have a little nap. As much as he'd enjoyed watching her take them off he still got a thrill from watching Lara, his second wife, put her clothes back on.

He was exhausted from his exertions but found his eyes lingering on the curve of Lara's hips. Indulging further would have to be a pleasure for another day. It would give him something to look forward to in these bleak times. His plan for the cadre of mages didn't seem to be working out. Marran was a constant worry and part of Choilan suspected the whole thing would blow up in his face. Then there was the pressing issue that Garvey had escaped from his cell and had not been seen since. He should have died down there, rotting in his own filth, but somehow he'd survived. As far as the public knew his mages had apprehended Garvey and then he'd been executed. Choilan regretted pressing him for a confession. He should have just cut his throat and hung Garvey's body from the palace walls.

Unless he found a way to secure his position on the throne he would be usurped by one of the other aristocrats lurking in the wings. Then he'd be nothing more than another footnote in history. Another leader who'd failed to leave his mark on Zecorria in the wake of the Mad King. Maybe they'd remember him for banning all Seekers. Then again, he'd quickly backtracked from almost banning all magic to embracing children with the ability. Would they speak of him fondly in years to come or call him the Two-Faced King? Perhaps being completely forgotten would be better than the alternative.

With so much uncertainty ahead Choilan wondered if it was wise to wait until tomorrow to indulge. He was just about to suggest Lara come back to bed when his bedroom door was flung open. Selina marched in followed by the greasy mage, Marran, and two Royal Guards.

Selina sneered at his second wife and casually backhanded her, splitting Lara's bottom lip. Anyone else would have fought back, but Lara just sat there in shock with blood running down her chin.

"What is the meaning of this?" roared Choilan, gathering the sheet about his waist. Perhaps this was a coup, although he never expected Selina to side with one of the others. If it was the end he wasn't going to face it naked. He quickly pulled on a pair of trousers and a loose shirt before moving to Lara's side.

"There's been a change," said Selina. "You're no longer in charge."

Choilan helped Lara to a chair before turning to face his back-stabbing wife. "Who is it? Who have you sided with?"

"You will remain here, in your rooms, until summoned," said Selina. "Later today you will be making a speech to the people, so dress appropriately."

"I will not," said Choilan. "I will not be someone's puppet and I don't deal with minions," he said with a sneer. "Tell that to your new Master or Mistress."

"Choilan—"

"What did it take," he asked, catching her off balance, "to betray me?"

"You don't understand."

"It can't be something as base as money. Was it power? A bigger network of agents so you can play at being a spymaster?"

He could feel the anger radiating from her whole body. Marran fidgeted behind her as if suddenly uncomfortable. Even the Royal Guards were having difficulty looking at her. "You need to understand. The only reason you're still alive is because you're useful. With a snap of my fingers they'll kill her," she said, pointing a finger at Lara. "Or, they could do something worse. Marran will enslave her mind."

"He'll do what?"

"Why do you think your cadre of mages are suddenly so happy?" she asked, raising an eyebrow. "He manipulated their minds. I've seen what he can do to the strong-willed. So, either you can do as you're told or he'll make you into a slave."

"I'll fight it," said Choilan, clenching his fists but Selina just laughed.

"It won't make a difference," she promised. "Perhaps a demonstration is required." Selina gestured towards Lara and raised that eyebrow again.

He had no idea if what she was saying was true but something had changed. Only yesterday they'd been discussing how much longer they could put up with Marran before having him killed. For Selina to side with the mage worried him a great deal.

"Leave her alone," he said.

"Then be a good boy," Selina said, as if he were an errant child. "Get dressed and tell Bettina to make the arrangements for a public speech. Take her away," she said, speaking to the guards.

The Royal Guards grabbed Lara by the arms and dragged her away. Marran lingered in the doorway, a smile pulling at the corners of his mouth. He was clearly enjoying the turnabout of events after Choilan had threatened him.

"What are you doing?" Choilan asked. Lara didn't even cry out as she was taken away. She was such a delicate little lamb.

"Providing you with some additional motivation." Selina's smile was so malicious Choilan wondered how he'd ever found her attractive. He'd known for many years that despite everything Selina was bitter about her position. Being the first wife of the ruler of Zecorria wasn't enough for her. He'd thought if he indulged her fixation with spying it might satisfy her. Clearly he'd been wrong.

Despite her denials he realised Selina had always been envious of how he treated his other wives. He doted on them, shared his bed with them and spent more time with them than her. To think that he was being overthrown because of a jealous wife almost made him laugh.

"She will be well treated, as long as you perform," said Selina. "And Choilan, you need to be very convincing, because people will be watching."

Selina turned and walked away, leaving him facing Marran. He expected the mage to gloat but instead he just closed and locked the door. The message was clear. His rooms, no matter how lavish, had now become his prison. It was exactly what he'd done to Marran.

Whoever was pulling Selina's strings was probably in the palace. Were they already sitting on the throne? And what had they promised her? What would satisfy her?

So far he'd only seen two Royal Guards doing Selina's bidding. How many were under her sway? Had they all been turned into mindless slaves? Every guard and every servant? He doubted Marran could have moved that quickly without him noticing. There would have been warning signs. Bettina or another of his other inner circle would have reported something. That meant there were factions within the palace.

He would have to speak carefully to his aide and find out how far Selina's betrayal extended. Once he knew who could be trusted Choilan would plan a coup of his own. He was not about to give up the throne without a fight.

CHAPTER 35

A large crowd of at least three hundred people had already gathered by the time Kimme and Baedan arrived at the gate. Kovac walked a little distance behind them, eyeing people around him with suspicion. No one was pleased to see them but without having to ask they made space for her and Baedan to reach the front. Those who'd been here the last time knew she would make sure everyone received an equal share of the food and other supplies. Kimme tried not to stare at individual faces and if she recognised someone she didn't acknowledge them. It only made it harder the next time when those faces were missing.

Kovac was receiving a fair number of glances because he openly carried a sword. They made room for him because of the weapon but also the look in his eyes.

When Kimme reached the gate a familiar stench filled her nose. Rot and decaying flesh. A middle-aged woman with grey hair and a blue dress was sitting in front of the gate. At first glance it looked as if she was merely asleep with her chin resting on her chest. The colour of her skin and the smell told Kimme otherwise. Perhaps the woman had arrived early this morning in the hopes of beating the queue and leaving with some food.

"Stand back," said Kimme, gesturing at those beside her.

Embracing the Source had always filled her with a sense of joy unlike anything else in her life. She used to love how it made everything sharper and brighter. The world seemed more real somehow. As if everything she'd experienced before had been a weak imitation. Now she was beginning to hate it. When the only things it made clearer was the smell of filth and the sight of dead bodies she was in no rush to use her magic. But it was necessary for what needed to be done and in this place her duty was everything.

As power from the Source flooded her body Kimme tried not to breathe too deeply. She didn't want the stink to get lodged in her nose all day. Cherry-red fire gathered in the palms of her hands before she extended it towards the dead body. Like a street magician pulling a series of scarves from her sleeve the fire continued to pour out of her hands. It briefly wreathed the woman's body before her clothes and hair caught fire. She poured it on until the colour of the flames changed from red to yellow and then to white.

She didn't know how many bodies she'd burned with her magic. At first she'd kept a tally but when it reached a hundred she stopped. It seemed perverse when she didn't even know their names. Everything was consumed by the fire. Their names, their faces, their memories.

It had bothered her at the beginning. Watching as the skin blackened and then split apart to reveal the guts beneath. Soon enough the rest of the flesh would melt like hot wax in the intense heat. The body fat would add fuel to the fire and not long after that the bones would crack and fall apart.

In the back of her mind she knew that the thing in front of her had once been a person with thoughts and feelings, but if she lingered on that idea for too long it would drive her mad. Dead children were the worst. It didn't take as long to burn their bodies to ash but those were the ones that stayed in her mind the longest. Some nights the dead haunted her dreams. Their faces always started out as normal, smiling and happy, before they fell apart from the inside or were burned up by flames. She was always the one wielding the fire and they always blamed her. She kept reminding herself she hadn't killed them but it didn't help.

A narrow plume of black smoke rose into the air as the fire consumed what remained of the woman. The last of her bones came apart, leaving only glowing ashes. A black stain marked the stones but it too would wash away with the rain. Kimme quickly severed her connection to the Source and turned away before taking a deep breath. The smell of burned human flesh had become familiar but it was no less grotesque.

The crowd had been watching her the whole time but there were only a few startled faces. The rest had been here long enough to know what happened. Usually it was done more traditionally, with a pyre and wood, but Kimme and Baedan often found bodies left for them in the middle of street.

A heavy rattle of locks announced the arrival of the supplies and instinctively the crowd pushed forward. They still left a pool of space around her and Baedan but she noticed those at the front were craning their necks to peer through the gate. Perhaps hoping to catch a glimpse of loved ones on the other side.

Sometimes a small group of people would gather behind the barriers. Kimme didn't understand it. Once someone came into the isolation zone they were as good as dead. To visit the gate seemed pointless. The best you could hope for was to see that your relative was still alive. The moment they stopped coming it was safe to assume the worst. Perhaps as long as they kept seeing them there was hope but on this side of the gate it was in short supply.

Before they'd left Corvin's Brow she'd thought it possible they might find a cure. After all, they'd beaten the raiders and their merciless leader Boros. Kimme knew Wren and the others were trying their best but now she doubted they could heal such an all-consuming disease. It resisted everything the doctors, herbalists and apothecarists threw at it.

They'd been so arrogant. To think that after studying the plague for only a short time they would succeed where others had failed. To think that magic would prove superior to skilled healers with decades of experience. If it wasn't so tragic she'd laugh at herself.

Maybe Wren and the others would prove her wrong but Kimme wasn't sure many of the people here deserved a cure. Her faith in humanity had been eroded in the face of all the misery, pain and violence they committed against each other, even here where they measured their remaining life in days.

With the gate opened she and Baedan stepped through to the edge of the barrier. A short distance away, members of the Watch and a ring of soldiers armed with crossbows kept a close eye on proceedings. Standing head and shoulders above them was the head Guardian, the Khevassar. With a nod at the women she started picking up the sacks and passing them back down the line into the isolation zone. Kimme waited until each sack had been deposited on the cart bed before trying to pick it up to avoid the chance of her touching anyone. Those unlucky enough to unload the goods all wore thick leather gloves and cloth masks to avoid the risk of contamination. From the look in their eyes she could see they were still worried about getting infected.

"How is it in there?" asked the Khevassar as she did every few days.

"The same," said Kimme with a shrug. This would be a lot easier if she could use her magic. She was strong enough to pick up several bags at once and float them through the gate but she knew it was likely to get her shot. One of the Watch might panic and think she was trying to escape. Any magic unnerved people and put them on edge.

"How is it out there?" she asked.

"The number of infected is continuing to fall," said the Guardian, rubbing at her eyes. Kimme thought she looked tired. She also noticed her gaze kept drifting to the mercenary, Kovac, who was distributing the supplies. "But the city is still on lockdown."

There was a lot she wasn't saying. Kimme wasn't particularly good at reading people like Wren, who seemed to know what you were thinking, but she could see the soldiers were tense. Some nights when she was starting fires Kimme spotted smoke in other parts of the city.

"Can I speak with him?" said the Khevassar, gesturing at Kovac. It was a strange request but Kimme shrugged and offered to change places with the mercenary. At first he was reluctant but then agreed and stepped through the gate to speak with the Guardian. Kimme heard the low rumble of his voice as he and the Khevassar chatted but her attention was drawn back to the waiting crowd.

Six people had been chosen to split up the supplies and they were now passing out items to different groups. Almost everyone in the crowd was reaching towards her with grasping hands, shoving and squabbling over what they were given. She could see everyone in the crowd was aching when they moved. There was strain on faces and people hissed in pain just moving around.

It could be worse. A lot of those with the plague couldn't even walk. There were perhaps three times as many people in the isolation zone as had turned up at the gate. Many were bedridden, writhing in agony as the infection consumed their body. A portion of all the supplies being handed out were packets of herbs to numb the pain. It was the only thing to do towards the end and a small mercy.

Kimme began to wonder if it was mercy. To let them continue to suffer. To give them false hope that a cure might be found in time. Perhaps it would be better if it was over. If it was quick then they wouldn't feel much pain and they wouldn't have to suffer for days and weeks. Surely that was real mercy.

Looking out at the countless faces in the crowd she could see the dead interspersed among the living. She didn't know their names but she recognised them. Every single one. She couldn't forget those she'd consumed with fire.

Embracing the Source was so easy. It seeped into every part of her body, filling her up with its boundless energy. Lately, whenever she used her magic the power seemed to fuel her rage and despair. It built up inside until every part of her skin itched. Like thousands of fire ants crawling across her body, stabbing at her flesh. Pressure from holding on to so much power built up until Kimme felt as if she might explode. Perhaps that would be mercy. For her. For all of them.

Kimme was aware that someone was talking softly but after a while their voice became louder. It didn't matter. They were in pain. She could end it. If she drew deeply enough the fire would reach all of them at once. She was strong enough to do it. It would be quick.

She wouldn't hesitate this time. The man who'd kidnapped Rue had deserved it but her resolve had wavered. Then Tianne had talked her out of it. None of them had deserved the mercy of a quick death and yet she'd been willing. She couldn't fail this time.

"Kimme," said someone loud enough to catch her attention.

She felt someone's hands on either side of her face and then something blocked her view of the crowd. It didn't matter. The dead were still there. She could feel them waiting for her. A sharp pain bit into her right cheek. Once, twice. The pressure in her head was mounting. Squeezing her temples, threatening to break open her skull.

"I must make it stop. Make it all stop," she said, not knowing if they could hear her.

"You won't come back from this. There's no way back," said the voice. It sounded like a man's voice. Was it her father? These people were already dead. When an animal was lame it was a mercy to put it down. It was cruel not to end its suffering.

"We killed Burr when he fell and broke one of his front legs, remember, Dad? I loved that horse but he couldn't walk any more. He'd have died a slow and painful death. This is just the same."

"These people aren't horses. They have families," said her father. Looking up she was surprised to see a beard. Had he always worn a beard?

"They're already dead and just don't know it. I can help them. I can end the pain."

"Everyone dies, Kimme, but you don't get to decide when it happens. I taught you better than that. You need to let this go."

Something red was flickering at the corner of her eye and she could smell burning. But where was the fire? Was she on fire? Was it the barn? The animals. They had to get them out!

"Dad, I can smell smoke. Is the barn on fire?"

"Let it go, Kimme. You need to rest." His voice was clogged as if full of tears. Maybe he was tired. She was so damn tired. She couldn't remember the last time she'd had a good night's sleep. It must have been after they'd built the first of the houses in Corvin's Brow. Her father was still talking, telling her to let it go. To rest. That sounded like a good idea. She'd go up to her room and lie down. Wren wouldn't mind if she had a little snooze. It was exciting, building a village from nothing, but there was always so much to do.

The pain was starting to ease and the smoke began to clear. If there wasn't a fire where had the smoke come from? And why was her dad here in their community? Or was all that a dream? Was she still back on the farm?

"Let it go. That's it," said her father, gently easing her to the floor. It felt cold and hard, not like her bed at all.

"Dad?"

"Yes?"

"Why is it so cold?"

"I'll get you a blanket," he suggested but she grabbed his arm.

"No. Don't leave me." She was afraid he'd never come back. That she'd die cold and alone. That the dead would drag her down into the earth with them.

"I'm here," he said, gently stroking her hair. "I'm right here. I'm not going anywhere."

Some of his body heat seeped into hers and she snuggled close to his chest. He mostly smelled of smoke, but she didn't mind. His strong arms were around her, his face was against the side of her head and she was safe. That's all that mattered. Kimme closed her eyes and slept.

Tammy watched in horror as Kovac approached the girl who'd set herself on fire.

Flames ran from her open palms, spilling over like water from a fountain, before gathering at her feet in a ring that was starting to spread across the ground. The girl was immune to the magical fire but those around her were not. The crowd was panicking and moved backwards, slowly at first and then in a mad rush. People were shoving each other aside to get away from the flames. A few of the most infected were unsteady and fell to the ground despite the crush of bodies.

The fire continued to creep forward and it became a full rout as people ran as fast as they could. All thoughts of the supplies were abandoned. They only wanted to get as far away as possible. Those underfoot were trampled and even from where she was standing Tammy heard screams of pain.

The other mage, the teenage boy, was the one who'd alerted them that something was wrong. Kimme remained in a daze and wouldn't respond to anyone when they spoke to her. Without being able to sense it Tammy could see from the boy's rising panic that Kimme was bringing more of her power to bear. There was a sudden change in the air like the moment before a lightning strike and she feared worse was about to happen. It wouldn't take much for a mage to cut down those fleeing in the street. If that should happen then even from this side of the gate she wasn't completely powerless. A crossbow bolt through the back of the skull would kill a mage the same as anyone else.

"No," whispered Tammy, willing Kovac to turn around as he approached the girl.

Seemingly unafraid for his own wellbeing he walked right up to Kimme until he was standing in front of her. He was just inside the ring of fire but still close enough that some of it landed on him. Almost immediately the fire licked at the bottom of his trousers, making them smoulder. She couldn't hear what he said but it didn't have the desired effect as he slapped Kimme hard across the face. That caught her attention as she began to talk. But all the while fire continued to spread, tumbling from her hands, turning the road black. The charred stone began to crack, fracturing the surface until more flames sunk underground through the gaps.

Kovac's clothes continued to burn but rather than catch fire instead they clung to his body creating a second skin. The teenage boy had fled in a panic with the others, leaving the fate of his friend up to Kovac. If he didn't stop her soon Tammy would have no choice but to put her down.

He was still talking, but with no more urgency as the fire reached his waist, cracking the leather of his belt. She saw his hands spasm in pain and he coughed a few times as the smoke clogged his throat. Once it reached his head it would quickly turn him into a living candle and that would be the end.

"Ready your weapon," said Tammy, turning to the soldier on her left. The woman must have known this was coming as she looked miserable at being chosen. Despite her reservations the soldier trained her weapon on the girl's head and waited for the order to shoot.

The fire running from Kimme's hands was now spreading in all directions like the living train of an exotic dress. The entire street was abandoned except for the girl and Kovac who continued to talk to her as if he wasn't suffering.

A sudden change in the air made Tammy's ears pop. Those around her stumbled and through the gate she saw the fire was beginning to fade. It had stopped pouring out of the girl and now Kovac had a hand against the side of Kimme's face. Tammy could see the girl's shoulders were shaking and then her whole body was trembling. The fire on the street started to fade layer by layer until all that remained was smouldering stone and black ash.

Kovac said something and the girl collapsed into his arms. He gently eased her to the ground and she appeared to fall asleep.

"It's over," said Tammy, gesturing at the soldier to lower her crossbow.

Tammy stared at Kovac on the far side of the open gate. It would be so easy to just hop over the barricade, walk through to the other side and help him with the girl. She didn't care that he was infected or even about the burns on his skin. She didn't even care that their time would be limited. At least they would be together.

Tammy took a step forward, fully intending to walk through the gate. Somehow Kovac knew what she was about to do and shook his head firmly. In that moment the city, its ongoing problems and even her position meant nothing. All of it was meaningless if she didn't have someone to share it with. All of the joys and triumphs. All of the losses and regrets. It was empty. The years ahead in isolation would be hollow if she were alone. And the man she loved had only days to live.

With a grunt of effort Kovac picked Kimme off the floor, slung her over one shoulder, and took a moment to steady himself. He glanced back once and their eyes met. There was a message there and she hoped it wasn't wishful thinking because she still felt the same about him.

Tammy had never prayed in her life. She wished she believed in the Maker, the Blessed Mother or any of the other gods. She wished there was a benevolent spirit that watched over them all because if she was a believer she would have prayed for more time. She hoped that this wasn't the last time they saw each other but her heart told her different.

Wiping her face the Khevassar turned away from the gate and walked back into the city.

Wren bit her lip to stop herself from crying in frustration at her latest failure. Another person had just died in front of her.

This time it was a middle-aged man called Borren who had continued to smile right up to the end. She didn't want to know about his life, his family and his job as a baker, but when you sat with someone for hours at a time eventually they started to talk. He'd done most of the talking as she'd been trying to concentrate but everything he'd told her had seeped in.

Now he was just another cold slab of meat and she was still fumbling around in the dark. Anger threatened to overwhelm her but Wren forced herself to breathe slowly until she felt calm. On the far side of the hospital Tianne was tending to one of the sick despite her own infection. Wren knew her friend was in pain. Her movements were stiff but Tianne was doing her best to hide it. So far she'd refused any of the herbal teas they brewed for other patients. It was the only thing they had to numb the pain. The stronger herbs were saved for those close to the end. She prayed it wouldn't come to that for her friend. It was a selfish thought but Wren couldn't help it. She didn't want her friend to die screaming in agony.

"We'll take care of him," said Andras, resting a hand on her shoulder. His endless compassion inspired her. Until getting to know him she'd never had much respect for priests. Those she'd met in the past seemed selfish or arrogant in their belief that their interpretation of scripture was the right one. They also seemed to spend a lot of time arguing instead of helping people. They lived in opulent homes, dressed in expensive clothes and ate fine food while preaching about the sins of desire, sloth and greed. Andras wore a faded old robe, ate the same food as everyone else and slept on the same cold floor but she never heard him complain.

Wren desperately wanted to find a cure but there were times when she was full of doubt. In those moments, when she thought about giving up, she only needed to look at Tianne and think of all that she'd been through. In spite of her suffering and betrayal in Zecorria she'd still chosen to be here among the sick.

Andras and another man wrapped Borren's body in a sheet and carried it out of the church. A short time later the priest sat down beside Wren and massaged his tired feet.

"Have you made much progress?" he asked and Wren almost laughed. Instead she just shook her head. If she started talking

the words would be bitter and angry. Right now the last thing she
wanted to do was add to his burdens with her problems.

"Tell me about the plague. How does it work?" he asked, intent
on drawing her into conversation.

"You've seen the effects. It targets the lungs and then other
organs. They struggle to breathe and tendrils of the infection
spread out into other areas, even the brain. It's almost as if it was
designed to cause as much pain as possible." Wren knew how
ridiculous that sounded but it was how she felt. She took a deep
breath in an attempt to repress the bitterness that was leaking
out. "Every time I try to push it back in one area of the body it
resurfaces in another."

"So why not work together with someone?" asked Andras.
"Fight the infection on two fronts."

"Magic doesn't work that way." She sounded confident but Wren
doubted her own words. As far as she knew it didn't work that way.
Healing was always one mage and one patient. Then again, what did
she know? She'd been a student at the Red Tower for less than a year.

Could two mages work together?

A skilled Healer like Master Yettle would have been able to
tell her if such a thing was possible.

They'd all been working in isolation to repress the plague, but
what if Andras was right? What if there was a way to combine
their weaves? She struggled with more than three layers but what
if she could combine her efforts with Val's? Would it be enough
to force back the infection? Or would they just kill the patient
more quickly?

A disturbance at the door drew her attention as Kovac stumbled into the hospital carrying Kimme over one shoulder. Several
people immediately moved to help, relieving him of his burden.
It also gave Wren a chance to look at his face.

The skin down one side was livid from fresh burns and all of his clothes were black and covered in ash. His trousers and shirt were falling to pieces and through the gaps she could see bright red skin underneath. Burns covered both of his hands and as she approached Wren felt intense heat radiating off his body.

"What happened? Where's Baedan?"

"Kimme almost lost control. I talked her down," he said, wobbling on his feet. She instinctively put out a hand to keep him upright and Kovac winced in pain from her touch. "Baedan ran. I don't know where he is."

"Sit down here," said Andras, producing a stool. Kovac slowly lowered himself on to it and breathed a sigh of relief.

Valmor and a herbalist called Murle were attending to Kimme but there was little to be done.

"There's nothing wrong with her. She's just deep asleep," said Val, biting her lip. "I'm more worried about what happens when she wakes up."

Kovac told them everything that had happened starting with Kimme going into a trance. When he was finished Andras and Murle carefully peeled or simply cut the clothes from his body. Wren stared with horror at the map of burns across most of his chest, legs and arms. The back of his body was barely touched but the front was a red mess of angry swollen flesh. Andras took Wren to one side while Murle offered Kovac some tea to numb the pain.

"I've seen burns like this before," said the priest in a whisper. "We can try to pick out all the pieces of cloth from his wounds but the risk of infection is high, especially in a place such as this," he said, gesturing at their grubby surroundings. "He'll be dead in a day—two at most—and the pain will be horrific. Is there anything you can do to help him?"

Healing the plague was one thing but skin and muscle wasn't nearly as complex. Wren had healed injuries in the past but none of them had been as severe as Kovac's burns.

"I'll try," said Wren, not wanting to offer false hope despite all that Kovac had done.

"That's all any of us can do," said Andras.

An idea started to form at the back of Wren's mind. She approached Valmor who was tending to a woman with a nasty lesion on her face. "Val, can you help me with something?"

"Of course," she murmured, tugging at the scarf around her neck. Most of those in the hospital had asked her about it but only a few knew the reason she wore it. Master Yettle had offered to heal the scar but she'd chosen to keep it. Much like Tianne, Val was determined to learn from the past. When she spoke above a whisper, which wasn't often, her voice had acquired a rasp from being hung.

"I want to try and heal Kovac. Together," Wren explained. Val just raised an eyebrow and gestured for her to keep talking. She had a far more delicate touch than Wren when it came to healing and what she was suggesting would play to both of their strengths. The idea of combining weaves was something to explore another day but right now Wren wanted to try something different. All of their patients had only days to live, but Kovac's remaining time was now among the shortest.

As she explained her idea Val's initial scepticism faded. "It can't make him any worse," she whispered.

Kovac had forsaken the tea and instead chosen a bottle of harsh spirits to numb the pain. A few days ago Baedan and Kimme had found a stash in one of the abandoned buildings. The ten bottles of colourless liquid were so rough none of the priests or mages wanted to drink it so they'd been using it to clean wounds. Kovac tipped back the bottle and grimaced.

"Worst stuff I've ever tasted," he said with a slur. He'd already put a good dent in the first bottle.

"We're going to try to help you," said Wren, choosing her words with care as the odds of success were small.

"I'd appreciate anything you can do," said Kovac, clearly aware of the severity of his burns and how much time he had remaining.

Wren drew deeply from the Source until her skin prickled with pain. "This is going to hurt. A lot," she warned him. Kovac took another long pull from the bottle.

"Ready."

At Wren's direction everyone else moved back, giving them plenty of space to work. She would lead and Valmor would follow.

Creating fire had become a relatively simple weave for her. By pulling heat from the air and then igniting it, the summoned flame could be maintained with a constant energy from the Source. Feeding more power into a simple flame could then be used to create a weapon. So much of what she'd learned with magic was destructive. It was only since leaving the Red Tower that she'd begun to learn how magic could be used in more practical ways.

What they were attempting was a lot more delicate and she had to work slowly or else risk killing Kovac before Val had a chance to heal his burns. At the moment the skin on his body was severely inflamed and warm to the touch. Focusing on the air around him Wren slowly drew the heat from it.

"That feels good," said Kovac, closing his eyes as the temperature around him fell. To begin with it would feel like the soothing balm she'd seen herbalists apply to minor burns, but a salve wouldn't save him today. Too much of his skin had been damaged and it was split open in many places.

Wren redirected the excess heat she was drawing away towards the ceiling where it naturally dispersed through small gaps. A few people shuffled further away from Kovac as icy motes drifted down through the air above his head.

Sweat gathered at Wren's fringe as she slowly drew more heat from the air. The colour of Kovac's skin hadn't changed but his face was now paler and he shivered.

"It's a little cold now," said Kovac, his teeth chattering together. His breath frosted and his whole body started to shake.

Wren was aware of Val embracing the Source but she didn't turn her head. If she lost concentration she might accidentally stop Kovac's heart. Lowering the air temperature was easy but keeping it at the same level required her full attention. The warmer air in the room kept mixing with the cold so it required her to make constant adjustments.

As Val made a flicking gesture with both hands Wren knew she'd placed the first weave across Kovac's body, just above the skin. He'd clenched his jaw against the cold and was now breathing hard. The air hissed in and out between his teeth.

Slowly the burned skin across one side of his face changed colour, fading from an angry red, but the underlying tissue was still damaged. Val made another gesture, adding another layer to the weave. Wren always tried to create several at once and then apply them to a patient, but Val built it up gradually one piece at a time.

When Kovac's skin was almost back to its normal colour Val added two more layers. These sank beneath his flesh and his whole body shook.

"Hold still," said Val, her own jaw tight with concentration. Kovac didn't reply but closed his eyes, perhaps to take his mind somewhere else away from the pain. Despite being so close to the cold air Wren felt sweat trickle down the sides of her face from the pressure. The power still sang in her veins but all thoughts of how it made her feel were pushed to the back of her mind.

Working beneath the skin Val was repairing damaged tissue so that for a long time it looked as if nothing was happening. But power continued to flow into Kovac and Wren could sense the complexity of the weave made from multiple layers.

Her awareness of time faded. Soon the only things in her world that mattered were the growing pain behind her eyes and the cold she was applying to Kovac. Even her awareness of the Source faded. She measured time in deep breaths and ignored everything else.

If she hadn't been so attentive Wren wouldn't have noticed the subtle change that rippled across the skin on Kovac's face and chest.

The burns were starting to fade.

"Ease up a little, Wren," said Val. She gripped Wren's shoulder hard enough for it to be painful, giving her the impression it wasn't the first time Val had said it.

Slowly Wren pulled back on cooling the air. Almost immediately more of Kovac's natural colour returned as fresh blood rushed to the surface. A long painful hiss burst from between his teeth as the new skin came alive. But it still wasn't done. Moving down his body, piece by piece, the burns were repairing themselves. Normally a burn left behind a scar made from smooth white skin. Kovac's was completely healed as if he'd never been injured. Every scar and blemish had simply vanished.

Working in tandem Wren gradually eased back again until Val finally signalled for her to release the Source.

The moment she let go Wren toppled over, her face slamming into the floor. The world turned black and all sound vanished.

When she woke up little time had passed as people were still helping her to sit up. Andras squatted down in front of her and said something but she couldn't make out the words. Someone put a blanket around her shoulders and pressed a mug of something hot into her hands. Her whole body was trembling from extreme cold and the sweat soaking into her clothes felt icy.

Gradually the blanket and the broth eased the chill from her body and sounds returned to normal. The hospital was unusually quiet, which made her fear the worst.

"Did it work?" she asked, trying to peer around the priest. "Is Val all right?"

"She's fine. Just tired," Andras said with a weary smile of his own.

"Kovac?" said Wren, a little afraid of the answer.

Andras moved to one side giving her a proper view of the hospital. Kovac was still sitting on the stool and someone had given him a blanket and a mug of something hot. He was greedily slurping it down, holding the cup to his face while inhaling the warm vapours. When he saw Wren watching him from across the room he raised his mug in a salute.

It was only then that she noticed the skin on his face. There were no burns at all and no scars. Without wanting to stare at his body for too long she saw enough to realise the rest of his skin was the same.

"You did it. You healed him," said Andras with a big smile. He gave her a hug and even went so far as to put two fingers to his lips and raise them towards her in the Drassi fashion.

"We did it together," said Wren, looking past him to where Val was sitting. She was staring hard at Kovac but then turned her head slightly towards Wren.

"He's cured," said Andras, laughing wildly. The full meaning of his words slowly sunk in.

There were no signs of the infection. As well as healing all the burns any lesions on his body were gone. He was healthy again.

Wren was about to celebrate when she noticed Val's expression. Her friend shook her head slightly as a single tear ran down her cheek.

Even though it was painful Wren reached for the Source and carefully extended her awareness towards Kovac. On the surface his body had been healed and he seemed healthy but when she probed beneath the surface the truth was revealed.

The infection was still there, buried deep in his lungs. They hadn't cured him, they'd merely delayed the inevitable.

CHAPTER 36

Vargus kept everyone moving as fast as possible without making them run. Everyone was still terrified by what they'd seen, with the exception of Munroe. She was watching the streets but he could tell her mind was elsewhere, no doubt trying to process what had just happened with Kai.

Walking beside the mortals Vargus could see Akosh was just as scared. She looked on the verge of panic and any moment he expected her to start running. Dox was shaking uncontrollably and clung to Munroe's hand. Exposing any mortal to Kai's real nature and appearance was dangerous. For such a young person, before their mind had finished developing, it would inform the rest of her life.

Only the boy had taken it all in his stride. He studied Herakion as a visitor arriving in the city for the first time. Danoph paused to take note of peculiar quirks of Zecorran architecture, remarked on the fashion of long tails on men's jackets and was charmed by a trio of local musicians performing on the street.

In Zecorria it was not uncommon to see jugglers and musicians performing for spare change. Danoph paused in front of an old blind man playing a mournful tune on a fiddle. The others had walked past him without noticing but the boy was visibly moved by the music.

The tune was mangled from the original but Vargus still recognised it. It came from a tragic story about heartbreak from two centuries ago. Supposedly based on a myth the song was an instructive tale about the dangers of young lovers making promises they couldn't keep. It had actually been adapted from a real story that no one alive would remember, yet somehow it had survived in oral history.

It made Vargus wonder what would be remembered from this era. What modern stories would people speak of in centuries to come? Would they know of their fight against Kai? Or would all tales be of the Mad King and the Warlock? Would magic ever be spoken about in public again, or would it truly become a curse?

"Where are we going?" asked Akosh, which was a fair question. His only thought so far had been to put some distance between them and Kai. It was unlikely he would come after them but Vargus had given up trying to predict what he would do. It was dangerous to underestimate him.

"We need somewhere safe to rest," he said. At the same time Vargus wondered if there was such a place in the city. If Kai had people everywhere, plus more thralls, it would be difficult to find somewhere out of sight.

Pointing down a small side street Vargus led them to a quiet tree-lined square. This late at night the whole place was deserted. Shops lined three sides of the square and the fourth was occupied by a battered old theatre.

The heavy shadows gathered in the square wouldn't normally concern him. Tonight he worried about who, or what, might be lurking within, sending whispers back to their Master.

"Rest here a moment," said Vargus, gesturing towards to a row of benches beneath the trees. When Danoph moved to sit with the others Vargus pulled him aside to speak in private.

"Danoph, I need you to use your power." He seemed to come

awake for the first time since entering the city. "We need to find a safe place. Somewhere he won't find us. I need you to look ahead and navigate us away from danger. Do you understand?"

There had been enough surprises today without revealing Danoph's true nature to the others. He suspected Akosh knew more than she was saying but so far she'd kept her mouth shut. They would find out soon enough but his first priority was a place to regroup.

Realising the danger they were in the boy's expression turned grim. Danoph raised his right hand and light blossomed upon his palm. It was pale and not very bright but still managed to ease the deepest shadows under the trees. They pulled back as if afraid of the boy's power and his potential.

When his eyes began to glow a scream started to build in the back of Dox's throat. "Silence her," said Akosh, nudging Munroe in the ribs. The mage was now staring at Danoph with a mix of awe and surprise. "Or I'll do it for you."

Munroe instinctively pulled the girl to her chest, turning her face away from yet another surprise. Dox had reached her limit. Her scream was muffled by Munroe's jacket and then it faded as she pulled herself tight against the mage with both arms.

"Follow me," said Danoph, his voice echoing around the square.

He led them with confidence down narrow streets and wide roads that would normally be busy with people. All of them were deserted apart from a few drunks or a patrol of guards but they always arrived when the squad was moving away from them. Vargus knew their timing wasn't by chance.

When they came across an inn that was still open with lights in the window Akosh moved towards it. "Why don't we go in here?" she asked.

The boy rested his left hand on the door and a faint smile tugged at the corners of his mouth. "The drunks won't remember but the burly man drinking at the bar is an apothecarist. He almost lost his home and shop then he embraced Kai as his patron."

Vargus saw some of the colour fade from Akosh's face. "He has people everywhere," he said. "We need to keep moving."

"Who is he?" hissed Akosh, jabbing a finger at Danoph's back.

"One of us," said Vargus. "But keep that to yourself for now, understood?"

Akosh nodded reluctantly. He knew it pained her to take orders from anyone.

"Munroe, I need you to use your old magic," said Danoph.

"Why?" she asked, immediately suspicious. Vargus didn't know if she'd met Danoph at the Red Tower but she was probably wondering why a teenage boy was leading their group.

"Because the road ahead is blocked by several groups of soldiers. They won't move out of the way in time without a distraction." Munroe peered down the dark road ahead but there was no one in sight. "I'll tell you when," he said, taking the lead again.

A short time later they came to the mouth of a narrow street where Danoph paused. Placing a finger to his lips he pointed down the road to their left. After peeling Dox off her for a moment Munroe peered around the corner and quickly ducked back out of sight.

"Seven guards," she mouthed, then her gaze turned inwards. Vargus felt her embrace the Source but he couldn't follow what she did. In some ways it mirrored the boy's natural power. Instead of revealing the future she was able to manipulate the odds in her favour. In the distance he heard a distinctive crack and the sound of breaking glass. Without waiting to see if they'd taken the bait Danoph led them on. Glancing to his left Vargus saw the last of the soldiers disappear around a corner.

Three more times Munroe was forced to use her magic to clear the way. Each time it was an immovable group of soldiers or criminals loitering in dark corners. Vargus didn't know if any of the people they encountered worked for Kai or not but Danoph was not taking any chances.

After an hour he led them to an area of the city populated by large homes belonging to the wealthy. Many of them were old families with deep roots in the city. Their obvious connections to the palace made everyone a little nervous. But the boy was navigating via channels only he could see and Vargus trusted him to steer them away from danger. The Weaver could see more than anyone.

His foresight, combined with Munroe's Talent, turned the impossible into reality. In such a large city, even so late at night, it was highly unlikely that they would go unnoticed and yet the path he'd chosen made sure of it.

When they arrived at one large walled house, much like those around it, Vargus was as confused as the others. He had no idea who lived inside or what kind of a reception they would receive at such an hour.

A pull-cord hung outside the gate and Danoph tugged on it sharply three times before anyone could protest. Vargus mulled over what he might say if anyone even bothered to answer the door. Eventually he heard the scraping of metal on wood. A hatch opened revealing the sleepy face of an old man.

"Do you have any idea of the time?" was the first thing he said.

"Tell your Master we seek an audience. I know he's awake," said Danoph.

"And who are you?" asked the servant.

"We support his family's claim to the throne and will stand with him against the Regent," said Danoph. The servant hissed through his teeth and quickly closed the hatch. Speaking against the Regent in the open was dangerous; however, Choilan hadn't been the only person vying for the position of Regent. There were many who resented him and the choices he'd made since taking the throne. The worst offence was his recent approach to magic and his cadre of mages.

Since the war magic had never sat right with Zecorrans, especially the notion of having a mage in a position of power. Having a dozen so close to the throne scared a lot of people despite reassurances from the Regent.

Keeping an eye on the street for signs of danger Vargus moved closer to the boy to double-check this was the right decision.

"Patience," said Danoph, before Vargus could ask him a question. The glow had faded from his eyes and yet he remained a different person. Someone that was both familiar and alien. He wondered if he'd unnerved people in the same way when he'd carried the mantle of the Weaver.

There was a scraping of bolts and the gate opened to reveal the old servant carrying a lantern. He was dressed only in a nightshirt, which showed off his bony legs, and a battered cloak.

"I can see your little soldier," said Akosh, pointing at the servant's crotch. He glared and pulled the cloak tighter around his body, concealing his modesty.

"Follow the path to the door," he said, gesturing to where another servant was waiting with a lantern.

The other servant was a guard who'd also been turfed from his bed but at least he'd pulled on a pair of trousers and a shirt. He glared at them all, especially the sword on Vargus's back.

"We're not here to cause any trouble," said Vargus, taking the lead. The boy had faded into the background again. His job was done for now. It was up to Vargus to find a way forward.

"Inside," said the guard, giving nothing away.

They walked through a short hallway to a richly decorated sitting room with a marble fireplace, tiled mosaic floor and metal tables topped with thick glass. Crystal lanterns hung on the walls and the padded furniture was crafted from rare woods Vargus had not seen in a long time. A selection of drinks sat idle in crystal decanters on an antique side table. Munroe helped herself without waiting for an invitation.

Dox sank down into one of the chairs and Danoph perched on the edge of another. Akosh moved to stand by the fire which had recently been lit, but it offered little warmth yet. Glancing up at the high arched ceiling Vargus saw paintings depicting scenes from early Zecorria. The wars. The building of Herakion. The old tribes coming together as one. The owner of the house had deep roots.

"My Lord Mallenby," said the nasal voice of a weasel-faced herald.

Sweeping into the room behind the herald came a plump middle-aged man dressed in silk pyjamas, a red gown and woollen slippers. Unlike the servants his eyes were clear, suggesting he'd not been asleep.

Lord Mallenby scanned the room with a calculating look. If he was surprised by having such a peculiar group of strangers turn up at his door in the middle of the night it didn't show. Vargus noted how their host's gaze lingered on him and Danoph more than the others.

"Who is in charge?" he asked, his voice unusually high-pitched for such a large man. The others looked towards him so Vargus stepped forward. This pleased Lord Mallenby as a wry smile tugged at the corners of his mouth. "It was very risky of you, to show up at my door, speaking ill of the Regent. I could have you arrested for treason."

"But you won't," suggested Vargus.

The air was ripe with tension as Lord Mallenby considered his response. Vargus was good at reading people but even he couldn't tell if Royal Guards were already on their way to arrest them.

"No, I won't," said Lord Mallenby with a giggle and the tension eased. "Pour me a big one," he said, waving a hand at Munroe who was lingering by the drinks table.

Vargus waited until Lord Mallenby had a drink in hand and was settled in a padded chair before speaking. It gave him a little time to think about why Danoph had guided them here and what to say. "We both want the same thing. The Regent off the throne."

"Go on," said Lord Mallenby, sipping his drink.

"You want more?"

"Either you're serious about this or you're wasting my time. Let's start with what you want," he suggested.

Vargus considered his words carefully. "The Regent is being manipulated by dangerous forces. I want them removed from the palace. His mages, too. They've become unstable."

Lord Mallenby harrumphed. "They should never have been there in the first place. Choilan was mad to think he could do better than those before him. I want every mage expunged from the palace and an end to this ridiculous amnesty."

"And how are you going to fight his mages without some of your own?" asked Munroe.

"My dear, I know some of you are mages," said Lord Mallenby. It was almost as if he'd been expecting them. "It's a necessary evil I can stomach, but once all of this is done, I want you out of Zecorria as well. There will be a national ban."

"It won't stop children from being born with magic," said Munroe, glancing towards Dox. The girl was huddled up in her jacket and her eyes were far away. Danoph was equally unaware of the conversation flowing around him.

"Perhaps, but magic doesn't belong in the palace or anywhere near the throne. Many people side with me on this. Their memories aren't as short as some. We still remember what happened during the war."

Munroe sneered but said nothing more. Instead she drained her glass of whisky and poured another. Perhaps she intended to drink Lord Mallenby into poverty.

"What are you offering in return?" asked Vargus.

"Before we get to that I want to be clear on something. I want Choilan alive so that he can stand trial. The people need to see him punished for his crimes. I intend to see that justice is served. He is not to be killed."

Akosh snorted. She was probably thinking they would skew Choilan's crimes to suit their agenda. Most likely he'd still end up being hanged or beheaded, but not until he'd been paraded around and made to suffer.

"Agreed," said Vargus before an argument could begin. "And what will your contribution be?"

Lord Mallenby raised his glass and sipped his whisky. "I'll provide you with money, dear boy. Enough to hire an army to storm the palace and bring Choilan and his cronies to their knees."

"We'll need Drassi," said Akosh. "No one else can be trusted."

She was right. There would be no way to trust any of the mercenaries available in the city. Vargus had no illusion about Kai not finding out what they were planning but he didn't want a spy in their camp.

"Agreed. What else?" said Lord Mallenby.

"A safe place to plan our strategy," said Vargus. It would also give the others a chance to recover from their ordeal. He knew Akosh would heal quickly but he wasn't sure about the others.

"The west wing has been empty since my daughter moved away. There's plenty of space to house all of you. I'll have a scribe sent over in the morning. He'll make a note of whatever you need, supplies and whatever. Cost isn't an issue."

"Why are we here?" said Munroe, unable to hold her tongue until they were alone to discuss this. Vargus had underestimated her talent for asking difficult questions at inopportune times. "Why are we trusting him?"

"He's the only one who's ready to act," said Danoph, startling everyone in the room. He had been listening after all. "The others will follow but they have too much to risk. Lord Mallenby has nothing. His children don't need him for his money. His wife is dead and his life is fairly empty. The only thing he really craves is power."

"I'm also a patriot," said Lord Mallenby.

"Liar," murmured Dox, coming out of her reverie.

"What's the real reason?" asked Vargus, crossing his arms.

"Fine. I just like a good fight," said their host. "But if this all goes wrong, you're on your own. I'm not going to end up in a cell."

"A true mercenary," said Akosh with a hint of admiration.

"A survivor, Madam," said Lord Mallenby, holding up his glass. "If we're done for tonight I'll have someone show you to the west wing. You can talk to the others."

"Others?" said Vargus. Akosh reached for one of her daggers and Munroe embraced the Source.

"Yes, they told me you would be coming," said Lord Mallenby.

Akosh was creeping up behind their host but Vargus waved her back. She lowered her arm but kept her blade ready. Raw power from the Source continued to radiate from Munroe as they cautiously followed a servant towards the west wing.

He led them through the house towards a heavy set of double doors. The old servant pushed open one and then stomped off, muttering to himself about unruly visitors at ungodly hours.

Vargus stepped through the door first with Akosh and Munroe following close behind. Dox and Danoph held back in case they needed to run.

At the end of a corridor lined with huge mirrors and expensive paintings was a sitting room similar to the one they'd just left.

The thick red carpet muffled their footsteps. Through a gap in the door Vargus could hear the murmur of voices.

Reaching over his shoulder he slowly drew his sword, wincing as the blade scraped the scabbard. Those inside didn't seem to hear as their quiet conversation continued without interruption. If this was a trap it was a peculiar one. There were rooms on either side of the corridor but Vargus didn't sense anyone lurking within. Taking the initiative he pushed open the sitting-room door and rushed inside with Akosh and Munroe a step behind.

Two men were sat in front of the fire with their backs towards him but they turned at the sound of hurried footsteps. When Vargus saw their faces he almost dropped his sword in surprise.

"You took long enough," said Garvey.

"Welcome to the rebellion," said Balfruss.

CHAPTER 37

Regent Choilan paced back and forth in his bedroom as he contemplated his situation. Since being confined to his rooms every Royal Guard he'd spoken with wore the same vacant expression, suggesting they'd been mentally enslaved. All of them had been given strict instructions to keep him locked up for his own safety leaving him with little to do but stew and await further instructions.

Yesterday he'd been forced to make a speech. The square in front of the palace had been packed with people, many of them looking puzzled, wondering what he was about to say. Choilan had been equally surprised until they'd delivered the text.

He'd been expecting something radical. A major change from his approach to magic or a declaration of war. Instead it had been a speech about patriotism and a list of names. He had no idea who most of them were, only that they'd been labelled as national enemies, were considered extremely dangerous, and any sightings were to be reported. A generous reward for any information turned the mood of the crowd from indifference to excitement and enthusiasm.

Posters had been nailed to walls and descriptions given to every guard and mercenary in Herakion. More posters had been handed out to the crowd to ensure the vicious criminals were brought to justice. Choilan doubted what he'd been forced to say was true, particularly the heinous crimes they'd apparently committed, but it had all been carefully planned so they had nowhere to hide. The whole city would be looking for them and Choilan expected the criminals to be locked up in cells within the day.

There was a brief knock at the door before his traitorous first wife, Selina, strode into the room. She wore a gold dress that clung to her shapely figure making him hate her all the more as he still found her attractive.

"Sit down, we have something to discuss," she said in a commanding voice. One of the Royal Guards was lurking at her shoulder, an eager look on her face, as if she was desperately waiting for something. Choilan was about to argue when he vaguely recognised the guard. She was someone he'd seen disciplined for something in the past. Chewing loudly or glaring at him on duty. Maybe it was because she had a lazy eye. Since then she'd been kept at a distance so he wouldn't have to look at her surly face.

Choilan did as he was told despite being ordered around like a child.

"You see, I told you he just needs a firm hand," said Selina, smirking at the guard.

The surly guard raised a fist. "Let me know if you need any help with discipline."

"Of course. Leave us," said Selina and the guard complied.

Choilan was about to tell his first wife what he really thought of her when she put a finger to her lips. She gestured for him to follow her into the bedroom and at first he hesitated. She rolled her eyes, pointed at the door and made a face he couldn't read. Curiosity, and a desire to strangle her where they wouldn't be disturbed, made him follow her into the bedroom.

"We don't have much time so listen carefully," said Selina.

"I should kill you right now," he said, looking around for a weapon. The serrated pear knife would do. He might struggle to find the shrivelled raisin that passed for her heart, but it would do well enough to cut her treasonous throat.

Her slap caught him by surprise and he stumbled back, holding a hand to his stinging cheek. "Shut up and listen," she hissed. He sat down on the edge of the bed. A knife was too quick. He'd call in a torturer to take her apart, piece by piece.

"Half of the guards in the palace have been altered with magic but I think many are still loyal. Marran and his Master make sure the two groups remain separate, but Bettina has been making a list of names."

"How dare you strike me," said Choilan.

"Did you hear anything I've just said? I had to play along or else I'd have ended up like the rest. Choilan, dearest," she said, moving towards him and he flinched backwards. With a sigh she picked up the pear knife and pressed it into his hand before kneeling down in front of him, offering up her throat.

"Here's your chance. Kill me if you want to, but without my help, you'll remain a prisoner and their puppet. I'm on your side," she insisted. "Either you trust me or you can stay here until you're no longer useful to them."

He almost did it, right then, cut her throat and ended her miserable life. It would be one less thing for him to worry about. On the other hand he could still kill her later if he thought she was lying. Choilan lowered the knife and she smiled.

"You hit me."

"Yes I did, dear, but that's the least of your worries."

"You hit Lara as well," he noted.

"I'll apologise to her later, if we survive. Buy her a new dress and she'll forget all about it. They expect me to hate you, so I'm playing a role. If I don't they'll take away my free will." Selina shuddered at the thought. "It's difficult to know who to trust so we need to get you out of the palace."

"How?" he said.

"I was going to use my agents, but Doggett is dead and they've replaced him with someone else. A woman named Nell. I can't trust her, despite what she claims."

Previously Choilan would have said Selina was paranoid but now it was healthy to be suspicious of new faces. "Then who?"

"Bettina."

"Are you sure she's not been altered?"

Selina snorted. "No. She remains as icy and aloof as ever. As long as they keep things orderly she doesn't care who's in charge. At least that's what she's told them."

Bettina had a cold and analytical mind. He suspected the only reason she'd chosen to side with them instead of the traitors was the amount of mess they'd leave behind. Once the dust settled it would be her responsibility to clean it up and restore order. Chaos of any sort was anathema to her.

"How do we get out?"

"It's going to be difficult. Our best chance is to recruit some Royal Guards and escape at night. They might have to fight their way out, but it can't be helped. We can always train more after."

"What about the mages?" asked Choilan. He couldn't believe after everything he'd done for them that they'd betray him. Marran was less of a surprise. His days had already been numbered.

"I think most of them are thralls for Marran. Yes," said Selina, holding up a hand to stop him saying the obvious. "It was a mistake to bring him in and we should have killed him weeks ago. We'll deal with him when the time is right. Today's problem is getting out alive."

"When?" asked Choilan, not wanting to spend another night locked up in his rooms. Once they were out of the palace he would rally supporters around him and they would come back with an army. He would have to denounce his cadre of mages. Perhaps if he claimed he'd been influenced by magic, much like his predecessor, they would believe him. But unlike the Mad King he'd come to his senses and was now fully against mages. It would require some careful negotiations with various families, and no doubt some sacrifices before they'd provide him with money and troops, but he was confident about remaining on the throne.

"Tomorrow night. The longer we wait the harder it will become. I've no idea what plans are already in motion," admitted Selina, nervously glancing at the door. "I'm not sure how long I can keep up the charade."

Selina was right to be scared. Without him she would be cast out of the palace and stripped of everything. If she wanted to continue living in luxury it was in her best interest to keep him alive and on the throne. No matter how much she claimed to hate him Choilan knew she needed him.

"Why are you smiling?" she asked.

"I'm confident you'll get me out alive."

"I'm not," she said. Something caught her attention and she gestured for him to stand up.

"I'm sorry about this," she apologised.

"About what?" he asked.

A moment later she kneed him in the groin. At first there was no real pain just a dull ache. Then it hit him and Choilan dropped to his knees keening like a wounded animal. He found himself lying on his side, curled up into a tight ball, staring at the dust that had gathered under his bed.

Several pairs of feet marched into the room before coming to stand beside him. All sound in the world was strangely distorted but he picked out two voices he recognised, Selina and Marran. She was saying something condescending, no doubt about him, and the greasy mage chuckled in reply. His next comment was met with a stony silence that Choilan knew only too well. Marran had tried to push something and had gone too far.

Choilan wasn't sure how long he'd been lying there but as the pain eased he heard the tail end of her frosty reply.

" . . . still wouldn't touch you. Do you understand?"

"You should be nicer to me," said Marran.

"You're revolting," spat Selina. "Your Master finds you repulsive as well. I could see it in his face. We all know about your disgusting urges."

The pain faded by another degree allowing Choilan to see the mage's bitter expression. "I could kill you right now, and no one would care."

"Go ahead," said Selina, stabbing Marran in the chest with a finger. "You'd still be a maggot."

"What's happening in here?" asked a new voice as a Royal Guard stepped into the room. It was the surly one from earlier with the lazy eye. She noticed Choilan lying on the floor and smiled. He'd make sure she was suitably disciplined once this was over.

Marran was on the verge of violence and Selina seemed intent on provoking him. Slowly the redness faded from his face and the mage stormed out of the room. Selina was pretending that Marran hadn't scared her but he saw her relief. She would only be able to bully the mage for so long before she went too far and he killed her, regardless of the consequences. Choilan wasn't the only one living on borrowed time.

In the middle of the night Choilan was shaken awake. The first thing he saw was two figures moving around in the dark. Instinct made him open his mouth to scream but someone clamped a hand over it.

"It's me," hissed Selina, waiting until his breathing had slowed before she released him.

"What are you doing?" he asked.

"We can't wait. We have to go now." Selina was terrified and he wondered if Marran had already threatened her. The other figure in his room turned out to be Bettina. As ever she wore a dress that showed as little bare flesh as possible, but this one and even her slippers were black. She lit a candle and threw several dark pieces of clothing at him before retreating to the sitting room.

"Get dressed. Quickly," said his first wife, leaving him to do it by himself. Choilan thought she'd at least stay to help him but she went to check the corridor with Bettina. He endured the slight and pulled on his clothes by himself.

"We have to move quietly," said Selina as he came into the sitting room. "Don't speak until we're clear of the palace. There are seven Royal Guards waiting for us."

"Seven? Is that all?" Normally there were over sixty stationed around the palace at any time.

"We couldn't be sure of the others," said Bettina, no doubt grimacing at the imprecision rather than the odds. "I am certain these seven are loyal."

"It will have to do. We just need to get out," said Selina, raising her eyebrows. Of course. None of the guards had to survive. They just needed to get in the way of any opposition so that he could make his escape.

"Not a sound now," said Selina. He swallowed a sarcastic comment and gestured for her to get on with it.

Outside his door was a pool of blood. As he watched a pair of feet disappeared into the doorway opposite and a moment later a slightly battered Royal Guard appeared. Choilan vaguely recognised him because of his bushy moustache but didn't know his name. For a moment Choilan thought his escape was over before it had really gone anywhere, but Selina gestured for the guard to take the lead. Blood dripped from the guard's sword, creating a line of red dots on the floor for them to follow.

At this hour the palace was silent and perfectly still. No servants roamed the corridors. Light came from widely spaced lanterns fixed to the walls but between them were deep pools of darkness. When Choilan stepped into the first it felt as if he'd passed through a doorway into another room. The air became bitterly cold. His chest ached and all sounds were distorted.

As he stepped out of the shadows the next lantern was so bright it dazzled his eyes. Selina gripped him by the elbow before he fell over while shading her face. Choilan followed suit to avoid being blinded again but the cold feeling inside wouldn't leave him. It gripped his stomach and he became conscious of his rapid breathing. He told himself it wasn't fear. It was excitement. It had been quite a while since he'd been on such an adventure.

The only sounds in the world were the thump of the guard's boots, the patter of blood dripping from his sword and the soft hush of their shoes. It was strangely peaceful and Choilan wondered if this inner calm was what the priests rambled on about in church.

A warning hiss brought them to a sudden halt. Up ahead the guard waved them back before ducking into an alcove. Selina shoved him towards an open door and they huddled together in a small room.

Not far away Choilan could hear the heavy step of several guards marching towards them. Someone gripped his hand, squeezing it so tightly he almost cried out. Instead he bit his lip and squeezed back. Not because he was afraid, merely to show support.

Breathing slowly in and out of his mouth he counted to fifty while urging the guards not to notice them hiding like thieves.

The notion of it, slinking around his own palace, made a mockery of his position but right now it was necessary. Tomorrow would be a day for setting things right. For cleaning all the vermin out of the palace from top to bottom.

The guards moved on without stopping and everyone heaved a sigh of relief. Selina quickly released his hand and refused to look him in the eye. She wouldn't admit to being scared and, worse, seeking comfort from him in her darkest hour. Choilan swallowed his smirk but made a mental note to use it against her at a later date.

Their moustachioed guard walked ahead, alert for danger, while they scuttled along jumping at the smallest noise. A faint whistle up ahead was echoed by their protector and six more guards appeared from the shadows. With their full complement of protectors surrounding him Choilan felt assured of their escape. At the very least if they encountered any trouble he could run while they fought to the death. Their sacrifice would be remembered and honoured, but only as long as he escaped. Their heroism would mean nothing if he died alongside them in a petty scuffle.

When they rounded the next corner the three guards in front cried out in surprise. Before they could warn him about the danger one of them stumbled back with blood gushing from a wound in her neck. She turned and tried to say something but her throat was clogged. Instead she spat blood over Choilan and collapsed on the floor.

There was a blinding flash of light and someone was shoving Choilan against a wall, shielding him with their body. Peering over the guard's shoulder he saw three of his protectors fighting with a number of Royal Guards in a frantic battle. Their blades were moving so quickly he struggled to follow who was winning until two of the opposition fell back. One stumbled to a knee holding a hand to his side while another simply collapsed on to her back. They were winning but then he heard more footsteps approaching from behind.

"We need to move," he said but was promptly ignored. The fighting continued in front while coming up the corridor from the opposite direction was another squad of Royal Guards. Standing in the middle of their line was Marran. The sneer on his face made Choilan sick to his stomach.

All but one of his loyal guards ran into the fight and the air rang with sounds of frantic battle. On one side of him he could feel Selina trembling while Bettina remained outwardly calm. She was watching the fighting with an air of disappointment. No doubt she was upset that her plan was not running to schedule.

At first glance the Royal Guards beside the greasy mage looked normal but they fought with such reckless abandon it became clear they didn't care about their wellbeing. They sustained severe injuries but just kept fighting until those standing against them were dead. In almost no time there was blood splashed all over the walls and the corridor was filled with the stench of spilled innards. Stepping over the dying guards Marran looked past Choilan to his remaining protectors down the corridor.

The greasy mage made a twisting motion with both hands and the resulting screams were bloodcurdling. One of the guards dropped to the floor, suddenly missing her head. It had simply popped off her body like a cork from a bottle. It rolled along the floor and stopped in front of Choilan. The second guard was flopping about like a puppet with cut strings. Those facing the injured guard showed no mercy as they immediately ran him through. Only the third Royal Guard appeared unaffected but when he turned around Choilan felt bile rise in the back of his throat. Blood ran from the guard's eyes, nose, mouth and ears which quickly soaked into his uniform. He managed two steps before his eyes rolled up and mercifully he collapsed face down.

A heavy silence settled on the corridor. Their remaining protector stood in front of Choilan between two groups of his peers. He was heavily outnumbered and on top of that was facing a ruthless mage. Nevertheless Choilan expected him to do his duty and die with honour.

Instead he dropped his sword to the floor and knelt down. "Forgive me, Regent," he said before asking his former friends for mercy.

Choilan was pleased when they didn't show any. Instead they cut his throat and the coward was left to die, choking on his own blood. Selina had stopped trembling and was now frozen with fear. On his right Bettina was staring down at Marran with a haughty expression that bordered on disgust. He wasn't sure what the mage would do next but as Regent he was not about to beg or plead for his life. If this was the end then he intended to die on his feet.

"Well, get on with it," said Choilan, lifting his chin. The mage said nothing. Instead he just stared at them with his beady little eyes. Choilan stared right back, refusing to be intimidated by such vermin. "What are you waiting for?"

An unpleasant smile developed on the mage's face. "Oh, I'm not going to kill you, but this disobedience can't go unpunished."

Choilan swallowed hard and prepared himself for the worst. Marran was going to change him into a mindless thrall. A living shell with no will of his own. Standing behind the mage one of the injured guards dropped to her knees and keeled over. She'd finally succumbed to her injuries or whatever spell he'd placed on her mind would only stretch so far. The survivors didn't react and remained immobile awaiting further instructions.

"I'm ready," said Choilan.

Again the mage smiled in a way that terrified him. Marran raised a finger and pointed it at Choilan's chest. He braced himself for pain and took deep breaths in readiness, but nothing happened. Instead that dreadful finger moved to his right until it was pointed at Bettina. He glanced at his assistant and she managed to raise a disapproving eyebrow before her head exploded in a shower of gore.

Hot blood splashed across Choilan's face and mouth and he gagged, spitting out blood. It was all over him, running down the inside of his clothes. There were bits of bone in his hair and pieces embedded in his cheek. He tried to wipe as much of it away as possible but it seemed without end, even in his beard. Eventually he'd cleared enough that he could see Marran's vicious smirk. The mage was focused on something between his outstretched hands but Choilan couldn't see anything. More magic. He should never have put his trust in mages. He should have brought in a national ban. All magic was inherently evil.

"Hold her," said Marran, gesturing at Selina who screamed and tried to run. Choilan was frozen with terror and watched his first wife try to escape but the treacherous Royal Guards quickly dragged her back. It took four of them to manhandle her as she was thrashing about like a wild animal.

"Help me!" she pleaded but he didn't know what to do. There wasn't anything he could do. The only sensible thing for him to do was to flee but as soon as the thought occurred another guard grabbed him around the arm. And all the while Selina was being dragged towards Marran and whatever he was creating with his magic. Selina's cries were almost deafening as the mage approached her. Then, for the briefest of moments, it looked as if she might escape his clutches. She kicked one of the guards in the face and elbowed a second in the throat. Their grip loosened but before she had a chance to break free the other two secured her again.

With a rising sense of horror Choilan watched Marran place a hand on either side of Selina's head. Her body stopped struggling almost instantly but her head continued to thrash from side to side. The fight had moved within as she tried to repel the invader that was eroding her will. There was a final long exhalation of breath and then she was silent and still. He could just make out the slight rise of her chest. The only other sign that indicated she was still alive were the tears running from the corners of both eyes.

The Royal Guards surrounding her showed no reaction to what was happening. Their eyes remained glazed and disinterested. Marran muttered something in her ear and then it was done.

The Royal Guards helped Selina to her feet and although she stayed upright she looked bewildered.

"Selina?" he asked but she didn't react. "Can you hear me?"

His first wife stared at Choilan as if he were a stranger.

"She can hear you, but you're not in charge any more," said Marran, turning to Selina. "Tell him who you serve."

"I serve you, Master," said Selina, placing a hand on Marran's shoulder.

Choilan turned away, unable to look at the smug mage any more. Two guards escorted him back to his rooms before locking him inside.

More than the blood on his skin and clothes, it was the silence that bothered him. The palace felt abandoned and yet it was still full of people. The difference was that none of them would come to his aid.

He was alone.

CHAPTER 38

It was a strange war council that gathered to discuss the assault on the Zecorran palace. Vargus had not seen the like in a long time.

Their host, Lord Mallenby, had been true to his word, providing them with everything they needed. A safe space to work where they wouldn't be discovered, comfortable surroundings and, most of all, peace and quiet. In addition, letters with credit had already been sent to numerous groups of Drassi to recruit them for the attack.

Zecorran Royal Guards were exceptionally well trained, which meant the fighting would be intense. They needed warriors who were equally fierce who could neutralise the palace guards as quickly as possible. It was going to be expensive but their host didn't care about the cost only the promise they'd made to him.

It would take at least another day before they had enough Drassi in the city for the assault. That gave them plenty of time to discuss a plan of attack.

After a good night's sleep in a comfortable bed and a filling breakfast everyone had recovered a little from their ordeal the previous night. Dox looked haunted by what she'd seen as her eyes kept drifting to stare into the distance.

Munroe's sharp tongue had regained some of its familiar edge and Akosh stared down her nose at everyone with her usual arrogance. No doubt the idea of working alongside mortals was abhorrent to her. However, given the circumstances, she had no choice. Without their help she would end up as a plaything and snack for Kai. Vargus knew it was that thought more than any other that kept her in line. Nevertheless she didn't trust anyone. One hand rested on a dagger at her belt and across the room Munroe sneered at Akosh. Another fight between the two of them was inevitable.

Finding two Sorcerers waiting for them had been the biggest surprise and a huge boon for their group. Their combined strength and skill gave Vargus hope that if they made it into the palace, and if they somehow managed to get past all of the guards and mages, they might have a chance of defeating Kai.

He'd never met Garvey before but the blindfolded man who sat across from him was not what he'd been expecting. The stories of the atrocities he'd committed after the destruction of the Red Tower were at odds with this calm and contemplative man. Others had described him as constantly simmering with anger but Vargus didn't sense that. Garvey was unusually still and often tilted his head to one side as if listening to something in the distance. If it were anyone else Vargus would've said he was mad but the Sorcerer was not an ordinary man. Long before he'd become a member of the Grey Council there had been rumours. It made Vargus wonder how much Balfruss knew about his friend's history.

Then there was the fact that both of Garvey's eyes had been burned out. Vargus had met blind people in the past but there was something peculiar about Garvey's lack of vision. He moved around the unfamiliar rooms with ease and never bumped into furniture or doorways. He'd gained much since losing his eyes.

Being part of such an unusual group made everyone uncomfortable, with the exception of Garvey, but it was Balfruss who seemed the most on edge. The Sorcerer knew more about Akosh and their brethren than anyone. From his expression and the way he kept staring at Akosh it was obvious he knew what they were facing. After all, Balfruss had spent time with Kai in distant Shael when he'd been pretending to be a plague priest. He already knew the full horror of what lay under Kai's flesh mask. Vargus would have to find time for a quiet conversation with Balfruss. The others were terrified enough by what they were up against without him adding to their woes.

There was more grey in his beard than Vargus remembered but that was to be expected given the events of the last few months. Deep lines etched into his forehead spoke of new sorrows and yet here he was again in the thick of it.

Without having to say a word the others drew strength from his presence. They all knew he'd faced remarkable odds in the past. Despite all that he'd endured he'd never used his power to abuse others. Whatever happened Balfruss would keep Garvey in check, giving Vargus one less thing to worry about.

Danoph sat in the room with everyone and yet he seemed apart from it all. Vargus knew he wasn't using his power and yet he'd begun to drift, which was a bad sign. He needed to remain tethered to the present and the people in this room. If he didn't have an emotional connection to current events and the repercussions, it would erode his humanity.

Kai mocked all of their brethren for appearing as humans at their gatherings instead of showing their real faces. He thought living alongside mortals had made them all soft and had eroded their true natures. Vargus was willing to admit that perhaps it had affected him and the others more than they realised but it was better to care than view mortals as nothing more than ants.

Each life Vargus took was not something he did lightly. There was always a reason and a cost, sooner or later. Despite not being a mortal his fate was intertwined with theirs. Without mortals all but a handful of his kind would exist. It was a simple lesson that many of his kind had forgotten.

Danoph had the ability to see what might happen but it was clear he'd not thought about his own place within the weave. He couldn't simply drift through the years as an observer, never speaking, never making a decision. He had to live. He had to interact with others and he had to accept the consequences of his actions. As did everyone else, mortal or otherwise.

"You all have an idea of what we're facing," said Vargus, drawing everyone's attention. "So we need to plan this carefully."

"Plans always go wrong," said Akosh, earning a sneer from Munroe.

"Then we'll prepare for that as well. How does that sound?" he asked, raising an eyebrow. She didn't take the bait and stared out of the window, pretending they were all beneath her.

"We should go in now. Not wait around," said Munroe. "Between us we can take care of anything."

"There will be Royal Guards and mages."

"We've got two Sorcerers and me. We can easily beat them."

Vargus would have said it was arrogance except they were three of the strongest and most dangerous mages he'd ever met. "Normally I'd agree, but I think you're going to need to conserve your strength. For him."

Munroe grimaced and Dox shuddered with revulsion.

"We need warriors we can trust. Kai has eyes and ears everywhere in the city, that's why I'm hiring Drassi. They'll take care of the Royal Guards. All three of you will have to neutralise the young mages."

"I can do it," said Munroe. "I don't need any help."

"They've been altered," he said, focusing on Balfruss.

"How?" asked the Sorcerer.

"Their minds have been enslaved. They're Splinters." The word sent a ripple through all of them. They'd all heard of Splinters because of the war. To them it was just a story but Vargus and Balfruss had lived through those events. Balfruss had lost good friends to the Warlock and his enslaved mages.

Balfruss clenched his jaw. "Will it never end?" he muttered. "It will take at least two of us."

"Why?" asked Munroe.

"One of us to control the Splinters. One to cut the head off the snake." His tone of voice made it clear he wasn't talking figuratively. Once Marran was dead the other mages would be negated.

"So once we get past the mages and the Royal Guards, then what?" Munroe asked.

"We must defeat him," said Vargus. There was a long uncomfortable silence in the room but eventually Munroe broke it.

"How do we do that?"

"Danoph will help us," he said.

All eyes turned towards the boy and he shifted uncomfortably under the combined scrutiny.

"The boy is an Oracle, not a weapon," said Balfruss. "He should stay here with Dox where it's safe."

"We can't defeat Kai without him," said Vargus.

Garvey smiled as if hearing a punchline. Vargus wondered how much he knew but none of the others noticed except Akosh. The pair of Sorcerers worried him a great deal and with good reason. They were almost as powerful as Munroe but considerably better trained. There had not been any mages like them for hundreds of years. Elwei had once told Vargus that Balfruss was "becoming". Now he wondered the same about Garvey. What had he become?

"How will Danoph help?" asked Munroe.

Vargus had to be careful. He couldn't tell them the whole truth but he also knew Dox would smell the lie if he tried to deceive anyone. "He's more than an Oracle. He has a rare gift that I've seen only once before. The fire at the Red Tower was just the beginning. He can see what is about to happen and anticipate what Kai will do next. His foresight will give us a rare advantage."

Dox was staring at him with an odd expression. He hadn't lied but was dancing around the truth and she knew it. Vargus waited for her to tell the others but she kept her mouth shut.

"How do you think we made it across the city without being seen?" he asked.

"Is this true?" said Balfruss, turning to the boy.

"There are roads that stretch into the distance. Crossroads of choices yet to be made. I can see them all." His eyes clouded over briefly but quickly regained their natural colour. Now everyone was staring at him with growing concern.

"It won't be that easy," said Akosh. "If it was me, I'd have other surprises. Traps. Poison perhaps."

"Which is why you're coming with us," said Vargus, showing his teeth in an approximation of a smile. "You and Dox are our wildcards."

"She's not coming with us," said Munroe, a moment ahead of Balfruss.

"It's too dangerous for the girl," said the Sorcerer.

Vargus took a deep breath before replying. "However we manage to get inside it's going to be a bloody affair. People are going to die, but not everyone in the palace has been enslaved. Many will be serving Kai and his people out of fear. We can't just kill everyone we meet in the palace," he said, holding up a hand before Akosh suggested they do exactly that. "There will be enough death without a massacre. Whatever we do it is going to draw considerable attention and leave a scar for a long time. We need to minimise the number of casualties."

At this Danoph frowned, which showed he was paying attention now. After all it would be up to him to repair the damage they left behind.

With so many deaths he would not be able to put everything back the way it was. Some pathways would simply vanish and others would be twisted into new and damaging futures. At the very least he would be able to avert the worst disasters. The boy sat upright in his chair, focusing more on the conversation than before. Everyone had their role to play.

"We need Dox to tell us who has been altered. It could save a lot of lives."

Munroe stubbornly shook her head. "No. I won't allow it."

"Allow?" scoffed Akosh. "You're not the girl's mother."

"Don't talk to me about family. Mine are dead because of you." Munroe reached for the Source and an instant later Akosh was on her feet, a dagger in each hand.

"Just try it. You won't catch me off guard this time," sneered Akosh.

Munroe laughed at her bravado. "We all know you're afraid of me, and you should be, because I'm going to destroy you."

"This isn't helping," said Balfruss but both women ignored him. The Sorcerer looked towards Vargus for help but he just shrugged. This was always going to happen at some point. Better that it happened now than when they were in the middle of the palace surrounded by Royal Guards and Splinters.

Akosh shook her head and laughed. "You're a mewling child. I've seen more in my life than you can possibly imagine."

"None of that will help you. In the end you'll beg," promised Munroe.

In the lull between insults a little voice said, "I'll go." Dox was trembling with fear but she boldly jutted out her chin. "I'm going with you."

Everyone was taken aback and the pending fight was suddenly derailed. Munroe released the power she'd been holding and Akosh sheathed her weapons.

"I won't be able to protect you," said Munroe. "You could die."

"I know," said the girl.

"Do you? Do you really?"

Dox looked at each person in the room, taking a moment to study their faces, before coming back to Munroe. "Everyone here is willing to fight. How could I do anything less?"

Dox was terrified and yet she was willing to go with them. It was one of the bravest things Vargus had ever seen.

A short time later, while everyone was preparing themselves for the coming fight, Vargus moved through the rooms to speak with individuals. He found Munroe sat alone holding a small wooden horse. It was crudely made but she was cradling it in such a way that he knew it held great significance.

"She's going to betray us," said Munroe, without looking up. "Akosh is right about one thing. No matter how many plans we make something will go wrong. And as we're scrambling around to fix it, she'll stab us in the back, or make a deal to save her own skin. It's inevitable."

Vargus stepped into the room. "I know."

"Then give me one good reason why I shouldn't just kill her now."

"Because we need her," he said, because it was the truth. "You know by now that Kai isn't normal."

"Neither are you," said Munroe, meeting his gaze. "And neither is Akosh."

He didn't deny it but also didn't elaborate. "We're going up against something that is a master of deception. He's been hiding his true nature and power for years. I honestly don't know how strong he is, but the only way we might have a chance is if we throw everything at him."

It wasn't a good plan but it was the only one they had. Sometimes brute force and ignorance would get the job done. The less the others knew about his brethren the better. The threat Kai posed to them, and all mortals, would keep them awake at night if they knew everything.

"The things she's done . . . " Munroe trailed off and stared into the distance. "She must die."

"I know."

"He's telling the truth," said Dox, coming into the room behind him. The girl was visibly intimidated but he smiled to show that he wasn't angry about her eavesdropping. They'd set this up to try and catch him out. If he'd told a lie it would have given Munroe an excuse to tear Akosh apart.

Another dose of the truth seemed in order. "I can't know how you're feeling, so I won't belittle your loss by saying you shouldn't kill her. All I can ask is that you delay it for a while. Once this is over, no one will stand in your way."

There was a very good chance that none of them would survive what they were about to attempt. Munroe knew that as well.

"I will wait," she said and Vargus heaved a sigh of relief.

"I wanted to ask you for a favour."

"Another one?" she said, which made him grin. A ghost of a smile drifted across her face.

"Get some sleep. None of you will be of any use if you're tired. I'll make sure she doesn't try to kill you in the night." He knew that Munroe had been awake all last night in fear of being attacked. By contrast Akosh had slept the whole night through. In her arrogance she'd probably not even considered the notion that Munroe would come after her.

Leaving them to rest he went in search of Akosh. Vargus found her staring out of one of the windows at the lush gardens.

"All I've done is trade one prison for another," she muttered. "At least this one has a nice view."

"Stop whining before I put my boot up your arse," he snapped. Akosh's eyes were blazing and he sensed her reaching for her power. "Do you really want to test your strength twice in two days against one of your elders?"

Akosh turned away and released her power. "What do you want?"

"Two promises from you."

He waited while she sullenly mulled it over. "Go on," she eventually said.

"Promise that you won't try to kill any of them, Munroe in particular."

There was another drawn-out silence but he was happy to wait. "And the second promise?"

Vargus moved to stand beside her at the window. She continued to pretend he wasn't there, staring straight ahead. "That you don't try to run."

Akosh didn't respond except to fidget in her chair. He knew she'd been thinking about it. It was the sensible option from her perspective. Everyone would be too busy fighting Kai and his army of followers to come after her until it was over. There was also a good chance that they would all die in the process. If that happened she'd be free to rebuild her group of followers and power.

"Everything that's happening is partly your fault, so you need to be here to clean it up. But if you run, if you make me hunt you down, I will destroy you. I've done it many times before." Coming from someone else it would have been a threat but she knew it was a promise.

"You're a bastard," she said, but there was no heat in her words only defeat.

"Do you agree?"

"Fine. I promise, now just leave me alone."

Vargus left her to sulk while he went in search of the two Sorcerers.

Balfruss stared at Garvey with a mix of guilt and revulsion. He couldn't forget what his old friend had done after the destruction of the Red Tower. The murder of innocents and the damage he'd done to the rogue students. They were young, impressionable, and he'd taken advantage by feeding their base needs, allowing them to gorge themselves. To delve into the darkest parts of magic with no repercussions. It didn't matter that Balfruss had either captured or been forced to kill all of them.

The swirl of emotions was overlain with a sense of guilt because whenever Balfruss looked at Garvey it was difficult to ignore his disfigurement.

"How can you be so calm?" asked Balfruss.

Garvey shrugged. "Vargus is wise beyond anyone we've ever met before. I trust him."

Apart from the obvious there was definitely something different about Garvey. Balfruss had been following up rumours of a rogue mage in Zecorria when a blind beggar had approached him on the street. The calm and quietly spoken man was so at odds with the Sorcerer he'd known for years it had taken Balfruss a moment to recognise him. Even though Garvey's persona had mostly been a mask it was what he'd become used to seeing. This new version was a man at peace. It was unsettling and alien.

In the past Garvey was quick to offer his opinion on any subject but now he was happy to listen to others. Balfruss wondered if he'd ever known the real Garvey.

"Why do you trust him?" he asked, sensing there was something more that Garvey wasn't saying.

Even though they were alone Garvey lowered his voice. "Because you're not the only Sorcerer to have visited the banqueting hall."

A chill ran down Balfruss's spine. "How much do you know?"

"A little about what Vargus and Akosh really are."

"How did you find that place?"

"An old Pilgrim showed me the way." Garvey realised his poor choice of words and laughed at himself.

"Why aren't you angry?" said Balfruss. "I've never known you to be this calm."

"Because there's no need to pretend any more. The time for deception is over." Garvey grabbed his hand, which startled Balfruss. "And I'm not angry with you, old friend."

"I took your eyes."

"I asked you to do it, and besides, you gave me a gift." Garvey turned his face away and appeared to be staring at something beyond the room. "All our lives, we've both felt like children compared to the old Grey Council."

"True, but I've learned the hard way they were flawed individuals. Just like us they were trying to do their best." Balfruss's thoughts turned to the desolate city of Voechenka and the secrets he'd buried there. The knowledge that had been accumulated over decades that he'd burned to ash.

"There's a story there."

Balfruss waved it away before realising Garvey couldn't see him. "I'll tell you another time. What's this gift you spoke of?"

"Do you remember the first day when we took their place? When we finally had access to the entire library at the Red Tower?"

As a boy attending the school he'd dreamed of becoming a powerful Battlemage. A famous mage who would loan himself out to those in need around the world. He would visit every nation, eat exotic food, have encounters with mysterious women and earn a fortune. Not once did he imagine becoming a member of the Grey Council. They were the elite mages in the world and he was just a student of middling strength and skill. So much had seemed out of reach. The older students had better control, more patience and those who excelled were allowed access to the restricted section of the library. Even then he'd heard whispers about entire levels of the tower filled with books that only the Grey Council were permitted to read.

On the first day of forming the new Grey Council alongside Eloise and Garvey he'd been given access to the entire tower. The celebration had been hollow. The rumours had been true. There were entire floors filled with ancient books, crammed full of knowledge, but many of them were in languages he couldn't read. Even worse, a portion of the library was so badly damaged from twenty years of neglect the books were unreadable. Many of them simply fell apart as soon as he touched them. The rest had all manner of information on rare Talents and feats he'd thought impossible, but the books held no instructions. The old Grey Council had merely recorded what was possible while keeping the means to themselves.

Towards the top of the tower there were two whole floors containing books he wished did not exist. The material within was so far from what Balfruss had been taught about magic it felt like sacrilege. They should have destroyed them all but instead had locked and warded the door so that it could never fall into the wrong hands.

"It was a bitter day," said Balfruss, coming back to the present. "I gained nothing from my title, apart from responsibility."

"All our lives we've been striving to live up to something that's unattainable. We'd elevated them to such heights." Garvey laughed at himself. "But now, everything is different."

"How?"

"It's difficult to explain," said Garvey. "The Source has opened up to me in ways I'm struggling to describe. The possibilities are almost without limit. My mind is suddenly awake like never before." He spoke with such fever it bordered on the spiritual. "I feel as if I've been looking through a keyhole my entire life and now someone has opened the door."

"You saw the same books as I," said Balfruss. "Some knowledge should stay buried or be destroyed. It's just too dangerous."

"You don't understand," said Garvey, shaking his head. "I'm not talking about using magic to hurt others. We've been finding new ways to kill each other for hundreds of years without magic. People don't need our help to do that."

"Then what do you mean?"

Garvey tried a different approach. "Did you ever think it was possible to stand in a room that only exists between heartbeats. One that is a part of our world and yet is hidden from sight."

"I never imagined anything like that."

"What about Vargus, Akosh and the others out there? Beings that have lived for centuries in hiding amongst us. We're dealing with powers we barely understand. There's so much more to the world. So many layers that remain hidden. But now, I'm beginning to discover them."

If not for the events of the last ten years Balfruss would have said Garvey had been driven insane. In that time Balfruss had witnessed many things he was still struggling to explain. After the war his time spent across the Dead Sea had opened his mind in a similar fashion, although it sounded as if Garvey's awareness went beyond his own. Even now, as they sat together in silence, his old friend was listening to something in the distance.

As he left Garvey to his meditation he ran into Vargus in the doorway.

"I was just coming to speak with you," said the warrior. He glanced into the room and saw Garvey staring into the distance.

"Let's take a walk," suggested Balfruss.

The grounds of the Mallenby estate were as lush and richly decorated as everything else. A network of stone pathways wound through a sea of exotic plants from places as far away as the desert kingdoms. Normally they wouldn't be able to survive in such cold conditions but thin glass boxes and huge jars had been placed over the plants to keep them alive. The air was buzzing with the sound of insects and brightly coloured birds fluttered overhead, hopping from one branch to the next.

At regular intervals along the paths were marble statues of familiar gods, dead monarchs and creatures from myth. The house was similarly littered with artefacts and expensive pieces of art in a haphazard fashion. It was all a ridiculous display of wealth that demonstrated Lord Mallenby had more money than he knew what to do with.

"I need to know something," said Balfruss. It had been weighing heavily on his mind ever since he'd discovered who they were facing. "And don't say you can't tell me. We're long past that. I want to know the truth."

Vargus heaved a long sigh but eventually nodded. "Go on."

"Do you remember what happened to me in Shael?"

"I do."

"Then you know that I saw his true face, back in Voechenka." The others had merely glanced a small portion of what lay underneath Kai's human disguise. His true self was huge, monstrous and so utterly alien Balfruss had nothing to compare it with. Balfruss would never forget what he'd seen for as long as he lived. It made him wonder what Vargus and Akosh looked like beneath their masks.

"I remember," said Vargus.

When he'd set off for the remote city in Shael Balfruss had thought Kai was nothing more than an eccentric drunk and a plague priest. As events in Voechenka became more desperate his suspicions about Kai had grown. When Balfruss had confronted the priest it was Vargus who'd brought them both to the banqueting hall where he'd revealed a little more about their true nature.

"What is your question?" asked Vargus.

"Given what I know about all of you, can we actually kill Kai?"

It was a long time before the old warrior answered. Eventually Vargus came to a decision as he gestured for them to sit down on one of the marble benches.

It was a beautiful spot that was teeming with life. From the orange fish in the pond, to the insects buzzing across the water, to the gold birds flitting around the trees. The sun was warm on Balfruss's back and the noise and chaos of the city seemed far away in this haven.

"No, you can't kill him but you can help weaken him. Then I can destroy him and scatter his physical essence."

"That's it?"

"Once his body is gone it will take him years to rebuild. In that time I'll make sure he doesn't come back. Once he's without followers feeding him power he'll fade away."

Balfruss was still sceptical. "Will that work?"

"It's what I was planning to do with Akosh."

"But he's not the same as you, is he?"

Vargus shook his head. His frown lifted when a blue and yellow bird swooped into the garden, splashed beneath the surface of the pond and flew away with a fish in its beak. "I'll find a way. I always do. Besides, this time I'm not alone."

"I hope that your confidence in us isn't misplaced."

"It isn't, but I was actually speaking about Danoph."

"There's something about him you're not telling me," said Balfruss.

"Danoph is more like me than you. All of my kind are born of mortal woman. We come into this world not knowing who we are at first, but over time we discover our purpose. One day, he'll sit at the great table in the banquet hall and be among equals, but he's not there yet."

Perhaps this was one of the reasons Vargus told him so little. Balfruss always felt out of his depth when he did get answers. "I think it would be best if the others didn't know about Danoph or Kai."

"I was going to suggest that to you," said Vargus. "They have enough to worry about."

There was so much more that Balfruss wanted to know and he suspected that, for once, if he asked Vargus would answer. But he was already struggling with what he'd been told.

All of his life Balfruss had sought knowledge, believing that it gave him power, but perhaps there were times when the old adage was true. Ignorance was bliss.

CHAPTER 39

As Wren stared at the infection growing inside Kovac's lungs
her heart sank. There were no physical signs, no cough or
lesions on his skin, but it was only a matter of time before they
developed. Before Andras could really begin to celebrate she'd
been forced to break the bad news. Even now, two days later, the
look of anguish on his face was burned into her memory. It wasn't
an image she would ever forget. The loss of hope.

He still put on a brave face, was as kind and patient with all
of the sick as before, but Wren knew he'd given up. Every day
the number of people dying from the plague was growing. And
every day Tianne and Val burned the bodies to ash. They did it
out of sight but everyone knew what happened to the dead when
they were carried outside.

In contrast only one new person had been sent to the isolation
zone in the last few days, which meant that the city outside was
almost completely free of the plague.

Andras probably believed what some cynical people had been
saying since the beginning. That the only reason they were
locked up in the isolation zone was to wait for them all to die.
Some believed the city authorities never had any real intention of
curing them. Having studied the infection Wren didn't believe

that. It was far beyond the skills of any doctor or apothecarist. Queen Morganse and the Guardians had been left with no real choice. But Andras didn't want to hear that. He needed hope. The atmosphere in the hospital had never been cheery, but there had been moments where people had laughed and smiled. Now every face was sombre and the only sounds echoing around the old church were cries of pain. Normally some of the sick would find comfort in prayer but every priest, apart from Andras, had now succumbed. He would whisper something over the dying if they asked but his words didn't comfort them as they once had.

Wren knew that the only person who might live longer than two weeks was Kovac. They'd pushed back the infection but eventually he would become sick and die. The other more pressing weight on her mind was Tianne, whose condition had grown worse in the last few days. Time was running out for all of them.

Tianne came back into the church from where she'd been burning the latest bodies when she tripped and nearly fell. She managed to catch herself on the doorframe and sit down facing towards the street.

"Are you all right?" asked Wren, coming up behind her.

"A bit light-headed. I just need to catch my breath." Outside the day was cool and fresh. A heavy rain had fallen last night and it was still chilly. Tianne's breath frosted on the air but so far this morning she hadn't started coughing. Last night she'd had a horrendous coughing fit and had spat up blood before it subsided.

"Come inside. It's too cold out there."

"Actually, it feels good," said Tianne, taking deep breaths. Wren suspected she was just putting on a brave face but she did seem to be breathing easier. It didn't make sense. It went against everything she'd learned from Master Yettle and the apothecarists since arriving in Perizzi. Tianne should be bent over double in pain from her cough.

A horrible and insidious thought slithered its way into her mind. What if someone had created the plague? It seemed impossible and yet every day she'd been at the Red Tower that word had been challenged. What if someone had built the infection with magic?

In a rush Wren pulled Val away from her patient and together with Tianne they urged Kovac outside. She moved everyone away from the door so that they couldn't see what they were doing.

"What is it?" asked Kovac, his eyes scanning for danger.

"There's something we didn't tell you," said Wren.

"It's all right. I know I'm still infected."

Wren didn't know how he could be so calm in the face of his imminent death. "We want to try to cure you again."

"Why?"

"Do you trust me?" said Wren, dodging his question.

"Yes," came the careful reply.

"Then with your permission I want to try again."

He considered her words and then nodded. "Very well."

"This is going to hurt."

Wren explained her idea and everyone looked at her as if she'd lost her mind. However, at this stage, they were willing to try anything. Conventional wisdom and everything else they'd tried had failed. It was time to challenge the impossible.

Working slowly and carefully Tianne cooled the air around Kovac until a light dusting of snow fell on his head and shoulders. Thankfully, this time, his clothes would provide a little protection against the chill.

"Hold it steady there," said Wren. Tianne gritted her teeth while maintaining the temperature. If she began to tire Wren would move to take over but she knew her friend could manage for a while. Last time Wren had made it so cold it had almost stopped Kovac's heart. This time it was not as severe. Not yet at least. She hoped it wouldn't come to that.

Once Tianne was settled Val crafted a healing weave. This time she focused solely on the infection in Kovac's lungs. Wren could see that it had started to spread to other parts of his body but the worst of it was centred there. With meticulous care Val drew together one layer and placed it over his body. It sank beneath his skin and drew together like a fishing net around his lungs. With a small gesture using both hands Val added another layer and then a third, slowly building up the weave. Almost immediately Wren saw the infection squirm. She could think of no other word for it. It knew it was under attack and was trying to spread.

As Val fed energy into the weave Wren saw fine threads of black decay start to branch out from the infection in Kovac's lungs.

"Lower the temperature a little," she said to Tianne who took a deep breath and drew more heat from the air around the mercenary. He hissed in pain and clenched his fists but didn't move. He knew what they were attempting was very delicate.

Nothing happened. Val continued to pour energy into the healing weave and the infection continued to squirm, attempting to spread into healthy tissue. She was just about to ask Tianne to make it even colder when there was a subtle change.

The delicate threads at the periphery of the infection had stopped moving.

It was almost as if they had paused in their search but after a while Wren realised they were frozen in place. Then the warm glow from Val's weave began to pulse in time with Kovac's heart. As power from the Source continued to flow through Val into her weave his body finally responded. The slender tentacles retracted and the infection in his lungs began to shrink. It seemed to be working.

Determined not to get too excited, as they'd been here before, Wren bit her lip to prevent herself from smiling. Tianne remained unaware as all of her attention was focused on keeping the air cool. Val could see that the infection was shrinking but her expression remained pensive. She was probably thinking about their first attempt as well.

Piece by piece the large black chunks of the infection curled up and broke apart before being washed away in his bloodstream. Kovac was breathing easier but Wren could hear the air hissing between his clenched teeth. She was afraid the cold might kill him but was also scared if Tianne eased up even slightly the infection might spread.

It seemed to take for ever but slowly they hemmed in the infection on all sides, herding it into one spot like a flock of sheep. All of the remaining poison, all of the pain and agony he'd been enduring for days, was reduced to one small black nodule.

And then it was gone.

Val was so surprised she almost lost control but instead clenched her jaw and maintained the glowing weave. Healing energy continued to flow through Kovac's body as she meticulously searched every part of him for the faintest trace. If the smallest amount remained it could regrow and infect him again. She checked him over a second time and then a third to be absolutely sure. By this time Tianne was starting to tremble and Val released her grip on the Source.

"Let go, Tianne," whispered Wren, shaking her friend by the shoulder. She had fallen into a trance and Wren remembered experiencing something similar. Instead of collapsing Tianne merely wobbled on her feet. Wren held on to her shoulders and slowly eased her to the ground where she caught her breath. It was still cool outside but Tianne was dripping with sweat. Another handful of white flakes drifted down from above Kovac's head and then the snow stopped.

"What happened?" he asked, looking at all of them for an answer.

Wren looked towards Val who gestured for her to speak. "It's gone. The infection is really gone."

Kovac tried to say something but had no words. Like everyone else who'd walked into the isolation zone he'd never considered the possibility that he might walk out again.

"We can cure the plague," said Tianne, realising what had happened.

After being hanged by the neck and left for dead Val wasn't someone who saw the funny side of life. Wren couldn't remember if she'd ever seen her smile. Val's laugh was unlike anything she'd ever heard before. A sound so full of joy that Wren found herself smiling. Then a horrible thought crept into the back of her mind. As their eyes met Val's laugh faded as she must have had the same thought.

"By the Maker!" hissed Val.

Leaving the others behind Wren ran into the church. Val and Tianne were already exhausted from their exertions but Wren hadn't used any of her energy. It was desperately needed now as she stood in the doorway staring at all the braziers. To make matters worse they had covered all of the windows and plugged holes in the roof, making it difficult for the heat to escape. Normally that would have been a good thing, as typically cold was the enemy, but in this case they'd only made things worse and sped up the rate of infection.

With a feral scream Wren lashed out, blasting the braziers with air that was so cold it extinguished all of them simultaneously. She was tempted to blast holes in the roof and open all of the windows but everyone immediately felt the effect of her magic. Instead she began pushing cool air into the church from outside to gradually lower the temperature. Patients and the healers probably thought she'd lost her mind. As patients huddled under their blankets for warmth Andras came hurrying over.

"Get rid of your blankets! You need to go outside and cool down," shouted Wren. "Don't cover yourself up."

"What are you doing?" demanded the priest, steering her away from the open door.

"The heat. It's making them worse. We have to make everyone cold."

"These poor souls have suffered enough. A warm bed and a safe space is what they need."

"You don't understand," said Wren, shaking her head. "We've cured Kovac. We arrested the infection with cold and then healed him."

Having been overly enthusiastic last time Andras was obviously reluctant to believe her now. "Wren ... " he started to say but she dragged him outside to see the mercenary for himself.

It was only then Wren noticed the other subtle changes she'd missed. Kovac's skin was flushed again from being out in the cold whereas before it had been pale and waxy. His cheeks were no longer as hollow and the dark smudges under his eyes were gone. His posture had also changed and he was carrying himself with more confidence.

Since Kovac's peculiar arrival at the church she'd never been intimidated by him but now she began to see him in a different way. There was a masculine intensity she'd not noticed before and when he smiled at her Wren had to turn away to hide her blush.

Andras quizzed him and Val for a while before allowing himself to believe, but with every passing moment it became more obvious. Kovac had been cured.

"Can you do it again?" asked Andras, carefully searching their faces. "Can you help the others?"

It was a fair question. Two mages working together had cured one person but Kovac's infection had already been severely reduced. It would be a different challenge to eradicate the infection from someone with severe symptoms.

"We have to try," said Wren. She was worried that the longer they delayed the smaller their chances became of curing other patients. If only they hadn't plugged every gap in the church so efficiently the heat wouldn't have been so intense. It was possible several of their patients would still be alive. There was no way to know but that didn't stop her feeling guilty.

"It could kill someone," said Val, surprising all of them. "He's big and healthy. Someone old and weak could die from the cold."

Wren hadn't considered that. As she'd just realised Kovac was quite a large and virile man. They needed to test it again on someone else.

"Test it on me," said Tianne.

Wren shook her head. "It's too risky." Tianne's skin was always pale but now it was an unhealthy shade. She couldn't risk losing her friend.

"I'm young and healthy," said Tianne with a faint smile. "And I know the risks involved."

The stubborn set of her jaw told Wren everything she needed to know. "We'll try it. Andras, could you please extinguish the fires and open some windows?" she said to the priest. It might help to slow the progress of the infection in others. Andras left Wren alone with her two friends who were looking at her for guidance. Once again she had become the de facto leader without really knowing why.

"I need to know if I can heal," said Wren. She was conscious of the fact that so far it was Val who had healed Kovac. They all needed to be able to copy what she had done by working in pairs. If Val was the only one capable of healing the plague many would die before they ever reached them.

"Healing one person at a time is too slow," said Wren. "We need to do more."

"How?" asked Tianne.

Wren was naturally averse to risk but all other attempts at a cure had failed. If what they attempted went wrong then it was possible she would kill the patients faster than the virus.

"Come with me," she said, leading the others inside the church. Wren was pleased when Kovac volunteered to remain on guard outside. It was one less distraction for her to worry about. It was also reassuring to think of him keeping watch. Pushing the jumble of emotions to one side she focused her mind on the challenge ahead.

"How wide can you create a healing net?" she asked Val.

The Seve girl shrugged, which wasn't too surprising. They had only been taught about healing one person at once with magic. Then again Master Yettle had told them to create the whole weave first rather than gradually build it in layers which Val had discovered by herself. Once again Wren felt uneasy about questioning the wisdom of her elders. It went against everything she'd been taught growing up. However, the ingrained Drassi tradition excluded one vital fact. Her teachers, parents and elders were all human. They were imperfect and could make mistakes like anyone else.

Wren took a deep breath and explained what she wanted to attempt. Andras had drifted up beside them but she didn't alter what she was saying, especially when highlighting the risks involved.

"It's still too slow," said Tianne. "Both of you should try to heal people in parallel."

"If we do that, who will cool the air?" asked Wren. "You can't do it at the same time as being healed."

"I can try."

"You can't," said Wren. Despite the stubborn set of Tianne's jaw it was clear she knew it wasn't possible. If she lost control, even for a moment, while they were healing the others it could kill everyone by accident.

"I'll do it," said Kimme. She must have been standing behind Wren for some time but it looked as if she'd not been awake long. Her clothes were rumpled and her hair a tangled mess. Worse than the familiar odour was the anguish in her eyes. Wren was about to mention the risk when tears fell from Kimme's eyes. "I need to do this. To make amends."

"You've nothing to be sorry about. No one died."

"I could have killed everyone," said the farm girl. "Let me do this."

Wren expected the others to object but once again they were all looking towards her to make the final decision.

"All right, but be careful," said Wren.

It took some persuasion but eventually all of the windows and doors in the church were opened wide. Cool air drifted in from all directions but it still wasn't cold enough. All of the sick were shivering but oddly the cries of pain had faded. It was as if the virus had become dormant. A dark thought crept into the back of Wren's mind and wouldn't go away. What if they were just tired of being in pain? What if they had accepted their fate and were simply waiting to die?

At Wren's direction Kimme embraced the Source, drawing power into herself until she was ready to burst. With both arms spread wide she drew heat from the air, channelling it out of the church through the windows. A thin layer of ice formed on every surface. Everyone's breath began to frost and their shivering became more noticeable.

Wren and Val would have to work quickly or else several of the weakest would freeze to death. Val took the lead and Wren did her best to copy the shape, drawing together one layer of a healing weave. When she was certain it was ready Wren placed it across the person nearest to her. Next came the most difficult part. She attempted to stretch the weave. Almost immediately there was some resistance and the weave began to shear apart. Val was having the same problem but after adding a second identical layer at an oblique angle the weave stretched.

Piece by piece, working with meticulous precision, Wren built up her weave until it covered ten or eleven people. All of her other problems faded away. The only thing that mattered was keeping the merged net in one piece. When she tried to pull it any wider Wren felt a sudden wrench and knew she'd reached her limit.

Her clothes were damp from sweating and the cool air made them cling to her body. None of it mattered. Not the cold, the itchiness of her skin or the growing pain in the back of her head. With the roar of the Source flooding her mind Wren was able to look beneath the skin of her patients and see the grotesque virus within their bodies. She was aware of each person as a separate being and yet the infection inside them all felt connected, as if it were the limbs of a much larger entity.

As power flooded into her healing weave it filled the air around her with light and bright colours. The cold air froze the twitch-ing black limbs in place and slowly the virus began to fold in upon itself. The smallest pieces broke apart first and vanished. Somewhere in the distance she could hear a sound but didn't let it distract her.

Black spots danced in front of her eyes and she felt the entire weave shudder, threatening to fall apart. Gritting her teeth against the pressure in the back of her skull Wren persisted, keeping her eyes locked on the remaining chunks of the virus. It had been reduced to a small core in each person's lungs and now she felt as if it were fighting back.

Wren had a moment of clarity where she drifted free of her body and could see herself hunched forward on her hands and knees. A layer of snow had fallen inside the church, painting everyone white. It was as if the snow was purifying the sick, cleansing the darkness from their bodies. And just as the pain became unbearable and she was about to black out, Wren became aware of a presence within the remaining seeds of the virus. And somehow, it became aware of her.

Her magic eradicated the core of the infection in each patient and they were cured of the plague. Something slapped Wren across the cheek and the shock sent her tumbling sideways. Someone caught her and she felt gentle hands guide her into a sitting position. It didn't seem to matter that she was blind and could barely hear. They were safe and she'd done it.

"Drink," said a voice and a cup was pressed to her lips. It tasted bitter and burned all the way down, then her stomach was on fire. Another sip and her eyes were watering but white spots turned into a patch of light and the world rushed in again.

Andras was holding her up while all around her people in the church were walking about. Everywhere she looked Wren could see smiling, healthy faces. Some were laughing, others crying in celebration, but their skin was completely clear of any lesions.

"What about the others?" asked Wren, thinking of her friends.

"They're fine, just exhausted. Rest," said Andras. His voice suddenly came from far away. "Rest," he said again and she thought it sounded like a good idea. Her body was so heavy and tired. They'd done it. They had found a way to cure the plague. A smile lifted the corners of her mouth before Wren blissfully sank down into the warm darkness.

CHAPTER 40

Dox stared at the grey sky and frowned. It wouldn't be long now. Today they were going to leave the comforts of the Mallenby estate and storm the palace.

From her vantage point in the gardens she could see the front gate and keep an eye on the others inside the house.

The sky looked calm enough, with only a few wispy clouds, but she could smell the rain. A storm was brewing but the source of energy around her was not just the weather. She was surrounded by some of the most powerful Sorcerers in the world. And if that wasn't enough there were also two human-shaped beings that were apparently immortal. Akosh and Vargus walked and talked like most people but after seeing what was lurking under the skin of the thing they were up against she couldn't trust her eyes. They were probably gross to look at as well and would give her fresh nightmares.

Akosh had been scary before, when she'd just been the creepy leader of a cult, but finding out that she wasn't even human made it worse. Munroe had brought down an entire building on Akosh's head and yet she'd survived. That should have made Akosh the most terrifying in their group and yet she wasn't even near the top of the list.

Whenever Vargus came into a room Akosh was less aggressive than normal and her biting comments all but disappeared. The old warrior only had to raise an eyebrow and Akosh became subservient and apologetic. From what Munroe had told her Vargus was significantly older than Akosh and clearly more powerful. Dox knew she should be scared of him, and whatever was lurking underneath his human mask, but being in his presence made her feel safe. She smiled when he came into a room and found herself standing taller. With him on their side Dox believed they had a chance against that thing. She knew its name but didn't want to say it or even think it. Names had power and it already had more than enough.

Last night she'd had another nightmare. In the dream something had dragged her into the shadows and then started to eat her. Dox had felt rows of razor-sharp teeth ripping into her flesh and she'd been powerless to stop it. Even more embarrassing was crying on Munroe's shoulder until the worst of it had passed. Eventually she'd fallen asleep again with Munroe still holding her. It had been a long time since anyone had rocked her to sleep. Neither of them had mentioned it this morning for which she was grateful.

Lately Munroe had been unusually calm and quiet. She was watchful and her eyes never strayed far from Akosh. Munroe hadn't forgiven Akosh for murdering her family. For now the rage had been shoved deep inside where it was waiting and growing. At some point it would all come boiling out and the scary anger that was so familiar to Dox would land on someone. After what had happened at the orphanage she wanted to be as far away as possible when Munroe finally let go. Dox wasn't sure if there was anything that could stop her.

"Are you all right?" said a voice, startling Dox from her reverie. Balfruss was another reason that she wasn't screaming out loud and running for the city gates. Everyone knew Balfruss. She'd grown up listening to stories of what he'd done during the war. Killing the Warlock, saving the lives of thousands and standing alone against an army which then surrendered. Now that she was a little older Dox suspected the truth wasn't quite that simple but he was still impressive in person.

"I'm fine," she said, trying to ignore the seething ball of terror in her stomach.

"I still get scared too," he said, sniffing the air.

"You don't show it."

"That's because I'm ancient and I've had a lot of practice." Balfruss was smiling but there was a deep well of sadness in his eyes.

"You're not that ancient," said Dox, even though he was old enough to be her father.

Their conversation was interrupted as the estate gates were pulled open by Mallenby's servants to reveal a small army of masked Drassi warriors. All of them were dressed in identical grey and black uniforms with the traditional white teardrop-shaped masks that rendered them anonymous. Only the leader of each Fist of five warriors had a slightly different mask. It left the bottom half of their faces uncovered making it easier to hear what they were saying. The others had no reason to speak.

Dox had seen many Drassi walking through the streets of Rojenne protecting clients or cargo. They all had the same languid walk, like a prowling dog, confident in its own power. Their eyes never stopped moving and when they drew their weapons someone else always died.

All of the Drassi had a sword strapped to their back but each also carried an additional weapon or two. Some wore a baldric of daggers, others carried spears and bucklers and several had a pair of small curved axes. They were incredibly adaptable with weaponry and their skill was known across the west. The masks still creeped her out a little but Dox was glad the Drassi were fighting on their side. She stopped counting the number of bodies when it reached one hundred. If the Drassi made Balfruss nervous he wasn't showing it, unlike Mallenby's servants who were staring.

One of the leaders stepped forward and Dox saw the old servant quickly shake his head, denying anything to do with what was going on. Vargus came striding out of the house and several of the Drassi reached for their weapons.

Much to everyone's surprise Vargus spoke to the Drassi leader in his native tongue. He produced a strange, colourful disc and their leader checked it against the one he was carrying, which seemed to be its twin. Satisfied he saluted Vargus and the warriors followed him into the main house.

Money was never given to a Drassi warrior. All contracts and payment were handled by Drassi women. Giving gold directly to a masked Drassi insulted their code of honour, besides, she couldn't see any pockets in their uniforms. A small army of Drassi was exactly what they needed against the notorious Royal Guards, who were allegedly trained from birth. Dox suspected that was another urban myth created to keep them in line. In a couple of hours she would find out the truth.

Danoph emerged from the west wing of the house to stand in the garden but then he didn't seem to know what to do. He looked up at the sky and Dox saw him go into one of his trances. Every now and then he would drift off and she'd catch him staring at nothing.

"Excuse me," said Balfruss, moving to speak with the boy.

Dox had seen people from Shael before with golden skin but she'd never met anyone like Danoph. Before her parents had died she remembered meeting a boy who'd been kicked in the head by a horse. He would do something similar from time to time.

Stand and stare at nothing with his mouth slack and his eyes far away, but with Danoph she knew it was different. His Talent, or whatever it was called, allowed him to see other places. No one in their group could fully explain it to her but all of them had spoken about it with awe.

Another figure emerged from the building and Dox involuntarily took a step backwards. It was Garvey. Out of everyone he scared her the most.

It wasn't just because of the grisly scars peeking out from the edges of his blindfold. It wasn't because of the stories she'd heard about him murdering whole villages of people, because she knew Akosh had done far worse. It wasn't even because he was a Sorcerer who used to be a member of the Grey Council, which made him one of most powerful mages in the world. Garvey scared her to death because of the darkness inside him.

None of the others had spoken about it. At first she thought they were ignoring it because they needed him but after a while she realised they couldn't see it. Balfruss had spoken about Garvey always being angry in the past but now it seemed as if he'd found an inner calm. When Dox looked at him she didn't see a blind monk-like man but a lion getting ready to rip out someone's throat. He wasn't at peace. He was simply waiting for his moment.

Danoph had spoken a few times about pathways and choices creating different futures. When she looked at Garvey it felt as if there was only one road. If Dox believed in fate or destiny she'd say he was being drawn towards a moment in time.

"Are you ready?" said Munroe, startling her. Dox had been so transfixed she hadn't heard her approach.

"I guess," said Dox with a shrug.

"You don't have to go with us."

"I'm still going," said Dox, although a large part of her thought it was a bad idea.

She followed Munroe to the gate and gradually one by one the others joined them. Vargus arrived last and behind him came their small army of Drassi warriors. Whatever happened today a lot of people were going to die. Dox tried to swallow the lump in her throat and considered turning around. Munroe grabbed her hand and Dox gave it a grateful squeeze before letting go. She was ready.

A sea of grey bodies scrambled over the palace wall, scaling it with apparent ease. At the same time Royal Guards were busy fighting more Drassi at the gate. Guards screamed in pain as spears were jammed between the metal bars but whenever one defender fell back another took their place.

By the time the guards noticed the Drassi inside the courtyard it was already too late. A moment later Dox heard the frantic clash of steel on steel. Men and women were screaming in agony but thankfully she couldn't see the wounds being inflicted as they were behind a wall. When the guards at the gate found themselves fighting Drassi behind and in front it ended quickly. The Drassi cut them down and the gates were thrown open. The rest of the masked warriors poured into the palace grounds while she and the others stayed back at a safe distance.

Only when the outer courtyard had been cleared did one of the Drassi leaders gesture for them to follow. Vargus led the way and beside her Dox felt Munroe and the others embrace the Source in readiness. There had been no sign of the Regent's mages but it was only a matter of time.

Grabbing on to the Source while moving was more difficult but Dox carefully ran through the steps in her head. It took her a while, with the sound of fighting in the distance, but eventually she heard the Source. As a small trickle of power seeped into her body she experienced a heightening of her senses. It actually came at the worst time as they had reached the palace gates.

Several broken and bloody bodies lay on the ground not far away. Sightless eyes stared at her. The liberally splashed blood was so red it hurt to look at it and the moans of the wounded were so loud.

Not far away on her left a Royal Guard lay on her back, dying. The guard's brightly polished armour was splattered with blood and one of her arms had been hacked off at the shoulder. It lay nearby on the ground and she was reaching towards it for some reason. As if she had to reclaim what had been taken from her.

The Source called to her and Dox struggled to keep its siren call at bay. A voice in her head urged her to draw more power and keep going as it would make her feel so good. She'd seen addicts lying in filthy alleyways, rotting on the inside and out, while desperately searching for another fix. She would never be like that. Gritting her teeth she let go of the Source and was glad when the desire faded as well.

As they approached one of the outer doors three Fists of Drassi engaged more palace guards but in no time they'd cut them down and the way was clear.

A portion of the warriors stayed outside to secure the perimeter while the rest followed them inside. Soon it would be Dox's turn to help. Fighting her instincts to run, she walked into the palace.

In the grand entranceway Vargus stepped back and gestured for Danoph to take the lead. He knew Vargus had been preparing him for this moment since they'd met but he was still nervous.

It was strange, using his powers in front of others, but the time for modesty was over. His childhood, and his life as he had known it, was at an end. He was the Weaver.

As he embraced his power the pathways appeared in front of

his eyes. There were several routes they could take through the palace and they hadn't changed since the last time he'd looked, back at the Mallenby estate. No matter which route he chose a lot of people were going to die. There were also some routes that ended abruptly, with ambushes that had been set up by Kai. In those futures everyone in their group died in agony.

As he stood at the first crossroads Danoph felt the weight of responsibility resting on his shoulders. The others were looking at him to make a decision. If only it were that simple. If only it were a single step. Not the first of many that started with this moment in time. Only Vargus could understand and his smile was tinged with sadness.

"We go left," said Danoph, choosing a path that looked slightly less bloody than the rest.

Vargus and several of the Drassi took the lead with weapons held ready. Their eyes scanned every shadow and doorway for signs of a trap. By now Kai and his mages would know they were inside the palace. There was also a considerable number of Royal Guards that had not been accounted for outside. Danoph could see several traps not far ahead, in choke points where they'd be outnumbered and overwhelmed. He gestured to the right, avoiding a tight stairwell where guards with crossbows waited. The path they were taking was strangled but no one else knew their final destination so they followed his lead.

"Brace yourselves," he said, giving the others a brief warning. As they came around the next corridor Danoph saw the back of several Royal Guards hunkered down behind a makeshift barrier made from overturned tables and benches.

Without waiting to see if anyone joined her, Akosh charged at the enemy. The Drassi followed in her wake on silent feet. Danoph had been expecting battle cries but no one made a sound until one of the guards noticed they were about to be attacked from behind. Dox turned her head away as one of Akosh's daggers bit into the neck of a guard. The woman made a garbled choking sound that quickly trailed off. The Drassi were more efficient in disarming the guards, slicing the back of hands or causing superficial wounds. As Akosh went to stab a second guard in the face Vargus caught her arm in mid-air.

"We need them alive, remember," he said. She tried to shake him off but he was too strong and held on long enough to make a point.

"It's a waste of time," said Akosh, surreptitiously rubbing her wrist. "I can cut their throats and we can move on."

"Dox, can you test them?" said Vargus, completely ignoring her.

All of the guards had been forced to kneel with Drassi surrounding them on all sides. Dox moved to stand in front of the first guard.

"Who is your Master? Who do you serve?" she said. The first guard hesitated before answering so Dox poked him in the stomach with the tip of her boot. "Answer the question or else you'll be dealing with her," she said, gesturing at Akosh.

"The Regent. I serve the Regent."

Dox grunted and moved to the next guard. She asked the same questions of all five but when the fifth spoke her reaction was different. Danoph saw her shoulders tense up and she bit her lip.

"She's lying," said Dox, gesturing at the last guard.

The woman's response was instantaneous. She surged to her feet and tried to strangle Dox but was immediately pulled back by two Drassi.

"I'll kill you!" screamed the guard. "You'll suffer endless—"

Munroe's boot connected with the guard's face, cutting her off. Blood trickled from the woman's mouth but her red smile was sinister. Trying a more subtle approach Balfruss stepped forward and tried to place a hand on the guard's forehead. She flinched back from his touch but the Drassi held her in place.

Balfruss closed his eyes and one of his hands hovered just above the guard's head. Danoph felt a brief murmur of power from the Source. He couldn't see what the Sorcerer was doing but it appeared to cause him pain.

"Her mind has been butchered," said Balfruss, wiping his hand against his jacket as if it were soiled. "Marran has repressed their free will but the cost is severe. She's dying."

"Can you heal her?" asked Vargus.

"No. I could heal her body but the damage to her mind is too severe," he said. As Balfruss spoke blood ran from the guard's nostrils.

"Kill her and let's move on," said Akosh. Balfruss tapped the guard on the forehead with two fingers and she collapsed. "That's the spirit."

"She's sleeping," said the Sorcerer. "It's the best I can do for now. It will slow the damage."

"The Regent has been bewitched. So now you all have a choice," said Vargus, addressing the guards they'd captured. "Fight with us to free him and save Zecorria, or sleep through it. If you choose the latter then tomorrow you might wake up and find that while you were sleeping your country was enslaved by a mad man. If only you'd taken a chance and come with us, it could have made a difference. So make your decision and make it quickly. Will you fight?"

The guards briefly conferred but in the end there was only one choice. They would fight. Looking into their history Danoph could see each of them had been worried about the Regent. They'd had suspicions about what was going on but some of their friends had been acting peculiarly too.

Vargus gave the guards their weapons and in return they

shared what they knew about other blockades. They need not have bothered. Danoph could see it all but the less they knew about him and the others the better it would be in the long run. They had four Royal Guards on their side. It was a good start.

"Let's move," said Vargus.

Danoph nodded and took the lead.

CHAPTER 41

Munroe watched as Balfruss put another pair of Royal Guards into a deep sleep. They'd picked up a dozen loyal guards but almost as many had been left behind on the floor to sleep through the next few hours. On top of that the Drassi had been forced to kill ten or more who'd refused to listen to reason.

Watching the Drassi fight she understood for the first time why they were held in such high regard. She'd seen people use weapons all her life, but not like this, with such grace and poise. It was as if their weapons were natural extensions of their arms. The only thing she could compare it to was once seeing a Vorga fight with a sword. It was instinctive in a way she couldn't begin to understand. The Royal Guards were skilled but they were soldiers who'd been drilled by routine. The Drassi used unconventional weapons and their technique flowed more like a dance.

There had been no sign of the other mages but she knew they were close. Munroe could feel the collective beat of their connection to the Source in the back of her head. She'd noticed it the moment they'd entered the palace and the sound had steadily been growing louder. Danoph was guiding them away from danger as best as he could but some confrontations were inevitable.

They'd reached the third floor of the palace and were now deep inside its labyrinth of hallways. As they passed through another set of double doors they entered a grand foyer. Directly in front of her was a wide marble staircase that rose to the back wall and then split in two directions to the left and right. Waist-high marble banisters extended up to the next floor and all around. The tiled floor was so highly polished she could see reflections of small movements repeated over and over. Royal Guards were lying in wait all around the room hunkered down behind the railing.

Looking towards the high ceiling she noticed it was painted with a colourful mural showing the Maker creating the world. Vast crystal candelabra hung down on silver chains where dozens of pure white candles sat waiting for the flame. The entire space was made of hard surfaces and sounds echoed.

The drumbeat from the Source increased and without being able to see them Munroe knew the Regent's cadre of mages were here as well. The others could feel it too as Balfruss wove a dense shield in front of them all. Even Dox had noticed as she was struggling to draw power from the Source.

There was no grand speech. No chance for surrender or parlay. Nine young mages rose from their hiding places and descended the stairs. Staring at their faces Munroe noticed a disturbing similarity in their lack of expression. Even though they were moving of their own volition the eyes were dead. She'd seen corpses with more personality. Thick black veins bulged beneath the skin around their eyes and across their foreheads like warpaint.

"What's wrong with them?" she asked.

"It's Kai's influence," said Vargus. "They're his puppets now."

Munroe didn't hear anyone give an order but moving as one the Royal Guards pointed their bows and fired. Arrows and bolts hammered into Balfruss's shield and were instantly destroyed, breaking into pieces or ricocheting around the room, burying themselves into walls or sometimes flesh. Half a dozen guards stumbled back with injuries. Before they had a chance to reload Munroe extended her old magic and made a twisting motion with both hands. All of the bows snapped into pieces and the crossbows exploded maiming some of those who held them. As screams filled the air weapons were drawn and the guards ran forward.

Drassi and their own Royal Guards ran to meet them while Munroe and the others prepared for an attack from the mages. Garvey escorted Danoph and Dox off to one side where he kept watch over them but seemed uninterested in getting involved in the fight. It didn't matter. She and Balfruss could handle the youngsters.

With a roar that was so loud it hurt her ears Vargus ran into the fray leading a Fist of Drassi. He fought with such brutality that his opponents were taken aback by his fury. In spite of his shouting and apparent recklessness Munroe noticed his precision. He was drawing a lot of attention to himself, creating a focal point for the fighting, which then moved off to one side.

Akosh had already waded into the fight with a dagger in each hand. The sounds of battle were amplified by the hard surfaces and every scream echoed over and over. The air stank of fear sweat, blood, piss and shit from spilled innards. Despite all of that Munroe could hear Akosh cackling with glee as she maimed and butchered those in front of her. When one guard tried to run away Akosh showed no mercy, stabbing the woman in the back of the neck. The only justice was the dagger became wedged and Akosh was forced to let go. Sadly she had several more blades and she was soon causing more mayhem.

Ignoring the chaos around them the nine young mages walked forward in a line. Munroe recognised a few of them but she knew today's fight would be very different from last time. Several of them had dried blood on the bottom half of their faces and their once pristine uniforms were soiled. Stories from the war ten years ago mentioned the decaying state of the Splinters who'd been the Warlock's apprentices. He'd controlled them like puppets, much as Marran and Kai were doing with these children.

There was a brief surge of power and then the Regent's mages started lashing out, hurling glowing comets of fire at her and the others. With a brief wave of one hand Garvey created a shield around him and the two children, which left Munroe free to focus on the enemy.

With a few twisting gestures of her left hand she created a shield strong enough to block the fireballs and the residual heat. Although she felt several impact against her shield there was no damage. Meanwhile with her right hand she focused on a section of marble banister above her head, searching for a weakness. One of the pillars immediately started to wobble and with a flick of her hand she sent it spinning through the air. It struck one of the mages on the back of his head, crushing his skull. He was dead before he hit the floor.

The barrage against her shield intensified and each blow now felt as if it would leave a bruise. None of the children had been this powerful before but it wasn't just their will she was fighting.

When the Splinters realised that fire wasn't going to work they tried to kill her in a variety of different ways. All of them were crude and repetitive, suggesting they had truly become puppets with no original thoughts of their own. Their expressions never changed even when she retaliated and killed a second of their cadre with a fireball of her own.

As she blocked a volley of icy spears Munroe became aware of something else. Every time she stopped one of their attacks with a shield it left behind a sort of mental residue. A sickly sweet taint that reminded her of rot and decay.

Pale grey smoke began to gather around her feet and at first Munroe thought part of the room was on fire. But as it spread with unnatural speed she saw it was pouring out of the hands of two Splinters. Their level of skill was far beyond what she'd seen in the past. In no time the whole room was full to the ceiling with grey smoke.

She couldn't see in front of her beyond the length of her arms and throughout the room sounds were distorted and muffled. Elsewhere she could hear that the fighting continued with Vargus and the Drassi battling against the Royal Guards.

She was about to summon some wind to drive away the smoke when someone lurched out of the fog wielding a dagger. Reacting with instinct she grabbed the person's wrist, twisted the arm and pulled them forward off balance, tossing them over her hip. The young mage landed hard on the tiled floor, driving all from her lungs, but the fight wasn't over. Something hot caught Munroe across her lower back and she span around, lashing out with her heel. It connected with something solid and another young mage stumbled back out of sight.

The Splinter on the ground was trying to bite her while they fought over the dagger so Munroe punched her in the face but it had no effect. The girl's eyes were frenzied and she was foaming at the mouth as blood ran from both nostrils. With her back still exposed Munroe grabbed the girl's hair and slammed the back of her head against the floor. It took three heavy blows before the girl's body went limp.

Another figure stumbled into her and Munroe cried out in surprise. She grabbed the person by their waist, fumbled with their belt and yanked them to the floor. The Royal Guard held up his empty hands over his face but she let him go as she recognised him as one of theirs. He was bleeding from a cut over one eye and one of his sleeves was liberally splashed with blood.

"Where's your sword?"

"I lost it," he said with a shrug. Munroe touched the sore spot on her back and came away with blood on her fingers.

"How bad is it?" she said, turning around. The guard checked her wound and gave her a thin smile.

"You'll live."

She pressed the Splinter's dagger into his hand. With a wry smile he stumbled off into the fog again with one hand extended in front.

Munroe was about to clear the fog when she felt a gentle wind against the exposed skin on her back. It started slow and then picked up speed, driving the fog out of the stairwell and down one of the corridors.

As it cleared two more Splinters ran towards her. One wielded a sword he'd picked up and the other held a crude spear formed from frozen ice. Summoning a blade made of molten fire Munroe sheared the ice spear in two, danced around the first mage and blocked a crude swing from the boy's sword. Her blade passed through the steel and then the Splinter's body with little resistance, severing him in two above his hips. Before the other mage could attack Munroe clamped a hand over the girl's mouth and drove her sword into the girl's back through her heart. As the bodies dropped to the floor she felt a pang of regret. They were only a couple of years older than Dox. She hoped the girl hadn't seen her kill them.

With so much going on around her a dreadful thought occurred. Now, while everyone was distracted, was the perfect time for Akosh to betray them. She would sneak away or stab them in the back to gain favour with Kai.

As the smoke dissipated she scanned the ongoing battle and much to her surprise Akosh was still fighting alongside Vargus. Her arms were soaked with blood up to her elbows and she still wielded a dagger in each hand. The look of glee on her face as she stabbed another guard in the throat and twice more in the chest, just for fun, was chilling.

She hadn't betrayed them yet but it was only a matter of time. Munroe would not let her escape. Balfruss was still fighting against the other young mages and was faring well. As she turned to assist him one of her knees buckled and she fell to the ground. At first Munroe thought she'd tripped on something but the floor was clear of obstructions. The wound across her back started to throb and icy fingers of pain ran down her legs.

The mage's blade had been poisoned.

As Balfruss stared at the young mages, and the black tendrils of energy flowing into them, he was taken back ten years to the war. Instead of Splinters controlled by the Warlock he now faced corrupted mages who were slaves to a monstrous being. The Splinters had been undead puppets capable of only the most rudimentary thoughts. By comparison he could see emotions flickering across the faces of the young mages but they were only brief windows into their prison. With each breath they battled against the hungry monster imposing its will upon them and with each breath the struggle was killing them. Even at a distance Balfruss could sense it. The degradation of their bodies and the rotting of their minds.

The black threads flexed and the young mages responded by drawing more power from the Source. Working together they tried to overwhelm him with their combined will. The pressure against his shield was intense but he didn't fight back and made no aggressive move. Normally they would not be able to challenge him. It had to be Kai's influence but the gift of additional strength was already causing severe damage.

Cracks appeared like open sores across the skin on their faces, but instead of blood the wounds glowed with sickly yellow light.

The harder they pushed against him the faster they would die. It brought up another memory from the war of watching a friend die because he'd channelled too much power. Finn Smith, the young mage who some had called Titan, had almost killed the Warlock and ended the war by himself. His power was unprecedented but it had been wild and untrained. In the end it had been his undoing and he'd died in a column of fire falling from the sky. Balfruss didn't want to see history repeat itself.

As much as he wanted to help them Balfruss knew their injuries were beyond his skill. Healing the body with magic was relatively easy compared to the mind. But, perhaps, those who fought alongside him, with centuries of knowledge, might know of a way. The best he could do was put them to sleep but so far his attempts to reach what remained of their minds had failed.

Holding back the tide of their combined will left Balfruss with little power of his own. But with his remaining energy he tried to grasp on to their fragile minds and send them to sleep. Every time Balfruss reached one of the Splinters he had a moment of shared thought. Commands rang through their heads to destroy, to kill and to obey. The voice was so loud it filled all their minds but somewhere in the recesses a tiny voice cried out for help. He strained to reach the core of the mage but it continually slipped away.

On his left one of the young mages started foaming at the mouth, her body spasmed and the girl fell to her knees. Any remaining will was not her own as power continued to flow against him through her unconscious body. The cracks on the girl's faces glowed brighter and he sensed a build-up of power.

"Clear the area," he shouted but his voice was swallowed up by the sounds of battle. Garvey had sensed it too as he pulled Danoph and Dox into a sheltered doorway and fortified his shield around them. Munroe was stumbling about as if drunk so he grabbed her by the armpits and dragged her through a doorway into the next room. The Splinters remained unaware of the danger and made no move to escape. Balfruss slammed the door shut behind him and fortified it with a dense shield.

The build-up of energy continued and then from under the doorway there was a sudden blinding flash. The explosion knocked Balfruss to the floor and the whole building shook. Cracks appeared in the walls and ceiling around the door and in the stairwell he heard the sounds of falling stone crashing to the tiled floor.

The moment Balfruss released his shield the door flew open and chunks of stone bounced through. Munroe was dazed but seemed uninjured so he left her to catch her breath while he went to check on the others.

The fighting had come to an abrupt end. Daylight showed through a gaping hole in the ceiling where the mage had exploded and piles of rubble littered the ground. He spotted a dozen or more bodies buried under debris and twice as many were scattered about with various injuries. Only a few Drassi had made it to their feet and they were busy disarming any Royal Guards still able to fight.

Vargus moved about the room helping where he could, lifting rubble to free the injured and assisting with the wounded. He was pleased to see Garvey and his two wards were uninjured but at first there was no sign of Akosh. Eventually he spotted a figure sat against a wall that vaguely resembled her. She must have been caught in the blast as part of her face was scorched down to the bone. Half of her body was covered with burns and if she'd been human it would have been fatal.

As he watched the flesh on Akosh's face began to repair itself, knitting together over the bone as fresh muscle grew across her jaw. One of her eyes had been melted by the heat but it too was regrowing. Balfruss turned away from her grisly regeneration to check on the fate of the young mages.

He found five that were still alive but the rest had been killed in the blast. Four were already unconscious so it didn't require much energy to calm their minds and put them into a deep sleep. They fell into a near-hibernetic state where their hearts beat so slowly it would appear as if they were already dead. They would stay there, resting and at peace, until he woke them. The fifth mage struggled and tried to fight back, forcing Balfruss to club him across the back of his head with his axe.

With that done he used his magic to lift heavy sections of rubble until all of their allies had been accounted for. They'd lost a portion of Drassi and loyal Royal Guards but the survivors were keen to press on and finish it.

Dead bodies littered the ground. Part of the building had been destroyed and there were patches of blood and pieces of people scattered over the floor and walls. Balfruss found himself looking towards Danoph for an explanation.

"Could none of this be avoided?" he asked, gesturing at the carnage.

Danoph shook his head sadly. "No. This was the best outcome."

That made Balfruss laugh. "What could possibly have been worse?"

"You all died." Danoph spoke with such certainty it was more than a little unsettling. "You were distracted and ripped apart by the explosion in one future. Munroe died from the poison before you healed her in another."

"What—"

It was only then Balfruss noticed Munroe wasn't with them. He retraced his steps and found her slumped against the wall.

"I thought you'd forgotten about me," she gasped. Her lips had gone pale and Balfruss quickly searched for a wound. Dox raced to her side and clasped one of Munroe's hands.

"Do something," screamed the girl. The others were looking at him and Garvey but his friend made no move to help.

With no time to waste he lay Munroe down on the ground and immediately pulled together a healing weave. It took him only moments to build, a testament to the training he'd received across the Dead Sea. Built from five layers, the first two were identical to target the poison, cleanse her blood and flush her kidneys. The rest would replenish her body's fluids while repairing any damaged tissue.

After placing it across her torso he immediately fed power into the weave. Golden light flooded the room and Munroe's eyes rolled back in her head.

"Hold her head steady," said Balfruss. Dox cradled Munroe's head in her lap to prevent further injury as her body jerked around. The poison was not one he recognised but it had already started to creep into her liver and lungs.

The Source called to Balfruss, urging him to draw more power into his body and channel it into Munroe. Ignoring the craving he maintained an even stream of energy as the magic removed the poison in her blood. It scoured it from her organs, herded it together in one place and then dissolved what remained into thousands of harmless motes.

Colour had returned to her face and she began to breathe normally. He checked the skin on her back and found that the wound had completely healed.

"We should leave someone behind to guard her," said Balfruss.

"Help me up," said Munroe, tugging on Dox's arm.

"You need to rest," said Balfruss. Healing had taxed him a little but it would have taken more from her. After a good night's sleep and a few meals her stamina would return.

"I'm coming with you," said Munroe through gritted teeth. Her eyes locked on to Akosh and she stood up with a little support from Dox. She would not let Akosh out of her sight no matter the cost.

"We need to keep moving," said Danoph.

"What about the mages?" asked Balfruss, turning towards Vargus. "Can you help them?"

"I can't heal them. That's not how my power works."

"We can't just leave them."

"Even I can tell their minds have been gouged apart. Nothing can be done. We should slit their throats and move on." As ever Akosh's suggestion was brutal and merciless.

Balfruss turned towards the boy, hoping for another choice. "What can we do?"

"There are only two paths and both of them are short. Either Akosh kills them or they fall asleep and never wake up. There's nothing else."

At that moment Balfruss hated the boy. He hated whatever he was becoming and his callous attitude. He also hated him because he was right. And he hated him because they both knew he would not let Akosh kill the mages, because she would enjoy it.

With a heavy heart he walked towards the prone figures and embraced the Source. They were already deep asleep and far from this world. Free of pain and further abuse. That was small comfort when Balfruss weighed it against all that they'd lost.

Exerting a small portion of will Balfruss forced them further from the light, down into the warm dark, until their heartbeats slowed and finally stopped.

CHAPTER 42

Vargus watched without regret as Danoph channelled the power of the Weaver. His eyes glowed and he led them away from the shattered remains of the marble stairs.

The choice he'd offered Balfruss had no favourable outcomes. It was only the first of many. Danoph would tell himself that he wasn't to blame. He hadn't enslaved the mages nor had he killed them, but over time the guilt would grow. No matter how many times he told himself it wasn't his fault, that he was merely an observer, the anguish of each decision would take a little bite out of him.

Over the years, and a lifetime of choices, the guilt would consume him until he sought the silence of the Void. A place without emotions or feelings. But then he would be reborn and the cycle would begin again. It was a hard road ahead but a necessary one. Vargus intended to make sure Danoph didn't walk it alone as he had for so many years. But none of that would come to pass unless they could defeat Kai.

Through the hole in the ceiling he could see storm clouds had gathered over the city. Somewhere in the distance came the rumble of thunder and he heard it getting closer.

"This way," said Danoph, leading them down a corridor on their left. Two Fists of Drassi roamed ahead to clear the way, pausing at each junction to await further direction from their guide. The surviving Royal Guards and the rest of the Drassi followed at the rear.

Vargus was directly behind Munroe and could hear her wheezing. She was leaning on Dox for support but he knew nothing short of death would stop her. All of the others were a little shaken up from the battle apart from Akosh and Garvey. She was more alive than ever, slathered in gore, red to the elbows and eager for another fight. Garvey had stayed apart, choosing to protect the children and conserve his energy for what lay ahead. He walked with the confidence of a sighted man and the bearing of a priest. Somehow Garvey knew he was being watched as he smiled at Vargus and bobbed his head.

Whatever happened today Vargus knew that Zecorria, and perhaps beyond, would forever be changed. So much overt magic, in the palace no less, would likely ensure that Lord Mallenby's wish came true with little resistance. Thoughts of the future distracted him to the point where he almost missed the ambush.

The Drassi turned left at Danoph's gesture but then the boy stopped suddenly, letting them roam ahead. A squad of Royal Guards burst out of a side door. Vargus barely had time to draw his sword before they were upon him. The Drassi were running back but they were too far away to stop the first attack. Vargus managed to knock aside one sword, elbow a second guard in the face and stun a third but two more guards were still unopposed. All of them had been targeting Danoph, which meant Kai knew the boy's real identity.

Time slowed. Vargus stabbed one guard in the shoulder and kicked him in the hip, spinning him around. The second was already lunging at Danoph who made no attempt to defend himself.

Akosh stepped in front of the boy, blocked the sword with

her daggers and disembowelled the guard. Two more appeared in the doorway with loaded crossbows but they stumbled back screaming in pain as their weapons exploded. Munroe made a twisting motion with one hand and their heads jerked to one side, snapping their necks.

The other guards were caught between the returning Drassi and were soon dispatched. There was no need for Dox to test their loyalty as Kai's influence clearly showed on their faces with black veins beneath their skin. Vargus was surprised that Akosh had saved the boy but Munroe was less impressed. Her sneer told him everything and she was right to be suspicious. Akosh was playing a longer game. One heroic act did not change who she was or what she'd done.

"We go left," said Danoph as if nothing had happened.

Instead of going up the stairs he took them down a narrow corridor used by palace servants. The Drassi were reluctant, as it was the perfect place for an ambush, but Danoph insisted and they complied. Three Fists now roamed ahead with a pair of warriors flanking Danoph on either side in case there were any more surprises.

When they reached a tight spiral staircase the boy paused and glanced up as if he could see through stone.

"Three mages are waiting two floors up. The moment we enter the stairwell they'll flood it with fire and kill everyone." Danoph spoke so calmly it was as if he were talking about someone else's fate. Vargus wondered if he'd been as dispassionate when he'd carried the mantle of the Weaver.

"Stay here," said Balfruss, gesturing for everyone to keep back. Vargus sensed him drawing power from the Source and a moment later he vanished. There was a mild ripple in the air and then it too faded.

They all waited in silence. The Drassi barely moved but he

could see from their posture they were nervous. Despite hating this plan they would follow it because that was the contract. Each warrior would rather fall on his sword than break it. The uncorrupted Royal Guards were less self-assured. They had followed Vargus with the sole purpose of freeing the Regent and now found themselves surrounded by mages. All of them had seen some of what Balfruss and Munroe had done. If not for the Drassi Vargus suspected the guards would have tried to kill them all by now.

From somewhere above their heads came a cry of surprise followed by a loud roaring sound. Despite being two floors away from the fire Vargus felt some of the peripheral heat. Anguished screams echoed off the stone walls and something heavy bounced down the stairs, quickly at first and then more slowly before finally stopping out of sight. He suspected they were better off not knowing exactly what it was.

A short time later Balfruss came down the stairs. The collar of his shirt was slightly black and he smelled of smoke but was otherwise unharmed. There was a splash of blood on his jacket but Vargus knew it wasn't his. From the hard set of his jaw he also knew what Balfruss had been forced to do in order to clear the way ahead.

They followed him up the stairs and Vargus urged the others not to look too closely at the charred bodies. From what remained of their uniforms they had been Royal Guards but three bodies were much smaller. One of them had been reduced to a burned skeleton. Only a small patch of charred skin remained where a hand stretched out as if pleading for mercy.

"Is it far?" asked Munroe from between gritted teeth. Her stamina was holding out for now but she was starting to lean more heavily on Dox.

"Just down there," said Danoph, leading them along more corridors before they arrived in front of a grand set of double doors. The Royal Guards with them perked up, tightening straps on their armour and getting ready for a fight. Vargus checked that everyone was ready then kicked open the doors to the throne room.

Munroe was exhausted. If she closed her eyes she was confident she could easily fall asleep on her feet. Balfruss had completely eradicated the poison in her body but in doing so it had severely depleted her energy. She needed a big meal and at least eight hours' sleep. She was leaning on Dox for support but when she saw Akosh watching she stood upright by herself, ignoring the sneer that followed.

She watched as Vargus took a deep breath and then kicked open the door to the throne room. Ten Drassi ran in first, spreading out around the edges of the room. She and the others followed Vargus who marched ahead.

Kai was lounging on the throne as if it belonged to him. Once more he resembled a handsome man with blond hair but she knew what was lurking beneath. At his feet, on hands and knees, was a middle-aged man dressed in finery who she assumed was Regent Choilan. Kai was using him as a footstool and the embarrassment on the Regent's face almost made her laugh.

Munroe had been expecting an army of Royal Guards but there were barely a dozen arranged behind the throne. The rest of the room was fairly ordinary with pale blue walls decorated with expensive-looking paintings, many of which were portraits of the Regent. Above her head was a viewing gallery but instead of finding it bristling with archers it was empty. The only remarkable feature about the throne room was the domed glass ceiling through which she could see heavy storm clouds overhead. Thunder rumbled and a moment later she heard another echo. It was almost on top of them.

A weasel-faced man stepped out from behind the throne. Marran. He looked anxious and Munroe could feel a dull echo of the Source coming from him. Three young mages hovered behind him with blank eyes.

"Do you really want to do this?" asked Vargus. Kai was enjoying holding court. He sipped from a glass of wine and ate fruit from a silver plate as if he were the Regent. "Too many people have already died."

"People?" said Kai, laughing so much he spilled his wine. Munroe was watching his guards but none of them made any move to attack. Their faces were expressionless and their eyes had become black voids that absorbed the light. "They're worthless maggots. They breed faster than rabbits and care only about themselves. Even an animal has more sense. But you don't see it, do you?"

"See what?" asked Vargus.

Munroe wasn't sure if Vargus was playing for time or genuinely trying to get through to Kai but she knew it was too late for that. As Kai was speaking she noticed Danoph moving among the group, pausing to speak to each person in turn. She couldn't hear what he said to Balfruss but the Sorcerer's jaw tightened in response. When the boy tried to speak with Garvey the blind man just held up a hand.

"I've made my choice."

Danoph hesitated, as if he wanted to say something more, but instead he accepted Garvey's decision and moved on. He bypassed Akosh who raised an eyebrow but most of her attention remained on Kai.

"You can't see what you've become," said Kai, pouring himself another glass of wine. "How long have you spent among them? How many centuries?"

Vargus shrugged. "Does it matter?"

When Danoph reached Dox's side he leaned close and

whispered in the girl's ear. Munroe thought about using magic to eavesdrop, especially when Dox bit her lip, but by then it was too late. He was moving on towards her.

"Of course it matters," said Kai. "You're more like them than me."

"No one is like you," said Vargus, which made Kai laugh.

"That's true, but I wonder, what would happen if I cut your skin? If I pared the meat down to the bone. What would I see? The real you, something inhuman and majestic, or just another old man?"

It was as Danoph reached her side that Munroe noticed Kai's shadow. It had started as a lithe figure but now it was spreading like a cloud of fog. It crept across the back wall, expanding until it had swallowed up the other shadows, and still it grew.

Danoph leaned closer until his mouth was almost brushing Munroe's ear. "Akosh is going to betray us."

"I know," said Munroe.

"Then did you also know that she's going to kill Dox?" asked Danoph, his hand tightening on her shoulder. "And that you'll let it happen."

Stepping back, she grabbed the boy by his shoulders. "What are you saying? I'd never do that."

"You will." He spoke so confidently it made her stomach twist into knots. She searched his face for the lie but didn't need Dox this time. As far as he knew, in whatever future he'd seen, it was true.

"Why would I do that?"

"When her chance comes Akosh will grab Dox and use her to barter. She will promise to let Dox go, once she's out of the palace, as long as you don't try to follow. She will swear it, by the Maker, give a blood oath, say anything to convince you that it's the truth. But you still won't believe her. You can't."

Munroe had sworn she would have her vengeance. She wouldn't

rest until then and nothing would stop her. She couldn't let Akosh escape this time.

"Your need for vengeance won't allow it," said Danoph, echoing her thoughts.

Kai and Vargus were still arguing. Kai was mocking the warrior while he was trying to find a peaceful solution. The writhing shadow continued to spread around the walls. The Drassi had noticed and were frantically scanning the room.

"Don't do this," said Vargus.

Kai shook his head. "It's far too late. You knew that one day this would happen. It was inevitable from the moment you saved me, brother."

"You're asking me to choose between my family and Dox!" said Munroe, shaking the boy by the shoulders.

"Your family isn't here. The girl is," said Danoph. "There are only two roads for her. One long, one short, and you will decide which one she takes."

"That's an impossible choice." Munroe hated him for telling her the future. There had to be another way. Something else she could try that would allow her to save Dox and destroy her enemy. If she stayed by Akosh's side then the moment she tried to betray them Munroe would strike.

"There's more," said Danoph. From his expression she knew he was already beginning to hate his gift. "I need to tell you about Marran. About the things he's done. To the Regent's cadre of mages and to children like Dox."

As he spoke Munroe found she was drawing power from the Source until her skin felt as if it were on fire. The pain mounted with every heartbeat but she just didn't care any more.

Balfruss had been watching Kai's shadow sweep across the room for some time. He knew what happened next. He'd seen it before, years ago, in Voechenka. Vargus made one last desperate plea for this to end peacefully but Kai just laughed in his face. It was an inhuman sound. A cackling screech that few had ever heard. It made the hairs on the back of Balfruss's neck stand up.

With a sigh, resigned about what must happen next, Vargus drew his sword. The Drassi and Royal Guards on their side readied themselves. They thought they were fighting just another mad despot but they were wholly unprepared for the truth.

Kai's eyes glowed red and as he smiled the skin across his face split open on both cheeks. His jaw yawned wide and something bright yellow protruded from inside his mouth. There was a moment when Balfruss saw two versions of Kai in one place. The handsome man and the many-eyed monster. Then the human was gone in an explosion of skin and bone.

The weight of Kai's real form squashed the throne flat as dozens of dark purple tentacles flopped out, stretching across the room, searching for prey. A hundred glowing red eyes blinked in unison while his beak gaped wide and then it screamed. A terrifying cacophony of sound that sent spikes of pain into Balfruss's head while the nerves in his arms throbbed. The windows in the dome shattered and a thousand glass daggers hurtled towards the Drassi who had just engaged Kai's guards.

With a flick of his wrist Balfruss sent the glass spinning into the wall to prevent injuries. The discipline of the Drassi warriors was the only thing that kept it from being a massacre. Those Royal Guards allied to them were frozen in terror, staring at the huge monstrosity filling the throne room. Two ran screaming from the room and one soiled himself.

The Regent had avoided being crushed and with surprising speed he scuttled across the room and hid beneath a stone bench. It provided little in the way of real protection but with all of the doors blocked it was better than nothing.

As Vargus and Akosh ran forward to attack Kai their bodies began to shimmer with translucent white light. It mirrored their attacks and trailed after each swing creating a disturbing afterimage.

With a scream of her own Munroe launched herself at Marran who nimbly ducked out of the way. A lance of glowing fire passed just over his head, burning a narrow furrow across his scalp. He yelped in pain but it was little more than a graze. A second spear was already hurtling towards his head and this one he blocked with a crude shield. Leaving them to it Balfruss checked on the others.

Dox had wisely moved off to one side of the room where she watched the battle at a safe distance. She held a dagger in one hand but only threatened anyone when they came too close.

That left only Danoph and Garvey. The boy had undergone a transformation of his own as now his eyes glowed with the same white light as Vargus and Akosh. With both hands raised he was making subtle gestures, as if creating something with magic, but Balfruss couldn't see what he was doing. The air around him was charged with energy which buffeted against Balfruss in waves.

Across the room one of Kai's tentacles was reaching towards one of the Drassi who'd fallen on to his back. Just before it grabbed the warrior by his leg something unseen nudged it aside. It gave the warrior enough time to reach his sword and retaliate. The warrior severed the nearest tentacle and the remaining arm recoiled in pain allowing the Drassi to escape.

While Munroe's ability allowed her to manipulate the odds Danoph's extended far beyond that. If what Vargus had told him was true, Danoph could not only see into the future like an Oracle, he could also manipulate it. Instead of nudging probability he was guiding the immediate future by narrowing the choices available.

The changes were subtle but Balfruss knew the danger was immense. The pressure showed on his face but Danoph gritted his teeth and persisted.

A knot of tentacles surged towards Balfruss but instead of using magic he lifted his father's axe from his belt and severed them with steel. This fight would not be the same as the last time. He was a different man.

For every arm they severed another sprouted from Kai's huge worm-like body. He appeared to be larger and stronger than the last time Balfruss had seen his natural form. Even with the Drassi as well as Vargus, Akosh and Danoph, they were struggling to contain Kai.

Not far away Garvey was standing with his head tilted to one side as if listening to something in the distance. He'd made no attempt to attack Kai but finally drew power from the Source.

On his first day of school at the Red Tower the teachers had shown Balfruss that magic was created from weaves. Each was made up of multiple layers which were woven together to create different types of lattice.

What Garvey was building didn't resemble anything he'd ever seen before. It was utterly alien. Building, or perhaps forging, was a better word to describe what Garvey was doing. Incongruous elements were slotted together which then interacted with one another in asynchronous orbits. He couldn't hear anything but he could see the pieces were vibrating as they spun about.

The complexity was staggering and each movement of Garvey's hands was precise like a dance. If his connection to the Source had not been so strong the amount of energy he was channelling would have killed him. And still he drew more power, trickling it into the constructs for whatever he was building. His echo from the Source was so loud it hurt Balfruss's ears despite the noise filling the room.

"We all have our role to play, Balfruss," said Garvey, never once pausing in whatever he was doing. "I'm not here to fight. That's your task. You must protect the boy."

Kai must have realised what Danoph was doing as several tentacles surged towards him. Moving with instinct Balfruss raised his father's axe which he imbued with magic. The weapon grew in length until it became a flaming battleaxe which he held aloft with both hands. With sweeping movements, like a Drassi folk dance, he span across the room whirling the great two-headed axe. The flaming blade hissed as it made contact with the purple flesh which writhed in pain. Each swing neatly severed and cauterised one of Kai's limbs. They immediately pulled back but he could see they were regenerating. He thought that Danoph was unaware in his trance but the boy turned his head and offered a smile of thanks. Whatever he was doing required a huge amount of concentration so Balfruss took up position beside the boy to defend him.

"I can see what you're doing, boy," roared Kai, struggling to keep Vargus and the others at bay. "It won't make a difference. Play the odds all you want. In the end, the house always wins."

Danoph smiled up at Kai. He was a vulnerable figure compared to the hulking behemoth. "Do you think the Weaver's power is so limited?" That made Kai pause and his eyes turned towards Vargus. "Of course he lied to you," said the boy, answering Kai's unspoken question.

A tentacle seized Vargus around the leg but he hacked it apart, spraying black blood across the floor. "I never trusted you," said Vargus with a laugh. "Not even from the start."

Kai remained unperturbed. "Even you have limits, boy. Not even the Maker could alter every path in the future. There are too many."

"Ah, but I don't need to change all of them." Danoph had the tone of a teacher lecturing a slow student. "I'm merely guiding the skein in my favour, so that beyond today, you won't have a future. There are already a dozen plans in motion beyond this room."

"You're lying," said Kai. He sounded confident but his many arms twitched with indecision.

Balfruss couldn't believe it when Danoph baited him further. "For one with so many eyes, your vision seems rather limited."

"I will tear you apart," shrieked Kai. With a ferocious roar he launched himself towards Danoph. The boy didn't try to run and a smile danced across his face, further infuriating the monster.

Stretching himself to the limit of his ability, Balfruss threw up a shield directly in the path of the charging behemoth. Drassi warriors and Royal Guards hacked at his limbs but Kai sent them flying, utterly focused on destroying Danoph. Vargus and Akosh fared no better and both went hurtling into walls hard enough to crack the stone.

Time slowed and somewhere nearby Balfruss heard a rumble in the sky. There was a brief flash of light overhead before the thunder rolled again. It was almost above their heads.

Kai bore down on them with incredible speed, his many arms driving him forward. Balfruss poured everything he had into protecting the boy and prayed to Elwei that it would be enough.

With a deafening crack that echoed around the room Kai slammed into the shield. Kai's many arms were splayed across it and his gaping maw turned aside. Several of his eyes burst like overripe fruit but he barely noticed. His momentum had been immense and yet the monster was merely stunned from the impact. Sweat was already streaking down the sides of Balfruss's face from the pressure of keeping the barrier in place but then Kai brought his will to bear.

Groaning in agony Balfruss felt a huge weight settle on his shoulders, driving him to his knees. Tendrils of chaotic energy were burrowing past his defences into his brain. His shield cracked and the air was driven from his lungs. As darkness crept in around the edges of his vision, and the barrier started to buckle, Balfruss saw a flash of light. Buried within were moments from his life.

He remembered as a young boy that the other children in his village had made fun of him for not having a father. He remembered hearing his mother cry at night but he'd pretended not to notice. He remembered watching his friends die, one by one, at the hands of the Warlock. He remembered leaving behind everything familiar to sail across the Dead Sea into the unknown. He remembered meeting his wife, falling in love and the joyous birth of their daughter. He remembered the heartache of his wife's death and the blame that fell upon him. He remembered the anguish of leaving a place that had become his home.

Hundreds of memories were laid bare before him in the space of a heartbeat. And with each memory came an echo of emotion. Shame. Misery. Heartache. Guilt. Wonder. Love. Rage and joy.

Drawing on the deep well of emotions inside he thought about all that he had endured to reach this moment. His will had taken him further than other Battlemage in more than a century. He was one of only four Sorcerers in the entire world and he refused to yield.

Stretching himself further than ever before Balfruss used the power of his birthright to hold back the darkness. The immense weight of Kai's will pressed against him, but drawing on reserves deep within, Balfruss held him back for one heartbeat and then another.

For one perfect moment a man pitted his will against a malevolent god of chaos and held it at bay.

Kai's many eyes widened in surprise and Balfruss found himself grinning at his hateful enemy.

The clouds broke overhead and Balfruss screamed in fury at the creature, lending his voice to the storm. Forked tongues of lightning burst through the high windows at his command and each bolt slammed into the huge body at the centre of the room. Balfruss's eyes were dazzled by the light and the air stank of burning meat. Kai shrieked as wild energy from the storm was focused upon him.

The moment passed. The lightning stopped falling but he refused to surrender.

Gritting his teeth Balfruss made it to a knee and then slowly forced himself upright. His whole body was shaking and his veins were on fire. Blood trickled from both nostrils from the pressure but he ignored it. He ignored everything but standing his ground while staring down the monster.

All of its tentacles reared back and Balfruss knew his shield would not survive another attack. Kai stretched to his full height but then stumbled back and fell over to one side crushing several guards. The pressure against his shield vanished and Balfruss collapsed on to his hands and knees. Across the room Vargus and Akosh were shaking off their dizziness, readying themselves for another attack. The fight wasn't over and he still had to protect his student.

"Thank you, Balfruss," said Danoph, touching him lightly on the shoulder. "You can stand down."

"What have you done?" asked Kai, staring at the boy with horror.

"I told you, I've been fighting this war on several fronts."

"What's happened?" asked Vargus, equally baffled.

"The plague . . ." said Kai.

"It's been cured in Perizzi," said Danoph. "The city is safe."

Danoph offered Balfruss a hand to stand up. Elsewhere Munroe fought Marran and some of the Drassi had resumed their battle with the enslaved guards. "Did you really cure the plague?" whispered Balfruss.

"No, it was Wren and the others," said Danoph, talking out of the corner of his mouth. "I was stalling for time as I knew it would weaken him."

"No matter, it's too little too late," said Kai. A portion of the skin on his lumpy slug-like body peeled away but instead of staring at his innards it had become a window to another place. Balfruss could see a sky full of unfamiliar stars and the outline of figures against the black. All of them rushed towards the light until they were pressed against the surface of Kai's skin as if it were a pane of glass. Unfamiliar faces begged and screamed for mercy but all of them were caught in a knot of tentacles within the alien void.

The arms flexed and each person convulsed as Kai siphoned off their energy. Each pulse drained them faster and faster, shrivelling up their bodies as all moisture was extracted along with their life force. Kai sighed in pleasure and the wounds they'd inflicted started to heal with alarming speed.

Kai's many eyes swivelled towards Danoph. "Like so many others, you will sustain me. In the end you'll be nothing more than fresh meat."

The boy had no cheeky reply this time, but Kai had already turned away to focus on Akosh and Vargus.

"Akosh, now is the time to make your choice."

She had a dagger in each hand but at Kai's words she sheathed her weapons and stepped back.

It was just as Munroe had feared. Akosh had betrayed them.

CHAPTER 43

As Danoph's words about Marran rang in Munroe's ears her fatigue evaporated.

Danoph had told her everything. The hideous crimes Marran had committed against helpless girls. The abuse he'd inflicted upon countless victims and the minds he'd destroyed with his corrosive magic. It stripped a person of their free will and they had to obey his commands while somewhere, deep inside, a small part raged against the enslavement. It was this conflict that would eventually kill each person he touched as they fought for their freedom.

She'd seen the vacant eyes of the young mages. Her previous fight with them had been one-sided but at least they'd been in control of their actions. Now they'd been reduced to mindless husks that had to obey.

On the periphery of her vision Munroe was aware of the others but her attention stayed on Marran. Danoph's words haunted her, going around and around inside her head like a tortuous mantra. "If he leaves this room alive, Dox will be his next victim." Every time it was repeated she felt her blood boil just a little more. She thought about the futures he'd stolen. The lives he'd taken. The trust he'd betrayed and the innocence he'd robbed.

Energy from the Source crackled all around her, filling the air with static. Part of her knew that Danoph had manipulated her, told her the worst of Marran's crimes to make her angry, but she didn't care any more. She needed to hear it. Marran was guilty and would never face justice in a normal court, but he would answer to her.

For the longest time she'd been told to be patient. That in time justice for her family would happen. Her usual approach, charging in head first, hadn't worked so she'd been forced to adapt. That meant forcing down her anger. Swallowing it like bile where it burned, gnawing away at her insides. But now she didn't have to hold back. Danoph's words stripped away her self-control. Being impulsive and violent as her first reaction no longer mattered.

The air around Munroe burst into flames and a wall of blue fire swept across the room towards Marran. He threw up a quick shield but it was poorly made and only blocked a portion of the fire. Flames licked at the edges of his clothing, singeing his boots and hair, while the overwhelming heat blistered the skin on his face and hands.

Marran screamed and made a twisting motion with both hands, forming a protective bubble around him. The three young mages, who had remained motionless, suddenly came to life. Their combined will was melded into one vast block of force with which they tried to crush her to death. Munroe pitted her strength against theirs and immediately found they were lacking. As they struggled to force her back she sensed Marran urging them on but also something else. Dark, alien energy ran through the mages like poison in their veins. Its corruption was causing as much damage to them as Marran's mind control.

The skin on their faces was already pale but as more of the darkness flooded their bodies grey veins protruded on their faces. Their mouths stretched wide in matching rictus grins and the skin split across their cheeks. Their injuries should have been bleeding but nothing seeped from the wounds. They had truly become puppets that felt nothing.

Their combined will, fuelled by Kai's magic, struck Munroe across the face, sending her across the room. She felt dizzy and black spots danced in front of her eyes but she quickly shook it off.

Another lash was coming towards her like the curl of a whip. Crossing her forearms above her head Munroe formed a shield which deflected the blow. The impact made her arms ache and ears ring. Gritting her teeth against the pain she targeted Marran since the others wouldn't react. Once she cut off his head the others would be free, or at the very least, allowed to die.

Making a twisting motion with her left hand Munroe focused her Talent on Marran's left knee. There was a satisfying popping sound and he squealed in pain and collapsed. Without direction the Splinters became immobile as Marran thrashed about holding his leg. The joint had been shattered but to make matters worse Munroe used her will to squeeze it. His mouth stretched so wide she thought he would dislocate his jaw. Anger kindled somewhere inside him as despite being in agony the Splinters came back to life.

Ducking a crackling bar of flame that would have cut her in two Munroe threw a hammer made of pure force directly at a Splinter's head. Anyone with a shred of self-preservation would have dodged the attack. The young mage didn't move until it was already too late. At Marran's command she tried to step aside. Instead of smashing her skull the hammer slammed into the Splinter's shoulder, tearing off the girl's right arm. Gristle dangled from the gaping wound and black sludge dripped on to the floor. Despite her injury the girl's expression didn't change.

A black and purple coil of energy wrapped itself around Munroe's right forearm pulling her off balance. As needles of pain shot through her body another whip struck her in the throat. She couldn't scream as the noose tightened and now she had a Splinter on either side. The pain was unbearable but even worse was that she couldn't breathe properly. Instead she had to take lots of short breaths which made her feel faint. Munroe tried to pull free of the energy coils but as more power was fed into them she fell to her knees. Her body refused to obey her commands. The Source was still there, on the periphery of her senses, but trying to embrace any power from it felt impossible.

Marran watched her from across the room. He was still in pain, leaning heavily on his good leg, but his smugness had returned. The leash around her neck tightened, burning her skin, while the other Splinter tried to tear her arm out of its socket.

Munroe's eyes swept the room, taking in the fight between the monstrous form of Kai and her friends. Balfruss was facing off against it alone while the others tried to hack away its sides. Their efforts were having little effect as Kai's momentum didn't slow. He would crush the Sorcerer and the boy. But somehow Balfruss survived and then it happened just as she knew it would. Akosh was offered a choice and instead of continuing to fight with them she put away her weapons. She betrayed them.

White-hot fire erupted from the palm of Munroe's hands, coiling around her wrists, racing up her arms to her shoulders. It flowed down her back like a living cloak, descending to the floor in a shower of sparks. Grabbing the two leashes she sent the fire down them towards the Splinters. Despite being nothing more than mindless puppets they noticed the churning heat that blackened the flesh of their arms before it set their clothes and hair alight.

Screaming in voices choked by smoke the two Splinters tried to release her but she grimly held on, ignoring the agony in her body, blotting out the burning in her mind. With a final whoosh the two Splinters exploded like firecrackers, spraying blackened lumps of meat and bone in all directions.

The leashes vanished and the pain inside her was replaced with a heaviness in her limbs from fatigue. Marran was leaning on his remaining Splinter but with a final flick of her right hand Munroe twisted its head around severing the spine. The body died and Marran collapsed to the ground.

Akosh was still in the room but she wouldn't be for long. She would run and hide and then Munroe would never get her revenge. She didn't have time for Marran but he had to be destroyed. Given the smallest chance he would slither away and once the danger had passed would revert to his old self. She owed it to his victims to make his death long and tortuous but she was out of time.

As she stalked towards him across the room he hurled things at her. A black cube crackling with energy. A triangular trap. A spear of ice. Moving with instinct she shrugged off each attack until she was standing over him. As she pressed down on his injured knee with her boot Munroe felt his connection to the Source evaporate.

"You deserve much worse than this," said Munroe, drawing together a spear of fire so hot that the end glowed white.

As he opened his mouth to beg Munroe stabbed the spear into the top of his head. Marran's eyes widened in terror as she slowly drove the flaming lance through his skull into his brain. He choked and thrashed about but she held on tight, forcing the spear down through his head deep into his chest. Thick red blood was trickling from his ears, nose and mouth while his eyes had rolled up in his skull. His body continued to twitch as the fire consumed him from the inside, turning his brain to grey sludge. Marran gasped his final breath and she let the spear evaporate, leaving behind a gaping hole in the top of his head.

Munroe spat on his corpse and turned away. Finally, the time for her revenge was at hand.

*

In spite of everything Garvey found himself smiling as his hands moved in a precise series of motions. He continued building, piece by piece, channelling a vast amount of energy into his construct. With every heartbeat he found himself balanced on a knife edge. It would only take the slightest distraction for him to fail. Then his heart would burst, or his head explode, or both. His smile stretched even wider until it hurt.

The others were still battling against the behemoth that pretended to be a man. They seemed to be holding their own, but he knew the monster was merely playing with them, like a predator teasing its prey. It had not yet drawn on its full strength.

He sensed it opening a window to somewhere else. A playground full of lesser beings that it tortured while absorbing their energy. With the end of the plague one of its strands of power was cut but Kai renewed his strength by draining the creatures inside. There would be no second chances. They were all gambling everything on this fight.

The moment was upon him. The Pilgrim had been right. It had all been leading up to this. Every decision in his life. The boy, Danoph, knew more than he realised.

Wherever a person was born, whatever their station, their life was but a road stretching out to the horizon. Along the way there were an endless series of choices. Tens of thousands of crossroads that gave a person the opportunity to change for the better or worse.

Over the years there were many things of which he wasn't proud. Words spoken in anger. Lives he'd taken as the Bane. Students he'd knowingly led astray. It had all been done to serve the greater good but such words were small comfort for the victims and their families.

Garvey suspected in some versions of his life he had not razed Garrion's Folly to the ground. But in this life he'd done it and so had to live with the consequences. It was a stain upon his soul. Something terrible that could have been prevented but in his arrogance he'd believed it was necessary.

There was always a price to pay but at least one good thing had come from the tragedy. If not for that heinous crime he would not have been blinded by Balfruss and then captured. Deep in the cells beneath the Zecorran palace, not far from where he was now standing, the guilt had found him. It started to eat away at him even while his mind expanded.

And so he had been compelled to revisit Garrion's Folly and bury the dead. Not to assuage his guilt or ask forgiveness, for there was no one left alive. Something else had driven him to revisit that empty place. Only now did he truly understand why he had bothered to ask Mayor Phelon about the half-finished bridge and his grandfather's story.

So many choices, so many opportunities to be someone else. To be somewhere else in this moment in time. The story Phelon had been told was true. The bridge wasn't broken or incomplete. Only half of it existed here. The other half was in a place beyond the Veil.

The final piece slotted into place. A vast river of energy continued to flow through him into the artefact. The bridge had taught him so much but the rest had come from the Pilgrim.

Making a final twist with one hand Garvey opened a doorway.

In a distant place beyond the Veil, wrapped in eternal darkness, drowned in sorrow and scoured of all joy, a portal opened. The pinprick of light shone upon the flesh of what lay slumbering within the emptiness; vast beings that were so old they appeared undying.

Somewhere in that endless sea of flesh, feathers and scales, an eye opened.

CHAPTER 44

Ever since Dox had started travelling with Munroe she'd had all manner of adventure.

Her life back in Rojenne, working for the local crime lord, had been tedious but occasionally peppered with danger. She'd always dreamed of getting out of the tiny city, exploring the world, and seeing its wonders. What she'd experienced in the last few months had been far more wondrous and terrifying than she'd ever imagined. There were times, like today, when she regretted leaving her quiet life.

A few days ago she'd been trying to help Munroe get revenge for the murder of her family. Now they were fighting alongside Akosh against a huge purple creature that had erupted from the body of a man.

As the tide of the battle shifted, and Kai faltered, Akosh's true nature reasserted itself. Just as Munroe had predicted, Akosh put her daggers away and changed side. Kai's strength returned, his severed limbs regenerated, and he readied himself for another fight.

But then something happened that no one could have anticipated. Whatever Garvey had been doing all this time was finally complete. She'd felt him working with so much power from the

Source it made her teeth ache. Garvey made one final gesture and then he tore a hole in the world. There was no other way to describe it.

A glowing ribbon of white light appeared in mid-air before it expanded sideways and then she was peering through a doorway to somewhere else.

Inside it was utterly black. At first Dox thought it nothing more than a featureless void but then she saw something huge moving against the darkness. As her eyes adjusted she realised the little that she could see was only part of something much larger. Her mind rejected the initial idea because of the scale. Nothing alive could possibly be so big.

But then, as she stared past the portal, Dox saw again the huge tentacled monster with glowing red eyes. Even so, whatever was on the other side dwarfed Kai by a considerable margin. Finally Kai noticed the glowing tear and paused in his battle with Vargus and the Drassi. Every one of his arms froze but the many red eyes swivelled to focus on the doorway.

"What have you done?" he hissed.

Several things suddenly happened. Someone grabbed Dox from behind, wrapping an arm around her waist and another around her throat. Something cold and sharp was pressed against her neck and the whole room shook under the power of Munroe's scream. The sound was deafening but when Dox tried to cover her ears, her captor held on more tightly. The air rushed past her and a groan of pain escaped her lips as the sound drove needles of pain into her head.

Slowly the scream faded and when the black spots stopped dancing in front of her eyes she saw Munroe standing not far away. Dox had never seen her so angry before. In the past she'd always held back but now Munroe's whole body was shaking with rage. Blue sparks of energy jumped from her fingers and motes of fire danced across her clothing. The strength of her connection to the Source was so strong it created a loud pulse in Dox's head.

"Let me pass," said Akosh, pressing her dagger more firmly against Dox's throat.

"You're not going anywhere," spat Munroe, slowly moving towards them.

"Don't come any closer or I'll cut her throat," said Akosh. Dox hissed in pain as the blade nicked her skin and a trickle of blood ran down her neck.

Munroe froze but the air around her was charged with energy. "Let the girl go."

"I'm going to walk away," said Akosh, "and when I reach the city gates I'll let her go. I won't hurt her."

Munroe shook her head. "No. We both know you'll kill her."

"I promise, I will let her live. Just let me go." Akosh sounded sincere but then she was a master of deception.

"I can't let you out of my sight. Not again." Munroe was adamant.

Dox couldn't blame her. Munroe had already been forced to let Akosh escape once at the orphanage. If she and the other orphans hadn't been trapped then it would already be over. Munroe would've killed Akosh and had her revenge for the murder of her family.

Sometimes, when she was particularly drunk or tired, Munroe would talk about her husband, son and mother. Sometimes it was the small everyday moments that still filled her with joy. Mostly she spoke of the agony of their loss and the pain she felt all the time. It never faded. The absence of them from her life. For Munroe it wasn't as if someone had cut off an arm or a leg. Her family weren't simply a part of her. They meant everything to her. Without them Munroe had no future. Once Akosh was dead that was the end. She would simply stop.

Dox instinctively knew that if Akosh walked out of the throne room, whether she kept her promise or not, Munroe would never find her again. There were too many people that wanted her dead. Akosh would disappear and Munroe would spend the rest of her life in a futile search. The death toll of Munroe's hunt would be catastrophic. She would never get revenge and never be at peace.

"Let me go, or she dies," said Akosh.

The anguish on Munroe's face was unbearable. Tears ran from her eyes and her jaw was clenched tight. The struggle within manifested without as cherry-red fire continuously ran from her fingers, scorching the tiled floor in a growing circle of flames.

Just before the fighting had begun Danoph had moved around the room whispering something to each person in turn. His words now came back to her and Dox understood what needed to happen.

"It's all right," said Dox, speaking directly to Munroe. "I don't blame you. I always knew it would end this way." She was trying not to cry but couldn't help it. While her dreams of a life full of adventure had changed she still wasn't ready to die. There was still so much she wanted to do.

"Don't say that," gasped Munroe.

"It has to end here. I know that," said Dox, closing her eyes. "I'm ready."

"Don't be stupid, girl," said Akosh, giving her a shake. Dox tried her best to ignore Akosh and kept her eyes closed. "Don't listen to her, Munroe."

"I never wanted this for you," said Munroe.

In spite of everything Dox found herself smiling. "I know."

There was more she wanted to say. So much more, but they were out of time. The throbbing in Dox's head became worse as Munroe drew even more power from the Source.

"I will kill her!" shouted Akosh. She was desperate now. She could feel it too. There was no going back. It had to end here.

"If she dies you'll have no leverage. Then I'll kill you," said Munroe. They all knew it was no idle threat. She'd almost succeeded last time.

Akosh was trying to drag Dox towards the door but Munroe stalked forward a step every time they retreated. "Choose now," said Akosh, readying her dagger. Dox still had her eyes closed but she felt the length of the blade press against her throat.

Elsewhere Dox heard an almighty shriek that was so loud it hurt her ears. The sounds of battle resumed but none of it mattered.

"I want your word," said Munroe.

She felt Akosh's whole body tense for battle. Then she hesitated. "What?"

"I want a blood oath that once you reach the city gates, you will release the girl, unharmed." Munroe spoke calmly but there was a tremor in her voice. The decision had cost her. Dox knew it was more than she would ever be able to repay. Fresh tears ran from her eyes.

Akosh eased the dagger away from Dox's throat. "I swear—" she began and that was when Dox struck.

Compared to everyone else her connection to the Source was weak and she'd only been practising for a few months. But today it was more than enough. While they'd been arguing, while magic filled the air all around them and fire dripped from Munroe's hands, Dox had opened herself to the Source and crafted something.

Shoving a hand backwards she summoned a globe of light directly in front of Akosh's face. Even with her eyes closed she saw the flash. With a screech Akosh reeled back, clawing at her eyes. Dox ducked under the dagger and rolled across the floor out of arm's reach. She didn't know how long Akosh's blindness would last but Munroe didn't hesitate.

The waterfall of fire stopped. In its place a glowing spear appeared in Munroe's hands. Its tip glowed white like the heart of a forge. With a scream full of rage and hate she hurled the spear at Akosh. It pierced her side and howling in agony the assassin stumbled back. One hand was wrapped around the spear and the other held a dagger which she whipped from side to side. She was still blind.

Dox watched as an evil grin stretched across Munroe's face.

In her dreams Munroe sometimes found herself back in Perizzi. The city had been her home for many years so it wasn't surprising. However, most often those dreams quickly became nightmares as once again she witnessed an insane Fleshmage tear a hole in the world. With help from others, including her husband, Choss, they'd managed to close it and save the city, but not before she'd seen what was on the other side.

Now, with her revenge at hand, Munroe's smile faltered. Across the room Garvey stood beside another hole in the world. Unlike the other, which had been a crude slash which constantly tried to close, this was more like a doorway. Lines of glowing alien runes that squirmed when she focused on them circled the rectangle of light on three sides. Inside the doorway she could see into another place and within huge shapes swimming towards her in the black.

Akosh was momentarily forgotten as she watched Vargus drive his sword up to the hilt into Kai's side then drag it sideways. Bright pink innards and white blood spilled on to the floor. Balfruss had been resting on one knee but with a grunt of effort he forced himself upright and lashed out with his magic.

The air cracked with a sound like thunder and a dozen tentacles were crushed from the impact of Balfruss's attack. A huge dent, the size of a horse, appeared in the monster's side. Drassi and Royal Guards were hacking away at Kai as well, chopping off tentacles but new ones kept spawning in their place.

All of Garvey's attention was on the doorway but Munroe could already see sweat soaking through his clothes from the strain. Even Danoph was engaged with the battle in his own way. His eyes glowed pure white and with both arms raised all of his fingers were twitching as if playing a musical instrument. She felt eddies in the air swirling around her, subtle shifts that she couldn't understand, but with each there was a ripple across her skin. She didn't know what Danoph was doing but it was hurting Kai along with everyone else.

They were trying to inch him towards the doorway but their progress was slow and everyone was already so tired. They were at a stalemate.

Once again Munroe found herself facing an impossible decision. To kill Akosh and let her friends die, or fight alongside them against Kai. And if she chose the latter there was a good chance that Akosh would escape.

A third option presented itself and with a cackle of glee Munroe lifted Akosh off the floor and hurled her towards Kai's head. As expected for something with so many eyes it saw the human projectile and caught Akosh in mid-air. Several tentacles immediately wrapped themselves around Akosh's arms and legs. She started babbling, trying to explain what had happened, but either Kai didn't hear or he simply didn't believe her. It looked as if she had chosen to side with the enemy against him. Her words were replaced with screams as Kai started to pull her limbs from their sockets.

An icy shiver ran down Munroe's spine and immediately her eyes were drawn to the doorway. It didn't belong. It was unnatural and its alien nature made her skin itch, but the source of her fear came from something worse. Something far more dangerous.

Something was trying to cross over into their world from the other side.

A huge spiny limb, the width of a tree trunk and covered with nodules, started creeping through the doorway. Munroe could see it pushing against a thick viscous membrane that stretched but refused to break. When it was six feet long there was a horrific tearing sound and the fleshy sheath finally came apart.

The impact was immediate as Munroe blacked out. She came to and found herself lying on the floor staring up at the storm through the broken windows. Thick black clouds had gathered directly overhead and sheets of rain hammered against the shattered dome. Thunder rumbled and less than a heartbeat later lightning answered. The air inside the room was unnaturally cold. Munroe's breath frosted in front of her face and her fingers throbbed with pain.

Everyone was disorientated and struggling to stand up while the huge spiny arm continued to move around the room, searching for prey.

Balfruss was the first on his feet and wasting no time he unleashed a hail of icy needles. They fell from the sky directly above Kai, impaling him over and over again. Vargus was glowing all over with pale white light. With a roar he charged into battle but now he was moving so fast Munroe's eyes were constantly one step behind. His sword created silver arcs of light and it cut through Kai's hide like it was made of paper. Munroe felt each blow of his sword deep in her bones. The sound it made was so low she felt the vibrations through her feet. Instinct told her that Vargus was doing far more damage than simply slicing into the monster's flesh. Kai tried to stop him but Vargus was moving too fast. He danced out of the way or swayed to one side before running back in.

Akosh was fighting to stay alive. Expending energy to keep her limbs intact. One of her arms had already been torn from its socket. A new arm was trying to regrow but the wound was closing very slowly.

Munroe closed her eyes and tried to blot it all out. Focusing only on the sound of the waves she drew power from the Source. She drank greedily, letting it soak into every part of her body, until she was saturated with energy. Until her skin burned, her head throbbed and she felt dizzy and sick. Until the drumbeat from the Source had merged with her own pulse to create one painful reminder of life. And with every beat she thought of all that she'd lost and would never have again. Base emotions flooded her mind and her veins sang with primordial power.

Only then did she open her eyes and unleash all of it towards Kai.

It started deep in her chest and as it rose up through her body she felt it gathering power and momentum, snowballing into something monstrous, until it exploded from her mouth in a piercing scream. The air in front of her vibrated and the whole room shook from the force which slammed into Kai so hard he was driven backwards across the floor.

The huge grasping arm reached a little bit further into the room where it made contact with Kai's flesh. As the sound continued to pour out of her mouth Munroe watched with growing horror as the end of the creature's arm split open like the overlapping petals of a flower. Inside was a gaping maw lined with teeth which bit into Kai's body. Her stomach turned over when it began to burrow inside.

Lightning fell from the sky inside the room bursting Kai's eyes and gouging black craters in his flesh. A hundred or more icy needles slammed into one part of his body until it resembled a pin-cushion. Vargus continued severing limbs while echoes of every strike made the room chime like a bell. Munroe took a deep breath and resumed her scream but now it was tearing the flesh off Kai's bones. A dozen red eyes exploded and, for once, were not instantly replaced by more.

The thing on the other side had a firm grip on Kai's body and it was slowly dragging him towards the portal. Balfruss added his power to the momentum and Kai started to slide across the floor. Akosh was now missing an arm and a leg, was drenched in blood and barely conscious. But Kai had an arm wrapped around her and was squeezing what remained.

With a screech Kai desperately tried to find some purchase to stop his momentum but Vargus continued to sever his limbs. A few brave Drassi and Royal Guards rushed forward and together they hacked and chopped at any tentacle that moved.

The room was swaying and Munroe knew she'd been pushing herself too hard for too long. But the battle wasn't over. Reaching deep inside she strained towards the Source. As its power seeped into her body it soothed away her aches and enhanced her senses, lulling her into a false sense of immortality. With her magic she could do anything. The only limit was her imagination.

After today she would hunt down every person who'd ever spoken ill of magic and make them pay. They would suffer as every child and Seeker had suffered. She would drown, burn and hang every single one. Magic was a gift not a curse.

"No," said Munroe, shaking her head. Such dark thoughts didn't belong to her but she couldn't stop them surging through her head.

She would start with Balfruss and the girl. Then hunt down Vargus and the boy. Her strength could not be matched. She would burn them up from the inside. Roast them alive like hogs. Fire. Fire was the answer.

"Munroe, what are you doing?" said a little voice.

The fog lifted. Dox was terrified and holding a dagger towards her. Kai had stopped moving towards the portal and everyone was now focused on her. It took a moment for Munroe to realise why. She was holding Kai in place with her magic.

Every single one of the monster's red eyes was boring into her skull and the weight of his will pressed against her.

"Get out," she hissed, sinking to her knees. The pressure inside her skull was intense. It felt as if her head was going to explode. "Get out of my fucking head!"

"Obey!" whispered a voice.

Fire was the answer after all. It devoured everything. It burned away the shadows bringing light into the dark. As Kai tried to control her mind she pictured the flames. The cherry-red and white-hot glow at the heart of a blaze. The gnawing, all-consuming heat. As Munroe focused on the fire within her body erupted with flames, turning her into a living candle.

She broke free of his control and hurled fire across the room which roasted Kai's flesh.

His massive body skidded across the floor and struck the portal, wedging him in place like a cork in a bottle.

The doorway was too small.

For a moment nothing happened and Munroe thought it had all been in vain. Then Kai's maw widened in agony and she heard an almighty popping sound. The crunching of bones followed as parts of the monster's body were folded up. Piece by piece he was being mashed together and pulled through from the other side. Something still had a firm grip on him and it was now doing all of the hard work. Munroe's connection to the Source vanished and she would have fallen if not for Dox supporting her.

Kai was thrashing about in desperation. His remaining arms searched for something, anything, to help. Akosh's broken and bloody body had been forgotten. It lay on the floor in front of Kai but he was more interested in saving his life than killing her. With her remaining arm Akosh was trying to pull herself away from the doorway.

More tiles fell from the ceiling as Kai slammed his arms on the ground in a vain attempt to break free. A series of loud pops followed before another section of his body was folded inwards and he slid backwards a little more. One arm snagged Akosh around her ankle and she was dragged towards the portal.

"Help me," pleaded Akosh, reaching out in desperation.

"Why would I help you?" asked Munroe.

"Because your son is still alive. I can help you find him!"

Akosh was truly desperate. "You would say anything," said Munroe, no longer surprised. Instead of getting angry she just felt empty.

Munroe watched with dispassion as what remained of Kai was crunched up and then yanked through the doorway followed by Akosh. She screamed until her head vanished through the glowing portal. The moment she crossed over it stopped and a heavy silence settled on the throne room.

Garvey made a series of complex gestures but nothing happened. The portal was still there. Munroe saw something else move closer to the threshold on the other side. Dox was keening in terror as something new started to pass through. It was scaly and dark blue. She saw an arm of some kind glistening with viscous fluid that steamed in the air. The girl's scream rose higher as a second smaller limb, adorned with bony hooks and lumpy yellow sacs, tried to force its way through as well.

Balfruss could barely stand but he forced himself upright and Munroe sensed him trying to embrace the Source. She reached for it as well but the sound of the ocean was so far away. Vargus readied his sword for battle and Munroe looked around for a weapon.

With a cry of triumph Garvey made a final twisting motion with both hands. The portal snapped shut, severing the alien limbs, and a blast of air knocked everyone from their feet. The limbs melted like hot wax, turning into liquid which then evaporated. Garvey dropped to the ground and she didn't know if he was just exhausted or dead. Balfruss could barely stand and Vargus was leaning heavily on his sword. Beside her Dox was staring at the space in the middle of the room as if she expected the portal to reopen.

Munroe stood for a while just staring up at the small piece of sky she could see through the broken windows. Somewhere in the distance thunder rumbled. The storm had passed. Akosh was gone and, finally, she could rest.

It was over.

CHAPTER 45

Balfruss gingerly eased himself into the bath, sighing with pleasure as the hot water enveloped his body. He rested his head against the back of the tub and closed his eyes.

It had been over a week since the events in the Zecorran palace and he was still recovering. He'd slept for a whole day and night immediately after then woken up ravenous the next morning. He still had more of an appetite than usual but in time it would return to normal.

The ride to Yerskania had been made at a leisurely pace and each night on the journey south he'd treated himself. Normally he stayed in modest taverns but for a change he'd indulged. Every night, as well as a hot bath and a comfy bed, he ate the best food. He wasn't used to such luxury and often felt a little out of place among the other guests. Most of them were wealthy merchants or minor nobles from Yerskania so he tended to keep to himself while listening to the crowd.

As expected all conversations were focused on what had happened in Zecorria. Everyone believed the Regent had turned out to be mad after all. The throne was cursed. How else could you explain three successive rulers going insane? To make matters worse the Regent had invited mages into the palace only for them to destroy it.

On the night of the battle all across the capital city people had huddled together in their homes watching a bizarre storm linger over the palace. Lightning had flooded the sky and unnatural screams had drifted through the air.

When it was over they found the Regent sitting among the ruins dressed in rags with wild eyes and wilder stories.

One merchant claimed that rather than face justice the Regent had thrown himself under a carriage and been trampled to death. Balfruss heard another story where the Regent had been locked up in an asylum. Apparently he'd been talking about huge monsters and invisible doors. Of course no one believed his stories. Everyone knew the damage to the palace had been caused by his cadre of young mages turning rogue. They were all gone now and so was any kind of magic. A national ban had been brought in across the country just as Lord Mallenby had wanted. There were now rumblings of Zecorria becoming a republic but at this point it was only speculation.

Part of Balfruss was disappointed that after all of his efforts at the Red Tower, and in the years before, magic was still seen as a curse in the west. The difficult truth was they weren't ready for it. Not yet. The war was partly to blame but deep-seated mistrust had existed in communities for a long time before his conflict with the Warlock.

It was a different story in the desert kingdoms where magic had been an integrated part of society for over two hundred years. Perhaps, in time, the west would adjust but he didn't think it would happen in his lifetime.

As the water began to cool Balfruss eased himself from the tub, dressed in clean clothes and went in search of food. After a hearty meal of lamb stew, roasted vegetables and rye bread to soak up the gravy he felt replete. Nursing a pint of ale he dozed by the fire, listening to the conversations with one ear.

A shadow moved in front of Balfruss and someone sat down at his table. At this point he was no longer surprised. The grizzled old warrior looked exactly the same as ever.

"Hello, Vargus."

"Balfruss," he said, slurping from his mug of ale. "What are people talking about?"

"What do you think?"

Vargus laughed. "That's good, because if they were talking about what actually happened I'd be worried."

They sat together for a while in comfortable silence letting other people's conversations wash over them. The atmosphere was relaxed but everyone was agitated about Zecorria and the wider repercussions with its ban on magic. Many people were speculating about mages in other countries. How would other leaders deal with them?

"Is it over?" asked Balfruss. "Is he ... dead?" They'd all seen Kai dragged through the portal to that other place beyond the Veil. A nightmare world populated by monstrosities of gigantic proportions. Beyond that he knew nothing about it.

"I think after everything that's happened you've earned the truth. But are you sure you want to hear it?" asked Vargus.

Balfruss believed that knowledge was power but there were times when it was simpler and better to remain ignorant. On this occasion not knowing would be far worse for him. It would gnaw away at him and this might be his only opportunity to get some answers.

"I need to know."

"All right," said Vargus, taking another drink. "It's over. He's gone."

"But is he dead?" asked Balfruss.

"That's more difficult to answer."

"Why?"

"The rules in that place are different," said Vargus. "Here, time is like a river, constantly flowing. Over there it's more like water trickling through wet clay. Kai will be fighting for his life against the others but I don't know if he's won or lost."

"Will he ever die?" asked Balfruss, thinking of the thing that had grabbed Kai.

"The creature you saw, it's one of the Nameless. Even I don't know where they came from or how they were trapped there. But they've been waiting in the dark for aeons. And in such a place, which is almost beyond time, even death ceases to have meaning. So they sleep and wait and whisper in the shadows. Some of their words cross over, reaching the ears of zealots, the insane and others whose minds have been cast adrift. Sometimes people seek them out, like the Fleshmage of Perizzi."

Balfruss hadn't been there at the time but he'd spoken to Munroe many times about what she'd seen.

"Before the tear in Perizzi was sealed something crept through from the other side. It was tiny but you saw what it became in Voechenka."

That seed had grown into the brood mother. A grotesque being, which in turn had spawned countless more of its kind to infect and enslave people.

"Can they open a door from their side?" asked Balfruss.

"No," said Vargus, which came as a huge relief.

He didn't need to say the rest. The Nameless would continue to whisper and one day someone else would find a way to open a door, but for now, it was over.

"I'm sorry about Garvey," said Vargus, raising his mug in a toast.

Balfruss sighed and took a long drink in honour of his old friend. The strain had been too much. The amount of power Garvey had been channelling from the Source should have killed him. Even now Balfruss didn't know how his old friend had sustained the portal for so long. It wasn't possible and yet his will had made it so.

In the end his heart had simply given out from the pressure. If not for Garvey they would never have defeated Kai but no one would ever know of his sacrifice. History would remember him only as a member of the Grey Council who had gone on a mad rampage. His name would become a curse for all of the innocent lives he'd taken and the blood he'd shed.

There had been no grand words at the end. No fond remembrances of their shared youth before he'd stopped breathing. One moment he'd been smiling up at Balfruss and the next he was dead.

"So, what are you going to do now?" asked Vargus, startling Balfruss from his reverie.

"I honestly don't know."

Balfruss had given it a little thought since leaving Zecorria but all of his plans focused on the short term. He wanted to visit Eloise in the far east, to see how the children were progressing with their training, but such a trip would be fraught with complications. The least of which was that, according to local tradition there, he and Eloise should get married.

There was also the mantle of the Bane that he had reluctantly taken on from Garvey. There would always be those with magic who would seek to exploit others. He didn't want the responsibility but there was no one else. And with magic under such a dark cloud he couldn't let a few make it even worse for those trying to help like Wren and her community.

"You must have some ideas," said Vargus.

Balfruss shrugged. "I'll wait for the next Warlock, I guess."

Vargus laughed until he realised Balfruss was serious. "Why would you do that?"

Balfruss shrugged. "What else am I going to do?"

"This conversation requires something a little stronger," said Vargus. He went to the bar and returned with a bottle of whisky and two glasses. He poured them both a generous measure which he downed and Balfruss followed suit. "I think that would be a waste," said Vargus, pouring them both another.

"All right. What are you going to do?" asked Balfruss.

"I'm going to live. The length of time I'm here is longer than you, but eventually, one day, I'll fade away. So right now, I'm going to drink this whisky, order some food, have a hot bath and get a good night's sleep. And tomorrow I'm going to pick a direction at random and see where the road takes me, because who knows what will happen? You can't live your life waiting for the next disaster, Balfruss. If you do that you'll never cherish what you have. Live for today, don't worry about tomorrow."

Vargus raised his glass and Balfruss followed suit. For the rest of the night they were just two men, drinking and talking. Tomorrow could wait.

CHAPTER 46

It had been a long journey back to Shael but when Corvin's Brow finally came into view Wren felt as if she'd truly come home.

The trip to Yerskania had been a success, in as much as they'd cured the plague, but it had not been without cost. All of them had been changed by the experience and she wasn't sure any of it was for the better.

Before leaving the city they'd searched the isolation zone and found Baedan's body. Out of shame, or perhaps guilt, he'd taken his own life. Wren didn't know if he'd been religious but she'd said a prayer before they'd consumed his body with fire.

The normally verbose Kimme had been unusually quiet since her episode. She'd more than redeemed herself in Wren's eyes, pushing herself so hard when healing others that a streak of her hair had turned white. It made her look older than her eighteen years or perhaps it was the pain behind her eyes.

Most nights Rue still had episodes where she shivered despite a fire. Andras had assured Wren that over time her withdrawal symptoms would fade. She'd never been particularly chatty before but now had become all but a mute. Most of the time Wren could see Rue's mind was elsewhere as she drifted along, going through the motions. She had much to think about and so far had only shared a little about her experience of being abducted.

Since being hanged by people in her village Val rarely spoke, which left Wren with Tianne for conversation. Sadly her friend had much on her mind as well. Along with everyone else she'd been physically cured of the plague but mentally it had left a number of scars.

All of which meant that for many hours during the day no one spoke, which made the journey feel incredibly tedious and long.

It was strange, Wren noted, that before coming to the Red Tower she would have been annoyed by Tianne's gossip but now she missed the sound of her friend's voice. Mostly she missed her smile as that seemed to have abandoned Tianne as well.

With time on her hands Wren decided to put it to good use. She spent long hours in the saddle working up a list of tasks that needed completing when they got back. There were many things she'd planned to do but had run out of time. Part of it came from having trouble delegating but as Wren had often told others she wasn't in charge. She sincerely hoped that in her absence the work had continued but also grown beyond her original plans.

Wren also spent a lot of time on the journey thinking about magic and its place in the world. For all that they'd done, curing people in Perizzi and dealing with bandits in Shael, she knew that magic had lost its place in the world. Going forward magic had to change because the methods of the past could no longer work.

One day there might be another school like the Red Tower but it would not be as isolated or mysterious. More than ever she knew the only way for people to accept magic was through familiarity and integration. The old notion of a village Wise was more important than ever before.

Those with magic, working hand in hand with those without,

was the way forward. Corvin's Brow was only the beginning and hopefully just the first settlement of its kind. It had to be or else they were doomed to repeat the mistakes of the past. A glance at Val's scar was a stark reminder that it was not going to happen overnight and they were not there yet.

Magic was a gift and a blessing. It was full of mysteries that she wanted to spend years of her life exploring but there had to be balance. The abstract and the practical. There also had to be control because the destructive side of magic was incredibly tempting. Garvey and his rogue mages had taught her that lesson.

Forging willpower into physical force was easy and the first thing a mage learned. It had to be different from now on. Young mages needed to be aware of the cost. Not only for themselves but also the way it affected everyone around them. More than ever Wren knew she couldn't do it alone.

"Tianne."

"I know," said Tianne, who must have been thinking the same thing. "We have to do this together."

Tianne knew that it was risky but the alternative, to wait and hope for the best, was not an option. Not after everything that had happened to her and the others. She and Wren had been discussing her plan for several days since coming home but from the start her mind had been made up.

Sour Crown was a fairly typical village in western Shael. It had been attacked by Boros's people and they'd suffered a loss because of her callous brutality. They understood far better than anyone else how alone they were and how much they needed allies. They'd also seen what one young mage could do to help and yet their fear of magic remained.

So when the Warden of the village agreed to meet, Tianne was convinced it was a trap. She found the stocky man sat outside the village tavern beside a woman of a similar age. The table and chairs looked a little peculiar on the street but she suspected the owner had not wanted a mage inside.

Tianne offered a wry smile as she sat down opposite the couple.

"What do you want?" asked the Warden, wasting no time.

"Sergal," said the woman and he winced at her tone of voice. "I'm sorry for my husband's rudeness. My name is Katria and this is Sergal."

"Tianne."

"Would you like something to drink?" asked Katria. "It's a hot day."

Sergal rolled his eyes. "Yes, drinks, why not? And perhaps we should make her a meal at our house tonight!"

"That's fair," said Tianne, before his wife berated him again. "I'm just here to talk. After that I'll leave you alone."

"At least let me get you a drink," said Katria, frowning at her husband. "I know I need one." She went inside while Tianne and Sergal sat in silence until her return. She set a mug of ale down in front of Tianne and had one for herself.

"Where's mine?" complained Sergal.

"I can only carry two," she said with a wink at Tianne. Grumbling all the while Sergal went inside to fetch his own. "So, what did you want to talk about?" asked Katria when her husband had resettled.

"I'm here to tell you a story. My story," said Tianne.

She started at the very beginning, growing up in Shael with callous parents who left her desperate for approval. How she was mocked and lied to by her peers, ultimately leaving her feeling alone and embarrassed. The Seeker coming to their village seemed like a curse to most people but when Tianne discovered her magic it was a second chance. She could be someone new and start over far away from those who knew her.

Tianne told them about the joy of magic and discovering some of the wonderful things it could do. Create light in the darkness and heal the sick. Looking back she realised it was a golden time. The Red Tower had been a sanctuary in so many ways, but it had also been remote and that bred fear.

When Tianne told them about the rising tension in the school Katria looked uncomfortable while Sergal feigned indifference. Then someone started blaming Seekers, spreading lies that they were infecting children with magic. That somehow Seekers were responsible for children losing control.

"Every day we heard more stories," said Tianne. "Seekers being attacked and chased out of villages. Then we heard about the first murder."

Perhaps the end of Seekers had been inevitable. The golden masks were just another barrier separating those with magic from those without. It also created another mystery and the Red Tower already had plenty of those.

"A few months later an angry mob of ordinary people, just like you," said Tianne, gesturing at them both, "marched on the school with weapons. A few brave people stayed behind to man the walls. It gave the children enough time to escape in the chaos. Then the mob killed everyone and burned the school to the ground."

Katria swallowed hard and wiped at her eyes but Sergal's expression remained grim. "That wasn't us. We didn't do it."

"I know. I don't blame you."

"Then what do you want?" he asked.

"Let her finish, Sergal," snapped his wife. "She's earned that much."

"Without the school some of the pupils turned wild. They were drunk on power and went on a rampage." Even now Tianne didn't know what to make of Garvey or how she felt about him. There was so much about him that didn't make sense, lies wrapped in truths. But he was dangerous, of that she had no doubt. Garvey was a mystery to unravel another day. "After the school was destroyed the rest of us tried to start over. To build something new, here in Shael, but then Boros and her people arrived."

There was no need to tell them about what had followed. They had lived through it while she had been in Zecorria. So instead she told them of the Regent's amnesty. It was a chance to return home in victory. To show them how much she had learned in her time away and how much she'd changed. She wasn't the naïve girl who'd fled to the Red Tower.

"It was all a lie. The Regent. His cadre of mages. The amnesty."

"I knew it," said Sergal.

Katria slapped her husband on the arm. "Let her tell it."

"He wanted slaves. He claimed the mages were to protect the people but really he wanted a private and unbeatable army that was loyal to him. With a handful of mages the Regent intended to keep himself on the throne indefinitely. But I didn't know any of that when I arrived. I thought he wanted patriots. It turned out I was still nothing more than a naïve child. At the palace I was beaten, starved and left to rot in a filthy cell full of water. After a few days I was miraculously rescued by the Regent. It was all part of an elaborate deception to earn my loyalty and guarantee I would do anything to please him."

Katria was crying now but Tianne had no more tears to shed about what had happened to her. Other people suffered through far worse every day. Her experiences were just a drop of water in an ocean of cruelty.

As she told them about the beating of charlatans, and the murder of those with real magic who wouldn't serve, Tianne realised the true depths of the Regent's cruelty. There was nothing he wouldn't do or say to stay in power. He would swear a blood oath to one person and immediately say the opposite to someone else. Being on top was all that mattered. His version of the truth was everything.

"Eventually I managed to escape and I came back home. Then I heard about the outbreak of a plague in Perizzi."

By the time she'd finished telling them about burning the dead, tending to the sick, the abduction of Rue and the loss of Baedan even Sergal had tears in his eyes. Somewhere during her story Katria had gripped Tianne's hand but she hadn't noticed until now. She squeezed the woman's hand and offered her a wan smile.

"We cured all that we could, but the number of dead is still being counted. And once again I've come home. We're not here to hurt anyone. We only want to live in peace. Magic is a part of this world. Sometimes I wish it wasn't, but when did wishing change anything?" she asked rhetorically. "Even if you killed every mage and child with magic it wouldn't make any difference. More are being born every day. I don't know what will happen in other countries but I believe there are two choices for us."

"What are they?" asked Katria, offering a friendly smile.

"You can continue pretending that magic doesn't exist and we can live a few miles apart from one another. I just pray to the Maker there are no children in your village born with magic."

"What's the other choice?" asked Sergal.

"We can try to find a way forward. Together. I can divert the course of a river. I can make it rain when the well runs dry or the crops need water. I can heal the sick and if someone should threaten the safety of the village, well, I have something for that as well. There's so much I still have to learn but every day I'm discovering something new. Why wouldn't you want such powerful magic at your disposal?"

"What are you suggesting?" asked Katria.

"That I live here as the village Wise," she said.

"You're just a child," said Sergal.

Tianne offered him a wry smile. "I'm young. I don't think I've been a child for a while." Having just listened to her story he had nothing to say to that. "Think on it. Speak to the others. I'll come back in a week for your answer."

Danoph had sensed Wren and Tianne long before they came into view through the trees. He overheard the tail end of their conversation as they approached.

"Do you think they'll agree?" asked Wren.

"I don't know, but I had to try," said Tianne.

They sat down beside him on a fallen trunk covered in moss.

"I'm sorry. I can't stay long," he said. There was much work to be done in Zecorria, unpicking the tangle left behind by Kai and Akosh, but he'd needed to see his friends. Danoph had no idea how long he'd spend in the north and the next time he returned to Corvin's Brow it could be in five, ten or even fifty years. He needed to see them as they were now. To fix images of them in his mind.

"You're always welcome here," said Wren. She didn't go so far as to say that it was his home. Danoph didn't know where he belonged.

"Will you come back and visit us?" asked Tianne.

"I promise."

For the last two days they'd been sharing stories. Danoph telling them a little about the events in Herakion while they'd told him about the plague in Perizzi. Some of it he already knew but pretended to be hearing it for the first time. He didn't want to lie but if they knew the whole truth about him, about what he was, it would change their friendship.

Vargus was right. He needed human connections to ground him. Whatever he was becoming Danoph knew he was still a person with flaws. His powers hadn't made him any wiser, merely given him a unique perspective. If they didn't know the whole truth his friends would still tease him and share stories, both their triumphs and failures. The emotional weight of their actions and those around his friends were important.

He needed them to see him as nothing more than a mage with a unique Talent. Without them it would be so easy to become untethered from the real world. Whatever choices he made in the days ahead to restore the natural order, there was going to be a cost in lives.

For whatever reason, perhaps because he'd never been that way since the start, Kai saw humans as nothing more than prey. The death of one or a thousand meant nothing to him. Danoph's worst fear was that over time he would become as callous.

Part of Danoph didn't want to leave. He wanted to stay and be an active part of what was to come not just an observer. He didn't need his power to know what they were building in Corvin's Brow was just the beginning of something.

After saying goodbye and promising again he would visit, Danoph walked out of the village. He wasn't surprised to see Vargus waiting for him beside a pair of horses.

"How much did you tell them?" he asked.

"Very little. Will it always be like this? Lying to my friends?"

The old warrior sighed. "Yes, because the truth would change everything."

"Did you do it when you were the Weaver? Manipulate people as I did in Zecorria?" asked Danoph, and Vargus gravely nodded.

Even now he couldn't stop thinking about it. As he'd delved deeper into his power, and the upcoming battle with Kai had unfolded, Danoph had seen a dozen ways they would lose. In one future they all died because Dox had decided to stay behind. In another Munroe expended too much energy destroying Akosh. So many possibilities. So many choices. So many lives at stake.

Danoph had manipulated everyone. Telling each of them what they needed to hear in order to nudge them in a preferred direction. There'd been no guarantee that any of it would work. Free will always created opportunities for chaos but, mercifully, in the end they'd banished Kai to a place beyond the Veil.

"Are you ready?" asked Vargus.

"No. I don't think I am," said Danoph, shaking his head.

His lack of confidence seemed to please Vargus. "That's a good start."

CHAPTER 47

Munroe was very, very drunk. The whole room was spinning and all the conversations were just a little too loud. Another drink. That's what she needed.

"Another," she said, slamming a coin down on the bar.

The woman behind the bar had a face only her mother could love. Munroe thought she looked like an ugly frog. Her eyes were just a bit too big. Her mouth too wide and it was fixed in a permanent frown.

"Beer!" said Munroe, tapping her empty glass. "Fill it up."

The barkeep said something but Munroe missed it. The room was just too damn noisy and bright. Why were there so many lanterns in the room? Then again the lack of shadows was a good thing. In the last few years she'd seen far too many things that lurked in dark corners.

At least it was over. That thing was gone. They'd sent it away to somewhere. She didn't know where and didn't want to know. What she'd seen on the other side would haunt her dreams for years.

Twice in one lifetime. How unlucky did a person have to be to see something like that once, never mind twice! Munroe hoped that was the end of it. But it was definitely the end of Akosh. For however long she survived Akosh would be tortured and feasted upon by powerful and monstrous beings. They would suck the energy and life out of her. Eventually she'd die but until then she'd suffer horrendous agony.

That thought made Munroe smile and raise her glass. Somehow it was still empty.

"I need beer," she said, looking around for the lazy barkeep.

"She won't serve you any more beer," said a familiar voice.

"Ah, Dox, get yourself a drink," said Munroe, fishing out another coin. "It's a celebration. We won."

Somehow the girl was older now. After what she'd experienced in the last few months it wasn't too surprising but Munroe thought it was more than that. She dressed less like a street urchin and had started taking pride in her appearance. Dox was still a little gawky but there was a determined glint in her eyes. She always tightened her jaw before making a difficult announcement, one that she thought Munroe wouldn't like.

"You're doing that thing with your jaw," she said, touching the girl on her cheek.

"You've had enough to drink. It's time for bed."

"Bed? It's still early, I think." Munroe had no idea what time it was but if the lanterns had been lit then it was probably night-time.

"Come on. I'll help you," said Dox, offering a hand. Munroe was about to wave her away but when she tried to stand up by herself the room tilted to an impossible angle. Dox caught her by the armpits and held her up. The spinning continued but at least the floor was no longer above her head.

"Some fresh air might be a good idea," said Munroe, trying to walk towards the door but her legs were really bendy for some reason. Eventually they made it outside and mercifully a cool breeze was blowing. It woke her up a little and the spinning eased.

Instead her head began to pound and black spots danced in front of her eyes. Leaning heavily on Dox they wandered through the streets of Perizzi towards bed.

Overhead the dark sky was broken up by a scattering of stars. Her son, Sam, used to think they were fireflies that were stuck in spider webs. The sky became blurry and Munroe wiped at her face.

The pain was still there, like a jagged piece of glass in her chest. In time she thought the edges might soften but right now it was still raw. She allowed herself to think of her family in a good way for the first time in months. To say their names out loud. To mourn for her husband and son. She missed her mother as well but her time had already been limited. At least her mother had gone out on her own terms. On her feet with a sword in her hand rather than dying in bed.

By the time Dox had helped her through the streets, up the stairs and into their room, all she wanted to do was sleep. Her head was pounding. Her heart ached for all that she'd lost and she just wanted the world to end. She wanted the quiet void of sleep and hoped that, for once, it would be free of dreams.

She fell on to the bed, closed her eyes and felt Dox pulling off her boots. Something warm and heavy settled across her body but it didn't matter. She was already drifting down into the black.

The next morning, after dunking her head in a cold bucket of water and eating a greasy breakfast of fried sausages, eggs, bacon and a fatty slab of beef, Munroe felt a little more human. She nursed a mug of herbal tea and hoped the stabbing pain behind her eyes would soon fade. There had been no sign of Dox since she'd woken up but the girl was old enough to look after herself.

By midday Munroe felt strong enough to take a walk down to the docks. For a while she just sat outside one of the cheap taverns nursing a mug of piss-poor ale. It wasn't for the taste or that she really wanted another drink. It just gave her an excuse to sit quietly without being harassed by the owner.

In the distance tiny specks on the horizon swelled until they became huge ships that slowly drifted into port. All around her hundreds of people raced about on important business like ants in a nest. Sailors were busy loading and unloading cargo. Merchants were arguing with Captains, while everyone was shouting at the dockside authorities. Working boys and girls walked up and down, winking and calling out to the sailors who were desperate to finish their business and get on dry land.

Vendors selling vaguely recognisable food from carts shouted about their wares, the air rich with the smell of dubious meat. Tavern owners bellowed room rates at sailors while urchins tried to sell fresh fruit to anyone who would listen. Several squads of the Watch kept a close eye on everyone, dragging away the occasional pick-pocket or breaking up fights that suddenly erupted.

Munroe watched people busy at work, racing around with purpose, and was a little envious. She didn't belong here. She didn't belong anywhere and that was the problem.

"I thought I'd find you here," said Dox, sitting down beside her. At some point every day Munroe came to the docks to watch the ships, although she wasn't sure why. Perhaps someone would recognise her. One of her old friends or, even better, an old enemy from her days of working for the Families. At the very least it would give her something to do.

They sat in silence but after a while Munroe noticed Dox was fidgeting in her chair. She was clenching her jaw again and this time her fingers were digging into her thighs.

"Spit it out," said Munroe. "Before you grind your teeth to dust."

Dox swallowed hard before speaking. "There's something I need to tell you. About your family."

Munroe raised an eyebrow. "What did you say?"

"At the end, just before she was pulled through the portal, Akosh said your son was still alive."

"At that point she would've said anything to save her skin. She was desperate." Munroe took a sip of her ale and immediately regretted it. She had to stop coming to this dive.

Dox bit her lip and shook her head. "She was telling the truth."

Munroe felt as if she was still drunk. The world rushed past her as if she'd been dropped from a great height. She gripped the edge of the table with both hands to hold herself upright. The girl was still talking.

"I don't know how, or where he is, only that Akosh wasn't lying. I didn't want to believe her, but I've gone over it again and again. Somehow he's still alive."

And just like that the world made sense. She had a place in it and a reason to live. The dragging sensation within her body subsided. Her stomach settled and her heartbeat slowed.

"What are you going to do?" asked Dox.

"Head back to Shael, to the Red Tower. Someone around there knows something or they saw something. I'll leave first thing tomorrow morning." Munroe was already planning what she would need for the journey. A good horse. Supplies and money. That meant a trip to the gambling dens tonight. She could win a modest amount at several without making it look too suspicious.

"I guess I'll go back to Rojenne," said Dox, snapping Munroe back to the present.

"Why would you want to go there?" asked Munroe.

Dox shrugged. "You need to find your son. Your family."

"And?"

"I didn't think you'd want me to come with you. I'd just get in the way."

All of the jaw clenching and distracted looks suddenly made

sense. Munroe sighed and found herself smiling at Dox. She kept looking away until Munroe lifted her chin, forcing eye contact. "Of course I want you to come with me."

"Why?" asked Dox.

"Family isn't always about blood."

Dox's eyes filled with tears and Munroe pulled her into a tight hug.

"We'll need a couple of good horses," said Munroe as they walked away from the docks. They had a long and difficult journey ahead but they would do it together.

CHAPTER 48

As Tammy walked through the streets of Perizzi she attracted a lot of attention. Some of it was due to her Guardian uniform and rank, but in the last two weeks she'd noticed a subtle change.

Guardians had always been respected by the public but during the quarantine she and her people had been forced to make some difficult decisions. Separating families. Keeping the peace when fights broke out and arresting those who flaunted the law. The Watch were the muscle but everyone knew who gave the orders. Her people had been shouted and spat at, assaulted and threatened.

In spite of everything the Guardians had done during the crisis people weren't scared of them. Lifting the quarantine and closing the isolation zone had eased tension that had been building up for weeks. The number of fights and murders drastically fell. The cells were no longer stuffed with bodies awaiting trial. A semblance of normality was returning to the city.

The exception seemed to be how the public saw her. Tammy was used to people staring. It was something she'd lived with all her life and had learned to ignore. When you were always the tallest person in the room it was natural that you attracted attention. But it wasn't those sorts of glances she'd begun to notice.

People were afraid of her.

Now that she was the Khevassar there were few places she could go in the city where she wasn't recognised. Most people were reserved but polite when they saw her. They nodded or smiled. A few of the braver ones called out a greeting. It was the moment she turned her back that their expressions changed. Some of it was hostile but most of the time she could feel their fear.

Hanging a murderer in front of a crowd had sent a clear message that no one had forgotten. She'd hoped it would have faded but the story must have spread. A little fear was healthy and it kept people on their toes.

The walk from the palace to her office was one she'd done so many times she didn't need to think about the route. Her last meeting with Queen Morganse had been about dealing with the aftermath of the plague. The latest challenge was what to do with the homes in the isolation zone. Even though the mages had cured all the sick no one wanted to live there any more. People associated the area with death and they avoided that part of the city.

Tammy hoped the Old Man had some ideas because she and the Queen hadn't come up with anything. She was due to call on him in the next day or so. It had been too long since her last visit but dealing with the plague had taken up all her time.

As Unity Hall came into view Tammy remembered the huge pile of reports that were awaiting her attention. One of them would contain the latest death toll, which was still an estimate. The rest would be reports from her people about recent crimes and she also had to review several applications from novices who wished to become Guardians. Her body was craving sleep but she would be up for at least a couple more hours.

Perhaps it was because of her exhaustion but Tammy didn't

see the man lurking on the corner until he subtly coughed. Her hand instinctively went to the sword on her hip but he didn't react. Big, with thick arms and a shaven head, a pair of daggers on his belt and a face marked with scars. The swagger and the calculating look in his eyes told her the man wasn't a common criminal. He was probably a senior jackal in one of the Families. The question was who did he work for? And why was he lurking outside Unity Hall?

Keeping his hands down at his sides the man approached at a sedate pace. Tammy scanned the surrounding streets before looking up at the buildings in case this was an ambush. She couldn't see any faces lurking in windows or arrows pointed at her.

"The boss would like a word," said the jackal. "She's waiting for you at the tea shop on the next street."

She knew the one. Most of the Guardians stopped there every day. The fact that his boss was a woman meant it could only be one of two people. Tammy walked beside the jackal to the tea room with a hand resting on her sword.

At this hour the shop would normally be closed but for such a special customer the owner must have been persuaded to stay open. Tammy spotted her hovering inside the shop nervously wringing her hands. Doña Tarija was sat at a table outside sipping tea while picking at a plate of pastries. As ever her clothing was elegant and expensive. Her fingernails had even been painted a pale blue to match her silk dress.

"Ah, Khevassar, thank you for joining me," she said, gesturing at the chair opposite. The jackal walked to the end of the street to keep watch. Tammy spotted three more lurking nearby. "I know this area is safe, but they're very protective," said Doña Tarija by way of apology.

It felt as if years had passed since her meeting with Doña Tarija and the other Family leaders but it had only been a few weeks. It was shortly after that she'd received a note from Doña Tarija thanking her. Tammy still wasn't sure if Doña Tarija knew she'd killed her predecessor or if she was being thanked for something else.

"Would you like some tea?" asked Doña Tarija. She rolled her eyes when Tammy didn't react. "The tea isn't poisoned. I'm not here to kill you."

"Then why are you here?"

"Because I received your note about the end of our temporary alliance."

The day after the end of the plague Tammy had sent identical notes to all of the Families. Whatever leeway she'd given them in return for their help was officially over.

"What about it?" asked Tammy, keeping an eye on the closest jackal.

"I've been asked, on behalf of everyone, to see if you'd consider extending our agreement."

"Absolutely not," she said.

"Are you sure I can't offer you something to change your mind?"

Tammy didn't even consider it. "No. Our alliance is over."

Doña Tarija shrugged. "I told them you'd say that, but I had to ask."

"I'm surprised that you would come in person, especially if you knew what my answer would be."

Doña Tarija offered her a sly and secretive smile. It made Tammy wonder how much the other woman knew about her past.

"Maybe I just wanted to see where you worked," she said, flicking a hand towards Unity Hall. "I'm sure we'll run into one another at some point in the future."

"Perhaps," said Tammy, not sure if that was a threat. Even with her resources she knew little about Doña Tarija compared to the other leaders. That would have to change.

"Until next time," she said, delicately wiping sugar from her mouth before getting up from the table. "I look forward to our next meeting," she said, touching Tammy lightly on the arm as she walked past.

Two of the jackals formed up on either side of Doña Tarija while the other two roamed ahead keeping an eye out for trouble. Once she'd disappeared around the corner Tammy sat down again. The meeting had left her unsettled and on edge. She didn't know what game Doña Tarija was playing.

She would need to keep a close eye on all of the Families in the coming weeks. They'd probably try to exploit or bribe a few Guardians to look the other way. She needed the Families to understand in no uncertain terms that the leniency they'd been enjoying was at an end. A firm hand was needed. It was something she added to her list to talk about with the Old Man.

Tammy knew she should go back to her office but right now she just couldn't face it. All of it would still be waiting for her tomorrow. It wasn't that she didn't enjoy the work but after the last few weeks she needed a little time to herself.

Her meeting with Doña Tarija had left her alert for danger. This time she spotted the man lurking in the shadows outside her building. It was a quiet street at the best of times but at this late hour they were the only two people on it.

When he realised he'd been spotted the man stepped out of the shadows and Tammy's breath caught in her throat.

It was Kovac.

At first she didn't want to believe it. Her eyes were playing tricks on her. She was tired and lonely. It made sense that she would see his phantom. But when he smiled she knew that it was real. It meant he'd been cured. It also meant that after everything she'd said about staying away he'd chosen to ignore her.

The future was uncertain but Tammy knew that because of

her job it would always be chaotic, busy and rife with danger. She would work all hours to protect the city and the people. She would push her body and mind to the absolute limit in the service of others for many years to come.

Much of what she did would go unnoticed. Most people would never know how many times they'd been saved from a disaster that threatened their lives. If she did her job well then the Yerskani people would live in blissful ignorance. She would do it because it was her job, but more than that, she needed to do it.

But all of that was for tomorrow. Today she found herself thinking about her decisions in the last few years.

If life was about taking risks and living with the consequences then she had to decide which were worth pursuing and which to ignore. What she could live with and what she couldn't live without.

Crossing the street she took Kovac by the hand, led him inside, and closed the door.

ACKNOWLEDGEMENTS

With thanks to my agent, Juliet Mushens. Six books and a novella ago, back in 2013, she saw something in my writing that she enjoyed. As a result she helped to make a lifetime ambition come true. Thanks to everyone at Orbit, those I know and those I've never met, for all of their hard work behind the scenes. A special thanks to Matt Addis for bringing my characters to life with his extraordinary skills for the audio books.

Once again, many thanks to my family and friends for always being there for me. I wouldn't be here without their love and support.

Finally, a big thanks to you, the readers. Getting published is tough, staying in the game is, perhaps, tougher still. So thank you for coming with me on the journey this far and I hope that you'll follow me as I start a new chapter.

extras

orbit

meet the author

Photo Credit: Hannah Webster

STEPHEN ARYAN was born in 1977 and was raised by the sea in northeast England. A keen podcaster, lapsed gamer and budding archer, when not extolling the virtues of *Babylon 5*, he can be found drinking real ale and reading comics.

He lives in a village in West Midlands with his partner and two cats. You can find him at @SteveAryan or visit his website at www.stephen-aryan.com.

if you enjoyed
MAGEBANE
look out for

COLD IRON
Masters & Mages: Book One

by

Miles Cameron

Aranthur is a promising young mage. But the world is not safe, and after a confrontation leaves him no choice but to display his skill with a blade, Aranthur is instructed to train under a renowned Master of Swords.

During his intensive training he begins to question the bloody life he's chosen. And while studying under the Master, he finds himself thrown into the middle of a political revolt that will impact everyone he's come to know.

To protect his friends, Aranthur will be forced to decide if he can truly follow the Master of Swords into a life of violence and cold-hearted commitment to the blade.

PROLOGUE

It was late in the day when Syr Xenias di Brusias was ready to leave Volta. Almost everything that could go wrong had done so, and he was rushed and was prone, even after the life he'd led, to forget things, so he made himself stand by his fine riding horse in his two-stall city stable and review everything.

He still had not decided what to do by the time he mounted. He set himself in motion, mostly to avoid thinking too much.

His mare was delighted to be ridden; she'd been cooped up for as long as he had himself, and as soon as she was out in the street behind his house she was ready to trot, or more.

He kept her gait down because it was very important that he not be stopped. He was a little overdressed for a common wayfarer, in tall black boots all the way to his thighs and a black half-cloak and matching black hat full of black plumes, but he liked fine things and he lacked the time to change.

He was riding out of a maelstrom, and he needed to stay on the leading edge.

He could hear screams from the north, where the Ducal Palace was. He patted the sword at his hip with his bridle hand then he turned his horse at the first cross street—away from the palace of towering brick on the hillside, and down towards the river, the bridges, and the street of steelworkers where he had a commission to collect.

It struck him that if he collected the commission then he had made his choice; he would never be able to come back to Volta.

It also struck him that a violent political revolution could cover a great many dark deeds. There were already looters on the streets;

two men passed him carrying a coffer, and neither looked up or caught his eye. The sound of breaking glass was almost as prevalent as the sound of screaming from the north.

He heard *gonnes* firing, and the snap of crossbows, and a sulphur reek floated past him and made his mare shy. There was the acrid reek of magik, too.

He let the mare trot, and her hooves struck sparks from the paving stones. Volta was one of the richest cities in the west, and it had fully paved streets and running water from the two great aqueducts, which was still nothing compared to the wonders of his home. The City.

Megara. Which he was about to help destroy.

Or not. He still couldn't decide.

The mare stopped abruptly. There was a corpse in the street, and the sound of steel crossing steel. He tugged at her reins, turned along an alley that ran across the back of the shops and emerged on the next broad, empty street, with tall houses tiled in red rising high enough to block the sun.

He looked right and left, but the street was empty. From long practice, his eyes rose, looking at rooflines and balconies above him, but nothing moved, and he gave the horse her head. They flew along the street, past the corner of violence, and down to the riverside, where he reined in and turned the mare into Steel Street, where the armourers were. He knew the shop well; Arnson and Egg, the two families on the gold-lettered sign, had made fine *gonnes* since the principle had first been developed far to the east.

He had a moment of doubt; the street seemed deserted.

But he saw a light burning, and smoke from the chimney, so he dismounted, tethered his horse to a hitching post and moved his dagger back along his belt from habit. Then he pounded at the door despite the darkening eve and the sounds of violence in the high town.

He heard footsteps.

"You came!" said young Arnson.

He pushed in beside the young man.

"I came for my *fusil*."

The lad smiled. "It is done." He pointed at a leather case on the front bar. "Pater is gone; he says it will be bad here. I'm to keep the doors locked and only eat food in the house."

"Very wise." The man paused to admire the case; the fine steel buckles made by hand and blued, and expert leather-work.

Then he took out the weapon.

"You made this?" he asked.

The young man grinned. "I did, too. Pater helped with the lock; I'm not that dab with springs, yet. And I hired the leather-work."

The boy was so pleased with himself that the man almost laughed.

He permitted himself a smile instead. "And the compartment?"

"Just as you asked," the young man said. "Not in the weapon, neither." He showed his visitor the cunning compartment built for keeping a secret.

"Superb," the man in the black cloak said, and slammed his dagger into the young man's temple, killing him instantly. The blade emerged from the other temple with admirable precision, and the man in the black cloak supported the corpse all the way to the floor, stepping away from the flow of blood. Then he filled the secret compartment with his deadly secret, wearing gloves; one tiny jewel skittered away across the table and he tracked it down, picked it up with coal tongs from the fireplace, and put it in his belt-purse. Then he threw his gloves—fine, black gloves—in the fire, where they sparkled as if impregnated with gunpowder. He left, satisfied, leaving the shop door wide open to the looters already moving along the street like roaches.

But then he paused. The decision was made; there was no point in being sloppy or sentimental now. He took the tiny jewel from his purse using his handkerchief, covered his horse's head with his cloak, and tossed it back through the open door. It was so tiny he didn't even hear it hit the floor.

He led his horse away. Only after he counted one hundred paces did he trigger the jewel's *power*.

The house behind him seemed to swell for a moment. Then fire, white fire, blew from every window, the glass and horn panes exploding outwards, the shutters immolating, the door blowing off their hinges. It sounded like a crack of thunder, followed by a rushing of wind, and then the fire began to catch the other old houses in the row, even as the first house collapsed inwards in a roar of sparks and a burst of thick black smoke.

He mounted his mare, who didn't like the smell of blood on him or the sound or smell of smoke, and he used some of his *power* to cast an *occulta*. It didn't make him invisible; it merely compelled most people to look elsewhere.

He drew a second pair of gloves from his belt and tried not to acknowledge that he'd always intended this.

The killing.

The secret.

The compartment.

The fire.

The massacre to come.

He had a little difficulty at the bridge; angry, unpaid mercenaries were holding the near end, and they wanted money and no amount of magikal *compulsion* was going to fool them. So he paid, handing over one hundred gold sequins—almost five years' wages for a prosperous craftsman—as if it was his entire purse. They wanted to open his case, the case with the secret and the little *fusil*, and he prepared to fight them, but they lost interest.

There were more unpaid sell-swords in the streets of the lower town, and they were killing. He had to wonder if the duke was dead; and if he was, if the plan was still valid.

He considered changing sides.

Again.

To his enormous relief, there was no one on the Lonika Gate. He rode through unchallenged, and he was tempted to let the mare gallop; he needed to put time and distance between himself and Volta. The weight of his secret was tremendous; he flinched from it, trying to occupy his mind so that he would not think too carefully of what he was doing or what it would mean. He knew this would end his relationship with his wife.

Myra, his mistress, wouldn't care. She might prefer him alone. She wouldn't even understand.

But he understood all too well what it would mean.

All too well.

People were fleeing the violence; he passed a long line of carts in the winter fields. He rode aside at a barn, dismounted, and took off all his jewellery and his dagger belt, and put it all in his leather case. Sell-swords might search the case, but at least his rings wouldn't give him away. He put his beautiful black doublet in the case as well and pulled on a smock. It was not as cold here as it would be in the mountains, towards the barbaric Arnaut lands, but it was cold enough, and refugees trudged past him carrying beds and bedding, blankets and furniture.

Lonika was five days away; Megara three or four more days beyond. But he had a fast horse, and the money to buy remounts at Fosse and Lonika; as soon as he was free of all the violence, he'd eat up the ground. Nine days travel for a man on foot would be perhaps three for him. He could arrive exactly on schedule, if he was fast. Dark Night. The night the ignorant feared. The perfect night, or so the Servant said. That was not his problem. Delivering was his problem.

He had to make the Inn of Fosse in two days; he'd managed as much on other occasions.

There were soldiers ahead, stripping a wagonload of a poor merchant family as a mother cowered with her children and a man held his split scalp together. Five men in rusting armour threw the family's worldly goods into the mud, rooting for coins. Ten years of falling grain prices and increasingly violent weather had already stripped the countryside of coin and brought out the violence in people.

This was going to be worse.

He rode down a farm lane and well around the soldiers, and emerged on the turnpike into near darkness.

It was a major risk to travel in the dark. But he could see a farm-house on fire off to the west, and it seemed to him that the whole world had come apart, which gave him comfort for what he was choosing to do. The world might end, but it would be far away and he'd be very well paid. Rich, even. And he'd have Myra. And other entertainments.

He left Volta on fire behind him and rode through the night.

By morning he was just twenty leagues from the Inn of Fosse. He knew the road and the hills, and he was wary, because the Arnauts, although they hadn't made trouble in a generation, were a race of degenerate cattle thieves and sell-swords.

He climbed into the snow-clad hills, his horse tired and hungry, and he was watching the trees either side of the road. But when the road curved sharply into an ancient gully, he had no sight line, and the unpaid mercenaries had chosen their spot perfectly. They had a tree across the road, and he had no warning to turn aside or prepare a *working*, and he had to halt.

He loosened his sword in the scabbard and reached to unbuckle his *fusil*.

He never saw the crossbow bolt that hit him in the chest. It took him ugly hours to die.

if you enjoyed
MAGEBANE
look out for

THE GUTTER PRAYER
The Black Iron Legacy: Book One

by

Gareth Hanrahan

The city of Guerdon stands eternal. A refuge from the war that rages beyond its borders. But in the ancient tunnels deep beneath its streets, a malevolent power has begun to stir.

The fate of the city rests in the hands of three thieves. They alone stand against the coming darkness. As conspiracies unfold and secrets are revealed, their friendship will be tested to the limit. If they fail, all will be lost, and the streets of Guerdon will run with blood.

CHAPTER ONE

Carillon crouches in the shadow, eyes fixed on the door. Her knife is in her hand, a gesture of bravado to herself more than a deadly weapon. She's fought before, cut people with it, but never killed with it. Cut and run, that's her way.

In this crowded city, that's not necessarily an option.

If one guard comes through the door, she'll wait until he goes past her hiding place, then creep after him and cut his throat. She tries to envisage herself doing it, but can't manage it. Maybe she can get away with just scaring him, or shanking him in the leg so he can't chase them.

If it's two, then she'll wait until they're about to find the others, hiss a warning and leap on one of them. Surely, between herself, Spar and Rat, they'll be able to take out two guards without giving themselves away.

Surely.

If it's three, same plan, only riskier.

She doesn't let her mind dwell on the other possibility—that it won't be humans like her who can be cut with her little knife, but something worse like the Tallowmen or Gullheads. The city has bred horrors all its own.

Every instinct in her tells her to run, to flee with her friends, to risk Heinreil's wrath for returning empty-handed. Better yet, to not return at all, but take the Dowager Gate or the River Gate out of the city tonight, be a dozen miles away before dawn.

Six. The door opens and it's six guards, all human, one two three big men, in padded leathers, maces in hand, and three more with pistols. She freezes for an instant in terror, unable to act, unable to run, caught against the cold stone of the old walls.

And then—she feels the shock through the wall before she hears the roar, the crash. She feels the whole House of Law shatter. She was in Severast when there was an earth tremor once, but it's not like that—it's more like a lightning strike and thunderclap right on top of her. She springs forward without thinking, as if the explosion had physically struck her, too, jumping through the scattered confusion of the guards.

One of them fires his pistol, point blank, so close she feels the sparks, the rush of air past her head, hot splinters of metal or stone showering down across her back, but the pain doesn't blossom and she knows she's not hit even as she runs.

Follow me, she prays as she runs blindly down the passageway, ducking into one random room and another, bouncing off locked doors. From the shouts behind her, she knows that some of them are after her. It's like stealing fruit in the market—one of you makes a big show of running, distracts the fruitseller, and the others grab an apple each and one more for the runner. Only, if she gets caught, she won't be let off with a thrashing. Still, she's got a better chance of escaping than Spar has.

She runs up a short stairway and sees an orange glow beneath the door. Tallowmen, she thinks, imagining their blazing wicks on the far side, before she realises that the whole north wing of the square House is ablaze. The guards are close behind her, so she opens the door anyway, ducking low to avoid the thick black smoke that pours through.

She skirts along the edge of the burning room. It is a library, with long rows of shelves packed with rows of cloth-bound books, journals of civic institutions, proceedings of parliament. At least, half of it is a library; the other half *was* a library. Old books burn quickly. She clings to the wall, finding her way through the smoke by touch, trailing her right hand along the stone blocks while groping ahead with her left.

One of the guards has the courage to follow her in, but, from the sound of his shouts, she guesses he went straight forward, thinking she'd run towards the fires. There's a creak, and a crash, and a shower of sparks as one of the burning bookcases topples. The guard's shouts to his fellows become a scream of pain, but she can do nothing for him. She can't see, can scarcely breathe. She fights down panic and keeps going until she comes to the side wall.

The House of Law is a quadrangle of buildings around a central green. They hang thieves there, and hanging seems like a better fate than burning right now. But there was a row of windows, wasn't there? On the inside face of the building, looking out onto that green. She's sure there is, there must be, because the fires have closed in behind her and there's no turning back.

The outstretched fingers of her left hand touch warm stone. The side wall. She scrabbles and sweeps her fingers over it, looking for the windows. They're higher than she remembers, and she can barely reach the sill even when stretching, standing on tiptoes. The windows are thick, leaded glass, and, while the fires have blown some of them out, this one is intact. She grabs a book off a shelf and flings it at the glass, to no avail. It bounces back. There's nothing she can do to break the glass from down here.

On this side, the sill's less than an inch wide, but if she can get up there, maybe she can lever one of the panes out, make an opening. She takes a step back to make a running jump up, and a hand closes around her ankle.

"Help me!"

It's the guard who followed her in. The burning bookcase must have fallen on him. He's crawling, dragging a limp and twisted leg, and he's horribly burnt down his left side. Weeping white-red blisters and blackened flesh on his face.

"I can't."

He's still clutching his pistol, and he tries to aim it at her while still grabbing her ankle, but she's faster. She grabs his arm and lifts it, pulls the trigger for him. The report, that close to her ear, is deafening, but the shot smashes part of the window behind her. More panes and panels fall, leaving a gap in the stained glass large enough to crawl through if she can climb up to it.

A face appears in the gap. Yellow eyes, brown teeth, pitted flesh—a grin of wickedly sharp teeth. Rat extends his rag-wrapped hand through the window. Cari's heart leaps. She's going to live. In that moment, her friend's monstrous, misshapen face seems as beautiful as the flawless features of a saint she once knew. She runs towards Rat—and stops.

Burning's a terrible way to die. She's never thought so before, but now that it's a distinct possibility it seems worse than anything. Her head feels weird, and she knows she's not thinking straight, but between the smoke and the heat and terror, weird seems wholly reasonable. She kneels down, slips an arm beneath the guard's shoulders, helps him stand on his good leg, to limp towards Rat.

"What are you doing?" hisses the ghoul, but he doesn't hesitate either. He grabs the guard by the shoulders when the wounded man is within reach of the window, and pulls him through the gap. Then he comes back for her, pulling her up, too. Rat's sinewy limbs aren't as tough or as strong as Spar's stone-cursed muscles, but he's more than strong enough to lift Carillon out of the burning building with one hand and pull her through into the blessed coolness of the open courtyard.

The guard moans and crawls away across the grass. They've done enough for him, Carillon decides; a half-act of mercy is all they can afford.

"Did you do this?" Rat asks in horror and wonder, flinching as part of the burning buildings collapses in on itself. The flames twine around the base of the huge bell tower that looms over the north side of the quadrangle.

Carillon shakes her head. "No, there was some sort of...boom. Where's Spar?"

"This way." Rat scurries off, and she runs after him. South, along the edge of the garden, past the empty old gibbets, away from the fire, towards the courts. There's no way now to get what they came for, even if the documents that Heinreil wants still exist and aren't falling around her as a blizzard of white ash, but maybe they can

511

get away if they can get out onto the streets again. They just need to find Spar, find that big slow limping lump of rock, and get out.

She could leave him behind, just like Rat could abandon her. The ghoul could make it over the wall in a flash; ghouls are prodigious climbers. But they're friends—the first true friends she's had in a long time. Rat found her on the streets after she was stranded in this city, and he introduced her to Spar, who gave her a place to sleep safely.

The two also introduced her to Heinreil, but that wasn't their fault—Guerdon's underworld is dominated by the thieves' brotherhood, just like its trade and industry is run by the guild cartels. If they're caught, it's Heinreil's fault. Another reason to hate him.

There's a side door ahead, and if she hasn't been turned around it'll open up near where they came in, and that's where they'll find Spar.

Before they can get to it, the door opens and out comes a Tallowman.

Blazing eyes in a pale, waxy face. He's an old one, worn so thin he's translucent in places, and the fire inside him shines through holes in his chest. He's got a huge axe, bigger than Cari could lift, but he swings it easily with one hand. He laughs when he sees her and Rat outlined against the fire.

They turn and run, splitting up. Rat breaks left, scaling the wall of the burning library. She turns right, hoping to vanish into the darkness of the garden. Maybe she can hide behind a gibbet or some monument, she thinks, but the Tallowman's faster than she can imagine. He flickers forward, a blur of motion, and he's right in front of her. The axe swings, she throws herself down and to the side and it whistles right past her.

Again the laugh. He's toying with her.

She finds her courage. Finds she hasn't dropped her knife. She drives it right into the Tallowman's soft waxy chest. His clothes and his flesh are the same substance, yielding and mushy as warm candle wax, and the blade goes in easily. He just laughs again, the wound closing almost as fast as it opened, and now her knife's in his other hand. He reverses it, stabs it down, and her right shoulder's suddenly black and slick with blood.

She doesn't feel the pain yet, but she knows its coming.

She runs again, half stumbling towards the flames. The Tallowman hesitates, unwilling to follow, but it stalks her, herding her, cackling as it goes. It offers her a choice of deaths—run headlong into the fire and burn to death, bleed out here on the grass where so many other thieves met their fates, or turn back and let it dismember her with her own knife.

She wishes she had never come back to this city.

The heat from the blaze ahead of her scorches her face. The air's so hot it hurts to breathe, and she knows the smell of soot and burning paper will never, ever leave her. The Tallowman keeps pace with her, flickering back and forth, always blocking her from making a break.

She runs towards the north-east corner. That part of the House of Law is on fire, too, but the flames seem less intense there. Maybe she can make it there without the Tallowman following her. Maybe she can even make it before it takes her head off with its axe. She runs, cradling her bleeding arm, bracing herself all the while for the axe to come chopping through her back.

The Tallowman laughs and comes up behind her.

And then there's a clang, the ringing of a tremendous bell, and the sound lifts Carillon up, up out of herself, up out of the courtyard and the burning building. She flies high over the city, rising like a phoenix out of the wreckage. Behind her, below her, the bell tower topples down, and the Tallowman shrieks as burning rubble crushes it.

She sees Rat scrambling over rooftops, vanishing into the shadows across Mercy Street.

She sees Spar lumbering across the burning grass, towards the blazing rubble. She sees her own body, lying there amid the wreckage, pelted with burning debris, eyes wide but unseeing. She sees—

Stillness is death to a Stone Man. You have to keep moving, keep the blood flowing, the muscles moving. If you don't, those veins .

and arteries will become carved channels through hard stone, the muscles will turn to useless inert rocks. Spar is never motionless, even when he's standing still. He flexes, twitches, rocks—yes, rocks, very funny—from foot to foot. Works his jaw, his tongue, flicks his eyes back and forth. He has a special fear of his lips and tongue calcifying. Other Stone Men have their own secret language of taps and cracks, a code that works even when their mouths are forever frozen in place, but few people in the city speak it.

So when they hear the thunderclap or whatever-it-was, Spar's already moving. Rat's faster than he is, so Spar follows as best he can. His right leg drags behind him. His knee is numb and stiff behind its stony shell. Alkahest might cure it, if he gets some in time. The drug's expensive, but it slows the progress of the disease, keeps flesh from turning to stone. It has to be injected subcutaneously, though, and more and more he's finding it hard to drill through his own hide and hit living flesh.

He barely feels the heat from the blazing courtyard, although he guesses that if he had more skin on his face it'd be burnt by contact with the air. He scans the scene, trying to make sense of the dance of the flames and the fast-moving silhouettes. Rat vanishes across a rooftop, pursued by a Tallowman. Cari...Cari's there, down in the wreckage of the tower. He stumbles across the yard, praying to the Keepers that she's still alive, expecting to find her beheaded by a Tallowman's axe.

She's alive. Stunned. Eyes wide but unseeing, muttering to herself. Nearby, a pool of liquid and a burning wick, twisting like an angry cobra. Spar stamps down on the wick, killing it, then scoops Cari up, careful not to touch her skin. She weighs next to nothing, so he can easily carry her over one shoulder. He turns and runs back the way he came.

Lumbering down the corridor, not caring about the noise now. Maybe they've got lucky; maybe the fire drove the Tallowmen away. Few dare face a Stone Man in a fight, and Spar knows how to use his strength and size to best advantage. Still, he doesn't want to try his luck against Tallowmen. Luck is what it would be—one hit from his stone fists might splatter the waxy creations of the alchemists' guild, but they're so fast he'd be lucky to land that one hit.

He marches past the first door out onto the street. Too obvious.

He stumbles to a huge pair of ornate internal doors and smashes them to flinders. Beyond is a courtroom. He's been here before, he realises, long ago. He was up there in the viewer's gallery when they sentenced his father to hang. Vague memories of being dragged down a passageway by his mother, him hanging off her arm like a dead weight, desperate to stay behind but unable to name his fear. Heinreil and the others, clustering around his mother as an invisible honour guard, keeping the press of the crowd away from them. Old men who smelled of drink and dust despite their rich clothes, whispering that his father had paid his dues, that the Brotherhood would take care of them, no matter what.

These days, that means alkahest. Spar's leg starts to hurt as he drags it across the court. Never a good sign—means it's starting to calcify.

"Hold it there."

A man steps into view, blocking the far exit. He's dressed in leathers and a grubby green half-cloak. Sword and pistol at his belt, and he's holding a big iron-shod staff with a sharp hook at one end. The broken nose of a boxer. His hair seems to be migrating south, fleeing his balding pate to colonise the rich forest of his thick black beard. He's a big man, but he's only flesh and bone.

Spar charges, breaking into a Stone Man's approximation of a sprint. It's more like an avalanche, but the man jumps aside and the iron-shod staff comes down hard, right on the back of Spar's right knee. Spar stumbles, crashes into the doorframe, smashing it beneath his weight. He avoids falling only by digging his hand into the wall, crumbling the plaster like dry leaves. He lets Cari tumble to the ground.

The man shrugs his half-cloak back, and there's a silver badge pinned to his breast. He's a licensed thief-taker, a bounty hunter. Recovers lost property, takes sanctioned revenge for the rich. Not regular city watch, more of a bonded freelancer.

"I said, hold it there," says the thief-taker. The fire's getting closer—already, the upper gallery's burning—but there isn't a trace of concern in the man's deep voice. "Spar, isn't it? Idge's boy? Who's the girl?"

Spar responds by wrenching the door off its hinges and flinging it, eight feet of heavy oak, right at the man. The man ducks under it, steps forward and drives his staff like a spear into Spar's leg again. This time, something cracks.

"Who sent you here, boy? Tell me, and maybe I let her live. Maybe even let you keep that leg."

"Go to the grave."

"You first, boy." The thief-taker moves, almost as fast as a Tallowman, and smashes the staff into Spar's leg for the third time. Pain runs up it like an earthquake, and Spar topples. Before he can try to heave himself back up again, the thief-taker's on his back, and the stave comes down for a fourth blow, right on Spar's spine, and his whole body goes numb.

He can't move. He's all stone. All stone. A living tomb.

He screams, because his mouth still works, shouts and begs and pleads and cries for them to save him or kill him or do anything but leave him here, locked inside the ruin of his own body. The thief-taker vanishes, and the flames get closer and—he assumes—hotter, but he can't feel their heat. After a while, more guards arrive. They stick a rag in his mouth, carry him outside, and eight of them heave him into the back of a cart.

He lies there, breathing in the smell of ash and the stench of the slime the alchemists use to fight the fires.

All he can see is the floor of the cart, strewn with dirty straw, but he can still hear voices. Guards running to and fro, crowds jeering and hooting as the High Court of Guerdon burns. Others shouting make way, make way.

Spar finds himself drifting away into darkness.

The thief-taker's voice again. "One got away over the rooftops. Your candles can have him."

"The south wing's lost. All we can do is save the east."

"Six dead. And a Tallowman. Caught in the fires."

Other voices, nearby. A woman, coldly furious. An older man.

"This is a blow against order. A declaration of anarchy. Of war."

"The ruins are still too hot. We won't know what's been taken until—"

"A Stone Man, then."

"What matters is what we do next, not what we can salvage."

The cart rocks back and forth, and they lie another body down next to Spar. He can't see her, but he hears Cari's voice. She's still mumbling to herself, a constant stream of words. He tries to grunt, to signal to her that she's not alone, or that he's still in here in this stone shell, but his jaw has locked around the gag and he can't make a sound.

"What have we here," says another voice. He feels pressure on his back—very, very faintly, very far away, like the pressure a mountain must feel when a sparrow alights on it—and then a pinprick of pain, right where the thief-taker struck him. Feeling blazes through nerves once more, and he welcomes the agony of his shoulders unfreezing. Alkahest, a strong dose of blessed, life-giving, stone-denying alkahest.

He will move again. He's not all stone yet. He's not all gone.

Spar weeps with gratitude, but he's too tired to speak or to move. He can feel the alkahest seeping through his veins, pushing back the paralysis. For once, the Stone Man can rest and be still. Easiest, now, is to close eyes that are no longer frozen open, and be lulled into sleep by his friend's soft babbling...

Before the city was the sea, and in the sea was He Who Begets. And the people of the plains came to the sea, and the first speakers heard the voice of He Who Begets, and told the people of the plains of His glory and taught them to worship Him. They camped by the shore, and built the first temple amid the ruins. And He Who Begets sent His sacred beasts up out of the sea to consume the dead of the plains, so that their souls might be brought down to Him and live with Him in glory below forever. The people of the plains were glad, and gave of their dead to the beasts, and the beasts swam down to Him.

The camp became a village in the ruins, and the village became the city anew, and the people of the plains became the people of the city, and their numbers increased until they could not be counted. The sacred beasts, too, grew fat, for all those who died in the city were given unto them.

Then famine came to the city, and ice choked the bay, and the harvest in the lands around wilted and turned to dust.

The people were hungry, and ate the animals in the fields.

Then they ate the animals in the streets.

Then they sinned against He Who Begets, and broke into the temple precincts, and killed the sacred beasts, and ate of their holy flesh.

The priests said to the people, how now will the souls of the dead be carried to the god in the waters, but the people replied, what are the dead to us? Unless we eat, we will be dead, too.

And they killed the priests, and ate them, too.

Still the people starved, and many of them died. The dead thronged the streets, for there were no more sacred beasts to carry them away into the deep waters of God.

The dead thronged the streets, but they were houseless and bodiless, for their remains were eaten by the few people who were left.

And the people of the city dwindled, and became the people of the tombs, and they were few in number.

Over the frozen sea came a new people, the people of the ice, and they came upon the city and said: lo, here is a great city, but it is empty. Even its temples are abandoned. We shall dwell here, and shelter from the cold, and raise up shrines to our own gods there.

The people of the ice endured where the people of the city had not, and survived the cold. Many of them died, too, and their bodies were interred in tombs, in accordance with their customs. And the people of the tombs stole those bodies, and ate of them.

And in this way, the people of the ice and the people of the tombs survived the winter.

When the ice melted, the people of the ice became the people of the city, and the people of the tombs became the ghouls. For they were also, in their new way, people of the city.

And that is how the ghouls came to Guerdon.